Books should be returned or renewed by the last date above. Renew by phone **03000 41 31 31** or online *www.kent.gov.uk/libs*

A TIME TO DIE

TOM WOOD

SPHERE

First published in Great Britain in 2016 by Sphere

3 5 7 9 10 8 6 4

A CIP catalogue record for this book
is available from the British Library.

ISBN 978-0-7515-5599-8

Typeset in Sabon by M Rules
Printed and bound in Great Britain by
Clays Ltd, St Ives plc

Papers used by Sphere are from well-managed forests
and other responsible sources.

MIX
Paper from
responsible sources
FSC
www.fsc.org
FSC® C104740

Sphere
An imprint of
Little, Brown Book Group
Carmelite House
50 Victoria Embankment
London EC4Y 0DZ

An Hachette UK Company
www.hachette.co.uk

www.littlebrown.co.uk

A TIME TO DIE

ONE

Killing was the easy part. Getting away with it was the true skill. Victor had been doing both for half his lifetime. The realisation came to him in a rare moment of self-reflection and was summarily dismissed because to be lost in thought meant to be unaware of his surroundings. Whilst thinking of his past he was not evaluating the people around him, judging angles of attack and lines of sight, deciding on the best choke, gouge or strike to neutralise threats, nor could he determine the best method of subsequent escape.

To kill required little more than the ability to point and shoot. Almost anyone could do it. To escape required the successful diversion of blame. As a professional assassin, Victor's motive for killing was either money or self-defence, the latter always related to the pursuit of the former. He killed who he was paid to, and who he had to. Because he had little-to-no connection with his victims he could sidestep almost all of the blame. That was focused at his clients – those who had the most to gain from application of Victor's talents.

The idea of blame was in his thoughts as his gaze shifted to assess the men and women in the carriage around him. There were families and couples, and of those travelling as singles most were too old or young or wore the wrong clothes. No one caused so much as a ping on his threat radar.

There was only one other man around Victor's age. He sat opposite Victor, nursing a cup of cold tea. Even without trying Victor saw there were nine brown rings in the cup and a scum had formed on the remaining tea.

The train was the famous Red Arrow that made the long overnight journey from Moscow to St Petersburg. It was a nine-hour trip north through the Russian countryside, and one the Red Arrow had been doing for over half a century. Modern rolling stock did the journey in half the time, but half the style. Victor's private cabin in the first-class carriage was small but opulent. It even had its own shower. An extravagant way to travel, but worth every penny to Victor, who placed considerable value on his privacy.

The man seated opposite Victor wore dark chinos and a loose shirt of thick white cotton, sleeves rolled up to the elbows. The shirt was creased from the day's wear. The man looked alert but also tired. It was nearing midnight and he had red in his eyes and dark circles beneath them but was wide awake and fidgeting. Victor allowed their gazes to meet, which the man took as an invitation to begin talking.

'This is how we were meant to travel.' The man was

2

British and had a deep, well-spoken accent. 'Flying? No, thanks. That's for those that don't know any better. A car? That's like being your own chauffeur.' He frowned and turned the corners of his mouth down. 'Trains are for the civilised chap.'

He smiled to show he wasn't being wholly serious, but Victor saw the smile as the probe it was, testing the boundaries of a stranger and hoping to find common ground and with it someone to while away the hours.

Victor remained silent. In his experience, less was more when it came to conversation.

'I've taken this trip before,' the British man said. 'I can let you know which window to look out of and when. For when it gets light, I mean. Like a tour guide. You don't have to pay me, of course. Unless you want to.'

This time the smile was genuine.

'I've always liked trains,' Victor said. 'Or rather, I used to. When I was a boy.'

'First time on this one?'

Victor nodded.

'Then you're in for a treat.' He offered his hand. 'I'm Leonard Fletcher.'

Victor didn't like shaking hands. He didn't like physical contact at all. People who wanted to touch him usually wanted to do him harm. He shook the hand anyway, because the man offered no threat to him and Victor needed to engage in such actions to maintain his façade of normality.

'My name's Jonathan.'

'Nice to meet you, Jon. I was worried it would be all

couples or old people. Sometimes it is. No one to talk to. Beautiful scenery is great and all, but you can't see it at night, can you? Going to bed early isn't an option; I'm something of a night owl. I'm not interrupting, am I?'

'Not at all,' Victor said.

'That's what I thought. I figured you were bored too. I hope you don't mind me coming over.'

'Not at all,' Victor said again.

An announcement emanated from the public address system. The dinner car was closing soon.

'Have you tried the Croatian red?'

Victor shook his head. 'I'm not much of a wine drinker. Unless it's a good dessert wine.'

The British man was undeterred. 'You really should. The Merlot is a treat. And cheap too, which is always a bonus.'

'I'll bear that in mind.'

They sat in silence for a minute. The British man began to grow agitated in the silence; he wanted to talk, but was struggling to keep the conversation flowing. Victor's stilted answers meant the other guy had to do the heavy lifting.

The man rewound through what had already been said and found something to roll with: 'You mentioned before that you liked trains when you were a kid. Were you a bit of a trainspotter?'

He grinned at the taunt. He wanted to provoke a response, whatever it might be.

Victor shook his head. 'I had more practical hobbies when I was a boy. I enjoyed making things, so I'm not sure why I liked trains. I would see them from my window, coming and going from the railway station. I watched them all day long sometimes. Maybe it was the noise; the steady rumble of trains can be soothing, like music.'

'Hold on, you're saying you literally watched them *all* day? Are you serious?'

Victor nodded.

'No television in your house?'

Victor shook his head.

The man said, 'Wow, your childhood must have been boring as shit. I feel sorry for you.'

'We don't miss what we never had, do we?'

'I wouldn't know. I was a spoilt brat. We had every gadget and toy. Mother drank and left us to the nanny and Father didn't know how to communicate with us, so parenting meant buying us stuff we didn't need. Funny you say you liked trains because he had a train set up in the loft. I guess it was his own toy. A good excuse to avoid the brats and have some quiet time. He could spend hours up there. He tried to get me into it once, but I didn't understand the point of it. You watch the train go round once, you've seen everything you're going to see. I don't know why anyone would think that was fun. That way madness lies, if you ask me.'

'That's the thing,' Victor said, leaning forward, 'it's not just about the train going round the track. It's about the miniature world. The detail. The perfection. It's about the static grass and the trees carefully crafted from twigs and coloured lichen and the tiny model people going about their lives in a timeless, idyllic landscape. There's an incredible beauty to it, but you have to want to see it.'

Fletcher sucked air through his teeth, feeling awkward.

'Oh right. Sorry, I didn't mean to offend. I didn't realise you had one yourself. I should have guessed, shouldn't I? You said you liked trains as a kid.'

Victor shook his head again, sitting back. 'No, I never had a train set either. I wanted one more than anything in the world. But no TV. No train set. Just the window I had to climb up on the sideboard to see out of. Nearest thing to a real train set was a picture that I tore from a magazine. When it was too dark outside to see the real trains I would use a torch I'd made and look at the picture and imagine the train was moving along the track, the electric motor whirring as I worked the controls.'

Fletcher stared at him. 'Are you winding me up?'

'Not even a little bit. Believe it or not, that picture was my most prized possession.'

'Well, that's a kid's imagination for you. Where does it go? I don't think I ever had one because I had a Nintendo. No reason for creating make-believe worlds for yourself when they're on the screen, is there? I don't think I read a book until I was seventeen, and then it was only to impress some girl at my college.' He laughed and tapped the table-top with his palm. 'I wasted a whole week reading this massive boring tome of shite and I didn't get so much as a snog out of it. Things we do for women, eh? So, what happened to the picture? Keep it in your wallet still?' He was joking.

Victor said, 'Not exactly. But it's sitting in an airtight bag inside a safety deposit box within the most secure bank vault in Switzerland.'

Fletcher laughed again, longer and louder, and had to

6

wipe tears from his eyes once he had taken control of himself. He then saw that Victor hadn't been joking.

'You're kidding me?' the man breathed. 'That must cost you a small fortune.'

He shrugged. 'I spent years hiding it from the others. The older boys would have taken it for themselves or torn it up just for fun. I'm not typically nostalgic. I don't think about my past if I can help it. But that picture of the train set is one link to who I used to be that I haven't been able to fully bury. If the picture was valuable to me then, now it's priceless. I suppose you could say I've never stopped protecting it.'

'I have to say,' Fletcher said, rubbing a finger on his chin, 'you might very well be the weirdest person I've ever met on this journey. And I've met a few. I don't mean that in a bad way,' he was quick to add.

'I didn't take it as such,' Victor said. 'I'm a difficult man to offend.'

'What's your story then? How come you're alone on a hellishly expensive overnight train?'

'Work,' Victor said. 'You?'

'I told you I don't like to fly. Well, the truth is I *can't* fly. My firm hates it, but they can't do anything about it because it's classed as a medical condition. We have some great employee protection in the UK. Yay for socialism, right?'

'Who do you work for?'

Fletcher hesitated – only for an instant, but Victor saw it – then said, 'An accountancy firm in London.'

'You're an accountant?'

Fletcher nodded.

Victor imitated the nod. 'You know, in my experience, people who don't want to be asked questions about their work often say they're accountants. No one wants to talk about percentages and liabilities, do they?'

Fletcher laughed once more despite Victor's neutral expression.

'I know this,' Victor said, 'because sometimes I too say I'm an accountant.'

The laugh faded to a smile while the man's gaze searched Victor for answers to questions not yet asked. Victor was silent while he let the man think. He didn't need long to say:

'You know who I am, don't you?'

Victor said, 'Yes.'

Fletcher considered this. His fingers tapped on the table-top. 'St Paul's Cathedral ...'

'Used to be one hundred feet higher,' Victor finished.

'*Cleric?*' Fletcher asked.

Victor nodded and said, 'The original spire was destroyed in the Great Fire of London. The lead from the roof formed a molten river of metal through the street.'

Fletcher stared for a while as he replayed events and realised Victor knew enough about him to know he would seek out a bored-looking man to chat to.

'I didn't know any of that about the fire,' Fletcher said. 'I just knew the code. I'm supposed to meet you in Helsinki.'

'Last-minute change of plan.'

A frown creased Fletcher's forehead. 'They never change

the plan. Do you have any idea how much effort – how much paperwork – it takes?'

Victor remained silent.

'You don't look as I thought you would,' Fletcher said. 'I mean: your file has no photographs or physical details.'

'Which was a condition of my servitude.'

'Servitude? You make it sound so sordid.'

'Isn't it?'

'I almost didn't believe some of the things I read about you. I expected you to be, well, terrifying. Yet . . . you look so bloody normal. Like you're just a regular no one.'

'I work very hard at that.'

'Well, you succeed. I never would have guessed you were Cleric if you hadn't made that clear. But, I suppose, that's why they pay you so much money.'

'That's not the only reason.'

Fletcher laughed a little to disguise his nervousness. 'Why did you engage in small talk first? Why not get the code in earlier?'

'I wanted to be sure you didn't know me. I wanted to know for certain that no photographs of me were on file.'

'Are you saying I wouldn't have been able to bluff it?'

There was a measure of offence in Fletcher's question.

'Yes,' Victor said. 'That's what I was saying.'

Fletcher's lips stayed closed for a moment and his face was rigid, but it relaxed as he decided to let the slight to his skills go. He said, 'So, why the train face-to-face and not in Helsinki as planned?'

'Chinese Secret Service are waiting to follow you when we get to St Petersburg.'

'Damn,' Fletcher said. 'They've never left me alone since I was stationed in Hong Kong.'

'Persistence is a Chinese virtue.'

'Isn't that the truth? Well, this carriage is as good a place as any to discuss your next assignment. I take it you've checked it?'

Victor nodded. 'No one is watching or listening.'

'Of course,' Fletcher said. 'Else you wouldn't have been talking about your childhood, would you?'

'That's correct.'

'But that could have been lies for all I know. There are no personal details in your file, after all.'

'I assure you that I was telling the truth.'

Fletcher accepted this and scratched the back of his neck. As before, Victor let him come to his own conclusion. It took longer this time, because Fletcher didn't want to come to the inevitable truth.

'There are no personal details in your file,' Fletcher said for the second time.

'There would be a lot of trouble if there were.'

'The photographs and physical description were omitted, as per your request. But aside from your work for us and what we know of your jobs for the CIA, there is nothing else about you because we don't know anything about you.'

'Good,' Victor said as Fletcher stared.

'There was a line like *subject values anonymity and protects this ruthlessly* ...'

'The information is accurate. It's a necessity, for protection against current threats and potential future ones.'

'I get that. You don't want us to know anything more about you than the minimum, in case we ever turn on you.'

Victor nodded.

'Yet now I know about the photograph of a train set in a Swiss vault.'

Victor said nothing.

'But it doesn't matter if I know,' Fletcher said, pointed and knowing. His gaze was locked on to Victor. The skin to the left of his Adam's apple trembled with the thundering pulse below it. 'It doesn't matter what I know about you because I'm never going to become a threat to you. Because you're here to kill me, aren't you?'

'Yes,' Victor said.

TWO

Fletcher was calm. He didn't bolt from his seat or attack. He just sat there, looking at Victor for almost a minute as he processed the fact he was facing his killer.

Fletcher cleared his throat and said, 'Can I know why?'

'Your mistress from Hong Kong has been passing on your pillow talk to Beijing.'

He thought about this, then said, 'That can't be the reason. That's no reason to have me killed.'

'London thinks you know,' Victor explained. 'They believe you are complicit. They believe you to be a traitor.'

Fletcher looked at his hands. His palms were on the tabletop and his fingers spread wide. He took a breath and spent a while exhaling.

'I wasn't at first,' he confessed. 'Not when I met her. I was a fool who thought this beautiful young woman was genuinely interested in me. God, it was such a basic bloody honeytrap. So obvious in retrospect. She approached me. In my regular bar, of all places. Can you believe I fell for that? She even drank the same whisky. *What a coincidence.* The Chinese are still using the spy playbook from the sixties, yet I didn't see it because I couldn't take my eyes from her lips. She has the most amazing lips I've ever seen. Of course, eventually I realised what was going on. She wasn't as careful as she should have been asking about work and my movements, which, given the sledgehammer subtlety of her approach, shouldn't have been any surprise. But it was. I couldn't believe it because I was already in love with her. Well, in lust anyway. Same thing though, right?'

'I wouldn't know,' Victor said. 'But I don't need to know any of this.'

'Well, I'm telling you, so you're going to have to listen. Unless you're planning on doing it right here in the open.'

'I'm not,' Victor admitted.

'My point, exactly,' Fletcher said with a measure of triumph, revelling in any victory he could claim while it was still possible. 'So, yeah, by the time I found out she was an agent I was too into her to break it off. I just couldn't, even though I knew deep down she only wanted intel, I carried on regardless. I needed those lips on mine, whatever the price. Shit, I'm such an idiot.'

Victor agreed, but he felt it impolite to voice agreement. Likewise, it seemed rude in this instance to tell a condemned man to watch his language.

Fletcher sat back in his seat. 'But even if London found out about me and Ling, that can't be the only reason they sent you. It can't be. Not for that alone. Not *you*.'

'That's what I was told.'

'Then they're lying to you.'

'I don't care,' Victor said.

Fletcher frowned. 'You don't care that you're being fooled and manipulated?'

'No one in this business ever tells me the truth. I get over it.'

Fletcher showed an angry smirk. 'So you're nothing more than a yes-man?'

'Yes.'

The smirk became a sneer that faded away to a sad sigh. 'Will it hurt?'

'Not for a second.'

'I suppose I should thank you for that small mercy,' Fletcher said. 'How are you going to do it?'

'Do you really want to know?'

Fletcher thought for a moment and Victor saw him going back and forth on the idea before he nodded. 'Yes, I need to know.'

'Suicide,' Victor explained. 'You're going to go back to your couchette and take an overdose of painkillers. You'll drift off to sleep and never wake up again. Quiet. Peaceful. No mess. No fuss. No pain.'

He set a bottle of prescription painkillers on the table. Fletcher stared at it.

'They're mine, for my bad back.'

Victor nodded.

14

'Your fingerprints are on the bottle,' Fletcher said, looking from the bottle to Victor's hands.

'No, they're not.'

Fletcher slid the bottle closer. 'I don't want to be a suicide. I don't want to die like that.'

Victor said, 'You don't really have a choice. I'm going to accompany you back to your couchette. Trust me when I say that it's in your best interests to take the pills willingly.'

Fletcher swallowed. 'No, you misunderstand. I'm not going to fight or run.'

'I don't worry,' Victor said. 'And it wouldn't make a difference if you did.'

Fletcher sighed. 'I know. Like I said, I read your file. I read the reports. I even saw a video of a massacre you committed in Minsk. I'm a pencil-pusher with a slipped disc who's terrified of flying. I know there's nothing I can do to stop the one they call Cleric. But what I mean is: I don't want my wife to think I killed myself. My wife is a good woman. She doesn't deserve to have to grieve for me and hate me for leaving her at the same time. Just because I can't say no to a beautiful woman doesn't mean I don't love her. I do, with all my heart, despite what you think.'

'I don't care if you love your wife or not.'

'And my daughter,' Fletcher said, composure starting to crack. 'Sweet Ella. She's too young to understand, but one day she'll find out what really happened to her dad and then she'll think I didn't love her enough to stay alive to watch her grow up.'

Victor remained silent.

Fletcher said, 'Can't you shoot me or break my neck? Anything but a suicide.'

'No. Beijing can't know the leak was found. London want to use your mistress without her knowledge. There can't be any blame.'

'Then an accident, for God's sake,' Fletcher said, talking faster than he was thinking. 'I can fall in front of a train at the station. I can tie my shoelace and slip and—'

'No,' Victor said again, insistent but calm and level. 'You'll look coerced on the CCTV recordings. It won't convince anyone.'

'There has to be some other way. There simply *has* to be. I'll do anything.'

Victor thought for a moment. It seemed only polite to consider the plea from a target to alter the method of his own death, whilst accepting the death itself as inevitable. In all his years as a professional assassin, he had never been in such a situation. People had begged before, to no avail, but always to survive, never to die in a manner of their own choosing. Pulling off an accident that attracted no suspicion was no small feat – hence the overdose, either with cooperation or forced – but an accident with the victim's assistance was a different matter.

'Go to the dining car before it closes,' he told Fletcher once he had thought through the particulars, 'and order yourself some dinner.'

'Dinner?'

Victor said, 'The dining car's open, but not for much longer. There is a steak option on the menu.'

'I don't understand.'

'When we've finished this conversation I'll sit here and you go order a nice slab of sirloin. Ask for it well-done. Cut off a big piece. Don't chew too much before you swallow. The rest will take care of itself.'

'Oh, I see. I'm going to choke to death. Shit.'

Fletcher was pale, as if the reality of the situation had only just occurred to him. His cheeks expanded and his lips pursed with heavy breaths. He touched his throat. After a moment, the inevitable question was asked:

'How long will it take?'

Victor had already worked it out. 'You're mid-thirties and out of shape, so maybe ninety seconds until you pass out and don't wake up.'

'That doesn't seem very long.'

Victor didn't say that it would seem like an eternity to Fletcher while his lungs burned for oxygen they were never going to get.

He shook his head. 'My wife doesn't let me eat red meat. We're trying to be healthy.'

'That's okay,' Victor said. 'It'll make it more convincing. You're not used to it.'

'God, when I think of all the pissing quinoa I've had to endure, and for what? I should have eaten nothing but bacon. It wouldn't have made any difference, would it?'

'I suppose not.'

'She could blame herself, couldn't she? My wife might think it was her fault for me not being used to steak.'

'Yes,' Victor admitted. 'At first perhaps, but people will help her through that. Choking kills almost as many people as fires.'

'And far better than to think I killed myself, right? That's like leaving her as well as dying. This way I just die.'

Victor didn't know. He didn't understand, but he nodded because he saw Fletcher wanted reassurance.

'Make sure you smile at the waiter while you make your order,' Victor said.

'I don't feel like smiling. Smiling is the last thing I want to do. Well, second last.'

'That's why I'm reminding you. This isn't going to work if you look like a condemned man.'

Fletcher nodded his understanding and agreement. He was quiet for a moment.

'Will it . . . ?'

'Yes,' Victor said. 'It will hurt. After the first forty-five seconds without oxygen it's going to be bad, very bad, so think why you're doing it; picture your wife and daughter. Not long after that it won't hurt at all, I promise. All the pain will go. You won't be afraid. Oxygen deprivation will make you feel euphoric. You'll pass out feeling good.'

'Like autoerotic asphyxiation,' Fletcher said in a monotone, eyes focused on a point somewhere on the other side of Victor's head. 'I didn't really believe that was true though. I always thought it was kind of an urban myth. Now, I wish I'd tried it. I wish I'd tried everything. I wish I'd told my wife I loved her more often.'

Victor said nothing. He watched Fletcher's face. He had aged ten years in ten minutes.

'Have you ever been strangled? Do you know what it's like?'

'Yes,' Victor admitted. 'A few times. But it never reached the euphoric stage, otherwise I wouldn't be here now.'

Fletcher said, 'Then how can you truly know I'll pass out feeling good?'

'It's part of the job description to understand how the body works,' Victor explained. 'And sometimes, when I've choked people to death, they almost look happy at the very end.'

THREE

Victor watched Fletcher stand and walk away along the carriage. He said nothing further, but before he turned around had worn the stern expression of both commitment and resolve. He was afraid, but he hid it with a straight back and his head held high. He left the bottle of painkillers on the table. He didn't need them.

Victor collected them up and slipped them back into a pocket.

The dining car was in the middle of the train. Fletcher would be there within three minutes. With only a short time waiting to be served at this time of night, then a moment for ordering, and then cooking and delivering of Fletcher's food, he should be choking to death in no longer than fifteen minutes. If there hadn't been an announcement for any doctor on board to head to the dining car within twenty minutes then Victor would go and find out why. The train journeyed nonstop through the night, so there were no scheduled stops to interrupt, and even an emergency one wouldn't make a difference.

Fletcher's acceptance of his fate left a curious impression on Victor, who was glad the job was to be completed as specified by his employer, but he didn't understand how. He knew enough about psychology and acceptance and fatality to understand that Fletcher would kill himself because he believed he had no other choice, but Victor didn't *get it*. His own survival instinct was ingrained so deep and so strong he didn't know any other way. Civilians lived through each day, thinking of work, families, sex or their favourite TV show, whereas Victor had to survive those same days, knowing one mistake, one unchecked angle or decision made for comfort over security would be enough. Surviving had become unbreakable habit long ago.

Fletcher stepped through the far door and out of the carriage. Ten minutes later, the door opened again and a man entered.

The man was all wrong.

Everything about him said trouble. On Victor's checklist of telltale signs of a threat, he ticked each and every one. He was the right age to be an effective operative; in this case early forties. He was in shape; strong but not bulky. He had the kind of clothes Victor would select: footwear with a decent tread for running and climbing, and an outfit that was smart but forgettable and on the larger side to aid manoeuvrability. He wore dark trousers and a black hip-length leather jacket, unbuttoned, over a thin sweater of brown wool. Victor didn't wear gloves because his hands were coated in silicone solution, but this man did. They were slate grey and thin, made of supple leather; maybe calf's. There was no innocent reason to wear them on a well-heated train that hadn't been on a cold platform for almost two hours.

The man had used his left hand to ease open the carriage door, but it was clear he was right-handed from his leading left step. Victor pretended not to register him just as the man pretended not to recognise Victor. The man wasn't aware he'd been made because he was at a considerable disadvantage: there were a dozen other occupants in the carriage competing for his attention. By the time his gaze found its intended target, Victor had already noticed, assessed and drawn his conclusions, and his eyes were diverted.

The primary response to any threat was to avoid it. On a train, escape was impractical. Not impossible, because Victor could pull the emergency alarm and when the train stopped and the doors unlocked he could disappear into the night. That, however, would be impractical because Victor's suit offered no protection against the Russian winter outside.

Inaction, or waiting, could sometimes be considered the next best option. A threat didn't always signify an imminent risk. Circumstances could change. A premature reaction would lose the advantage of surprise that might better be exploited at a future point.

The man approached.

His hair was short and greying. He had a neat beard that was darker than his hair. The skin between was pale; another sign of a threat in a Caucasian because it meant he didn't see much sunlight because he most often operated at night.

With distance and seats between them, the man would need to close in if he intended to fire a gun, and come closer still if he had a knife or other melee weapon to employ. Going up against an enemy with a firearm was always complicated, the more so when Victor himself was unarmed, which was the norm. He had passed through far more metal detectors, and undergone far more pat-downs or wand searches by bodyguards or security personnel than he ever had encountered gunmen. In this instance, Victor had only the door behind him as a means of escape, and to reach it he would have to leave the cover of the seats and make a straight line down the aisle to safety he had next to no chance of reaching because he had yet to encounter an assassin too poor a shot to miss his back at that range.

But Victor saw the assassin was not going to attempt the fulfilment of his contract here and now. The man knew how to dress so he wasn't stupid, and only a stupid killer would strike in a crowded train carriage monitored by CCTV. This was reconnaissance. He was locating his target.

The man tried to hide it, but his shoulders squared a fraction as he spotted Victor. The gait didn't change, and he continued walking along the aisle, moving in a half-shuffled step because the space between seats was too narrow for a man of his size to pass through without skewing hips and shoulders.

As he neared, Victor remained stationary, his head tilted

and his eyes in the direction of the window and the black world outside of it, but his focus on the moving shape in his peripheral vision and reflected on the window glass.

The man passed him and Victor listened to the footsteps until they were lost within the ambient train noise and the door hissed open at the end of the carriage.

Waiting in this instance could not be considered a wise choice. It was another seven hours to St Petersburg. Circumstances could not improve in that time, only worsen as the killer had ample opportunity to put into practice whatever he had planned.

Victor waited for two minutes and stood to follow.

When escape was impractical and inaction unreasonable, attack was always preferable.

FOUR

Victor left the carriage and stepped through the narrow vestibule that bridged the gap to the next carriage. The door hissed open and he felt the change of air pressure on his face. He detected a faint scent of deodorant, left behind by the assassin. The new carriage was identical to the one where he had conversed with Fletcher. It was occupied by a sparse spread of travellers – Victor counted nine individuals with a quick glance. Other night owls, like himself or Fletcher.

At the far end of the carriage the man with greying hair was stepping through the doorway.

Victor followed him, moving down the aisle while picturing the layout of the train – seven carriages, three of which were seating, one dining car, with the rear three housing sleeping compartments. The assassin had entered the first of the three sleeping carriages. Victor's own cabin was in the first-class carriage at the rear of the train.

Which particular cabin would be a difficult thing for an

enemy to find out, but no more difficult than ascertaining his whereabouts in the first place. He had to assume an assassin who had tracked him down to this particular train would know.

The reconnaissance had not only been to locate Victor but to make sure he was not in his cabin at the present time. The assassin could then enter and wait for Victor's return, for the purposes of both surprise and privacy.

A simple enough ambush, but an effective one if executed well. Had Victor not identified the threat, the chances of dealing with it would have dropped by an exponential degree if he first became aware of it upon returning to the cabin.

He slowed his pace when he reached the narrow corridor to the right of the line of sleeping compartments. He wanted to give the assassin more time to prepare his ambush. A false sense of readiness would work in Victor's favour. Overconfidence was a killer.

Victor's cabin was the third of four occupying the first-class carriage. It was not his preference to have cabins either side of him, but his options had been limited at the time of booking.

He pictured the interior of the cabin: a comfortable space in which to travel but a confined box in which to ambush someone. A padded bench occupied the wall on the right perpendicular to the doorway, which converted to a cot to sleep on. There was space underneath it for luggage. A separated water closet was opposite the bench, with a door that opened inward. The cabin's door opened outward and to the right.

The space for luggage beneath the bench could accommodate a person lying down, and was low enough that they would be hidden from view. That would be Victor's preferred strike point, but only if he was there to kill a civilian. A fellow professional would check such a space before settling down to sleep.

The next logical point would be the water closet. Due to the inward-opening door there was insufficient room for an attack, but these deluxe cabins had their own shower cubicles. They were tiny, even for a man of Victor's leanness, but would enable the assassin the advantages of standing upright and being forewarned of the target's presence, first by the cabin door opening and then their imminent appearance as the water closet door opened. A knife attack would be next to impossible to defend against when employed in those confines with the benefit of surprise, while a gun could be aimed in anticipation and no shot could miss at such a range.

Even taking away the assassin's advantage of surprise did not negate the danger. With a gun of his own, Victor could open the bathroom door and expose only his hand and part of his arm. There would be no way of cleaning up such a mess or removing the body, however, and a shot-dead assassin would disrupt the narrative of Fletcher's subsequent accidental death. Chinese Secret Service would never believe the two to be unrelated.

Victor opened the door to his cabin and stepped inside. To his left, no more than three feet away and separated by only two inches of aluminium and plasterboard was a man who wanted to kill him.

He closed the door behind him, blunting the rattling noise of the train that was amplified in the narrow corridor outside. He knew the assassin hiding in the shower cubicle had heard the door open and close, and maybe even detected the sound of Victor's footfalls on the cabin floor. It was a little warmer inside and the air was still.

He checked under the bench seat because he was thorough, unsurprised to find the space empty. Beneath the cabin window on the opposite wall was a small table on which rested complimentary snacks, sachets for hot beverages and cutlery. Victor took the knife and fork from their napkin and held one in each hand in downward ice-pick grips – the fork in the right; knife in the left.

He stood before the door to the water closet.

The assassin with greying hair was six feet tall. Standing in the shower cubicle put him about one metre from the door, therefore if he had a gun he would not have his arms extended, since that would place the gun far too close to the target, making the shot more difficult and increasing the risk of being disarmed. The gun would be near to the assassin, secondary hand supporting the primary from beneath the grip. At point-blank range it wasn't necessary to aim, so the muzzle could be as low as chest height. Victor was the taller man, so the muzzle would be at an angle to shoot him in the heart or head. Victor expected the assassin would go for the heart. Less chance of the bullet over-penetrating. Even a low-powered handgun round could blow a hole out of the back of the skull. The bullet might then go on to break a window or bury itself in a wall, leaving behind more evidence, along with the blood, bone and brain matter.

Aiming for the heart meant there was a safe area of space up to four feet from the floor.

Victor bent his knees and used the fork to twist the door catch.

He lowered himself further, took a breath, released it, and powered forward, knocking the door open with his left shoulder and twisting into the water closet as he sank even lower, below four feet, whipping out his right hand to throw the fork as distraction to give him an extra split-second to cover the distance and drive the knife into the assassin's neck.

The fork struck the waterproofed wall and clattered on the cubicle floor, rattling against the plughole guard.

No assassin with greying hair.

Victor rose and turned, realising his mistake. The reconnaissance hadn't been reconnaissance at all. It had been a lure. The man with greying hair had wanted to be spotted and followed.

Victor had done the hard work for him. He had trapped himself.

He darted out of the water closet in time to see the assassin enter the cabin, closing the door behind him as a drawn pistol rose to fire.

FIVE

The assassin with greying hair had been smart to trick Victor, but he had made a mistake with his weapon. It was a long-barrelled Glock automatic made longer still with a suppressor. At such close confines all that length slowed down target acquisition. The shorter the gun, the faster it could be aimed.

By the time the muzzle had swung Victor's way he was close enough to disarm it, striking the assassin's inner wrist to shock and weaken the hand's grip before batting the weapon free. The gun bounced off the padded bench and skidded beneath the cabin's table.

The assassin slipped Victor's subsequent knife thrust and directed his momentum into the closed door. The swaying motion of the train aided the stumble and Victor had to drop the knife to use the palm as a brake and pivot to spin back around in time to ward off an elbow meant for the back of his skull.

Though a little shorter and a little older, the assassin was the stronger of the two. His free left hand hammered into Victor's flank, compressing ribs and driving the air from his lungs to interrupt any attempt to grapple, forcing him to sidestep away from the power of the blow and the intense pain.

There was no room to create distance and give himself an instant to recover, even without the unsteady floor that fought his precarious balance. The assassin took advantage of this and launched a barrage of strikes.

Victor hunkered over with his left hand gripping the back of his own neck so the folded arm guarded the side of his face and head, whilst his right hand held on to his left wrist, forearm creating a shield across his lower face. The assassin tried to punch and elbow through these defences but struck only solid skull, damaging his own knuckles more than he did Victor's head.

The assassin tried an uppercut – the only way to get past Victor's guard – but it was an inevitable punch that Victor knew was coming. He blocked it by snapping his elbows together, catching the fist between them, but releasing it a split-second later because the move left him defenceless to the assassin's free hand.

He didn't attack with it, however, instead scooping up the dropped butter knife that had landed on the padded bench within his reach.

A combat knife with a razor edge would have caused Victor to dodge away, but a slash to the inner wrist or neck from the blunted blade would fail to cut deep enough to sever even the most delicate of arteries. Only a direct thrust

31

delivered with huge force posed any real risk, and this was the option the assassin chose, aiming at Victor's groin.

The blade glinted in a fast upwards arc. Unconcerned about the knife's edges, Victor used his forearm to intercept the attack, only realising it had been a feint to open his guard when the assassin body-slammed him backwards.

Victor hit the small table with his lower back while his upper body continued backwards until his head smacked off the cabin's window. He saw stars and his senses faltered. He still had the instincts to kick out at his attacker, catching the assassin's inner thigh with a heel before he could exploit Victor's vulnerability.

A grunt escaped the assassin's lips – the first noise he had made – and hearing it energised Victor enough to propel himself forward and land an elbow.

It hit the jawbone and the assassin's head twisted away with another grunt.

Vision blurry, but knowing he had the advantage, Victor snapped out some fast strikes to stop the assassin recovering.

The flurry worked, forcing the assassin on the defensive, enabling Victor to position himself to get his enemy where he wanted him – overwhelmed and concentrating on blocking so he wouldn't see the chokehold coming until it was too late.

Four carriages away, Leonard Fletcher had swallowed a piece of well-done steak far too large for him to have any reasonable chance of swallowing it. Within twenty seconds a concerned diner, having heard Fletcher choking, pulled the emergency alarm. In reaction the driver deactivated the accelerator and applied the brakes. The train was old and some of its mechanics outdated, but it was maintained to impeccable standards. Metal screeched and sparks brightened the night and several hundred tons of moving train rapidly decelerated.

The sudden change in momentum took Victor from his feet and he fell through the open doorway to the water closet, where he collided with the sink, before collapsing to the floor.

The assassin hit the doorway, and only fell to his knees. He ignored Victor, prone on the water closet floor, and went for the fallen gun, now sitting nearby after sliding out and into view from under the table.

To reach it, he turned away from Victor, who threw himself through the doorway and at the back of the assassin, who twisted over as they tipped forward, bringing the gun round to fire.

Victor grabbed the suppressor before it could be aimed at his face and for a moment they remained a frozen tangle on the cabin floor as they struggled for control of the weapon. The assassin might be stronger, but Victor was above him and had gravity on his side.

No stalemate could endure for ever, and Victor felt the assassin starting to weaken beneath him. While he was breathing hard from the exertion, the assassin was gasping.

The assassin's arms began to shake. His face reddened. Soon, Victor thought.

His enemy knew it too, and his eyes, until then staring

unblinking at Victor's own, darted to the left, then to the right – looking, searching.

They widened. The assassin let go of the gun and his arm snapped out while Victor tore the weapon free from the remaining hand. He twisted the gun around, taking the grip in his palm, index finger slipping inside the trigger guard, angling the muzzle down at the assassin's face, and—

A sickening wave of agony exploded through him as the assassin drove the butter knife into his thigh. The blunted blade didn't penetrate far into his flesh, but was well-aimed and struck the femoral nerve.

The shock and incredible pain made Victor recoil and throw himself off his enemy, his central nervous system overloaded in a maelstrom of electrical signals, all thoughts of the gun and killing the threat overridden by base instinct to flee.

He realised the gun had come out of his hand as he scrambled to his feet, the explosion of pain short-lived and dissipating.

Fatigue meant the assassin was no faster to his feet and they faced one another across the small cabin as an announcement came over the public address system. There was less than two metres between the two men. The assassin still held the knife in hand, the blade now smeared with an inch of Victor's blood.

The gun was between them, but closer to Victor. If he went for it, he would grab it before the assassin could, but would Victor be fast enough to angle it and shoot before he was stabbed again?

34

He saw the assassin was asking himself the same question. The train slowed to a stop.

'Do you speak Russian?' Victor asked.

The assassin didn't answer, but his eyes said yes.

'So you understood the announcement. They're asking for anyone with medical knowledge to go to the dining car. Someone's in trouble. They need help.'

The assassin didn't respond. He looked from the gun to Victor's eyes and back again.

'That's why the train is stopping,' Victor continued. 'The authorities will be coming, police. Do you want to end up in a Russian jail? I don't.'

'What are you saying?'

The assassin's Russian was excellent, but Victor recognised the German accent behind it.

'Whatever your out was, you didn't count on police being on the train when you tried to slip away. If you try and get off before they arrive, there's snow-covered wilderness in every direction. It's sub-zero out there. You'll die long before you make it to safety.'

'What's it to you if I freeze to death or end up in prison?' the German asked.

'You're a professional,' Victor said. 'You don't hate me. You've been hired to kill me. I'm a job. That's all.'

'So?'

'So the job's over. Because even if you're the one to walk out of this cabin instead of me, you're going nowhere. I'm not worth a lifetime in prison and I'm not worth freezing to death for. You've failed, so give it up and we can both walk away.'

There was no pause to deliberate because Victor was right and they both knew it.

'How do you propose we do this?' the German asked, civil and polite – two colleagues discussing a work problem.

'I reach behind me and open the door,' Victor explained. 'Neither of us will act then. We don't want witnesses.'

'Correct,' the German agreed with a nod.

'Then I'll kick the gun under the bench and go. Which gives you the chance to take your weapon back and come after me, of course. But by then I'll be out in the corridor with CCTV watching.'

He saw the German thinking about this for a moment before he shrugged, accepting the fact he could pursue Victor and finish his contract, but not with any hope of getting away with it clean.

'So, we're in agreement?' Victor asked.

'Okay, I accept your proposal,' the German said. 'There's no reason we cannot behave like gentlemen, like professionals.'

'My sentiments.'

Without taking his gaze from the German, Victor reached his left hand behind his back to work the door open. Cool air and noise rushed inside.

Victor waited, because whatever the assassin claimed, he wasn't about to trust his word. When Victor heard voices in the carriage as other passengers responded to the announcement by coming out of their cabins for more news, he kicked the gun behind the bench.

A smile played on the German's lips, because maybe he

had been debating whether to shoot Victor anyway and take his chances with the CCTV, but he wasn't going to risk eyewitnesses too.

The German said, 'I'll see you again soon.'

Victor said, 'I have no doubt,' and backed out of the cabin.

SIX

Krieger watched his target disappear through the doorway and out of sight. He did not pursue him. There were cameras and witnesses and a host of other problems not conducive to a successful completion of his contract. The mission had been unsuccessful. Chasing a lost cause was beneath the German. There was no dignified way of running after a departing bus. More than that, they had an agreement. Krieger was a man of his word. An insignificant degree of honour when considering the nature of his profession, he knew, but humanity was not a binary equation.

He waited in the target's cabin until the train stopped at a small rural station to allow paramedics access. Krieger took his leave.

Krieger disposed of the Glock and stared at the moon, bright in the clear night sky, for answers. In return, it was silent. A wise decision, even for a celestial body.

He was not sorry to get rid of the pistol. A decent

all-round handgun, but it offended him with its very being. Russia was not his primary field of operations. He had acquired the Glock in country from a fixer in the suburbs of Moscow. Krieger had requested a compact pistol as he would be operating on a train. He would be at close quarters. The fixer had assured him he could fulfil such requirements. The fixer had lied or had been incompetent. Krieger couldn't tell which was the case because he had strangled the fixer to death for the failure. As a man of his word, the assassin expected – demanded – the same from others.

That failure had cost Krieger. The contract would have been fulfilled otherwise. He would have shot the target in that orchestrated instance of surprise, neat and simple. Instead, the split-second delay had been enough to save the man's life.

Krieger, who believed in the hand of fate, had a hard time rationalising such interference, but at the same time took comfort instead of anger. If that was to be his script, there was little he could do to alter it.

There would be other opportunities to exploit, he knew. Until then, he had another contract to pursue.

He tasted something both sweet and bitter. Salt. Glucose. Iron. He touched the tip of his tongue to the back of his hand, leaving a smudge of orange spittle behind. Blood. He had a cut in his mouth.

Krieger was stunned.

He knew the taste of blood well, but only that of his victims or enemies. He had never tasted his own before. Maybe once as a boy he might have fallen and cut himself, but any such incident was so far back in the swirling mists of time that he had no memory of the taste to draw upon.

He found he liked the taste of his blood. It was rich with platelets and strong with minerals.

Krieger prided himself in having no ego. That no one had ever hurt him like this was a statement of cold fact. Every violent encounter was met on his terms. People didn't hurt him. He hurt them. That was how the world spun. It was an immutable law of the universe. That law had been broken. He was not happy to have his reality altered.

But as an enthusiast of mythology he reminded himself that Odin, king of the Norse gods, the All Father, had elected to give up his eye to acquire the most precious treasure of all: wisdom.

A little blood was a small price for Krieger to pay for his own.

SEVEN

'I still don't believe it,' Banik said in a quiet voice. 'Fletcher choked to death on a piece of sirloin in a dining car full of witnesses who all swear he was eating by himself. No man fitting your description was even in the same carriage. The CCTV is irrefutable. No hint of foul play. No one to blame.' Banik was wide-eyed. 'Coroner's report: accidental death. How the devil did you manage to pull that off?'

Shadows danced and swayed on grass. The air was saturated with noise.

Victor raised an eyebrow. 'A magician never reveals his tricks.'

Banik shook his head as if there was no possible explanation and took a bite from his meat pie. It steamed in the cool air and Banik chewed with his mouth open in an effort to expel the excess heat.

'I like that they call it a meat pie,' he said between openmouthed chews. 'Not a pork pie or beef-and-onion or chicken-and-mushroom. Just meat. It's comforting to know I could in fact be eating badger.'

He was a thirty-six-year-old case officer in the British Secret Intelligence Service who spoke with a cultured accent befitting his private education and Oxford credentials. Victor knew the man's background and personal details in the same way he would know about a target, in part thanks to his own research, but the majority of information came from Banik himself in the form of his SIS files.

'I want you to trust me,' Banik had explained before their first face-to-face meeting. 'Or this arrangement is never going to work.'

The file was an act of good faith. It said: *I wouldn't give you this if I meant you ill.* Even so, Victor didn't trust him, of course, because anyone he dealt with in a professional capacity was untrustworthy by association. But Banik had yet to show himself to be the kind of problem Victor couldn't deal with.

He was the son of Indian immigrants and the eldest of seven siblings. He was also a diehard West Ham United fan. Which was why they were sitting amongst a crowd of over thirty thousand supporters who were enjoying the winter sunshine more than they were their team's performance. It had been a limp, lacklustre game and was nil-nil with less than fifteen minutes to go. Banik, like a true fan, refused to give up hope.

'They haven't had a single decent shot on target against us,' he said between open-mouthed chews. 'All we have to do is commit to the attack.'

'If you say so,' Victor said.

'You're really not into *soccer*, are you?'

Victor raised an eyebrow at the American pronunciation and the bad accent that delivered it, playing along with a little ambiguity because he knew Banik was playing too. The SIS man was acting as if he had somehow deduced Victor's true origins, pretending to be a little dumb, a little naive. It was all part of Banik's effort to prove that he posed no threat. So Victor – never one to forget that loyalty was a closer cousin to convenience than it was to trust – allowed Banik to believe he'd succeeded in being underestimated.

With supporters singing and shouting all around them, there was no legitimate chance of being overheard, but after Banik had finished his pie, he leaned closer to further reduce the possibility. This required Victor to tolerate the intrusion into his personal space. Though he could control the instinct to cripple Banik, it was impossible to stop his mind rehearsing the moves to break and maim.

'So,' Banik said, oblivious, 'how did you do it?'

Victor said nothing.

'*Oh, come on,*' Banik roared, but not to Victor.

A West Ham midfielder had volleyed the ball from eighteen yards out. It sailed so high over the crossbar the goalkeeper stood and watched it go. The opposing fans jeered.

'Why do they bother? When does that kind of shot ever go in?'

Victor sat without expression.

Banik looked at him. 'Are you a fan of any sport?'

'Do you mean: do I enjoy observing organised physical

activity that serves no purpose but to perpetuate itself indefinitely for profit?'

'And they say we Brits are stuck up.'

Banik hunkered forward to watch the game, elbows on his knees and chin in his palms. 'Three points at home should have been a breeze. We'll have to settle for one.'

Victor didn't respond because, although he knew the rules and how the league worked, he didn't care. He let Banik do the watching while he waited. They were here to debrief the last contract and brief the next one. Though all the details would be sent through electronic channels, Banik liked to meet in person as often as it could be arranged. He liked face time, as he called it. Victor never met contacts if it could be helped, but it was unavoidable when working for SIS.

'If this arrangement is going to work then it can't be done properly online,' Banik had explained. 'We do things old school at MI6.'

'In other words,' Victor replied, 'you can't keep the NSA from reading your emails.'

When he grew bored of watching the ball being kicked back and forth to no avail, Banik said, 'You know, I was never really sure this would go as smoothly as it has.'

'I'm good at my job,' Victor said.

'Such a modest man. Well, three contracts in and I can't disagree. But that's not what I meant. After all that drama in London last year, I didn't think you would stick to your side of the deal.'

'I don't blame your whole organisation for the actions of one individual.'

Banik nodded. 'That's very gracious of you.'

Victor raised an eyebrow. 'Modesty is not my only virtue.'

Banik smirked, then said, 'How's your Serbian?'

'*Nije loše, ali moglo biti bolje,*' Victor replied.

'You could have said *the monkey is up the tree* for all I know.'

Victor shook his head. '*Ja ne znam srpsku reč za* monkey.'

'Well, if your language skills are up to scratch I need you in Belgrade. There's an odious individual named Milan Rados we would really rather appreciate you removing from this fair Earth of ours. Rados is wanted for war crimes committed during that little tête-à-tête that we call the break-up of Yugoslavia. He was a top boy in a Serb paramilitary outfit that liked to burn civilians to death in their own homes.'

'Then why is he still walking free?'

'He has been in hiding for the last six years since an SAS rendition team tried to take him into custody.'

Victor thought about this and said, 'It's not like the Regiment to fail. What happened?'

'Well, that depends whether you're a glass-half-full or a glass-half-empty kind of chap.'

'I would say the glass's capacity is at fifty per cent. What are you trying to say?'

Banik said, 'I mean: if you're a cynical person you might say that Rados was tipped off by sympathetic nationalists in the Serb security services, or, alternatively, if you are a trusting soul, he merely happened to flee his stronghold an hour before sixteen double-hard bastards from Her Majesty's 22nd Special Air Service came a-knocking.'

'I see,' Victor said.

'He's been in hiding ever since. Which, as you might imagine, surprises no one. Most of the high-profile warlords wanted for war crimes have been sent to The Hague and sentenced to not-enough-time in not-harsh-enough-conditions, but for every one of those scumbags there are twelve of their subordinates who actually conducted those atrocities and have escaped prosecution. Rados is one – and one of the very worst – but like the rest of his ilk he's a hero to some powerful Serb ultranationalists who still believe their very existence as a people was at stake back then. Also, let's not forget that NATO would go on to bomb the holy hell out of Serbia and the locals are still pretty sore about high explosives being dropped on their country, which doesn't help when it comes to convincing certain Serbs that their own people were ever war criminals. Now that the headline-grabbing warlords have been rounded up, Serbia as a whole would rather forget about the rest of its dirty linen. Of course, there are thousands of corpses who aren't able to do that.'

'If Rados has disappeared, what can I do?'

Banik said, 'Rados has only disappeared if you believe the Serb party line. Me, I'm not so trusting. Even without hard intel we know that, like a lot of his kin from that era, he's moved into organised crime and heads up a sizeable network in Belgrade. He stays off the grid himself, but we know he's still in country and probably still in Belgrade itself, or in a big old mansion on the outskirts.

He's probably not even trying very hard to hide, given we believe he's being protected by his powerful friends.'

A fan in the seat behind Banik knocked into him as he got up from his seat. 'Sorry, mate.'

Banik raised a hand to show it was okay and the man shuffled away. He had had enough of the Hammers' display.

'So,' Banik said to Victor when the man had gone. 'You'll take the contract?'

'I'll wait for the particulars before making my decision.'

'Which is why they're waiting in your inbox right now.'

Victor didn't comment on Banik's presumption. He thought of Fletcher's words: *You're nothing but a yes-man.*

'Why do you want Rados dead? Why not send people to track him down and bring him to the ICC?'

Banik shrugged. 'What's the point of trying? The Serbs won't cooperate, so any raid is doomed to fail. Or they will cooperate officially, but someone involved will tip Rados off again. And if we don't tell them it will be seen as an act of war. So, old boy, we need a man such as yourself.'

Victor nodded, accepting the explanation. 'But what's in it for British Intelligence? The war was over a long time ago. There are no political points to score assassinating Rados, are there? So why bother?'

Banik looked offended. 'Why bother? This is an evil man, plain and simple. That's not to mention we have obligations to NATO and the International Criminal Court as well as the Society of the Fucking Civilised. Excuse my language.'

'Excused. This time.'

'If we can't bring Rados to justice then we're going to send justice to him courtesy of a lovely shiny gift-wrapped 9 mm hollow point. Or feel free to use an FMJ, if that's your preference.'

'Somewhat ruthless for a nation without the death penalty, don't you think?'

'We didn't rule the world by being nice.'

'You haven't ruled the world in a long time.'

Banik sighed. 'And look at the mess it's been in ever since.'

They sat in silence for a moment.

'There is another reason why I wanted to see you,' Banik said. 'Since Fletcher's unfortunate accident we've found out he wasn't just whispering secret nothings into his mistress's ear to keep her affections. He had recently started trading intel with other parties. This time for cold hard cash.'

'Why do I have the feeling some of that intel was about me?'

'Because you're a perceptive soul.'

'Go on,' Victor said.

'Apparently, there is an open contract on your head. Fletcher learned of this – I'm not sure exactly when. Instead of passing his discovery on to me, he decided to pass on information about you.'

'To whom?'

'An independent broker. As yet unidentified, but known by the handle Phoenix. He's been brokering a long time, and while he is a dab hand at hiring the right killer for the

48

job, he's even better at staying off the grid. No one knows who he is, where he is, or who his clients are.'

Victor thought of his most recent contract before his work for Banik began. It, like many others before, had done nothing for Victor's popularity amongst the powerful and vengeful. Maybe this bounty on his head was fallout from that, or it could be from any one of the many enemies he had acquired over the past decade-plus as a professional killer.

'I've heard of Phoenix,' Victor said.

'Have you ever done any jobs for him? Actually, I don't know why I'm asking. You wouldn't tell me if you had, would you?'

'That's right,' he agreed. 'But I also wouldn't confirm it if I hadn't. What has Fletcher passed on?'

'That, I don't know. Could be nothing, could be everything.'

'Such a range of possibility isn't particularly useful to me.'

'If I learn more I'll let you know,' Banik said, 'but for now I'm just giving you a heads-up.'

'You mean you're concerned I might get killed before I can kill Rados for you.'

Banik laughed; it would have been ridiculous to pretend otherwise. 'I do also think of you as a friend.'

'Of course you do.'

Ignoring the challenge, Banik said, 'You don't seem very concerned to learn that someone wants you dead.'

Victor shrugged. 'It's nothing new. Acquiring enemies is part of the job description. If nothing else, it means I'm doing something right.'

'Funny, because the way I see it the more friends I have, the better I'm doing at life.'

'Ah,' Victor said, 'but friends can be bought. Enemies are always earned.'

EIGHT

As promised by Banik, the dossier on Rados was waiting for Victor when he logged into the email account he used only for communications with his SIS handler. Whatever he had joked, Victor knew British Intelligence were more than capable of maintaining secure electronic communications. He wouldn't risk dealing with them if they were not. His own security precautions were extensive and required constant changing and updating that was both time-consuming and expensive. They helped guard against his employers as much as his enemies, because one could become the other.

He had a room in the Covent Garden Hotel, where he studied the literature on his target. It was an extensive electronic document summarising everything that SIS knew about Rados and contained photographs and video files, lists of known associates, family information, war history, suspected criminal activities, rumours and hearsay. There was no such thing as too much intel, but as Rados had been in hiding for six years, almost all of the dossier could be dismissed as out of date and of that which remained Victor could take little as provable fact.

Rados was now fifty years old and listed as five foot ten inches tall and one hundred and sixty pounds in weight. His eyes were dark, as was his short curly hair. But aside from his age – accurate due to a copy of his birth certificate – the description offered nothing that could be relied upon. Victor knew as well as anyone how a skilled cosmetic surgeon could alter a person's appearance because his own had changed so many times he no longer had an accurate mental picture of his original face. If he closed his eyes and tried to imagine what he looked like he would see a blurring shift of features, indistinct and ever-changing. The face in the mirror was a mask he could never remove.

Six years ago Rados had been strong but lean. Now, age and inactivity could have stripped away that strength. He could be thin and weak with the stress of living in hiding and under the constant threat of his past or current crimes catching up to him. Or he could be a bloated mass of soft indulgences, having lived the good life for over half a decade as one of Belgrade's organised crime kingpins. Even his height could have changed. Ill health might have shrunk the cartilage in his vertebrae or bowed his legs to make him shorter, or the five foot ten inches might be inaccurate in the first place. His dark hair, short and curly, could now be grey or bleached or shaved or receded or long or straight. His dark eyes could be disguised with contact lenses.

He had been married and was the father of four children when the SAS had stormed his stronghold estate. The family had gone into hiding with him and, impossible as it seemed, had not been seen since.

Rados' alleged criminal activities were in the staples of narcotics and extortion. He had been no mafia boss six years ago, but according to SIS he had spent the last half decade or so expanding his business to become one of the most feared players in Belgrade. Which was a tall order for a man supposed to be in hiding, but Rados' empire was run by his chief lieutenant, free to roam the streets in his stead, and in command of a sizeable crew of criminals who had fierce, unflinching loyalty to their boss. The intel on these was sketchy, since they were considered supplementary figures, but as they were solid links to Rados, Victor wanted to know more.

When Victor had finished with the dossier he headed to the hotel's wood-panelled drawing room, where antique armchairs and sofas were arranged for use by the guests. He nodded a hello to a suited man of about sixty and his twenty-something female companion, and poured himself a bourbon in the drawing room's honesty bar. He noted the drink and his room number in a handwriting that was not his own and sat down in the seat that enabled him to see the entrance in his peripheral vision. He selected a newspaper from a coffee table and opened it up while he considered the contract offered by Banik.

Rados was a hard target, because executing the boss of an extensive criminal network would be dangerous on many levels, and a difficult contract because so little about Rados could be verified, including where or how to find him. Victor would have to track him down, while trying to learn enough about Rados and his movements to be able to orchestrate a successful assassination. But nothing Victor wasn't used to. Anyone capable of squeezing a trigger could be a professional killer, but Victor's contracts were never that simple. If they were he wouldn't be able to charge an exorbitant fee for his services.

Such fees permitted him to stay in hotels like the Covent Garden, which was perhaps his favourite in London. This was his second stay. The last had been five years before, and he would not use the hotel again for a similar length of time to ensure CCTV recordings had long since been destroyed and any staff still working there had forgotten about him by the time he returned. Otherwise, it would be difficult to explain why he had a different name and nationality to his previous visit. With other hotels he deemed four years between stays a sufficient interval to avoid such problems. But with the Covent Garden he wanted to make extra sure no one recognised him. He didn't want to deal with such a problem here. He was far too fond of the amiable staff.

Victor was halfway through his second bourbon while reading about West Ham's disappointing 1-0 loss at home when a woman entered the drawing room. She didn't so much walk, as glide in an effortless gait. The sixty-year-old man watched her without blinking as she selected a place to sit and he received an elbow in the arm from his companion.

The woman's hair was brown. Halfway between blonde and black. Victor didn't know if this particular shade had a name, but he knew where it sat on the colour spectrum.

Such details were important to note. As was her height: five feet five inches. Her limbs were slim but toned. He estimated she weighed forty-five kilograms with a trim 17 per cent body fat. He accepted he could be off by a per cent either way and a kilo or two, but no more. Her age was more difficult to tell. The bar had soft lighting and make-up and creams and cosmetic procedures and supplements were improving all the time. She looked about thirty, but he guessed she was a little older than he was. He looked younger than people thought, even before his face had been cut and filed and filled and re-contoured countless times by the same surgeons who kept Hollywood stars ageless. His work had been done at intervals over the past decade not for vanity but to keep him ahead of his enemies and the ever-increasing presence of CCTV and facial recognition technology.

Victor recognised the glances that she cast his way and he returned them. She was attractive and alone. She wore no wedding ring but she was tanned and even across the room his keen eyes could see the paler band of skin around the finger. He imagined her as a corporate executive by the cut of her suit and the shoes he estimated had cost more than his entire outfit.

He took his drink over to the other side of the room and said, 'May I join you?'

She took her time responding, in a play of making up her mind. 'Why do you want to?'

'Because I'd rather talk than read.'

She didn't expect such a response. 'You don't like newspapers?'

'The news is depressing.'

'You don't look sad to me.'

'That's the bourbon.'

She gestured. 'Please, have a seat.'

'Thank you.' He sat opposite her. 'I'm Leonard.'

'Abigail.'

She offered her hand and he took it. Her nails were manicured and polished. Her skin was cool and so soft it was almost without texture.

'I'm so glad you have a normal name, Leonard.'

'Why's that?'

'I have this theory about people with unusual or exotic names. In my experience they're all utterly, mind-numbingly boring.'

'Please explain,' Victor said. 'I'm something of a fan of names.'

'What a curious thing to be a fan of, Leonard. My theory is that people who have interesting names are never interesting themselves because every time they introduce themselves to someone new there inevitably will be a conversation about their name. *Oh, what an unusual name you have, I must know where it comes from . . .*'

'I see,' Victor said. 'So they have the same conversation every time they meet someone and as a result never learn the art of small talk.'

'Which is absolutely an art in my opinion.'

'I would disagree, but only in that label. Small talk is more of a science, because it can be learned and mastered, whereas art relies on innate talent.'

She considered. 'Hmm. Seeing as I always consider

myself to be right I'm not fond of being disagreed with, but you may have a point there.'

'And in finding such middle ground we are able to continue the small talk and not digress into argument.'

'We can always negotiate,' Abigail said with a smile. 'And yes, I was hoping you'd notice that little piece of conversational acquiescence, especially as I'm entirely self-taught.' She grinned, pleased with herself, and he humoured her with a small smile of his own. 'Aren't you glad your parents didn't give you an interesting name now, Leonard?'

'I have a confession to make: Leonard's not my real name.'

'And my name isn't Abigail. So we have something in common already. Besides being equally good at chit-chat.'

'I wonder what else we'll be equally good at.'

Her lips pursed for a moment. 'I hope you're not going to be lewd, Leonard.'

'Not yet, at least.'

She examined her nails. 'How has your day played out? Mine has been a tiresome bore, so I do hope we haven't both suffered.'

'I've been working late.'

'Tut, tut, Leonard,' she said. 'You know what they say about all work and no play.'

'I do, but I have a new job offer I'm considering.'

'You must be very much in demand to have such a luxury. What's to consider? I take it they're offering you sufficient remuneration.'

'Substantial remuneration,' Victor said. 'But a former employee warned me the company doesn't play fair with its people.'

She arched an eyebrow. 'And do you with your employers?'

He shook his head. 'Never.'

She winked at him. 'Then there's no problem, is there?'

'The company is under the assumption I'll take the job. They think I can't say no.'

She said, 'Ah, I see. So, it's only your ego keeping you from saying yes. Is that a decent enough reason to turn the job down?'

'I don't like to be predictable.'

'Ah, but you're not by virtue of the fact you're unsure whether to say yes. They, however, *believe* you to be predictable. That's exactly where you want them to be.'

'Do you want to know what I do?'

'Not really. I don't like getting to know someone via their CV. I hope there's more to you than just your profession, Leonard.'

'I'm not sure even I know.'

She smiled a little, as if she had set a trap that he had walked into of his own free will. 'Do you like to take risks, Leonard?'

'No.'

'That sounds like a surprisingly honest answer.'

Victor nodded. 'That's because it is.'

'I would suggest that most, if not all, men would say yes when asked that question by a strange woman they approached in a hotel, don't you think?'

'It felt like the right moment for veracity.'

'I like your use of words, Leonard. A man under forty with an expansive vocabulary is something of a rarity I've found. Why is it that you don't like to take risks? No, don't tell me: you like to be in control. Or would saying you like to be *in charge* be more ... accurate?'

'Now who's being lewd?'

'I never said I was a lady. Is that a problem for you?'

'Quite the opposite.'

'Excellent, then you won't have a problem with me inviting myself back to your room.'

She watched his eyes with a careful stare.

'Let's go back to your room instead.'

He watched hers with as much care.

'Sure,' she said after a moment for deliberation, and stood. 'Let's go.'

NINE

Her room was identical to Victor's own, but one floor higher. A little small, because the hotel had stood for a century or more, but decorated and furnished to a grand taste that teetered on the brink of extravagance yet managed to remain understated.

Like his own room, Abigail's appeared almost unoccupied. The bed had not been slept in and her belongings were either still inside the wheeled suitcase that lay in one corner or had been distributed amongst the wardrobe and drawers available. The scent of her perfume lingering in the air and the suitcase were the only signs of habitation besides a single pillow on the king-sized bed that had been disturbed.

She reached out to him and he allowed her to grip his arm while she stood on alternate single legs to remove her shoes. She placed them by the door.

She asked, 'Would you like something from the minibar?'

'Sparkling water, please.'

'Nothing stronger?'

He shook his head. 'I've already had a lot to drink.'

Her gaze searched him. In the dimly lit drawing room he hadn't noticed, but she had amazing dark eyes, full of joy and energy. 'You don't seem drunk to me.'

'Can't be too careful.'

She smiled, playful. 'Wise.'

Squatting, she took a glass bottle of water from the room's minibar and a miniature bottle of vodka for herself.

'Could you pour while I use the facilities?'

Victor said, 'Sure.'

She took her clutch bag into the room's en suite and left Victor alone for almost four minutes. When she returned he had poured the vodka over ice into a tumbler and was sipping from the bottle of water.

'No glass for you? How uncouth.'

'I'm yet to be civilised.'

'That sounds delightfully intriguing.'

He handed her the tumbler and she finished the vodka in one swallow. He took the glass back from her and set it down while she slipped off her dress. She faced him.

'Don't keep me waiting,' she said.

He didn't.

After, he dressed while she showered and he waited for her to return. She was quick in the shower, and exited the en suite wearing one of the hotel robes provided. It was brilliant white and thick. She had washed her brown hair and it sat wrapped in a bun at the back of her head.

'Wouldn't you like to shower too?' she said when she saw him in his suit.

Victor said, 'I don't shower as a general rule.'

She laughed in surprise and distaste. 'You don't?'

'But I'll bathe later in my own room.'

Her nose wrinkled as she crossed the room with a hair-dryer and plugged it in a socket near the right side of the bed. She took a seat. She switched the hairdryer to her left hand and thumbed a switch while her right hand moved out of Victor's line of sight.

The hairdryer roared and she looked his way. Her right hand appeared a moment later with an automatic hand-gun in her grip. It was a .22 calibre SIG with a suppressor, small and compact.

She aimed it at his chest and squeezed the trigger.

Victor didn't hear the click of the hammer falling because the hairdryer blocked out any other sound, as she had intended it to. Even a low-powered .22 wasn't silent when suppressed.

While she sat still in a moment of confusion he placed a single .22 cartridge on to the room's desk. It had a conical slug and a steel core for piercing body armour. The low-powered bullet would have no chance of penetrating even the slimmest of Kevlar vests otherwise. The shape meant less physical trauma and hydrostatic shock to the body as a result, but a shot to the heart was still a shot to the heart.

She deactivated the hairdryer. 'I'm not used to the weight,' she said, referencing the SIG. 'I couldn't tell it was empty.'

Victor was silent.

'While I was in the shower?' she asked.

62

He nodded.

'That's why you *let* me go first. I thought you were being a gentleman.'

'I am a gentleman.'

'How did you know?'

Victor saw no harm in explaining. 'You hadn't slept in the bed but the right pillow wasn't perfect. In a hotel like this they always are.'

'I thought I'd put it back as I found it.'

'You're no maid. You shouldn't have hidden the gun between the mattress and headboard.'

'I wanted it close by.'

Victor didn't respond. He wasn't a teacher giving a lesson.

'Do you want to know who sent me? We don't have to get unpleasant. We can always negotiate, remember.'

'I already know who: open contract, brokered by Phoenix.'

'Biggest contract I ever competed for. There must be a dozen separate killers gunning for you. What did you do to piss off the client?'

'I can't even be sure who the client is this time.'

'This time?'

'You're not the first assassin to come after me. You're not even the first this week who tried to kill me.'

'That explains that nasty cut on your thigh. Popular boy, aren't you?'

'It's my winning personality.'

She said, 'Did you suspect before? When we were chit-chatting in the drawing room?'

'You did nothing wrong.'

'That's not answering my question.'

Victor said, 'I suspect everyone I encounter will attempt to kill me.'

'Too much of a stretch for the pretty girl in the hotel to find you cute?'

'Call it professional paranoia.'

She smirked. 'But it's not paranoia if they're really after you, is it?'

He nodded. 'It's saved me plenty of times before.'

'Why even come back to my room if you knew I was a threat?'

'I didn't know, not for sure. But I find it's better to test my paranoia in a private setting.'

'I can't argue with that.' She then frowned for a second, thinking. 'But if you noticed the pillow, why did you go through with having sex with me?'

'I'm a man.'

'A man who doesn't like to take risks, you told me before.'

'My survival depends on not taking risks,' Victor explained. 'But, every once in a while, I'll roll the dice so I can feel alive.'

She accepted this with a small nod. 'Now I understand why you didn't want to go back to your room. You didn't want any evidence of my presence left behind.'

'That's correct.'

Her voice was even, but quiet. 'You're not going to let me go, are you?'

His was the same. 'No, I'm not.'

She took a breath and stood to face him. Her amazing eyes seemed polished in the dim light. 'Don't keep me waiting.'

Again, he didn't.

When it was done he moved her body to the bathtub and placed the privacy sign on the bedroom door. Even for London it was too late for stores to be open so he sat in the room's armchair until morning before leaving in search of hard-shell luggage, a hacksaw and waterproof refuse sacks.

TEN

It wasn't raining, but the clouds over London looked ready to drench the city. Victor's counter surveillance took him all over the city, on buses and on the tube, walking and in cabs. He had no specific destination so could allow himself to be directed by randomness – alighting a bus after four stops because he boarded with four people; asking a black cab driver to pull over after nine minutes and seven seconds because the vehicle's radio was tuned to 97 FM, and so on – and he found himself in an area he had once operated within.

Not ideal, but not a significant problem either because it didn't take Victor long to find what he was looking for. Occupying a paved square, under the shadow of a clock tower, was a small market with stalls selling fake designer clothes, faded and furled paperbacks, counterfeit movies in several formats, cheap shoes and food produce. It was like any other market in any poor area of any European city. Traders shouted over one another and local residents shuffled between stalls, browsing and haggling. There were two stalls selling what he needed and he ignored the overselling while he perused the range of mobile phones that the original owners had sold for cash to buy the next handset as well as those that had been stolen, unlocked and presented for sale for what he needed. There were plenty to choose from, ranging from ancient handsets that looked like relics but would survive the apocalypse to sleek smartphones only months old that wouldn't survive being sat on.

Victor bought the cheapest he could find because he wanted a phone that was a phone and nothing else, and the greater the functionality of the device the greater the risk of compromise. He paid extra for a charger held together with electrical tape and bought credit from a nearby store. He charged the phone in a coffee shop while he enjoyed a red-hot double espresso, surrounded by young people on their laptops.

By the time he had finished, the phone had more than enough battery charge for his requirements. He left the coffee shop and entered the international calling code for Germany, the Hamburg area code, and a local number that he had memorised what seemed like a lifetime ago.

He would ditch the phone as soon as the call had been ended. A second-hand phone that used prepaid credit was close to untraceable. Victor didn't carry a phone unless he needed it for a specific reason. At best phones were portable tracking devices; at worst they were portable recording devices. Even if there had been some way to stop the GPS ping and ensure no outside body could hack the firmware, Victor wouldn't carry one. He had seen the effect they had on other people. He imagined some future subspecies of human with neck muscles so weak from millennia of atrophy that eyes no longer pointed forward, but down.

Victor had no friends and few acquaintances. He did, however, have access to the services of many individuals across the world who offered skills or assistance to him that ranged from useful to essential. Some of these he had been using for the duration of his professional career; others he knew of and what they could provide but had never called upon; a select few he had encountered during contracts or their preparation and had made sure to remember for when he needed them.

The dial tone sounded for seven rings before a click announced the receiver answering.

'Who is this?'

Victor recognised the female voice that answered the phone. He had spent enough time with her to know she was in her mid-fifties, but a lifetime of smoking had given her an ancient-sounding growl.

'A man you owe,' he said.

The woman replied with a snort. 'You must be mistaken. I am in no one's debt, though there are many people out there who are in mine.'

'Then you might want to see a neurologist because your memory is failing.'

'I don't have time for this,' she said. 'I'm going to hang up now so you can harass someone else.'

'No, you're not going to hang up. You're going to stay on this line and listen to what I have to say.'

The line stayed connected. She said, 'Why would I do that?'

'Because I can tell from the tone of your voice that there is a seed of recollection germinating in your mind as we talk and it is growing roots of memory of the dark and suffering and sound and fear.'

She didn't respond.

He continued: 'There is a man you owe everything to. You owe him for the breaths you are now taking. You owe him because he once handed you a phone while you lay dying.'

He pictured blood glistening on plastic sheeting.

There was a moment of silence and all he could hear was rapid breathing before she said a single word: 'You.'

'Hello, Georg.'

She said, 'I don't use that name any more.'

Victor said, 'You're still Georg to me, and you always will be.'

'It's been a long time. I didn't expect to hear from you again. I *hoped* I wouldn't hear from you again.'

'That's a very peculiar way of thanking me for saving your life.'

She grunted. 'You did save my life, that's true. But why do I now think you only did so to create a debt that you could collect at a later point?'

'You must not believe in the innate goodness of your fellow human beings.'

She grunted again, louder. 'What do you want? Why are you contacting me after all this time?'

'I'm just calling to see how you're doing.'

'I'd forgotten about your strange sense of humour,' Georg said. 'But if you have even the slightest interest in my well-being then you should know I can almost walk unassisted again. I'm not dead, thanks to you, but I still need physiotherapy.'

Victor said, 'I would like a delivery to Belgrade and I would like it fast.'

'You can order pizza online these days. You don't need to call.'

'I'm lactose intolerant.'

Georg said, 'How do you know I'm still in that business?'

'Because physiotherapy isn't cheap and cigarettes cost almost as much.'

'Maybe you should send me a shopping list.'

'I was thinking the same. Email address?'

She gave him one, which he committed to memory. 'How are you going to pay? I'm sure you're in no rush to visit me in Hamburg after last time. And I do not travel well these days.'

'I would like to think that I've already covered the bill.'

'Would you indeed?'

Victor remained silent.

The sound of breathing returned. 'Okay, let's say for argument's sake that I agree I have something of a debt to you and you're entitled to cash in.'

'For argument's sake,' he agreed.

Georg said, 'But I don't yet know what you want. I'm not a charity.'

'I understand,' Victor said. 'You're not a charity and I'm not someone who likes to feel cheated in an exchange.'

'Yeah, I get what you're saying. Very subtle, as always. But if you're reasonable in your request then I'll be reasonable in honouring it. Is that acceptable to you?'

'It is,' Victor said. 'Please do your best to expedite the dispatch.'

'I offer a special courier service for valued clients.'

He ignored the sarcasm and said, 'I appreciate your kindness.'

'And if my kindness is sufficient, will you consider us even?'

Victor hung up.

ELEVEN

Victor travelled light. The fewer items he carried the fewer things could be discerned about him from his possessions. A small suitcase, attaché case or overnight bag was his luggage of choice. A change of clothes and basic toiletries were all he required beyond his silicone hand gel. He preferred to swap clothes as soon as it was possible. Items bought in the area he was operating within helped him blend in with the locals. Foreign labels in his clothes gave away his movements. Removing them made him look like he had something to hide. When time was limited or he knew he was heading somewhere he would have a hard time finding the right attire, he travelled with clothes bought from global brands available across the world.

He napped on the flight because no one was going to assassinate him while on a commercial airliner. Perhaps they would bring the whole plane down to fulfil the contract, but no professional good enough to pose a threat would be so reckless as to try on board, and if the plane was going to crash he'd prefer to sleep through it anyway.

He awoke a moment before the shadow fell across his face. His eyes focused on a woman in a business suit and for a second he found himself looking at the assassin who had called herself Abigail. He blinked and the face changed, softening to that of a younger woman.

'Hey,' she said, cautious and nervous. 'I don't suppose I can take that seat next to you? I saw no one is sitting in it and the douche in the seat behind me keeps kicking me in the back. Sorry to wake you, by the way.'

'That's okay,' Victor said in return. 'I was only dozing.' He shifted, sitting more upright. 'Sure, be my guest.'

The young woman was overweight and awkward in her movements. She squeezed past his skewed knees and he watched her hands the whole time. The woman had a plastic bottle of mineral water in one and the other was a closed fist. She opened it to help her balance and the need to watch her disappeared. She didn't so much sit as fall into her seat.

He was suspicious at first that she had chosen to sit next to him when other free seats were available. His usual posture and expression sent out subtle messages that put off most people from engaging with him, but he had no control over himself when asleep. It seemed he was approachable like that.

The young woman continued their small talk and though she was pleasant enough the experience at the Covent Garden hotel was a solid reminder that he could trust no encounter, no matter how innocent it appeared. Even if this woman wasn't a professional killer she might be some other kind of threat – law enforcement, spy or watcher.

'What about your bag?' Victor asked, because he had never seen a woman on a flight without a purse or handbag or other carry-on luggage.

'Overhead locker above my seat. I'll get it when we land. If I hadn't got away from Mr Footsie back there then I might have done something I'd no doubt pretend to regret.'

Victor nodded. She seemed genuine and after half an hour of chatting about her Tibetan mastiff he was content to file her away as nothing more than a talkative civilian. Even if she prevented him sleeping, she helped pass the time.

They said their goodbyes as they disembarked the plane and Victor began scanning the faces waiting at arrivals.

The terminal was hot and the air stifling. Outside it was winter but the heating system was set to tropical. Rich women were carrying their fur coats and their husbands were sweating. Victor changed his watch for the new time zone. He planned to trade it for cash – it was a $10,000 Rolex – but he didn't want to give the jeweller or pawn-broker a clue as to where he had travelled from.

Victor ignored the car-hire services. Belgrade was small and its public transport adequate for his needs. Renting a car left a paper trail he preferred to avoid. He took a cab to the city and had the driver drop him off near Trg Repub-like, Belgrade's most prominent square, where he could disappear among the tourists.

It was cold and windy in Belgrade. He was happy being

uncomfortable to gain some other advantage, but the temperature let Victor's hands keep their feeling even without gloves. Most other people wore them or mittens, which had the added benefit of helping him identify threats. No competent assassin would wear thick gloves or mittens if they had a gun to use.

With no known location for Rados, little could be done until Victor had found him. That would take an indeterminate amount of time – days, or even weeks, depending on how off the grid the Serb was living. Victor needed somewhere to lay his head when he was not hunting down his target.

Hotels were his primary choice of residence. They offered security and a reasonable degree of privacy as well as convenience. For this job, he wanted somewhere else. The two recent attempts on his life had to be a consideration. He could not rely on his anonymity as his first line of defence this time. With every job he took he increased his exposure, but it seemed Fletcher's treachery had done immeasurable damage. He had numerous identities and aliases and legends to draw upon, but none were ironclad, as the two assassins had demonstrated.

Victor didn't want to leave any record of his whereabouts, which was impossible with a hotel. Finding a private landlord who was happy to accept cash and not ask questions was easy when he was paying three months' rent upfront. It was more than he would have liked to pay because marking himself as wealthy also made him memorable, but it was balanced out by not having to provide any documentation.

The apartment occupied the top floor of a townhouse within the walled old town. It was more space than he needed – enough for a whole family – but he liked the fact his footsteps echoed loud and clear on the hardwood floors of the building's corridors and staircase. The other benefit was the basement the landlord lamented could not be rented because of damp. Victor agreed it was a shame as he noticed the padlock securing it was one he could pick in under fifteen seconds.

The building was ten storeys of late eighteenth-century architecture in a neighbourhood built to house rich merchants and minor aristocracy. Two hundred years later and it was a fine place for an assassin to make a temporary home. The landlord owned several of the apartments and rented them out to tourists and business travellers, whom he could charge premium fees for short stays. Victor liked that. It meant he would have fewer neighbours than he might otherwise. With a dusting of snow on the ground and the temperature hovering around zero the temporary residents were even fewer. The landlord didn't like the winter for this reason, but with undisguised glee explained how he made up for it during the summer when he raised the prices in line with the increasing temperature.

It had been listed as part-furnished, which equated to a sofa, coffee table and bed. There was a mouldy cardboard box containing crockery left by the previous tenant in the kitchen and little else but dust. The landlord assured him the entire apartment had been cleaned by professionals. Victor nodded.

He paid the landlord with an envelope of cash, which

made the man lick his lips with delight. He was too busy calculating how much more profit he would collect by failing to inform the taxman to consider that his new tenant might also want to avoid a paper trail. Cash was always the preference for transactions, but there was only so much Victor could travel with without causing problems in airports. He supplemented this with expensive watches and jewellery that could be worn across borders without raising suspicion and then sold for cash at his destination. Not all transactions could be completed with cash, and so he had prepay credit cards as backup. The handful of solid identities that he used to hold bank accounts and be a registered director of offshore shell corporations were never used while working. They were harder and harder to establish all the time and the number he kept active had diminished in recent years.

'What are you planning to do during your time in Belgrade?' the landlord asked once they had concluded their business.

'I'm writing a book. This will be my home-slash-office. I need to lock myself away from the world to get it finished.'

'Oh,' the landlord said, surprised and disappointed not to have a more exciting tenant. 'What kind of a book are you writing?'

'It's a fictionalised account of the death of Archduke Ferdinand.'

'A historical novel then. How interesting. You understand a lot about the assassination?'

'Well,' Victor said. 'They do say to write what you know.'

TWELVE

The first night in the apartment Victor didn't sleep. He stayed awake until dawn, passing the time by reading a Serbian translation of a novel he had read before. It helped with his language skills. He spent the night sitting on the sofa, pausing reading for every sound that echoed and seeped through the old building. The near-empty apartment amplified the ticking of pipes and clatter of shoes. He kept all the doors open flush to neighbouring walls to aid his ears and so no enemy could hide behind them.

It had been years since Victor had slept like a regular person. The night was the most dangerous time. Killers operated then as preference, both to remain unseen and to catch their target unawares. As equal parts killer and target, Victor took his rest in the morning whenever he had the choice, in the afternoon if that choice was compromised and in the evening as a last resort. The time between midnight and dawn were the prime hours to both hunt and be hunted.

When enough sunlight had seeped into the apartment for him to see the fine hair on the back of his hands, he set the novel down on the floor next to the sofa, made himself comfortable, and slept.

If he dreamed, he had no memory of it when he awoke a few minutes after midday. He lay still for a moment and listened, identifying no sounds to suggest an enemy was present and registering no physiological reactions to advise his subconscious had become aware of danger while his consciousness was compromised.

Satisfied, he sat up on the sofa and breathed in the cold air. He shivered and rubbed some warmth into his arms. He slept without the comfort and constriction of bedding and his suit was no protection against the ambient chill.

He woke alert and refreshed because he knew his own body and the rest it required as well as his body had grown used to his sleeping habits. He made himself coffee regardless, because it had become habit long ago and, needed or not, he liked it and little vices made life worth living. Coffee drinkers lived longer, he'd once read whilst recovering from multiple lacerations caused by a custom-crafted combat knife.

He nudged open a blind enough to peek outside. Looking north, he could see the Danube and the far bank. Somewhere in the grey haze of winter clouds a plane was passing overhead. Cargo containers, sun-stained and rusted, were piled on a barge that made its slow passage along the river to the port. Gulls rested on top of the containers and cleaned their wings. Relying on his eye alone it was hard to be sure, but it looked to be seven hundred metres to the nearest conceivable sniping nest. If he was fortunate enough to spot the flash he would have two-thirds of a second to move before the high-velocity round smashed through the window and killed him. If he didn't see the flash then he would be dead before the broken glass reached the floorboards.

Victor rubbed his hands and exhaled, watching the vapour condense on the cold window glass. He didn't open the window. Precautions, no matter how small and insignificant alone, worked in conjunction with others, building and combining to form a pattern of behaviour that had saved his life before and could do again.

He stepped away from the window after a short moment in case there was a marksman on the other side of the river preparing a shot.

He washed, then applied a new dressing to his thigh, burning the old one in the kitchen sink. The wound was healing well. It was still painful, but not debilitating.

The front door had two quality locks, but the landlord no doubt had his own set of keys despite assuring Victor this was not the case. He had slept with the sofa barricading the door, and once dressed he found a locksmith and had the locks changed for the most secure ones available. The landlord wasn't going to be happy when he came to inspect the property in a month's time, but Victor would either be gone without a trace by then, else he would reinstall the original locks the morning of the landlord's inspection.

Once the new lock was fitted he set about securing the rest of the apartment. Retrofitting the windows with armoured glass was not a realistic option, but the height from the ground would make entry through the windows impractical. Not impossible, because Victor knew he could scale the exterior, and even if his strength and climbing skills were exceptional, there were others like him out there. The many scars hidden beneath his clothes were proof of that.

The apartment was on the building's north side. Not ideal, because he would have preferred direct sunlight to shine on the windows for most of the day, creating glare and making the job of watchers or snipers more difficult. He had taken it anyway, because compromises always had to be made, and the apartment's other benefits balanced out this imperfection.

The landlord had suggested Victor acquire some thick rugs because the bare floorboards would get cold underfoot, and though he agreed it was a good idea, he had no intention of adding muffling agents to what was a great line of defence. Years before when he had lived in one location he had emulated medieval Japanese lords and used 'nightingale' floorboards that sang underfoot to protect him from assassins as the daimyos had been protected from ninja. Polished hard flooring was an acceptable middle ground. Footsteps would be loud unless an intruder removed shoes or boots, but then would lose traction in socks or barefoot.

With his new tools Victor lay on the floor and began prising up floorboards at strategic locations – before the front door, under the windows and in the threshold of doorways. Even without the freedom to replace the flooring he could create a range of tones that would allow him to identify the precise location of an enemy by which sound reached his ear; any warning was better than none.

Quality cameras were easy enough to get hold of through legitimate channels and he installed one to cover every window and door of the apartment. Like the replacement locks, they could be removed before the landlord returned. He couldn't disguise them without considerable work knocking holes into walls or ceilings, but no one was going to spot the cameras unless they broke in. In which case it wouldn't matter, because they would either succeed in killing him or would themselves be killed.

The cameras, marketed for covert surveillance, had extensive wireless ranges. Even with obstructions from thick old Serbian masonry, they provided clear images at twenty-five frames per second to the laptop Victor had bought to receive the signals and act as his security hub. He kept it by the sofa at all times. He had selected the model with longest battery life in case of an outage. The cameras themselves were motion-activated and so consumed an insignificant amount of power. They would last far longer than he might need them.

The building's basement was as damp and mouldy as the landlord had claimed, but the space was valuable and the landlord was using it to store a multitude of items that were not susceptible to water damage: paint cans, synthetic brushes, rollers, sacks of cement and other building materials. There were also piles of rotting cardboard boxes, timber and wooden furniture.

He navigated the basement with a torch, looking for

somewhere to hide the waterproof backpack over his shoulder. He heard the quiet drip of a leaking pipe, a constant three-second rhythm. Drip. One. Two. Three. Drip.

The stacks of paint cans would provide the best cover, but he didn't know the state of the other apartments. He didn't know what the landlord was planning. Decorators might arrive tomorrow to start work on a recently vacated apartment. Instead, he opted to stash the backpack in a narrow gap between some rotting boxes and an old dining-room table and chairs. A keen observer might spot the hiding place if they were looking for it, but anyone who came down to access the paint and brushes – which was the greater risk – would remain oblivious to its presence.

The backpack and its contents formed a go-bag that Victor could access without returning to his apartment, in the event he found it necessary to leave Belgrade in a hurry. Should that contingency arise, the go-bag held a passport and accompanying documents to get him across borders, five thousand dollars in a cellophane-wrapped package and a titanium Tag Heuer to exchange for currency, plus a shaving kit, deodorant and face wipes. The latter wouldn't help if he was covered in blood, but he wouldn't attempt to pass through airport security in such a state. The grooming kit would however guard against body odour and a face slick with sweat, both of which were certain to draw attention. He let his facial hair grow between jobs so it could be shaved off if he required a change of appearance. A beard changed the whole shape of the face and its presence or absence made a considerable difference to his chances of being spotted by enemies or the authorities. *We're looking for a man – tall, dark hair, beard.*

There was no weapon because he had none yet available and a go-bag was to run with, not fight. If he grabbed it and ran straight into the cops, he was clean. They might be suspicious of the contents if they searched him, but he would be in far worse trouble if they found a firearm on his person.

With his safe house all set up and his go-bag secured, he could turn his attention to the next part of his preparations.

It was time to gather information.

THIRTEEN

Victor didn't know Belgrade. He didn't know its neighbourhoods and its idiosyncrasies, but he knew criminals. They were the same all over the world. They all wanted to make maximum money from minimum effort, same as everyone else. The ways they went about it might be different from regular citizens, but underground capitalism was universal.

He was well practised at asking the right questions, but finding the right people to ask was the difficult part. By the end of the first day he had gone from knowing no one to having half a dozen names in his head. Some had cost him money, others had been volunteered in exchange for a cigarette or anecdote. Different people had different needs.

After a second day on the streets he had narrowed those half-dozen names down to one.

Victor found the man in a back alley behind a traditional

kafana bistro, sitting on an upturned beer crate, playing cards with a boy of maybe eleven.

As Victor neared, the man waved the boy away; he offered no protest but scurried through the open kitchen entrance.

The man didn't look like a fixer. He looked like a no one. He was dressed in clothes that didn't fit right and needed a wash. His hair was thinning and cut short. Even without seeing the dirty fingernails, Victor's sense of smell told him the guy hadn't showered in a while. He didn't relate competence to cleanliness, however. Some of the fiercest and most dependable men he had known had cared least about their appearance and personal hygiene.

'I heard someone was asking about me,' the fixer said.

'I'm told you know all about Belgrade,' Victor replied. 'I'm told you know how the city works.'

The fixer exhaled by way of an answer. His face was pallid – iron deficiency and lack of sunlight. His eyes were bloodshot. The skin of his cheeks was marked by acne and broken thread veins. His lips were thin and cracked. When he opened his mouth, Victor wasn't surprised to see the man's teeth were disgusting.

'If you help me,' Victor said, 'I will pay you very well.'

'What do you need?'

'Many things, but I hope you can help me with a couple of them.'

The fixer looked him up and down. 'No, I don't think I can help you with anything.'

'No problem,' Victor said. 'I'll take my money elsewhere.'

The fixer shrugged like he didn't care and watched Victor go. When Victor had made it to the end of the block he heard the sound of hurried footsteps behind him.

He turned to see the fixer jogging along the alley in his filthy trainers. The man moved with an awkward, almost pained gait – it was hard to tell whether it was the result of injury, or an utter lack of physical fitness. Only as he drew closer could Victor be certain it was the second. Victor didn't understand that. No one expected a car to run without the right fuel and proper maintenance.

The fixer was panting when he stopped. He spat out a rope of saliva on to the pavement and wiped his brow with the back of a hand.

'Are you going to vomit?' Victor asked.

The fixer shook his head, but couldn't answer. He fumbled in a pocket for a cigarette he'd rolled earlier.

'That'll help,' Victor said.

The fixer ignored him and straightened out the roll-up that had become bent and creased. He lit it with a disposable lighter.

'Take your time,' Victor said.

'I can help,' the fixer said after he'd taken a couple of deep inhales. He coughed as smoke was expelled from his nostrils. 'I know this city. Whatever you need, I can get.'

'Why pretend otherwise?'

He shrugged. 'In case you were a cop.'

'Do I look like a cop to you?'

The fixer studied him as if seeing Victor for the first time. He shook his head, but it took a while for him to do so because if Victor wasn't a cop the fixer had no idea what to make of him. He didn't ask, however, which showed promise.

'What should I call you?' Victor asked.

'Hector. What about you?'

'Achilles.'

The fixer didn't react. Victor didn't know if Hector was the fixer's real name or a fake one, but he thought it had been a pretty good joke. There was no pleasing some people.

Hector offered his hand. Victor didn't shake it. The Petri dish of microorganisms no doubt clinging to his palm didn't encourage Victor to break protocol for the benefit of improving social connections.

Hector didn't seem to be offended. 'Were you followed here?'

Even for a man of Victor's experience and skill such a thing was impossible to be sure of if there was a professional crew of watchers involved, but his response was a simple, 'No,' because the fixer would never have dealt with anyone approaching professional standards. His only concern was avoiding cops or fellow criminals.

'What do you need?' Hector asked.

'The same thing everyone needs: love.'

The fixer said, 'I can get you a woman. No problem. Blonde? Tits. Whatever. Or a boy, if you like. Or both even. I don't judge.'

'I was joking,' Victor said. 'I want a car.'

Hector looked dumbstruck.

'You do know what a car is, don't you?'

Hector shook himself out of the daze and nodded. 'Of course. You can't rent one?'

'I don't want the paperwork.'

For this job Victor was operating under a Hungarian legend that was clean and he wanted to keep it that way if at all possible. Albert Bartha was a thirty-five-year-old resident of Taksony, a town to the south of Budapest. He had been born with a prolapsed umbilical cord that had caused severe oxygen deprivation leading to long-term cognitive problems. He required twenty-four-hour care and had never had a job, been to school, or owned a passport until Victor had applied for one in his name using a copy of Albert's birth certificate and forged documents. Victor had used Bartha's identity before and would again if this job was completed without complications – genuine identities were hard to come by and difficult to maintain, so he preferred not to discard them after use. If compromised, however, the Bartha ID would be buried like so many others had been over the years.

He had a spare identity, a backup, that he had picked up from a post office in the city centre, having mailed it to himself days before leaving London. It was the safest way to travel with multiple identities. Victor had a few ways of limiting the odds of being searched by airport security, but there were no guarantees and getting caught with bogus identification was not a risk worth taking, especially when he had no genuine identification. The spare was now in his go-bag should he need it.

'You don't know how to steal a car?' Hector asked.

Victor said, 'Do you want my money, or not?'

The fixer shrugged. 'Sure, if you want a car I'll get you a car.'

'I'm also looking for work.'

If Hector thought he was stupid before, now he thought he was crazy. 'You think I'm hiring people? For what? To run my empire?'

'I didn't say you,' Victor pointed out. 'But maybe you know people. Maybe you can put the word out.'

'What kind of people are you talking about?'

Victor said, 'You know exactly the kind of people I'm talking about.'

'They don't hire men in suits.'

'So you do know such people.'

The fixer didn't respond.

'Get me a car,' Victor said. 'Something that won't be missed. And while you're doing that you can make enquiries on my behalf, for which you will receive a substantial finder's fee.'

'How substantial?'

'Enough to get your teeth fixed at the very least.'

Hector said, 'What kind of work can you do? You look like a lawyer to me.'

'I'm a man of many talents. If there's work going, I can do it. You know exactly what I'm talking about.'

The fixer swallowed. He nodded. 'I'll ask around. See what I can do.'

Victor took out a roll of cash. 'Just make sure everyone knows I'm not cheap, but I'm worth every penny.'

FOURTEEN

A cab dropped him half a mile away from his destination because Victor wanted the driver to know where he was heading about as much as he wanted to turn up there without proper recon. It was cold and wet and the cab had been warm and comfortable, but some rules could never be broken.

Victor trusted no one. He expected to be betrayed. Even when logic suggested betrayal was improbable, his caution persisted, fuelled by protocol, necessity and the knowledge that no one was dependable. A kind man had once told him he should never assume malice when he could assume incompetence. The philosophy, like many, made a lot of sense in the normal world, but would get a professional killed in record time.

Georg, like Hector, was an underworld fixer. But whereas Hector was a middleman of sorts, Georg's speciality was trading in illicit materials. Victor had first dealt with her when the requirements of a particular contract demanded explosives only she could supply. She'd had protection in the shape of a couple of heavies with guns, but had Victor not been present when her former business partner's crew had ambushed her, she would now be dead. He was confident that not only would she remember her debt to him, she would recall that he had been the only person to walk away unharmed that night. Even if she viewed Victor as a serious threat – which made sense, because he was – she had neither the resources nor stupidity to attempt to neutralise that threat. Doing what he asked was a simpler and more effective way of staying alive.

However, there was a German assassin out there who had found him once and an unknown number of others seeking to claim the large remuneration offered in return for his life. *Biggest I've ever competed for*, Abigail had said. Maybe someone had found out about his connection to Georg. The odds were against it, but caution hadn't killed him yet.

The neighbourhood was quiet. It was an industrial area along the river. Between a junkyard and a martial arts dojo was a strip of brownfield land guarded by a high chain-link fence topped with a spiral of razor wire. A length of heavy chain bowed between two posts created a gate of sorts. Victor stepped over. Disused shipping containers, old tyres and rusted car body shells formed an uneven backdrop against the dark sky.

Cracked concrete on the ground told of some building long-since demolished, but the land had been left to rot, used as a dumping ground and place for drug addicts and the homeless to loiter. Victor watched his step, avoiding broken bottles and the occasional syringe. Now, in the dead of winter and without shelter, it seemed empty of humanity. Which was why Victor had chosen it. The icy wind blowing in from the river would ruin any junkie's fix.

He took his time, regardless. Maybe those sleeping rough or seeking the blissful escape only narcotics could deliver were absent, but the cold would not deter Victor from striking a target so it would not deter someone like him.

Hampered by lack of ambient light and a howling wind he moved at a slow pace, unable to rely on his eyes or ears to detect an enemy until he was in close proximity. He circled the shipping containers and stripped-down cars, checking the best ambush spots. He checked the worst ones too, because he couldn't know who might be waiting; being killed through overestimating an enemy's competence was an indignity he couldn't bear.

When he was confident he was alone – because it was impossible to be certain – he found the bald and frayed tyre he had carved with a letter G earlier that day after learning the shipment was imminent. It sat alone, but near to a pile of other tyres that had been abandoned here. The tyre lay flush to the ground, and an observant person might note the G, but the likelihood of such a person having passed through here in the intervening hours was negligible.

He examined it for tampering and saw nothing amiss. The courier had returned it to its rightful place, as per Victor's instructions. Behind the nearby pile of tyres was a beam of rotting wood about two metres in length. It was there because Victor had placed it there after carving the G. He used it now to prise up the tyre and flip it over while keeping his distance.

He backed off and waited ten seconds in case any explosives set beneath the tyre had a built-in delay once a pressure sensor was tripped. No bomb went off so Victor dropped the beam and approached.

Beneath where the tyre had rested was a hole that he had dug. The rocky soil had been deposited far away so as not to draw attention. The hole was wide and deep enough for a medium-sized suitcase to sit within, and that's what he found.

The case was a hard-shell Rimowa made of grooved aluminium magnesium alloy still with its price tag and a set of two keys attached. He lifted it out of the hole. Even empty, the case weighed three kilos. Victor estimated the contents weighed almost twenty more.

He used the telescopic handle to roll the case out of the shadow of the shipping containers, pleased the Rimowa had large multi-direction wheels to traverse the uneven terrain so he didn't have to carry it. He placed it flat on the ground and examined it with both sight and touch for any sign of tampering. He then used the four-number sequence given to him to unlock the two combination locks and open the case. The leverage lock had not been engaged.

Georg hadn't been able to acquire his first choice, or even his second or third, but she had managed to get him a sniper rifle. It was a Nornico EM351 rifle, a Chinese version of the Russian Dragunov he had asked for. Close enough, he thought. The Chinese copy would be sufficient for his purposes. Both were designed for a battlefield marksman, not an urban sniper, but Victor needed a rifle that would kill at up to five hundred metres and this weapon would do that.

The case also contained a parabolic microphone and a smaller case made of black polycarbonate. Inside this case was a handgun suspended in foam rubber. The weapon was a Five-seveN made by Fabrique Nationale of Belgium. It was as close to Victor's preferred firearm as there could be. Circumstance usually dictated what weapon was available for use, but the Five-seveN would be his choice to use in most situations. It fired an unconventional 5.7 mm round that was tiny in bore compared to more common pistol rounds almost twice the diameter, but the small size and considerable gunpowder charge combined to create a supersonic bullet with exceptional range, accuracy and stopping power.

He checked the magazine, somewhat disappointed to find it had a ten-round capacity instead of the twenty a Five-seveN could accommodate, but the larger magazine was only available for law enforcement or military purchase, even in nations where handguns were legal. The bonus was that Georg had supplied a second magazine. Ten in the gun and ten spare was still plenty of ammunition when it took but a single bullet to kill.

There was a suppressor too, along with boxes of both subsonic and standard 5.7 mm ammunition elsewhere in the Rimowa.

The weapon and ammunition were of prohibitive

expense, and rare as a result. Rare weapons were harder to obtain and traffic. Victor doubted Georg had such items lying around. She would have gone to a lot of trouble to secure this for Victor. He recognised the gesture. Even if she had not said so on the phone, the Five-seveN said it for her: *Thank you for saving my life.*

He smiled. *You're welcome.*

FIFTEEN

Victor had been in Belgrade for five days before contacting Banik. He sent the message from a second-hand tablet computer he bought from a pawnshop, using the free Wi-Fi at a railway station. The email account was only used to contact the MI6 man and was bounced twice around the world through numerous other accounts with preset forwarding scripts as well as anonymous redirection servers to disguise its origin. It was next-to impossible to hide electronic communication from the supercomputers of the world's spy agencies, but intelligence had to be actionable to be useful. The pre-established codes Victor used would first need to be cracked for any message to be deemed worthy of attention, and by the time it had been traced back to its origin, Victor would be long gone.

The encrypted email to Banik stated Victor was accepting the contract and would begin preparations in earnest. It didn't hurt to have a head start, and now that he was armed, with his safe house and go-bag prepared, it was almost the truth.

The port of Belgrade was set near Pancevo Bridge in the centre of the city, in the shadow of the hilled fortress. Like the city itself, the port was small and compact, stretching just over a kilometre along the south bank of the Danube. Even so, there was two hundred thousand square feet of warehouse space inside its borders and triple that space for outside storage to cater for the ships, boats and barges that came and went year round.

The MI6 dossier on Rados stated he was believed to own one of the warehouses, though his name did not appear on any paperwork. A trading company in Croatia was the official holder of the lease and paid the fees to use the port's facilities. Rados' name didn't feature in the list of directors or shareholders of the Croatian shell company, but his chief lieutenant, Ilija Zoca, was listed as the chief financial officer.

Victor left at 9 p.m. It was a thirty-minute journey to the docks, extended to ninety minutes to account for counter surveillance, which left him another ninety minutes to get into position and prepare. A comfortable amount of time, given the expected security. He was dealing with criminals and civilian guards, not professionals.

The docks were busy round the clock, but less so at night. So as not to appear out of place as he made his way through the compound, he wore blue overalls and a hard hat purchased earlier in the week. A high-visibility vest would have added to his disguise, but would have made slipping away unnoticed all the more problematic.

He had no pass and no identification, but the lack of credentials did not concern him. There were many firms operating within the port, plus an ever-changing rotation of ship crew and contractors. Unfamiliar faces were as common as familiar ones. Legitimate port workers had no reason to question anyone else's presence, and the security guards were there to discourage criminal acts, not check IDs. If someone was on the right side of the fence, it was assumed they were meant to be there.

Victor carried a clipboard as an extra layer of defence. It was a psychological weapon, lending him an air of authority and at the same time diverting attention from the bag, which might otherwise have seemed out of place. The first thought of any onlooker would be: *What is he checking?* Not: *What's that he's carrying?* And afterwards it would be: *Did you see the guy with the clipboard?* Not: *Did you see the guy with the bag?*

Prevention over cure, and it worked. No one asked him to show identification or tried to make small talk or even gave him a second glance. He appeared busy and important, and that was enough.

The warehouse was simple to break into. It was no fortress and relied on the port's own security, which was basic even by civilian standards. The building was modern and well made, equipped with a number of CCTV cameras, but to cover the entire structure would have required at least twice as many. He doubted Rados had anyone watching them full-time. They were for show, at best. They might not even be recording.

The sturdy new build meant that the drainpipes were

galvanised steel and bolted securely in place, while the walls were corrugated steel. The construction was suited to climbing; Victor selected an area that wasn't covered by the cameras and faced on to the river, where the chances of being spotted were negligible. He was on the roof in less than two minutes.

The roof was sloped but the incline wasn't steep enough to impede movement. It was made of transparent polycarbonate to let sunlight pass through and provide illumination during the daytime. The polycarbonate wasn't clear, so those inside would be hard pressed to make out his silhouette against the night sky. Access to the various air conditioning units and vents and aerials dotting the roof was provided by a stainless steel door. The lock was a good one and took Victor longer to pick than the warehouse had taken to climb.

There was no alarm, and he slipped inside. He found himself on a metal walkway suspended high above the warehouse floor below. It was linked to a series of walkways and ladders that crisscrossed the space, enabling access to the roof and offices above ground level.

Victor took off his shoes before he moved any further. Even with careful steps the vast interior space would echo the noise of footfalls on the metal walkways. There was little to no ambient noise to disguise the sound, and as there was no cover on the walkways, anyone glancing upwards was sure to spot him.

No one was going to see him, however, and no cameras were going to record, because the warehouse was empty. There were no drugs stored here, and no legitimate products to provide cover. There were no employees or security guards or even office stationery.

However Rados operated his business, it was not from here.

Zoca's name also appeared on the ownership deeds of a property just outside of the city. The scrap yard, or car breakers as the sign translated to, occupied a triangle of land: its north point fed into a used-car dealership; to the west lay train tracks.

The scrap yard was surrounded by a stainless steel chain-link fence, twelve feet tall, with posts spaced every six feet. The top of each post bent outwards at an angle of forty-five degrees and forked into two spikes. Between the spikes hung coils of razor wire, galvanised and sharp. The sections of fence facing the surrounding streets were reinforced with a haphazard collection of corrugated iron sheets, bolted and welded and jammed and wedged together to block a passer-by's view of the yard. Scattered throughout the arrangement were occasional sheets of plywood, presumably where there hadn't been enough corrugated iron to hand, or to fill gaps when the original iron sheets became too rusted and full of holes to do their job.

Signs advertised the easy money to be made by trading in old cars, white goods and other scrap. Spare parts for vehicles were also available on enquiry. It was hard to know whether the business was run for profit or as a front or even as a base of operations. Organised crime had many needs that such a place could fulfil.

The scrap yard was a blight on the riverbank, huge

and ugly, hiding the river behind towers of rusting car shells, crushed cubes that had once been cars and a host of unidentifiable parts. The dealership operated only during business hours, so Victor waited for nightfall to check it out. Unlike the warehouse, which was protected by the security of the wider ports, this had none. There was no one keeping watch overnight, no CCTV cameras or prowling dogs. It was left to the fence alone to keep out intruders. Which Victor found interesting.

The chain-link fence surrounding the scrap yard was topped with coiled razor wire. A formidable barrier to the average person, but nothing Victor hadn't scaled with ease a dozen times before. He had even climbed one with his hands bound with plasticuffs. He tossed up an old rug so it covered the razor wire and climbed the fence, using one of the posts for support.

He scaled the barrier with only a short-lived increase in heart rate and waited in a crouch on the other side for his eyes to adjust to the darkness. There was little ambient light to pierce the shadows of the high fence and the towering mounds of scrap.

No security could mean there was nothing worth stealing – though the scrap metal clearly had sufficient value to make it worth trading in, else the business would cease to exist. Or it could mean that local thieves knew who owned the place and whatever could be stolen would not be worth the wrath it would unleash. But it could also mean that what went on here was not to be recorded by CCTV cameras or glimpsed by anyone's eyes but members of Rados' crew.

There were no signs of human activity, but Victor took his time regardless. He crept through the compound, watching his step, careful not to disturb anything that might reveal his presence. A horn sounded in the distance as a barge passed along the river.

The air stank of iron and motor oil and something else. Something organic. It wasn't hard to imagine rivals crushed into cubes and buried beneath the car towers. Victor imagined rats scurrying beyond his sight, watching him from the darkness.

Twisting pathways rounded the mountains of car shells and scrap metal. One pile consisted of what had to be thousands of firearms, presumably left over from the wars – mostly old automatic rifles, long since discarded or collected in armistices. Even if they hadn't been deactivated, they were useless now. They had been left to the elements for years. Metal and alloy had corroded. Wood had warped or rotted. They would be half-full of water and dirt. Parts would be missing.

At the centre of the yard was a portacabin office the size of a large caravan. It stood on locked wheels and stilts, half a metre off the ground, with a short set of aluminium steps leading to its single door. There were two small windows on each of its long sides. Nearby stood a pair of chemical toilets, and then a line of three shipping containers.

Victor tried the office door. It was locked, which was no surprise, but it wouldn't have been a surprise to find it unlocked either, given the lack of other security. The lock was basic and survived ten seconds of raking tumbles before it clicked open.

Inside, the cabin offered nothing Victor hadn't expected. There were a couple of desks and chairs, phones and computers to go with them, filing cabinets, a kitchenette and a calendar on one wall featuring topless women and sports cars. He used a small torch to look around. He had used superglue to stick red acetate over the lens to change the colour of the light and preserve his night vision.

The computers had been shut down and he left them alone. Rados was not listed in the company records, so Victor didn't expect to find his name on any electronic file or hard copy. He didn't expect to learn of his location at all, but he wanted to explore every avenue as he gathered intelligence on Rados' organisation. He checked the desk drawers and petty cash box, riffling through receipts and documents. He searched the filing cabinets. He found purchase orders and invoices and letters and tax forms, but nothing he could use. The scrap yard and scrap metal dealership was legitimate and profitable. If it was used for illicit purposes, those were well hidden and undocumented.

He swept the torchlight over the calendar. Apart from the obvious titillation, it was used to mark important dates; thumbtacks held in place scraps of paper and card. There were notes of deliveries and orders, and some were marked with a scribbled letter Z along, every week or so, with a sum of money and a time, always in the late evening, anywhere from 9 p.m. to midnight.

The next entry was for tomorrow night.

Victor flicked off the torch and listened. He heard no approaching vehicle or footsteps, but he couldn't afford to hang around. He would have liked to set up a hidden recording device, but Georg had only been able to supply so much. He would have to make do with the parabolic microphone.

He slipped out of the office and used his lock picks to relock the door. There were no signs of anyone on the premises or on their way. He would hear the scrape of the gate opening long before he needed to be hidden.

He made his way back to the fence.

Rados stayed hidden because he didn't need to expose himself. His business, managed by his loyal men and headed by Zoca, grew year on year, running unopposed and efficient and making Rados a fortune. He was the figurehead and gave the awe of his name and reputation to his organisation, but he wasn't involved in the day-to-day operations. Everything was taken care of for him. Everything ran smoothly.

But what would happen if it didn't run smoothly ... ?

SIXTEEN

The sunrise was pale and yellow, blocked and filtered by clouds so it was hard to locate in the grey sky. A poor sunrise by any qualification of beauty, but Victor appreciated it. He had always liked sunrises. Seeing one meant he had made it through another night.

He liked Belgrade. He liked the way the city felt, the combination of cold and beauty fused together well, as if by tactile design. Serbs seemed polite and had an earnest nature, but were quick to laugh and joke. There had been so much recent turmoil that the country's rich history had been almost forgotten outside its borders. It was still a young nation post communism, but old enough for its culture and customs to have created as strong a national identity as any of the more recognisable states. People here had good manners, and he respected that.

The city was both old and new, ugly and beautiful;

historic sites nestled between communist concrete; modern offices overlooked white-washed churches.

He had Hector out there making enquiries on his behalf and a chance to observe Rados' chief lieutenant tonight, but there was still work to be done. Victor wanted as many potential avenues to his target as possible. His advance research had provided him with the location of a club for former armed forces personnel. Rados hadn't been in the regular Serbian army, but he had fought alongside it.

The city changed the moment Victor crossed a wide boulevard and the park that lay beyond it. On the far side of the park the neighbourhood seemed all concrete and grime. The pretty pastel buildings of the old town were nowhere to be seen. Here was the poverty and the neglect. The people changed too. It wasn't their clothes, which were cheaper and didn't fit as well. It was their movements, which were slower. They were weighed down by everyday existence; in no rush to get on with it. That weight was as palpable as if it hung in the air.

A homeless guy hassled him for change. His suit and overcoat made him stand out here. People watched him everywhere he went. It was impossible to watch them all in return.

He straightened his back to add strength to his posture. His expression, usually neutral and forgettable, hardened to radiate the willingness to use that strength. He had no fear of opportunistic criminals, but it was better not to have to deal with them in the first place.

Some buildings looked abandoned. Others were occupied though they appeared unsafe and uninhabitable. He passed a wall covered in beautiful graffiti. Someone had spray-painted swirling galaxies and glowing nebulae. He stood before the wall for a moment to better appreciate it.

He moved on before he wanted to because other pedestrians were nearing. On another wall someone had painted a crude outline of a soccer goal, complete with skewed posts and a net with holes large enough for a ball to go through. Hanging around the goal was an old man in a sweater three sizes too big who offered him homemade slivovitz plum brandy. The old man was selling it in wine bottles repurposed for his business. Some bottles still had labels – Pinot Noir, Rioja and more, in a multitude of languages. Victor bought a bottle because the old man looked like someone he had once known and whom he wished he could still know. The old man, so used to refusal or being ignored, insisted on giving Victor an additional bottle to show his appreciation of the rare sale. Victor took the second bottle but was equally insistent on paying for it. The old man was wiping tears away when Victor left him.

The club was located in a neighbourhood with few residential properties. This was an area where no one would choose to live. It was rundown and industrial, derelict and unsavoury. Traffic was rare and foot traffic rarer still. Even the homeless knew to stay away.

It was inevitable, he realised after the fact. He felt it coming long before it happened. He was a stranger here. His clothes, so useful for blending into the background of most urban environments, made him stand out here. He was a respectable-looking outsider in a bad part of town. Still, he should have avoided it – he knew how these things worked – but he had been too focused on the real danger posed by professional threats to spot an amateur one in time to sidestep it.

They were a trio of local degenerates without fortune or brain cells enough to notice the signs he emitted that a fellow professional would have read. It was cold, yet his coat was open and his gloveless hands hung at his sides. His eyes never stopped moving, and his clothes, though of some quality, were not as suited to his frame as they could have been.

None were big and all three were out of shape. They weren't even real criminals. They were opportunists, drunk or high or looking to be. They took him to be an easy target – someone to scare into handing over a wallet or phone and making their week a little easier as a result.

One showed a blade. 'Give us your valuables and we won't hurt you.'

'Run faster than you've ever done before and I'll let you.'

They didn't.

He left them alive, but he would be flying out of Belgrade long before any of them were walking again.

SEVENTEEN

The setting sun was unobstructed and the nearby clouds had haloes of orange and red. They looked on fire. Victor walked below them, his shadow out before him in a long, jagged smear. The wind blew behind him, pushing against the back of his neck and flattening his hair forward from his crown.

He couldn't risk asking questions at the club, not after he had hospitalised three locals. Word of such things spread fast. He had no bruised knuckles – one of the many reasons he had used only the palm for hand strikes – but he was a stranger and his questions would make him suspicious enough without the potential link to the recent violence.

So he'd spent the rest of the day in his safe house, waiting for night to fall before making his way back to the scrap yard. Unlike the previous night, it showed signs of human presence – lights and vehicles.

A crane, used to stack cars and other scrap, offered a

perfect vantage point to watch the portacabin. Victor lay on top of the crane's cab, his silhouette blending into the night behind.

Zoca himself appeared a few minutes after midnight. Bright headlights flashed in the distance and white cones illuminated the tall heaps of scrap metal, glistening with rainwater. The headlights bounced up and down as the vehicle crossed the broken ground. They disappeared out of sight behind one of the towers of wrecked cars, leaving only the disembodied beams visible, before appearing again a moment later. The vehicle neared the office cabin, and the light emanating from its windows revealed it to be a rugged Land Rover caked in mud.

The cabin door opened before the Land Rover had come to a stop and a couple of guys came out to greet the new arrivals. One tossed a cigarette away. The burning end glowed on the wet ground and faded to nothing.

Zoca disembarked from the Land Rover at the same time as his men. No one opened the door for him. He dressed like them and acted like them. He was no older, and there was nothing in his behaviour to suggest he was their senior. There were handshakes and pats on the arm, but carried out in an organic order based on who was closest. Had Victor not seen a photograph of the man in the dossier it would have been impossible to identify him as the boss.

There were three heavies who had arrived with Zoca, and together with the two who had been waiting, they all went inside.

At this range, Victor could not see the telltale bulges and

creases of hidden weapons, but it was highly unlikely they were unarmed. He gave it two minutes after the cabin door closed before he moved. Though it was dark, he didn't want to risk being caught out descending the crane if some-one from the Land Rover had forgotten their phone, so he moved fast, sliding down the ladder until it was safe to drop. There was no great need for stealth as they wouldn't have a hope of hearing him until he was in the immediate vicinity of the cabin, and he wasn't planning on getting anywhere near that close.

The parabolic microphone was an old model, out-of-date and well-used. Given that Georg's base of operations was Hamburg, Victor suspected it had been in service with the local police until, surplus to requirements and destined for the scrapheap, it had been sold on by an enterprising cop or official. Newer models were half the size and had twice the range, but this one was more than adequate for Victor's requirements.

Having judged the angles and lines of sight from the cabin, he made his way to the spot he had chosen. It was in the shadow of one of the junk mounds, with a clear view of the cabin's west side. The door was on the eastern side, but there were two windows facing west.

Victor settled into the darkness and removed the para-bolic microphone from his rucksack. Though intended for covert surveillance, for some inexplicable reason this model was coated in white plastic. Victor had used spray paint to darken it to a matt grey finish. He set the earpiece in place, switched it on, and directed the microphone at the first of the two windows.

It worked by picking up the sound vibrations on the windowpane and in his earpiece Victor could hear a distorted version of the conversation going on inside the cabin. As he had expected, they hadn't yet turned to business. Instead they were catching up and swapping anecdotes. Victor used this time to adjust his aim and to modify the settings on the microphone to improve the signal.

Even at its best, in the hands of a specialist operator, the parabolic microphone was limited. Aside from the difficulties posed by obstructions, they were affected by air pressure, precipitation, humidity, ambient noise and wind. And if two people spoke at the same time it was almost impossible to separate the words. Nevertheless after twenty minutes Victor was sure there had been no mention of Rados.

It was a full hour before Zoca turned the conversation towards business. Again, Victor could not decipher all that was said, but four words in particular held significance:

Tonight. Three a.m. Shipment.

EIGHTEEN

The word shipment comes from a nautical source, and though it is used nowadays for land-based deliveries, in this case Zoca really did mean it in its literal sense. The port of Belgrade dealt with trade from all over the Black Sea. A shipping container full of hashish or heroin from Afghanistan or Kazakhstan was the first possibility that sprang to Victor's mind.

From the snippets of conversation Victor could decipher he came to understand Zoca and his men were responsible for looking after the merchandise. They were relaxed and there was no mention of needing to go to the warehouse at the port, so it had to be delivered to them here at the scrap yard. The warehouse itself would be used as nothing more than a way station – somewhere the shipment could be dismantled out of sight and put on a truck. He had seen nothing there to indicate it had any purpose other than a front.

Rados hadn't been mentioned by name but Victor thought he caught the Serbian word for boss on a few occasions. He had no expectations of finishing the contract tonight, but there was always a chance that Rados himself would come here to oversee the delivery of the shipment. If so, Victor was more than happy to take advantage of the situation.

A saying existed in the military: no plan survives contact with the enemy. Victor lived by the same principles. It was impossible to control the world around him. The ability to improvise was key. A reliance on seeing a plan through increased the chances of an unfulfilled contract in the best case. In the worst case, it would get him killed.

At a little after 2 a.m. another vehicle turned up. It was a flatbed truck without a trailer. Two men climbed out of the cab while one stayed behind the wheel with the engine running. It was heading out again soon. One of the guys who climbed out went inside the office cabin.

At first it seemed he was going to converse with Zoca, but he reappeared a moment later with a two-wheel trolley, the kind delivery men used, on which the second man stacked three shrink-wrapped cases of bottled mineral water taken from the truck's cab. The first guy wheeled it next to the office cabin and left it there, then both climbed back inside the cab.

As they did so, Zoca and his men filed out of the office cabin. Zoca's hair was bone white, cut short and brushed forward. The hair was so white and the skin so pale it was hard to see where they separated. His eyebrows were two narrow strips of pure black. He was thin, with prominent cheekbones and chin, but fit. He looked both old and young at the same time. Danger radiated from him.

The noise of the rumbling truck engine rendered the parabolic microphone useless, but Victor read *only seven this time* on Zoca's lips. Some of his guys shrugged or scratched while they considered this. Everyone started smoking as they watched the truck perform a long three-point turn and make its way out of the scrap yard.

It took so long that by the time it had gone the cigarettes were finished and the smokers were heading back inside. One used the chemical toilet first.

With the three from the truck, Zoca had eight men at his command. A sizeable number, even for a valuable shipment. No sign of Rados himself though, so whatever the shipment's value it wasn't worth his presence. Perhaps because he stayed away from any hands-on part of his business, or perhaps because Zoca was more than capable, or maybe this particular shipment was routine and unworthy of his attention. Whatever the case, the shipment had to be valuable, judging by the number of heavies in attendance. Its loss would be significant. It would necessitate Rados' involvement. If his chief lieutenant failed with so many men, whom then could he trust?

A noise made Victor turn, and he watched without surprise as a cat dragged itself from beneath one of the junk piles. It was thin and its black fur was ragged and dirty. He didn't know much about cats but he could tell this was a stray. He expected it to run away from him, but it seemed happy to hang around near to his feet. After a moment, he realised it was trying to get his attention and he squatted down and offered the back of his hand for it to rub against. It purred.

'How's the hunting?' he whispered, even though he knew the answer. A cat this thin wasn't having much success catching mice or rats, or maybe it didn't like how they tasted. He had no foood to give to it.

He moved his hand away because, even if the cat didn't have the time or inclination to keep its fur clean, he didn't want to coat it with silicone in case it was toxic to the animal. He didn't want to make its life any harder.

The cat arched its back against his shin and wandered away. After a moment, it had disappeared into the shadows.

The truck returned at 3 a.m., this time towing a trailer, on top of which sat a shipping container. Zoca and those inside the portacabin filed outside to await it. Victor couldn't be sure from what he heard via the parabolic microphone.

Victor thought about the large number of guys and the bottled water and realised his plan wasn't going to work because he now knew what merchandise was inside the container.

It wasn't drugs.

NINETEEN

It was people. The shipping container had enough space for forty people standing up and packed in tight, or fifteen with space to lie down, or for about eight with a modicum of supplies and room to sleep and use buckets in one corner for bodily functions.

In all, he saw seven women brought out of the back as he watched from the shadows nearby. They squinted against the glare of the artificial lights, holding up their hands to shield their eyes. They could have spent days in near darkness, journeying across the Black Sea and along the Danube. Apart from the sensitivity to light they seemed unhurt and healthy. They were all under thirty, and half looked to be under twenty. In addition to youth, they had beauty in common, despite their dishevelment. Judging by their dark hair and olive skin tone, they were probably a mix of Armenians, Georgians and others from the South Caucasus. Victor might have mistaken them for refugees or illegal migrants had it not been for the fact they were all women and it was clear they had not undertaken this journey of their own free will.

Nowhere in the dossier on Rados had it been suggested he was involved in anything but the usual organised crime staples. MI6 had no idea he was a people trafficker.

One of the men tore into the shrink-wrapped packages and began handing out the bottles of water. There was no kindness in the gesture. This was Rados looking after his product. Dehydration would lessen the value of the women.

While the women were unscrewing caps and drinking, Zoca paced back and forth in front of them, evaluating. He gestured and pointed and his men separated the women out into three groups – two of two and one of three – based on age range.

The women were distressed and scared but had no choice other than to comply. The group of three, which was made up of neither the youngest nor eldest women, could take some solace in their number. The two young-est women, little more than girls, were most upset. Victor noted one of the older two women seemed more angry than afraid. He was curious as to why she didn't cower, but instead scowled. Unlike the others her hair was cut short and choppy. She moved to comfort one of the youngest women, but was dragged back into place.

She struck the man who moved her with a slap to the face. The sound echoed and the guy retaliated with a slap of his own, dropping the woman with short hair to her knees.

A ripple of terror spread through the others. They

gasped and recoiled and cried, while shock and expectation registered on the faces of Rados' crew. Zoca approached the man who had slapped the woman. He knew what was coming, and didn't fight back or try to protect himself as Zoca grabbed the back of his head and doubled him over, then slammed a knee into his face.

The man dropped, spitting blood.

Zoca then helped the woman to her feet, in a show of apology, only to punch her in the solar plexus. She fell once more, gasping for air.

'Not. The. Face,' Zoca hissed to his men.

If the women had been scared before, now they were terrified. Zoca addressed them as his men kept them subdued.

'Do as we ask and no one need be hurt,' Zoca explained, his voice quiet and almost soft. He spoke in Russian, which was a common second language in the part of the world the women came from. 'We are kind men. We are gentle. We will respect you and treat you like royalty, provided you do the same in return. If you are unpleasant to us, if you are disrespectful, we will be the same. We can be kind or we can be cruel. It is your choice which we will be. But know this: we are now your employers. You work for us, and if you do your jobs well then you will be rewarded well. You will stay here tonight, and tomorrow you will be given new clothes and make-up and jewellery. You can take hot baths and sleep in soft beds. Some of you will remain here in Belgrade. Others will journey to far and exotic lands. Work hard and in time you will earn much money. In time you will be able to go home. Think of this as a holiday.' He grinned at them, but the smile could not hide his psychosis. 'Think of this as one great big adventure.'

Zoca gestured again and his men began leading the women away to the three shipping containers, one group to each.

He took the arm of the woman who had hit him and dragged her to her feet from where she had been slumped on the floor, stunned by pain and struggling to breathe.

He used a finger to raise her chin so he could look into her eyes. 'It's so nice to see you again, my dear. I see you didn't learn your lesson last time when you worked for me. I see that I must take it upon myself to teach you how to behave like a lady. I see that I must instil some manners into—'

She spat in his face.

Zoca blinked, but his expression didn't change. He let the saliva slide down his cheek and into his white stubble.

The absence of reaction induced terror in the woman with short hair. She had expected to be hit again – she had been willing to be hit again to have that show of defiance.

Zoca said, 'I hope you enjoyed that, my dear. I really mean that. I want you to breathe that moment in deeply. I want you to hold it and feel it. Hold it here' – he touched the left side of his chest with two fingers – 'close to your heart. Only then, when we will once again be alone, can you truly know if it was worth it.'

TWENTY

Victor watched as Zoca's men secured the women in the three static shipping containers that sat near to the office cabin, padlocking them shut. Some headed back inside the office cabin while others stayed outside to smoke and make jokes and re-enact the slap and punch and spit.

Then Victor waited. He waited because there was nothing else to do. He was here to sabotage the shipment, to harass Rados' organisation and in doing so learn more about it and lead him closer to his target. Heroin or hashish, he could destroy, but not seven women. He had the means to, of course, but killing unfortunate civilians was not in his playbook.

Assuming he was prepared to cross that line, it was still an impractical course of action. He couldn't hope to kill them all undetected. Zoca and his men would become involved. It would lead to a firefight.

No, Victor wasn't going to destroy Rados' shipment. But he could still disrupt it.

He waited until the men outside had finished their cigarettes and began to leave. Three climbed into the truck's cab while two set off on foot to where a car was parked outside the scrap yard, as was evident a few minutes later when Victor heard an engine start.

Zoca and the others remained inside the office cabin. But for how long? It was nearing 4 a.m. By 5 a.m. Victor had decided that these guys were here for the duration, which made sense. They couldn't leave the women unguarded.

He couldn't know when the women would be taken away, but he only had a couple of hours of darkness left.

He broke cover and backed away. He looped around the mountain of scrap metal and crept to the boundary of the site, following the chain-link fence to circle the centre area as far from Zoca and his men as possible. He wanted to be far out of sight and sound. In the dark it was possible, even likely, he would disturb some unseen piece of metal, making noise that could give him away, or shifting the angle of some chrome or glass to catch and reflect what little light there was.

By the time he had made his careful way back to the shipping containers and office cabin there was no sign of anyone outside. Victor could hear them inside the office, noisy and carefree, their work for the evening done. Now, they were relaxing. Tobacco smoke drifted out of a window. He heard glasses clink in toast. It sounded as if they were comfortable and complacent.

No time like the present.

He kept to the darkness, moving from shadow to shadow, dropping to a crawl when crossing areas where light penetrated, muddying and tearing his clothes on the wet and stony ground. The three shipping containers differed only in degrees of corrosion. He selected the one holding the two youngest women because it was furthest from the office cabin. It had a fat padlock sealing the door shut. Not the best model out there, but far from the worst.

Victor withdrew his pick and torsion wrench. His fingers detected that the pick had deformed a little in his pocket when he had crawled across the ground, so he spent a moment re-straightening it. The end result was less than satisfactory: a pick that was not quite straight and weakened from being bent back and forth.

The padlock was in deep shadow, making his job more difficult still. He couldn't risk using his torch, even shielding the light with his body, so he worked the pick and wrench in pitch-black darkness, keeping as quiet as he could. He didn't want to alarm the women inside into making noise that would bring attention.

He inserted the torsion wrench and began raking the tumblers with the pick, but miscalculated the pressure required.

The pick snapped.

It only made a small amount of noise, but he waited a moment to see if there was any reaction from inside the container or elsewhere. Nothing.

By working the wrench like a pick he managed to drag out the sliver of metal that had snapped off. That solved one problem.

He backed away, but not into the shadows. From one of the mounds of scrap metal he selected an aluminium can that was dented but not crushed. He held his breath and lifted it from its perch. There was a clink of metal. He paused, motionless. No reaction.

He crept back to the shipping container door, crouched in the shadows and spent a few minutes twisting and tearing the can apart until he could fashion a sliver of metal to the appropriate shape. He wrapped the sliver of aluminium around the arm of the lock and pushed it down in the slight gap between the arm and the lock. He worked it further down into the hole until he felt resistance. He pushed harder down and the mechanism clicked. The lock was open.

After glancing around to make sure he was still unobserved, he gripped the looped arms and pulled them free. Metal scraped against metal in a quiet scream as he withdrew the padlock from the container door.

There was no noise from inside. The women were asleep or hadn't heard him. But there was no way they wouldn't react when he opened the door. Maybe they would scream in fear of their captors or perhaps attack him. Even if they didn't, the hinges would make a hellish rusted wail when he pulled open the door.

He thought about the river and the barges and the occasional horn that sounded. One would cover any noise he made, but it was impossible for him to know when a ship or barge would pass, and he would have no warning. It wasn't an option.

He paused for a moment, thinking.

Victor rapped his knuckles on the container door with as light a touch as he could manage. He waited.

He did so again, but with a little more force and a little more noise. He waited. Still nothing.

A third rap, harder still, produced nothing but silence. He was preparing for a fourth attempt when there was a noise. Someone had rapped from inside the container.

He had heard no hasty discussion or murmur of conversation. Only one of the women had heard.

'I'm here to help you,' Victor whispered, speaking Russian as Zoca had. 'But you must keep quiet. Don't speak. Rap twice if you can understand me.'

Two quiet – if louder than he would have liked – clangs followed.

'Good,' he said. 'Don't say anything. I'm going to release you. When I open the door you need to be ready. Explain to the other woman what I tell you. Once the door is open you need to go immediately left and run as fast as you can. There will be a twisting path between piles of scrap metal. You will reach a fence. You're going to have to climb it. There will be razor wire at the top. It will cut you. It will hurt. But you'll be free. Rap twice if you understand.'

Two more clangs answered, quieter than before because the woman inside the container now knew what to expect.

'Okay,' he said. 'Once you're on the other side of the fence, keep running. If you see a car, flag it down. If you see a shop, run inside. Get help as fast as you can, but don't come back and don't stick together. Split up and they won't catch you. When I open the container it's going to be loud and they're going to hear, which is why you need to run as fast as you can and climb and not worry if you cut yourself getting over the wire. The cuts will heal and you'll be free. Whatever you do, don't look at me, and don't look back – just keep running, whatever happens. Go and tell the other woman what I've told you. Make sure you tell her absolutely everything. Once you've done that, come back and rap twice more to let me know you're both ready.'

He waited. After ten seconds there was nothing. After twenty there was still nothing.

A few seconds later he heard the two raps of confirmation.

He took the door in both hands and heaved it open.

TWENTY-ONE

He tried to ease it open as softly as he could, but despite his best efforts it made the predicted loud screech as the rusty hinges scraped and grinded. In the stillness of the scrap yard the sound pierced the night, echoing and unmistakable, impossible to ignore or rationalise as some innocent sound. Even inside the office cabin, amidst loud conversation and laughter, it would be heard; it would be recognised.

Victor had planned for this. He had told the women to run.

The first appeared, running and stumbling, bolting out of the container with everything she had. The ground was wet and slippery and her feet were bare. She kept from falling, but lost some speed before she recovered. She did as he had commanded. She didn't look back.

The second woman was right behind her, dashing out of the container as fast, but then stopping, abrupt and without warning.

She glanced back over her shoulder, then turned to face him. There was nothing he could do to stop her seeing his face. He could tell by the look in her eyes that she was the one he had communicated with through the door. Up close she was even younger than he had thought. A teenager, maybe not even eighteen. She was thin and malnourished, but fuelled by the will to survive and the promise of freedom. Her face was dirty and her hair a tangled mess, the blonde hidden beneath a paste of oil and grime, but her eyes, though red-rimmed and moist with tears at that moment, were the bluest he had ever seen.

They reminded him, despite himself, of a beach and breaking surf and similar eyes he had once gazed into, wet skin pushing against wet skin and promises broken and a debt he could never repay.

'Thank you,' she whispered, stealing him back to the present he should never have allowed himself to leave, however briefly.

'Go,' he urged. 'Hurry.'

She said, 'What's your name? I want to know who saved me.'

The other woman had disappeared out of sight, running hard.

'There's no time,' he said. '*Run.*'

She nodded. 'Thank you,' she said again.

Despite her fear, she was elated by his perceived kindness. She thought he was a hero. She thought he was saving her out of the goodness of his heart. As the girl turned away from him, her eyes seemed to leave a trail of incandescent blueness in their wake that shifted colour, darkening into red.

Blood, arcing from her neck in a sudden swathe.

Gunfire destroyed the silence.

He was blinded, the blood splashing in his eyes, and between the visceral assault of noise in his ears and the curtain of red pulled across his vision he lost his bearings.

Victor didn't need to see the weapon to identify it as an AK47. The concussive crack of each high-velocity bullet gave it away. His instincts were strong, honed from countless battles, and dragged him low, to the shadows behind the container, to safety, as sizzling hot rounds pierced the air around him. The shooter was aiming for the girl with blue eyes, but a stray round hitting him would be just as lethal as an aimed shot.

One of Zoca's men had exploded out of the office cabin, reacting to the commotion with fully automatic gunfire. Maybe he knew he was shooting at the escaping women – the fleeing shipment. Maybe he didn't.

Victor hit the ground before the girl. She fell a moment later, but while he dropped in a controlled descent, breaking the fall with arms and legs as shock absorbers, she was a loose collection of limbs, uncontrolled and without grace, flopping down into the mud.

He swiped the blood from his vision in time to see her last gasps and splutters, fighting to continue existing; desperation and terror and agony as the blood fountained from the gaping tear in her throat.

Her last words were mouthed: *Help me.*

He didn't. He couldn't. Had he been able, he would

not have. He would not have risked exposure even if there had been anything he could do for her. He wasn't a hero, whatever she had thought.

Those blue eyes never stopped staring at him.

Bullets were slicing through the night air, aim shifted to chase the other escaping woman, still alive and running faster than she would have thought herself able.

The shooting stopped, sudden and abrupt, and he heard screams – not of pain or fear, but anger.

Zoca, berating his man for opening fire, for being rash and impetuous and stupid. He backhanded the shooter in the face and stabbed the air with his fingers, pointing to where the second woman had run to, and ordering two of his men to pursue her.

'Bring her back or don't come back,' he called after them.

The other two, and Zoca, headed towards where Victor lay hidden – but hidden only because of the angle. If they moved laterally it would only be shadows that hid him. They stopped at the corpse.

The two men stood still but Zoca circled the body.

Victor was less than two metres away. He remained still in the cover of the shadows, a dark uneven shape against a dark uneven backdrop. They didn't see him.

'Shit,' Zoca spat.

'Is she dead?' the shooter asked, cautious and quizzical, and afraid.

The girl was still staring at Victor, but she was dead. Escaping air from inside her bubbled and frothed the blood at her neck and made a low whistle.

'Is she dead?' the shooter asked again.

Zoca snapped out a pistol and drove it into the man's abdomen in a sudden, savage strike. Rados' lieutenant was fast and he was strong.

The man dropped to his knees, heaving for breath, his face tight with pain.

'Are you dead?' Zoca asked, mimicking the man's tone.

The man, gasping, could not respond even if there had been a real question to answer.

'No?' Zoca asked. 'You're not dead, are you? You're still alive. Why are you still alive?'

He used the handgun to club the man in the side of the head, striking his temple with the muzzle, the blow as fast and vicious as the one to the abdomen.

The man tumbled over, dazed and panting, his eyes glazed and cloudy at the same time.

'Are you dead?' Zoca asked again.

He leaned over the man and clubbed with the pistol and stamped with his heel, interspacing the blows with the same mocking rhetorical question:

'Are you dead?'

'Are you dead?'

'Are you dead?'

He stopped only when there was not enough of the head left to strike with any degree of accuracy. Then he passed his pistol to the other man, who had stood watching in silence. The gun was drenched in blood and glistening bone and brain matter. The man took it without word or grimace.

Zoca was gasping from the exertion and rage. His face was flecked with blood, made all the more vivid in contrast to his bone-white skin and hair. He wiped his boot on the dead man's jeans.

Chest rising and falling, Zoca gestured to the man he had beaten to death. 'I just wanted an answer. Why wouldn't he answer me?'

The other man could only shrug. It was a shrug of indulgence rather than ignorance. He knew that Zoca was crazy.

The other two men returned a moment later, red-faced and puffing. Rados' crew were not fit. They smoked and drank and didn't exercise. One of the two returning men had the other woman flung over a shoulder. She was dead or unconscious, and her arms and legs were red with fresh blood.

'What happened to her?' Zoca hissed.

'She climbed the fence,' one explained, still huffing to get his breath back. 'She got tangled in the wire and cut herself. That's where most of the blood is from. I dragged her back down, but had to hit her once to keep her quiet.'

Zoca examined the cuts and took a fistful of hair to raise her head and examine her face.

'You broke her nose.'

The man was quick to defend himself. 'I had to hit her. She wouldn't stop screaming.'

'You flattened it. She's ruined now.'

'I had to,' the man said, but quieter. He took a nervous step back.

Zoca, having neither a gun in his possession to beat the man nor the stamina to do so, had to settle for baring his teeth in a maniacal expression of rage. It was short-lived: there were more pressing matters to attend to. He looked from the unconscious woman to the two corpses and then to the shipping container itself. He walked towards it.

'How did they get out?'

None of the three men answered.

He paced in front of the container, looking at the ground. He made a clicking sound with his tongue as he searched. When he had located the padlock, he bent over to retrieve it from a puddle.

'It's intact,' he said, turning to face his men.

One said, 'I don't get it.'

'How did they unlock it?' another asked.

'Unlock it? You think they managed to unlock it from inside the container?' Zoca's eyes were wide. 'You think they reached through the steel and used a magic key?'

The man didn't respond.

'Remind me,' Zoca began, 'which of you locked this particular container?'

No one answered. The three men glanced at each other.

Zoca asked, 'I suppose it was locked by magic too. Or rather, I think we can safely say that it was not locked *at all*.'

One of his men said, 'I think he locked it,' pointing to the corpse with the smashed-in skull.

'How very convenient,' Zoca said.

He approached the dead woman, coming close to where Victor lay hidden. He seemed to look directly at him, but his focus was elsewhere.

Zoca stretched his arms out wide at shoulder level, spreading his fingers into the night and darkness. The fingers of his right hand glimmered with blood, still wet but drying fast. He tilted his head backwards and exhaled, loud and deliberate in a controlled scream. His men watched, but their demeanour revealed this was something they had seen him do before.

When he had finished, he tilted his head upright once more and pushed his fingers through his hair, leaving a smear of blood through the white strands. The blood acted like styling product, leaving the affected hair sticking up in clumps while the rest lay flat.

His men shifted, uncomfortable.

'This is a serious setback,' Zoca said, his eyes still aimed at Victor, but the words directed at his men. 'He will not be pleased. All of us will suffer for this.'

The three remaining men shifted, even more uncomfortable. They might be tough criminals, former paramilitaries, but they were scared of Zoca and even more so of Rados.

Zoca approached the other two containers. 'Did you hear that?' he shouted. 'One of you is dead. That's what happens if you try to escape. You will die. You will be shot and killed. Worse, if we catch you alive. Take this as a warning and do not test me.'

He gestured to the man with the unconscious girl slung over his shoulder. 'Put her back in the container for the time being while I think about how to fix this.' To the other two he said, 'Get this mess cleaned up, and do so fast.' He headed to the office cabin, but then stopped, and said without looking back, 'And make sure the door is locked this time.'

Victor remained stationary. Each second that passed

increased the risk of discovery, but Zoca's three men weren't looking for him. They didn't know he existed, let alone that he was lying almost within touching distance. He stayed motionless while they talked and complained amongst themselves in hushed voices; about Zoca and his craziness and how the women managed to escape and whose fault it was and which of them would take the blame and what Rados would do to them.

They had two bodies to move and a lot of blood to clean up, as well as an unconscious woman. She was put back inside the container, and while the focus of the three men was on her, Victor backed away, crawling on his stomach, so by the time the container door was closed he was hidden from view.

It didn't take them long to wrap the bodies in black plastic and duct tape. They had done this kind of thing before. Next they picked the larger bits of skull out of the mud, then poured a sack of sand over the blood. They worked using the ambient light from the portacabin, but one used a torch at intervals to check their progress.

When they were satisfied with the clean-up, they took the bodies out of Victor's sight and headed back inside the office cabin. He took that as his cue to move out.

He had come here with the intention of destroying a shipment of drugs to disrupt Rados' organisation. It hadn't worked out that way, but Rados had lost a man and a quarter of a shipment tonight. Unplanned and messy, but the end result might even be better for Victor's purposes.

The price had been a girl with blue eyes.

Help me.

TWENTY-TWO

The sign outside said it was a famous kafana. The plastic chairs inside said otherwise. It was warm and full of hungry Serbians quite content with the dirty walls and cheap furnishings. The food looked appetising though and was piled high on plates delivered by a svelte waitress with boundless energy. The air smelled of smoked meats and strong coffee.

Victor had slept through most of the day, and spent the rest of it trying his best not to think about a dead girl with blue eyes.

Hector was seated at a table, alone, midway through a plate of sour cabbage rolls stuffed with chopped meats and rice. He didn't notice Victor's approach until he pulled out the chair opposite. Hector was maybe forty years old, but looked a decade older. There was no fat to plump out his skin and a lifetime of smoking and poor diet had taken a hard toll. The bags under his eyes were as dark as his irises.

His hair was thin and sparse in places from a lack of protein and nutrients.

'She hasn't brought my brandy,' Hector said with a look towards the waitress.

Victor settled on to the plastic chair. 'An essential of any nutritious meal.'

Oblivious to the irony in Victor's tone, Hector took an electronic vapour device from the jacket he had hung over the back of his chair. The device looked new – still shiny and clean.

'I'm trying to quit,' Hector explained.

Victor said, 'You'll feel better for it.'

'You smoke?'

Victor shook his head.

'Ever smoked?'

Victor shook his head again, thinking of the last cigarette he had smoked and how glorious and satisfying it had felt.

'Then how do you know I'll feel better?'

Victor looked him up and down. 'Can you feel any worse?'

Hector frowned. 'I've never had a day off sick in my life.'

'Have you ever worked a day in your life?'

The frown deepened, but then became a grin. 'Hustling doesn't count, does it?'

'No,' Victor said. 'It doesn't count.'

Hector fumbled with the vapour device and sucked in a lungful. He exhaled, disappointed. 'It's not the same without the burn.'

Victor resisted adjusting his seat. He didn't like having

his back to the rest of the space, but he wasn't about to show that he was aware of such vulnerabilities, nor that he was concerned about them. Instead he watched Hector's eyes because Hector was watching the room over Victor's shoulder. The fixer was a nervous man, weak and fragile, dealing with ruthless people; tolerated as long as he was useful to them; making more enemies than friends because in his business, like Victor's own, there were no true friends. Alliances were only ever based on mutual advantage. Loyalty was in direct correlation to personal benefit.

'Wherever it is,' Victor said, 'you need to take out seventy-five per cent and hide it elsewhere.'

Hector's bloodshot eyes were wide with incomprehension. 'What?'

Victor looked at the greasy hair and unwashed, shabby clothes; the plastic watchstrap and the old shoes. 'You obviously don't spend money on your appearance, but you don't work for free. And if I heard about you, then you must be doing something right.'

'So?' Hector responded, guarded and unsure.

'So,' Victor echoed, 'you have a stash somewhere – earnings from your *hustling*. Hidden away and growing all the time, waiting for you to take and run with, to go buy that beach hut in Fiji and live the good life.'

Hector's lips stayed closed.

'If I know you have it after meeting you only twice, then sooner or later someone else is going to realise it too, and they're going to knock on your door in the middle of the night, and you're going to let them in because you think you know them. But you don't. You think they like you. But they don't. And if you're lucky they're going to point a gun at your face, but at worst they're going to tie you up and go to work on you with a pair of pliers and a box cutter because you won't give up your life savings when they ask where it is. So, what I'm trying to tell you is, split your stash in two, one small and one larger. That way, when the knock on your door comes, you won't need to get cut up trying to protect your dream of a better tomorrow. You can give up the smaller stash and stay in one piece to collect the true stash.'

Hector hadn't blinked in a long time. 'Why are you telling me this?'

Victor shrugged. 'I'm not entirely sure. But I always root for the underdog.'

'You don't want my stash?'

'No,' Victor said. 'I want to know if you did as I asked.'

Hector should have hidden his relief better, but Victor didn't comment. He had given him enough advice already.

Hector said, 'I have a car for you.'

'Tremendous.'

Hector fished a set of keys out of his pocket and dropped them on the table. Victor saw by the badge that the fob was for a BMW, and it was at least twenty years old.

'It's parked across the street. Beige.'

'My favourite colour. What about the other request?'

'I put the word out,' Hector explained. 'Nothing too obvious or try-hard, but I've made the right people aware that I know a guy who can get things done. The firms in this town don't like using outsiders, just so you know.'

'Every firm likes to use outsiders for the kind of jobs I'm good at.'

'Well, it's funny you should say that.' Hector glanced around to make sure no one was listening. A useless check, considering what had been discussed thus far, but he had something more sensitive to say. 'It's funny because some-one got back to me. They want to meet you.'

'Who wants to meet me?'

Hector shook his head. 'No names. Not at this stage. You've paid me, yes, but this isn't your town, people don't know you like they know me. I have to think about that first.'

'Yeah, yeah, I get where your loyalties lie. But I need some information about who wants to meet. Are they a serious player or a wannabe?'

Hector licked his cracked lips. He nodded. 'Definitely more of the former. You can meet them tonight.' He gave an address.

'What's there?'

'Auto-parts shop. Near the port.'

'I want my money back,' Victor said.

'What? Why do you?'

'Because you're giving me nothing.'

'No refunds,' Hector said. 'No money-back guarantee.'

'Then I'll take your stash,' Victor said. 'All of it. I know where you live.' He didn't. 'I know your stash is there. You couldn't bear for it to be out of reach, could you? That's not smart. Why don't we have a race and see which of us can get there first? But by the look in your eyes I guess you don't fancy your chances of outrunning me. So you're going to need some backup, aren't you? Do you think you can call in enough favours and get some friends together to help you out before I find the stash and disappear with it?'

Hector was silent because he had no idea what to say.

'But it doesn't have to be like that,' Victor said. 'I'm a reasonable person. I expect you to be the same. So far you've given me an address. That's an expensive piece of nothing, unless you manage to assure me you're being straight and this person is worth meeting. The kind of people I work for are not street thugs.'

'Trust me.'

'Never words I like to hear.'

'Okay,' Hector said. 'I'll tell you the truth.'

Victor sighed. 'It's getting worse, not better.'

'What do you want from me?'

'Am I supposed to go alone tonight?'

Hector nodded. 'Of course.'

'Then you're coming with me.'

Hector didn't respond.

'So I can *trust* you,' Victor said. 'If this is a legitimate lead, there is nothing to worry about.'

Hector took a moment to think, then nodded. 'I'll meet you there.'

'No,' Victor said. 'You'll meet me here an hour before and we'll go together.'

'It's only a ten-minute drive.'

Victor said, 'I like to be early.'

TWENTY-THREE

Victor disliked meeting unknown people at unfamiliar locations as much as he liked being early. It was a good way of walking into an ambush, which happened now and again. The risk was inevitable when dealing with people like Hector – criminals who were always looking to make money or gain favour. Intimidation and threats were no help in such situations. Without revealing more about himself than he wanted people to understand, it was difficult to make the Hectors of this world more afraid of him than they were of those people they did understand. Monetary payment was a double-edged sword. The more he handed over, the more he advertised himself as a worthy target.

But there were few ways of learning about a city's underworld without a contact such as Hector, who was right when he said organised criminal networks didn't like outsiders. Setting aside racial, regional and national prejudices, outsiders could be undercover cops or rivals. Victor could embed himself in the city for weeks on end, talking and listening and learning; gathering knowledge and improving his understanding of its underworld, but he would always be an outsider, always mistrusted. He could never acquire what Hector had. Besides, to stay in one city that long would be to write his own death sentence. He had to keep moving, working or not.

Victor was waiting for Hector for an hour before he turned up at the appointed time. He wore the same shabby clothes, but they were hidden somewhat by a smart leather jacket. He was making an effort in his own way.

Hector sucked on his vapour device while he stood on the pavement outside the restaurant. He was nervous and couldn't stand still. If he was scared of Victor then that might mean he took the threat seriously, but equally it could mean that he was setting Victor up. At this moment, there was no way of knowing which was more likely.

No one joined Hector, and Victor had spent long enough waiting to know no one had been put in place beforehand, so he left the shadows and made his way along the street to where Hector stood. Again, he didn't notice until Victor was close by. Hector's success as a fixer must come from his contacts – putting the right people together; sellers and buyers; services and customers – because his street smarts were non-existent. How he had embedded himself in the underworld for so long without falling victim to it was a mystery.

'You're late,' Hector said, slipping the device back into his inside jacket pocket.

Victor didn't defend his apparent tardiness.

'Where are you parked?' Hector asked.

'We'll take your car.'

'Why?'

'Because I said so.'

Hector didn't argue. He shrugged as though it didn't matter and gestured for Victor to follow him. Hector's ride was close by, parked at a skewed angle against the kerb on a quiet side street. The car was an old hunk of junk.

Hector unlocked it. 'Do you want to drive?'

Victor shook his head.

'You want me to be your chauffeur?'

Victor didn't react to the sarcasm. He climbed into the back.

'Let's go.'

Hector had said it was a ten-minute drive, and it was. Past a traffic island near the port Hector drove down a dark street lined by commercial and industrial properties – Victor glimpsed signs for a self-storage unit, a van-hire firm, a solvent factory – until they slowed as they approached a used-car lot and the auto-parts shop that lay next to it.

A low gate blocked the entranceway, so Hector parked on the adjoining street. Victor saw no one around, but lights were on at the auto-parts shop, filtering through a pebbled windowpane and blinds.

'We're here,' Hector said.

Victor climbed out of the car first. It wasn't his nature to trap himself in a confined space with a potential enemy, however weak, outside. Hector was slow getting out of the driver's seat, but only because of the unaccustomed exertion.

Victor drew his Five-seveN from his waistband. Hector backed away at the sight of the weapon.

'What's that for?'

'Car keys,' Victor said.

Hector panicked, breathing hard, but handed them over. Victor dropped the handgun into the compartment of the driver's door and locked the car.

Near the river and with only low buildings for protection, the wind was cold and fierce. The latter was always welcomed by Victor – it meant any sniper waiting to kill him would have a much harder shot to make. He let Hector lead the way across the used-car lot to where the auto-parts shop stood beyond a token divide formed of short wooden posts painted white.

Victor noted the two vehicles parked out front. Both were immaculate Range Rovers with blacked-out windows.

Six to eight guys, Victor said to himself.

One of whom appeared in a rear doorway as they drew closer, having seen them through a window or on a CCTV camera. He wouldn't have been able to hear their approach over the wind.

The man was dressed in black jeans and a blue denim shirt. He looked tough and capable, and Hector tensed when he saw him. The man in the denim shirt gave a look of recognition as he glanced at Hector and then one of confusion as his gaze found Victor. No words were exchanged but the man gestured for Victor to raise his arms for a pat-down. It was done with competence, if not to professional standards. Victor wouldn't have been able to hide a gun from the search, which was why he had come unarmed, even without knowing what he was walking into. He hadn't wanted to relinquish his only handgun, as he would have done now had he brought it along. Better to have it nearby than to lose it completely.

The guy in the denim shirt pushed open the door and gestured for Victor and Hector to go inside. They did, Victor letting Hector go first. They made their way along a short corridor that smelled of oil and paint fumes, and out on to the shop floor, where three men were waiting.

Two of whom Victor could tell were hardened criminals from the way they stood. They were mob soldiers – enforcers; muscle. They were there as a show of strength and to provide protection for the man Victor was to meet. He was hoping to make some progress in the hunt for Rados, but was willing to waste his time tonight on the off-chance Hector knew the right people. It was a gamble, but not a lottery.

Victor had anticipated tonight's meet would be with a better-connected fixer, or maybe a low-level lieutenant from a mid-sized crew. If the fates were smiling on him, that person would have connections with Rados' organisation, or at least know someone who had the kind of connections Victor needed. Hector seemed to know Belgrade's underworld well enough to provide such a link in the chain.

In between the two enforcers was a man who had his back to Victor. The presence of the three heavies was telling, as was Hector's bowed head and hunched shoulders – reverence and fear. This man wasn't a fixer and he wasn't any low-level lieutenant.

The man turned around as they neared.

Milan Rados said, 'So you're the one who wants to get hired.'

TWENTY-FOUR

Victor was as unprepared as he had ever been. It hadn't occurred to him that he would be talking to Rados at this stage in his preparations – a man who had been hidden for six years; a man whose organisation had just come under attack; a man who relied on subordinates to handle the day-to-day running of his business.

His target was standing before him, within point-blank range, but he might as well have been a mile away in a concrete bunker. Victor was unarmed and surrounded by at least three armed threats with the possibility of more nearby. Even if he grabbed a tyre iron and managed to slay Rados with a well-placed blow to the temple, Victor couldn't hope to survive the aftermath.

Given that he was an assassin now at the mercy of the very man he was trying to kill, it was not a given he would survive the enounter.

Rados didn't look like a gangster and he didn't look

like a former warlord. He looked like a fifty-year-old businessman, or maybe a politician. His build was average and his manner neutral. It was the smile that gave him away. It was an imitation of a smile, because Rados was a psychopath.

He wore a tailored navy suit with brown brogues and white twill shirt. The suit had a sharp, tailored cut. The lining was bright red satin. His tie was woven silk, steel grey. His cufflinks were miniature gold shovels – maybe because he had buried so many bodies.

His eyes were a washed-out blue, as if once they had been bright but the colour had leached out of them, leaving only a memory behind. His skin was smooth and seemed younger than the grey hair indicated. The eyebrows were thin, but still dark, as was the five o'clock shadow.

It was as if he had aged since the picture of him in Banik's dossier, but at the same time grown younger. No one added a decade to their lives without paying a price, but wealth could buy many things, including health. Rados looked healthy. Like a man who exercised every day and had his personal chef cook him nutritious meals using only the best ingredients – grass-fed, free-range, organic and unprocessed. He didn't seem vain, but careful of his well-being. More than most, he knew how fragile life was, or maybe he feared death and what might lie beyond.

'Do you know who I am?'

Victor nodded. 'You're Milan Rados.'

'Good,' Rados said. 'That saves us some time. But how do you know who I am?'

'Everyone in my business knows who you are.'

150

Rados tried to hide it, but his eyes smiled. Psychopaths were usually narcissists.

'I don't like fame,' he pretended. 'I don't chase it, but it has its benefits, I suppose. I don't have to wait in line very often, for example. It's the small things that make the most difference, don't you agree?'

Victor said nothing because his first impression of Rados was that he was not the kind of man who liked to surround himself with yes-men.

'Did you know you were meeting me?'

'I had absolutely no idea.'

It was perhaps the most honest answer to a question Victor had ever given.

Rados spent a moment studying Victor, then gestured to Hector. 'What are you doing here?'

Hector stuttered and gestured at Victor. 'He, uh, wanted me to accompany him.'

The washed-out eyes stayed locked on Hector, but the question was to Victor: 'Scared to come alone?'

'I prefer stepping into the unknown with a bargaining chip.'

Rados looked his way. 'And you think my wife's only brother qualifies as such a chip?'

At last Victor understood how Hector had managed to survive in Belgrade's underworld. He had the best protection anyone could ask for. He walked around with a bulletproof vest made of Rados' reputation.

'No,' Victor said. 'Because I didn't know who I was coming to meet. But if this wasn't what I had asked for, he would be his own bargaining chip.'

Hector was slow to understand what Victor meant, but Rados grasped it straight away.

'And is this what you asked for?' the Serbian asked.

Again, there was no harm in honesty here, so Victor said, 'Yes.'

Rados gave a smile, then commanded Hector, 'Leave.'

The fixer looked more than happy to do so.

When the back door slammed shut, Rados said, 'You're looking for work.'

'That's right.'

'Have you ever killed a man?' Rados asked. He spoke as if the question was insignificant, even if Victor's answer would not be.

Victor said, 'One or two.'

'What are you?' Rados asked. 'You don't strike me as the bone-breaker type.'

'I think of myself as a counsellor.'

'And what is it on which you offer counsel?'

'Whether a person remains alive or not.'

'I see,' said Rados. 'Any notable hits you can tell me about?'

'No.'

'Why not?'

'Because it's my job to make sure they're not notable.'

'Then how do I know if you're any good?'

Victor said, 'You'll just have to take my word for it.'

Rados' nails drummed on a worktop. 'Hector told me that you are Hungarian. Is this correct?'

'That's what my passport says.'

'I don't like Hungarians as a general rule. I find their

sense of humour is too dissimilar to our own. I find them impolite.'

'You don't need to like me to hire me,' Victor said. 'My humour isn't going to help grow your business. My politeness offers no protection.'

Rados' head rocked from side to side as he thought about this. He said, 'But I do have to like you to let you live.'

Victor shook his head. 'You're not going to kill me. You need men. That's why I'm here. You don't interview someone if you don't have a position for them to fill. And when you need to bolster numbers you're certainly not going to lose more taking me down.'

Rados considered for a moment. 'You're pretty full of yourself, aren't you?'

'Not really,' Victor said. 'I know what I can do. I'm pretty good at working out what other people can do too. Usually, I hide both those abilities.'

'But not now with me?'

'Would you be more likely to hire me if I undersold myself? I don't think so. You don't want guys at your side who are modest. No one in your business respects the meek.'

'How do you know what I want?' Rados asked.

'You wouldn't even be here if you didn't need new recruits.'

Rados took his time responding. 'You're right, I do need men. Normally, I would not deal with such things, but a recent setback has caused me to undertake a little ... let's call it corporate restructuring. If I can't trust people to run my business properly, how can I trust them to repair the damage they have caused?'

'Is that a rhetorical question?'

'Of course,' Rados said. 'But why would I consider hiring someone I knew so little about, and an outsider, a foreigner, at that?'

'Because we're talking, so regardless of those concerns, you must be considering hiring me.'

Rados swiped some imperfection from his lapel. 'Or maybe I'm waiting for more of my men to turn up, to make sure I don't lose anyone taking you down.'

'In which case you don't believe these three are enough to deal with me cleanly, even if I am unarmed, which means you think I'm dangerous, which means you think I'm someone who could be useful to you.'

Rados stared. 'Are you as crazy as you appear to be?'

'I've been toning it down,' Victor said.

Rados held his gaze. 'Let's play a game. A hypothetical one. No winner, no loser. Purely for fun. You say you're a proficient killer, so how would you complete your mission if you were hired to kill ... me.'

Victor didn't blink. 'With a rifle, after I had worked out your movements.'

'So you're a good shot.'

'I learned to shoot long before I knew how to write.'

'Headshot or body shot?'

'Body,' Victor said. 'Chest.'

'Why not the head? You said you were a good shot.'

'I'm an exceptional shot,' Victor said, without hubris. 'But I'm hired to do a job, not show off. Dead is dead.'

'Wouldn't you be concerned about a bulletproof vest under my jacket?'

'There's no such thing as bulletproof. And even the most state-of-the-art covert body armour isn't going to stop a large-calibre, high-velocity round.'

'What kind of a rifle would you use?'

'First choice would be a Dragunov. I'd settle for a Chinese copy.'

Rados said, 'Why? There are more accurate weapons.'

'I like Soviet weapons. I like reliability. The most accurate gun in the world is no use if it misfires.'

Rados said, 'Okay. But why kill me with a rifle at all? They're hard to move. They're hard to hide. Why not a bomb or a pistol?'

'I don't like explosives if I can help it.'

'Why not?'

'I don't like killing people I'm not paid to.'

'But you like killing those that you are?'

'I don't mind killing them.'

'Funny. So why not a knife? Simplest weapon to use. Easiest to hide.'

'I don't work with knives as a general rule,' Victor explained. 'I don't like to make a mess, especially on myself. A knife isn't the weapon of a professional. They're for people who enjoy their work too much, or for those who have no self-restraint.'

Rados gestured and one of his men reached into his jacket, drew out a shiny Beretta gleaming with polished nickel plate, and presented it to Rados. 'Okay, why not a handgun like this? I take it you don't have any objection to handguns? Less risk of mess than with a knife, but easier to conceal than a rifle.' He took the weapon from the man's grip and pointed it at Victor's head with a swift, graceful motion. 'Faster to aim too.'

Victor couldn't see them, but he sensed the two heavies were nervous. Maybe because they were worried Victor might attack in response, or maybe concerned about getting his brain matter on their clothes.

He remained casual and said, 'With a pistol I would need to be close. You have a whole crew for protection and I'm not especially suicidal these days.'

Rados was quiet for a moment. He stared at Victor along the iron sights of the pistol. At this range, the Serbian couldn't miss.

All Victor heard was the shuffle of feet from the heavies. Like Victor, they had no idea what Rados was going to do or say next.

Rados flexed his thumb, drew back the hammer, and the weapon cocked.

TWENTY-FIVE

For almost a minute Rados held the gun steady, aiming at Victor's face, his index finger wrapped around the trigger, tensed and applying pressure, but maybe four of the required six pounds. Victor didn't know if the Serbian was testing his resolve or his patience, but he knew he had to maintain both.

'What's your background?' Rados asked.

'I've worked in Minsk and London in recent years,' Victor answered.

'Who for?'

'Danil Pentrenko in Minsk and Andrei Linnekin in London.'

'I don't know this Linnekin, but I'm familiar with the name Pentrenko. King of Minsk, he liked to call himself. Our paths crossed a few times. But not since he disappeared a few years ago.'

'That's when I stopped working for him.'

'What about before that? You didn't always work for criminals.'

Victor said, 'I was in the military.'

'I knew that from the way you stand. Special Forces?'

Victor nodded. 'For some of my service, yes.'

'And which particular unit would that be? Spetsnaz? SEALs? GIGN? GSG9? SAS?'

'You know your berets.'

Rados shrugged, but the pistol remained steady. 'Which one?'

'I'll keep that to myself,' Victor said.

'Soldiers are for the battlefield, but this is civilisation. At least, a watercolour of civility. Your drill sergeant didn't teach you how to watch a room and where to stand to keep my bodyguards in your peripheral vision.'

Victor remained silent.

'So . . .' Rados began, thinking. 'You were seconded to an intelligence agency while you were in Special Forces or else that's where you ended up after you left the military. Before you went into business for yourself, I mean. Which is it?'

'Perhaps both.'

'I'd like to know which unit we're talking about. I'd like to know who you spied for.'

'I'll keep that to myself, if it's all the same to you.'

Rados said, 'Because you're not Hungarian?'

'I'm whatever my passport says I am.'

'Funnily enough, I believe you mean that. I believe you're a lycanthrope, shifting your shape to whoever you need to be.'

158

'Something like that.'

Rados stepped closer. 'Do you even remember who you really are?'

'I remember a time when I remembered.'

Rados smirked and lowered the Beretta. He set it down on the worktop and stood still and quiet for a moment. His jaw was set and his lips tight. His gaze burned into Victor's own.

'Your Serbian is excellent. Where did you learn it?'

'I've worked with quite a few Serbs in the past.'

Rados pursed his lips for a second. 'In the war?'

'I didn't say that.'

'But you're not denying it either.'

'I'm good with languages. It doesn't take me long to pick one up. I could speak three before I set foot inside a classroom.'

'Which languages were those?'

Victor didn't answer.

Rados said, 'You want me to hire you without knowing you.'

'The only person we can ever truly know is ourself,' Victor said. 'For everyone else we put on an act. I am at least honest about my disguise.'

'Some acts are easier to see through than others.'

Victor remained silent.

Rados said, 'I too was a warrior, once. You may not think it to look at me now, but I was fearsome. Never the biggest or the strongest, but a warrior's might comes not from his muscles but his mentality. The will to win and the fortitude to swallow fear are your two most important weapons. Unlike you, a mercenary, I fought for a cause. And yes, I looted and I gained glory, but I went into that battle to protect my people. Have you ever done such a thing?'

'No,' Victor said, with as even a voice as he could muster.

'Then you do not know the clarity of righteous combat. You cannot comprehend the strength you gain from the unshakeable knowledge that you are pure and your enemy is sullied.'

'Napoleon said God is on the side with the best artillery.'

Rados laughed. 'I like that quote, but Napoleon was a fool, drunk on his own perceived invincibility. He could have ruled the world had he but known humility.'

'Are you humble?'

The Serbian thought about this. 'I have no desire to rule the world.'

'Just this corner of it?'

Rados smirked, but didn't answer. Instead, he said, 'Weakness draws only aggression from the strong and sympathy from the weak.'

'I don't know what you're trying to tell me.'

'You will,' Rados said with confidence. 'You will.'

Victor said, 'My time is valuable, Mr Rados, so if you only want to chat I'm afraid I need to leave.'

'You can leave when I say you can and not before.'

In his peripheral vision, Victor noted that the two guards, who'd become relaxed and even bored during the conversation, had now straightened. They recognised the tone of their boss's voice.

Rados stared at Victor. Victor let him.

'Okay,' the Serbian said after a moment. 'I can indeed use a man like you in my organisation. I'm an emperor surrounded by barbarians, so perhaps it's time to diversify.'

Victor remained silent.

Rados said, 'If I hire you, it would be on a trial basis.'

'Naturally.'

'I'll test you.'

'Of course you'll test me.'

'If you fail . . . '

'I won't fail.'

Rados reached into his inside jacket pocket. Victor didn't react because the Serb had a gun within easy reach on the worktop; there was no need for him to pull out another weapon. Rados dropped a strap of currency next to the Beretta.

'Yours,' Rados said. 'Think of it as a retainer.'

'You're hiring me then.'

'I'm willing to put you on probation, yes. The money is an act of faith. An aperitif for banquets to come – provided you prove yourself. Take it.'

Victor stepped towards the worktop, pretending he didn't notice the watchfulness in Rados' gaze. Victor reached a hand out towards the money and the shiny handgun along-side it, pictured grabbing the weapon at the last instant and shooting. Not at Rados, but his two men, taking them down with double-taps. First the one on the left because Victor wouldn't have to turn to face him – reaching across his chest would be enough. Then swinging his right arm in a wide arc as he twisted his hips and changed his footing to face the guard on the right. He would kill them quicker in that order. He could then kill Rados at his leisure.

An act of faith.

He watched Rados watching him, and took the money, leaving the pistol where it lay on the worktop.

Victor knew a test when he saw one.

He slipped the strap of cash into an inside jacket pocket. He didn't count it, but there was two or three thousand there. Some useful spending money, if nothing else.

Rados raised his eyebrows, as though he had half expected Victor to take the gun, but there was no hint of relief because he had been in no danger. The gun was empty or loaded with blanks, Victor was certain of it.

Rados said, 'I'll need your phone number.'

'I don't have a phone.'

'You need one if you work for me.' He gestured to one of the guards. 'Give him your phone.'

The guard didn't argue. He reached into a trouser pocket and came out with an old handset. He handed it to Victor.

'No smartphones,' Rados said. 'No personal calls, and no business discussed on the phone. Just details: times, locations, orders. You destroy the phone after a week and buy yourself a new one. Understand?'

Victor nodded. 'I understand.'

Rados stepped closer and regarded Victor. 'Meet me at my club in an hour and we can discuss how to move forward.' He gave the address and Victor made a mental note of it. 'I'm looking forward to seeing what you can do.'

'I look forward to showing you.'

Rados nodded and Victor took it as his cue to leave. One of the guards saw him out of the auto-parts shop.

'Get lost,' the guy said.

Victor said, 'Pleasure to meet you too,' and headed towards where the old BMW was parked at the dealership. Hector was leaning against the boot, smoking a cigarette.

'No vapour device?' Victor asked.

'I need the real thing,' Hector said. 'How did it go?'

'I walked out of there in one piece.'

Hector nodded. 'You understand why I couldn't tell you, right?'

'I do,' Victor said. 'But you would have made my life a lot easier if you had.'

It was a shame not to have been ready to take advantage of this encounter, but if Rados hired him then there would be other, better situations to exploit. He could gain the valuable insider intelligence about Rados' organisation that he wanted, but also learn more than he could have hoped about his target in the process.

Hector was nervous. He was rightly scared of Rados, but now he was scared of Victor too. His senses were sharp. 'You're not angry with me?'

'I don't get angry,' Victor said.

TWENTY-SIX

The auto-parts shop was quiet. The faint rumble of an engine could be heard as a car drove by, then a soft scrape of metal as the man in the denim shirt took the nickel-plated Beretta from the workshop. Rados' men said nothing when their boss said nothing; in part out of reverence, in part fear, but one could not hold his tongue any longer.

The man in the denim shirt said, 'I don't like him.'

Rados tilted his head to acknowledge the comment, but said nothing in return. Instead, he thought. He pondered.

The man in the denim shirt continued: 'He's dangerous.'

This time Rados chose to respond. 'I dearly hope he is.'

Rados' man knew when it was in his best interest to shut up.

'Let's see how our guests are getting on,' Rados said.

He strolled across the empty space to a door that led to

a corridor, which in turn led to a storeroom. The interior was cold and furnished only with steel shelving units holding cans of oil and spray paint, tools and spare parts. The smell of motor oil was strong and hid the stink of blood and urine.

Four of Rados' men cowered against the far wall. They were naked, bruised and bleeding. One had pissed himself. Another's face was slick with tears. These were the men who had failed him at the scrap yard.

'I'm sorry to have kept you,' Rados said, his tone soft and almost reasonable. 'I hope you have found the facilities here to your satisfaction. I hope you have no complaints about the level of service. We value all feedback.'

No one answered. Only one of the men – Zoca – was brave enough to look Rados in the eye.

'I have been thinking how to handle this,' Rados said, brow furrowed in careful consideration. 'One girl dead. Another girl ruined. Plus, there were cops who had to be paid off to ignore reports of gunfire. That is the part I dislike the most. Not losing almost a quarter of a shipment. Not your failure. But having to bribe police officers. They steal from me and I have to let them. I have to smile as they rob me.'

'*We're sorry*,' one of the men cried out.

'Words are meaningless,' Rados replied. 'Voltaire said we use words to hide our thoughts. I think Voltaire was wrong. We use words when we are too lazy or incompetent for actions. It is what we do, not what we say, that defines us. Your words of apology need not exist had your actions been sure.'

Rados gestured and was handed the nickel-plated Beretta by the man in the denim shirt, but the pistol was loaded this time. He studied it, weighing it in his hand while he listened to the panting and whimpering.

'Do you know how a Roman general would punish his soldiers when they failed him?' Rados asked the man who had handed him the gun.

The man in denim said, 'With death.'

Rados sighed, disappointed he had to explain everything to his barbarians. 'It was called decimation. The soldiers who had fled the battlefield were divided into tens. Every tenth man was then beaten to death by the other nine. Unfortunately, we do not have the numbers here for that. We must improvise. Hold out your hands, please.'

The man in the denim shirt was confused, but did as instructed. Rados ejected the Beretta's magazine and thumbed out bullets until twelve clinked together in the man's cupped palms. Rados dropped the magazine at his feet. It clattered on the cement floor.

'There,' he said to the naked men cowering on the opposite side of the room. 'Three bullets between four of you, and a single gun.' He held up the empty Beretta. 'I'll be waiting outside for one of you to return it to me.'

Rados gestured for his other men to leave the room. He followed too, until he was in the doorway, then turned and tossed the Beretta at Zoca, who was quick to catch it in both hands.

The other three men looked at Zoca, fear in their eyes. Zoca's showed only confusion. As he had been in charge of the shipment, his failure was greatest.

'Because you met my gaze,' Rados explained, and closed the door behind him.

For a moment, the four men were still and silent, then Zoca lunged for the magazine on the opposite side of the room and the other three men rushed to stop him.

TWENTY-SEVEN

The address Rados had given Victor turned out to be a boxy concrete building from the communist era, low and long and disused. It stood surrounded by parking spaces. Vegetation had pushed itself up through the asphalt, cracking and transforming the once-smooth surface into a moonscape of bumps and craters. A chain-link fence rattled in the wind.

Victor parked the old BMW and crossed the lot, his gaze sweeping back and forth to search the darkness. No lights shone from the building itself. Only the ambient city light provided any illumination. Clouds blocked out the stars.

It didn't look like any kind of conventional club. The building was obvious in its semi-dereliction. There were no neon signs and no thump of bass in the air. No doormen in tuxedos outside and no line of would-be revellers in inappropriate winter clothing. Only a handful of heavies loitering around the entrance.

Nature had started to reclaim the land. Grasses had pushed their way up through the asphalt. Mosses and lichens were growing on the building's exterior. The ground-floor windows were boarded up with plywood that had long since started to rot. It had been built cheap and fast, and even when brand new the stark lines and featureless concrete and pebble-dash couldn't have looked good.

There were no cars parked in the lot, so Rados must not want to draw attention, although nearby residents must have noticed the influx of cars parked on nearby streets and unsavoury men congregating in a building long-since abandoned.

The men in front of the building clearly worked for Rados. Their uniform of jeans, leather jackets and sportswear gave them away, along with their matching buzz-cuts, in various stages of regrowth. None of them were clean-shaven. There was a glint of gold from neck chains and signet rings as they stood smoking and talking. Victor had an idea what kind of club this was.

They saw him approach a long time after they should have made him, but these were criminals, not professionals. Several sets of eyes watched him as it dawned on them who he was. It was too dark to read their lips with any accuracy but he could guess the nature of their whispers.

That's the new guy ...

No one spoke to him or offered any gesture of greeting beyond a stare. He passed through a thin haze of cigarette smoke. It had been years since Victor's last drag, but the smell still made his mouth water.

The cold didn't seem to bother Rados' men. They were used to it; more than that, they did not want to appear weak by donning warmer clothes. Even the most hardened of criminals was in thrall to peer pressure and the need to fit in. The human longing for social acceptance was something Victor understood from observation rather than personal experience. True loners like him were against nature.

Two men flanked the entrance. Neither was tall, but they looked big and useful, with hands that had delivered plenty of beatings and faces that had received plenty too. They made a show of looking him up and down, acting as if they didn't know who he was. Victor stood his ground, letting them have their moment. They wanted him to be intimidated but instead he regarded them with an even gaze. As a rule he preferred potential enemies to underestimate him, but there was nothing to be gained here by showing submission. They wouldn't respect him that way, and the character he was playing – Bartha, the Hungarian killer – wouldn't be intimidated by a couple of street-level thugs.

'I'm here to meet Rados,' he said when it was clear they were not going to speak first.

One gestured with a thumb. 'Downstairs.'

They didn't try and frisk him, which was no real surprise. Criminals were never as thorough as professionals, and at least every other guy here would be carrying. Some would have guns, and those that did not would be armed with blades or their preferred melee weapon. Even if Victor had a sub-machine gun under his coat, he would be outgunned.

Neither moved out of the way to let him pass. He saw what they wanted – for him to have to force his way between their shoulders – so they could resist and make him work hard to gain entry.

He said, 'Can I get a smoke?'

There was a moment of hesitation, but he knew they would agree. To refuse said they couldn't afford to give away a cigarette, or worse that they disliked him without knowing him, which translated to them being intimidated by him.

The one on the left nodded, but the one to Victor's right was quicker fumbling with his packet. He shook one out and Victor took it. The guy activated his lighter and Victor pulled the smoke into his mouth, making the embers glow red and hot.

He exhaled the mouthful of delicious smoke and flicked the cigarette at the one who'd given it to him.

The man flinched in fear as the cigarette hit him square in the chest and dropped out of sight. Where it landed wasn't important; the terror of it hitting his crotch was enough for the guy to jerk away, patting himself in a frantic attempt to find the burning cigarette before it found his balls.

Victor strolled through the gap.

He was halfway down the stairs by the time the guy realised he was safe, and the other one was busy laughing and mocking his panic.

The club itself was below ground, down an echoing stairwell and through dim corridors and a white-tiled changing room, past wall-mounted showers, and out to where a swimming pool was sunk into the basement floor.

The room was lit by freestanding halogen lamps. There were at least three dozen men hanging around the floor space overlooking the shallow end of the empty pool. In addition to Rados' crew, there were maybe twenty who were better dressed and had the air of civilians. Some wore suits and had heavies of their own.

Rados was mingling, smiling and laughing as if he was having a good time in their company, and not out to exploit or cheat or steal. He saw Victor enter and gestured for him to approach.

Victor did, threading his way through the crowd and past the pool. It was twenty metres long by ten wide. It sloped to a depth of two metres, and was half that at the shallow end. It had been drained a long time ago and never refilled. There was no trace of chlorine in the air. Instead, it stank of bodily fluids, old and new: sweat and blood, urine and faeces.

It was the stench of violence Victor knew so well.

Rados said, 'Welcome to Disneyland.'

TWENTY-EIGHT

'Gentlemen,' Rados said, 'this is my newest associate, Mr Bartha.'

He spent a minute introducing the men in suits to Victor, and Victor was surprised by the interest they showed in him. Maybe it was because, like them, he wore a suit, which was something of a novelty amongst Rados' crew.

After a few minutes of small talk, Rados singled out one of the suits and they stepped away to converse.

'This is Mr Dilas,' Rados introduced the suit. 'One day he will be president of Serbia.'

Dilas laughed as if it was a grand joke, but that laugh was for show – he wanted, and believed, that one day he would indeed run the country. 'Milan likes to say such things to make me look foolish.'

'I wouldn't dare,' Rados said, smiling along. 'Because when you are president you would enjoy nothing more than taking your revenge with all your new might.'

He flexed his bicep for emphasis. Dilas chuckled.

'I won't forget my friends, Milan,' Dilas assured, smirking, 'when I'm sitting on a gilded throne.'

'Gilded, maybe,' Rados said. 'But a throne made of bones and polished with blood.'

'You're needlessly dramatic, Milan,' Rados replied. 'My hands are clean.'

He showed his palms – pink and soft.

Rados rubbed his own together. 'Yours are clean because mine are so very dirty.'

'An arrangement that suits our respective talents, let's remember.'

Palms pressed together before him, Rados bowed his head – a playful or mocking gesture, it was hard to tell which. 'I am your humble servant, my liege.'

Dilas smiled as if he took it as a joke, but the heavy swallow that followed told Victor the politician only pretended he and Rados were on any kind of equal footing. Suits or not, both men knew this was but a veneer of civilisation that could be stripped away at any moment. Here, strength was the only thing that truly mattered.

Rados said, 'I'll be back in a moment,' and left Dilas and Victor alone.

Dilas was young for a politician. He was somewhere in his thirties, but his cheeks were plump and smooth, making him look younger. His suit didn't quite fit. He was tall and slim, with narrow shoulders and a narrower waist. The suit was expensive, but it was off the rack, a designer brand, and the generic size, even in a fitted cut, was too big for Dilas' width, while at the same time too short for his height. He had enough money to pay for the designer label, but didn't yet know the money would be better spent having a suit made to measure.

His hair was dark and curly, but cut short enough that it didn't bloom away from his head. He wore glasses with dark, rectangular rims. They had a designer's logo on the arms. His shoes were polished to a high sheen and had extended, pointed toes that made his feet look clown-like.

'You don't seem like one of Rados' usual men,' Dilas said to Victor.

'I wouldn't know anything about his usual men.'

Dilas thought about this. 'He's lost a few recently. Maybe he wants to widen the gene pool. Criminal Darwinism, you might say.'

His voice was low, but the words came fast and stumbling. He believed in what he said but wasn't convinced other people would too.

Rados returned and excused himself from Dilas to steer Victor clear of the crowd so they would have more privacy.

'What do you think of my club?' Rados asked.

'I was expecting music. Maybe some strobe lighting.'

Rados smirked and looked down at the empty pool. 'This is my Colosseum. Perhaps not quite as grand, but you get a better view.'

The empty pool had once been white, but the tiles had darkened with grime and were marked in many places with blood – smears of old blood, brown and flaking; newer patches and flecks that were the colour of rust; fresh splashes, bright and glistening under the halogen lights.

There was nothing else in the pool apart from sand that had been used to soak up the mess before being swept into the corners where it formed dark dunes and had caked into the grooves of the floor tiles.

'No weapons,' Rados explained, 'and no shoes. Otherwise, there are no rules.'

Victor nodded, picturing two men pummelling each other into a bloody mess at the bottom of the pool. With no rules there would be groin strikes, bites and gouging. It wouldn't be anything resembling sport.

'I don't smoke and I don't take narcotics,' Rados said. 'Violence is my drug of choice.'

Another man arrived. Victor didn't see or hear him at first because of the crowd and the noise, but he noticed the reaction of those who did. Faces changed. Voices became hushed.

It was Zoca. He moved with awkward steps, almost shuffling. His face was a mess. It was swollen around both eyes and the mouth. His left cheek was bruised. He had stitches in one eyebrow.

'I take it he's one of the fighters,' Victor said.

Rados smiled. 'He fell.'

Zoca didn't approach, but he acknowledged Rados, who nodded his head to return the acknowledgment. Even with a messed-up face, Victor could tell Zoca regarded him with curiosity mixed with contempt. Zoca looked away and shuffled over to join some of Rados' other guys. No one shook hands or hugged or patted him. He looked as if every movement was painful and a slap of welcome on the shoulder would cause unbearable agony.

'Trust,' Victor said, still watching Zoca.

Rados followed his gaze. 'Those who show my trust in them to be misplaced have a tendency to . . . fall. But after this their balance tends to improve dramatically. It is only under the rarest of circumstances that this solid new footing proves unsteady.'

'And then they fall for a second time?'

'Yes,' Rados answered, 'they do. The difference being, they don't get up the second time.'

Victor watched Zoca's slow, pained movements and humbled body language. He didn't look like the ruthless hard man who'd terrorised the women in the scrap yard.

'Does *falling* breed loyalty?' Victor asked.

'I wouldn't know,' Rados said. 'I cannot see into the hearts of my men and know their true selves. But I believe it is only through our mistakes that we learn. I also believe that if we don't learn after our first mistake, we never will.'

'Everyone deserves a second chance.'

'And what about you?' Rados asked Victor. 'How many second chances have you been given?'

'I've had my share.'

'But how many second chances have you given out?'

Victor remained silent.

Rados smiled at the lack of answer. He said, 'Let's find a better spot. The fights will be starting soon.'

Victor asked, 'When is a bout over?'

'When the winner decides his opponent has had enough. A knockout or submission, usually.'

'Fatalities?'

'If we are lucky,' Rados said, and it was difficult to know

whether he was serious or joking. 'Few fights end that way though. Most show mercy before that point.'

'But not all?'

'No, not all,' Rados said.

Victor asked, 'When do the fights start?'

'Soon. I want you to know something first. There are certain things I value,' Rados explained. 'Fortitude, obviously. A man who cannot handle himself is no use to me. Intelligence ... not all my men possess it, but those that do stay closest to my side. Strength of will matters more than both. Confucius said it's not the fall but how we rise from the fall that matters. But even more important than will is loyalty, for without that we are nothing but barbarians. Homo sapiens became the dominant force on this planet not through individual might but because we worked together for the common good. We showed loyalty to our people. I expect the same of my men. I expect them to put aside their own wants and needs for the needs of our tribe. Then, and only then, will I reward them with more wealth and women than they can handle, for I am generous. And should their loyalty prove false ... then my generosity will become wrath, and I am every bit as cruel as I can be kind.'

Victor said, 'That sounds a fair deal to me.'

Rados regarded him. 'You're not scared of me, are you?'

Victor didn't answer. He wasn't sure what Rados wanted to hear.

The Serbian said, 'Fear is physical. It has a smell of its own and you don't have to be a dog to detect it. The stench of fear is almost sweet. I like it. But I smell none from you. Why is that? Why can I not smell your fear?'

'It'll be the aftershave.'

Rados' face didn't change. 'I deal with the worst of humanity, the most brutal and the strongest. Men who behave as though nothing scares them, as if it is the world that should be scared of them – but even from such men I can smell fear. Even if they are too stupid and arrogant to know fear, their bodies are not. The fear is there. It leaks out of their pores. They cannot stop it because their bodies know when they stand before the devil.'

Victor was quiet for a moment. He didn't believe Rados could smell a person's fear, but he believed Rados believed it. There were many signs a person was afraid and Victor knew them all – adjusting feet, creating distance, defensive posture, swallowing, sweating, dilated pupils, facial flushing. Rados might think he could smell fear, but he was deluding himself, turning an innate ability to read body language into a supernatural power.

Victor's hands were down at his sides, relaxed. He curled his fingers a fraction, as if he were about to make fists. Rados' eyes glimmered.

'Ah,' he said with a big inhale, 'now I can smell it. It appears that you are human, after all.'

'You sound disappointed.'

Rados shook his head. 'No, not disappointed, but I admit I am relieved. One devil in this city is more than enough.' The hum of the crowd quietened to a murmur and Rados checked his watch. 'Ah, it's time for the first fight.'

Victor could tell by Rados' tone what was going to happen next, even before the Serbian said, 'Take off your shoes.'

Victor said, 'I'm not going to fight.'

'Because you can't or don't want to? Because a man who cannot use his fists is of no use to me.'

'You didn't hire me to be an enforcer or an entertainer.'

'I hired you to be whatever I decide you to be. For tonight, you are a gladiator.'

Victor didn't have to look around to know Rados' men were in close proximity and paying attention to each and every word their boss uttered, as well as Victor's reaction. If he refused to fight, he couldn't expect to walk out of the building in anything resembling one piece. Even if they were all unarmed, he couldn't take on so many opponents. Far better to fight one-on-one in a semblance of a fair contest than to face a dozen without that semblance.

'Well?' Rados asked.

Victor unlaced his shoes, one at a time, before taking them off.

Rados said, 'I am disappointed in your reluctance.'

The socks followed. The tiled floor was cold beneath Victor's bare feet. He didn't respond to Rados' taunt.

'Who am I fighting?' Victor asked, removing his jacket.

'That depends what you mean,' Rados said. 'Existentially? When we fight the true opponent is always ourselves. But physically, you're fighting the Beast.'

TWENTY-NINE

The Beast lived up to his name. He was a monster of a man with a face that seemed almost Neanderthal. His skull was a bowling ball of dense bone with a sloping forehead and prominent brow. His jaw jutted out under fat lips lined with stubble. His ears were shrivelled cauliflowers, the cartilage so deformed by blunt trauma no clear hole was visible. There was more hair on his back than his head. His gut was massive, but his shoulders were wide and hard. The knuckles on both hands were a mountain range of bony lumps, hardened and thickened with repeated use. His face was red from high blood pressure; no human heart was designed to pump blood around a body that weighed three hundred pounds. Though he appeared well-balanced and comfortable on his feet, his size would make it impossible to move with real speed.

Victor watched as the Beast entered through a doorway on the far side of the crowd, standing a clear head taller

181

than any of Rados' men. Judging by their reaction, he was something of a celebrity. The suits responded with an uneasy mix of fear and revelry.

'He only fights the new recruits,' Rados began, 'because no one ever wants to fight him.'

'I'm not surprised,' Victor said.

'He's not really part of my organisation. He's more of an entertainer for my men, as well as the well-dressed criminals who run this town from boardrooms and swivel chairs.'

Victor assessed the Beast. There was no point waiting until the fight began to devise a strategy. Then it would be too late. He had to make every second beforehand count.

The Beast's strengths were obvious, but it was his weaknesses Victor was interested in. Agility and stamina would be poor. The second wouldn't matter at first, but would become apparent as the fight wore on. Knowing the Beast would tire fast made no difference if Victor couldn't defend against the initial onslaught. The Beast's agility, or lack thereof, was the most important weakness. No man that heavy could be fast, except in a straight line. Once in motion, the incredible force created by all that mass powered by so much strength would be too great to control. The Beast would be an unstoppable bulldozer rushing forward, and just as slow and awkward to turn.

'I knew his mother,' Rados continued. 'I'm not sure what she put in his cornbread, but he's as crazy as he is big. If he eats at one of my restaurants, we barely break even that evening.'

Victor smiled, as if he cared.

'I tolerate his appetite and his idiocy for two reasons. As I said, his fights entertain my men and my friends in important places, but they are also invaluable to me in learning about potential employees such as yourself. Anyone who can survive a beating from him will be an asset to my organisation. They may spend a month in hospital and walk with a limp for the rest of their lives, but I will know for certain that they are going to do as I say from that point onwards. If they climb willingly into that pit, anything else I ask of them will seem like a holiday.'

'What use is a broken man to you?'

Rados had been expecting the question. His answer was smooth and rehearsed, as if it had been delivered to every new recruit he made face the Beast. 'I value mental fortitude over physical prowess. The latter is only temporary. It will degrade with time, whereas your mental strength will only improve.'

Victor said, 'I wasn't talking about myself.'

Rados chuckled.

Victor removed his shirt and set it down with his jacket. He could move well enough dressed – he never wore anything restrictive – but he didn't want to give his opponent an easy means of grabbing hold of him. If they ended up in a grapple, it would be over.

'You've seen your share of confrontation,' Rados said, his gaze moving back and forth over Victor's collection of scars.

He didn't comment. The scars spoke for themselves. Rados knew enough about combat to recognise how he had come by them.

The Beast had no facial injuries Victor could see. No scar tissue above or below the eyes and his nose was unbroken. Victor didn't believe that was because the Beast possessed some kind of Kevlar skin; more likely he'd never been hit hard enough or often enough. Given his obvious slowness, that wasn't because he had the ability to dodge and block blows but because his fights were always over too fast. None of his previous opponents had lasted beyond the opening flurry. They'd not had the chance to hit the Beast with anything meaningful because he was too big and too strong to defend against. Most would have been too hesitant to attack first, even if the Beast let them, and that passivity worked against them, giving the Beast the advantage. Then, with each quick victory the Beast grew more confident in his own power to overwhelm his opponents and dispatch them with minimal effort. He didn't get hit in return, so he never had to worry about defending himself. He didn't know what it was like to fight on the back foot. His slow fists could bludgeon their way through a guard, but could they snap up to defend against a fast jab?

The Beast approached and stared at Victor. He didn't have to be told that Victor was his opponent – Victor was the only new guy in the room and the only man also shirtless.

'This the Hungarian?' he asked Rados.

'I'm him,' Victor said.

'You're not small, but you're not big either.'

The Beast's voice was a booming growl. A whisper from lungs that size was an oxymoron.

Victor said, 'They say it's not the size of the dog in the fight but the fight in the dog.'

'I like dog fights.'

'That doesn't surprise me,' Victor said. 'The weak often enjoy suffering.'

The Beast slapped his barrel chest. Fat rippled over the muscle. 'I'm not weak.'

'Then when was the last time you fought someone bigger than yourself?'

The Beast didn't answer. His nostrils flared and his jaw flexed. He walked away and set about working up the crowd, who were in reverence of their champion. They patted him on the arm or back and parted for him wherever he walked.

'Quite the specimen, isn't he?' Rados said.

Victor nodded.

Like the rest of him, the Beast's hands were massive. Ideal for punching and pummelling, but not so useful for finding pressure points and making small, important movements. He wouldn't kick; he was too top heavy. His height came from his torso and head, not his legs. They were thick and solid and able to support him well enough, but on one foot? Doubtful. Big guys didn't tend to kick; their natural reach meant they didn't need the extra range, even if their physique was more in proportion than the Beast's.

The ambient noise of shouts and cheers grew loud. The crowd was ready.

'It's time,' Rados said.

Victor climbed down into the empty pool.

THIRTY

The floor of the swimming pool was not the smooth, tractionless surface it appeared from the outside. Instead, it was grippy and coarse with a thin spread of the sand thrown down to soak up blood. Victor doubted it had been an intentional effect, but the fighters would benefit from the extra traction. They would slip less and their balance would be better. As a result they would throw harder punches, which would make for a better spectacle. He paced around for a moment. Down at fight level he could see the texture of the sand and where it was denser and finer. Some areas had more grip than others. The centre of the pool, where the fights began, had the least grip; the shallow end of the pool had the most coverage and it fell away towards the deep end. That made sense. The fights would take place at the shallow end of the pool where the spectators were closest to the action. No rules, Rados had said.

While the Beast worked up the crowd and the crowd roared for their champion, Victor judged distance and shuffled backwards, legs further than shoulder-width apart, sweeping the ground with the soles of his feet to shift away the thin spread of sand.

The Beast roared along with the crowd and pumped his giant fists into the air to whip them up into a frenzy. They chanted his name.

Beast. Beast. Beast.

Victor ignored the noise and showmanship, and kept sweeping with the soles of his feet until they squeaked against smooth tiling.

The Beast continued the preamble, roaring and shouting, fist-pumping and flexing. This routine might last longer than a typical fight. It would be an essential part of his popularity amongst Rados' men, whom he had beaten, one by one. At first, they would hate him for smashing up their faces and breaking their extremities, but men, fundamentally pack animals, were usually happy with their place in a hierarchy once it was established who was the alpha. Dogs were the same. These men had survived the Beast, which was an achievement in itself, and violent men liked to watch violence. There was no entertainment if the Beast's fights were over in seconds. The showmanship beforehand compensated for the lack of suspense over what might happen – everyone knew who the winner would be – by raising expectations that they were about to see another foe smashed.

When he deemed himself ready, the Beast climbed down into the pool. It was a spectacle in itself. He was huge and awkward using steps and rails designed for someone half his size. Victor was aware of Rados' intense gaze, as if the Serb was analysing Victor's own analysis.

They had climbed into the empty pool-turned-arena at the shallow end. Victor now stood towards the centre and the Beast, having received an impatient nod from Rados, stalked forward to meet Victor. The spectators lining the sides of the pool edged along to make sure they had the best view, careful not to impede Rados' line of sight of the coming action.

The Beast couldn't whisper, but he could produce a low growl. 'I'm going to kill you for what you said before. Once you go down, I won't stop until your skull is mush. We'll see who is the weak one.'

Victor smiled, because he was pleased to have got under the Beast's skin and because the smile would only antagonise the man further. He wanted the Beast angry.

The fighter's face was already red from his high blood pressure, which had been elevated by the adrenaline coursing through him after all the posturing and showmanship. The effect was now further intensified by his anger towards Victor.

The cheering spectators hushed, sensing it was almost time.

Victor backed away, and so did the Beast. They faced one another across the empty pool. The spectators quietened until they were almost silent. Then Victor winked at the Beast and the big man charged.

He roared as he powered forward, Rados' men breaking into an explosion of noise, screaming their support as the Beast shot across the empty pool.

He was faster than anticipated, but that only helped Victor, who waited until the last instant, as the Beast lowered his head and opened his arm to collide into Victor to take him to the ground, timing his dodge so that he darted out of the way once the Beast was committed to a battering-ram grapple. Victor was fast for a man of his size, but moved like lightning compared to the Beast.

All that force met no resistance, and as Victor had deduced, could not be stopped even by the Beast himself, who tried to slow himself and manoeuvre – something he was capable of, if not graceful at, but not when his bare feet met smooth tiles free from sand and the grip he was used to.

Victor had made sure to stand with his back to the deep end so the sloping floor of the pool worked against the Beast as he attempted to regain his balance. He stumbled and flailed and slid and tumbled and fell, hard. The crowd's screams of expectation became shocked gasps.

The sloping floor took something from the impact, letting the Beast slide away some of the energy instead of absorbing it all, but not enough to stop his face whipping into the tiles, crushing his nose and scattering teeth across the pool floor.

He stayed conscious, however, and tried to get purchase with his palms to push himself upright as blood rained from his flattened nose and wrecked mouth. His palms slipped on the blood-slicked tiles.

He was dazed but still fast to get to his knees, and with his opponent behind him, he spun around first before attempting to stand and risk exposing his back longer.

He turned in time to see Victor's hand blurring towards him, striking the side of his face with an open-palm strike, delivered like a hook with every ounce of power Victor could generate. The sound of impact was a monstrous slap and the Beast's head spun ninety degrees until the neck couldn't rotate any more and the remaining force travelled up and rocked his dazed brain around inside his skull. His eyes rolled backwards and he tipped over.

Victor grimaced. His palm was bright red and stinging, but the pain would subside without injury. His knuckles would not have fared as well against the Beast's Neanderthal bone structure.

The crowd were silent.

Victor walked back the way he had come and climbed out of the empty pool while Rados' men watched him under a cloud of disbelief.

Rados was waiting for him.

'Well done.' There was no praise in his tone.

Victor ignored the tone and nodded to show thanks.

Rados said, 'I'm not sure whether to be impressed or enraged. Beating him wasn't the test. You were supposed to take a beating to show loyalty to me, and to show your strength of will.'

'You said yourself there were no rules.'

Rados didn't respond.

Victor gestured to where the Beast lay on his back, unmoving, his face smeared in bright blood as one of Rados' men knelt by his side, checking he was still alive. He was, but he would be eating nothing but pureed food for a long time.

'If you're unhappy with the result,' Victor said, 'when the Beast wakes up, I'll gladly fight him again.'

Rados stared hard, and Victor couldn't tell what thoughts were playing behind those washed-out blue eyes, but then Rados chuckled.

'I think I'm actually starting to like you.'

'I'm surprised it's taken so long.'

Rados patted him on the shoulder. 'Come on, let's get out of here. I've had enough of sport for one evening.'

'Where are we going?'

Rados said, 'Somewhere quiet so I can get to know you.'

For a brief moment it seemed as though it would be only Victor and Rados leaving together, but some of his men fell in behind them. Rados didn't order or gesture, so Victor knew it was what was expected of them. They were to stay at their boss's side at all times. Close protection detail. That was going to be another problem.

Rados climbed into the back seat of a waiting Range Rover and a man took the seat either side of him. Victor took the passenger seat. The other four men were in the second vehicle.

These guys weren't the same as the others. They had the same casual clothing; the same jewellery; the same clipped hair and stubble; the same smell. The difference was in their age. These were older than the rest. Victor was the youngest man in the vehicle. The men who were closest to Rados were late thirties to early fifties. They were carrying more weight than their contemporaries – a little more useful bulk and a little more around the waists to go with it – but they looked competent and confident.

They were from Rados' era, from the war; they may not all have fought with him, but they had fought. They were hardened criminals now, but they had once been hardened paramilitaries. Their eyes had the glaze of men who had killed and were proud of it, and would not hesitate to do so again. These were warriors. As Rados had said: men who had given up their humanity, like he had himself. Rados was different still, with his nice suit and healthy living, his philosophy and his intelligence. He appeared civilised in comparison to these men – as he had said, he was an emperor guarded by barbarians.

They didn't like Victor. That was clear. They didn't like the accelerated way he had joined the exclusive inner circle. They had earned their places. They had proved they belonged with Rados. Victor had not, and he wondered why Rados was willing to upset his loyal men for an outsider. He had to know his men well enough to see their reaction to Victor. Having been in the company of some of them for twenty or more years, he should have been able to predict their resentment. Rados was not stupid. If his men were unhappy then he was prepared to accept that in return for ... what?

THIRTY-ONE

Victor had been in the inner sanctum of many reprehensible individuals – politicians, warlords, crime bosses, arms dealers, dictators and royalty. He had found that where they spent most of their time revealed much about their personalities, the same as any civilian. Wealth and power were scalable and understandable because they were observable, but personality disorders and psychosis could be disguised and hidden. Rados' office was lavish and spoke of extreme wealth from the crystal chandelier to the huge desk made of red oak with gilded carvings. The walls were panelled with wood and decorated with a range of contemporary artworks. A circular Persian rug occupied the floor before the desk.

Rados took a seat behind the red oak desk. There was nowhere for Victor to sit even had he wanted to. Two of Rados' men flanked Victor from opposite sides of the wall. Their usual spots, he saw from the scuffed areas on the dark-stained floorboards. Victor adjusted his own footing in response, taking a half-step back and angling his head so he could keep them both in his peripheral vision. There was no way he could get to Rados. The two heavies were alert and watching, if unconcerned. They were armed and Victor was not.

Near to Rados' desk, under a wall-mounted spotlight stood a magnificent suit of medieval plate armour. The gauntlets rested on the pommel of a sword from the same era. Victor recognised the Milanese detailing of the armour, judging it to be early fifteenth century. The armour would have cost a small fortune, affordable only to a landowner or minor noble. He found it interesting that Rados owned such a set, which though beautiful to Victor's eye for the expertise of the workmanship and the superb protection it offered, was not an attractive set of armour by aesthetic standards, either today's or those of the 1400s. The warrior who had commissioned the armour – for all such suits had to be made to order to fit their wearer like a glove – had ignored fashionable convention and used a close-faced helm instead of the sleeker, lighter basinet with visors that had superseded it. He hadn't cared about fashion or convention and had wanted only the best protection. Understandable, of course, but curious that Rados was displaying an ugly set of armour when his obvious wealth would allow him to buy any he desired.

'What do you think of it?' Rados asked, seeing where Victor's gaze lay.

'Impressive,' Victor said. 'I like it.'

'Do you happen to know anything about armour?'

Victor shook his head. 'Not really.'

Rados looked disappointed, as if everyone he invited into his office gave the same answer and he longed to engage in conversation about one of his interests, but each disappointment made it harder to bear instead of more tolerable.

'Unfortunately, it's not my size,' Rados said. 'Else I'd never take it off. I don't have the shoulders for it.'

'Can't it be adjusted?'

Rados responded to Victor's feigned ignorance with a smile that conveyed both sympathy and contempt. 'That would defeat the point of a made-to-measure suit, even if the process would not ruin the antique.'

Victor nodded as if he was learning a lesson. 'Looks cumbersome,' he said, because he knew it was a common misconception that such suits of armour were heavy and limited the wearer's range of movement.

'A knight wasn't a tank. Whoever owned that would have been able to vault up on to his horse from behind the beast as well as perform handstands and cartwheels. The plates are thinner than you would think and the weight distribution is incredible.'

'I didn't know that,' Victor said, because he did.

'That piece is from Milan, as all the best plate was in those days, but made for a Teutonic knight. He wore it at the Battle of Grunwald, where his order met defeat.'

Victor didn't ask for more information. He wasn't here to discuss history even if he would have liked to know more about the knight. He stood silent as if he was not interested.

Rados didn't register the disinterest or didn't care. 'There was honour in war in those times. To kill a man you had to face him, sword to sword. You had to risk your life to take his.'

'Unless you used a crossbow, of course.'

'Once banned by the Pope,' Rados said, telling Victor something else he already knew. 'It was deemed unfair that a peasant with little training could kill a king.'

For a moment, no one spoke. Victor noticed there was no clock on any of the walls. Rados wore no watch. Even in the case of a man who waited for no one and who in turn everyone waited for, the absence of both was telling. Rados had a phobia, else feared time itself.

'I have several suits of armour. One in each of my offices.'

'You have several offices?'

He nodded. 'Scattered around the city and beyond. For security purposes.'

Victor nodded too because the precaution was going to work. He couldn't use this office as a strike point, not knowing when Rados might return.

Rados reached into a desk drawer, took out a small plastic bottle and squeezed antibacterial gel into his palms. He rubbed it in. 'I don't shake hands,' Rados said. 'I touch my wife. I touch my mistresses. I refuse to touch anyone else.'

'Frightened you'll catch something?'

'Not at all, but I'm scared they'll realise I'm just like them; nothing more than human.'

'Then why tell me?'

'Because I see through your disguise of humanity because I wear one too.'

Victor didn't respond.

'I know all about you,' Rados said after a moment. 'Not from what you say – or don't say – but the way you stand and the set of your shoulders and how you hold your chin and where your hands hang and how you keep your fingers open.'

'What are you trying to say?'

'Let me explain,' Rados began. 'Once, at the height of the war, I was with a small group of my most loyal warriors. We engaged in a firefight with a contingent of Croat irregulars. We were lightly armed – assault rifles only – but the Croats had a couple of machine guns. They had us pinned down in a forest outside Sarajevo. Machine gun rounds were taking great chunks out of the trees. The forest was raining branches and splinters and shredded leaves down upon us. The Croats were well-practised and knew how to fire in controlled bursts, staggering their volleys so only one machine gun was firing at a time, allowing one to reload while the other was firing. It was relentless. We thought we would never get out of there.'

Victor asked, 'How did you?' because that's what Rados expected of him.

'We tried to fight our way out, of course. A few of us were cut down as a result. The machine guns were .50 calibre. Have you ever seen what a bullet the size of your finger can do to a man?'

Victor had seen, of course, but he shook his head.

Rados didn't elaborate. 'When it became obvious we were outgunned and outnumbered, we did the only thing we could do: we surrendered. The Croats, for all their faults, had humanity, and did not fire on us when we threw down our arms. They even gave us water and food and some expensive brandy they had looted from a mayor's cabinet. They were just like us, fighting for their nation in a war they didn't really understand. We were all humans, all scared. One of the machine gunners even cried when he saw what was left of the men he had shot. He begged us for forgiveness.'

'You spent the rest of the war as a POW?'

Rados shook his head. 'I didn't even spend one whole night as a POW. A unit of Serbian commandos happened upon us and surprised the Croats. After a brief firefight we were free. We repaid the kindness of our captors by splitting them into pairs. We told them that only one of each two would be spared.'

'You made them fight one another.'

Rados nodded. 'They were reluctant, of course, so we executed one pair to show the others they had no choice. We used their own machine guns. We drank their brandy and cheered as they fought with their bare hands and teeth until half of them were dead and the others were half-dead with exhaustion and injury and wailing because they had killed their brothers. Then we made those who had survived split into pairs to fight again. But they refused. They knew then we would not let them go. So we locked them in a house and set it alight.'

'What's the point of this story?'

'Because maybe, just maybe, we might have let those who survived the second fight go. Instead, we killed every single one of them.'

'I don't think you would have, whatever you say now.

You were never going to let them go. Maybe you look back in those rare moments when your conscience speaks out and think you might have done.'

Rados laughed. 'Are you talking about me or yourself?'

'I'm not conflicted. I don't have nightmares. I'm just not a very nice person.'

'Exactly,' Rados said. 'Look at my eyes. Do you see but one hint of shadow beneath them? I sleep like a baby. I never wake up in the night in a cold sweat. Do you know why?'

'I think it doesn't matter what I believe because you're going to tell me.'

'It matters because I'm going to tell you. Because everything I have ever done, regardless how foul and inhuman another might think it, has been entirely justified.'

'Even what you did to those Croats?'

'Especially those Croats. Each one of my men lost friends and loved ones in that war and watched our comrades shot and blown to pieces. In taking our revenge on our captives we could forget that hell and salvage our broken ... not humanity, but our sanity. The Croats tried to hold on to their humanity by showing us mercy and kindness, but there is no humanity in war. Once you take a life, you are a warrior. From that point you either toss your humanity aside or you are killed by it, as those Croats were. We, however, found peace through cruelty.'

'I still don't understand.'

Rados said, 'I think you do understand, though you pretend not to. Once you have been cruel, you are forever cruel. There is no going back. Once you have taken one life, all life becomes worthless. I told you that story precisely because you do understand. You're not conflicted. You don't have nightmares.'

Victor was silent.

Rados regarded him with a measured smile. 'More than anything else, evil recognises its own reflection.'

THIRTY-TWO

Rados' Range Rover was a new model. The interior was cream leather and smelled of tobacco. Neither the bodywork nor windows were armoured, Victor had noted. Still, Rados was protected by the three heavies, including the driver, who travelled with him. Victor rode in the passenger seat, as instructed by Rados, who was squeezed into the back between two of his men. He didn't seem to mind. The Range Rover had plenty of space and the two bodyguards flanking him did their best to give him as much room as possible.

He hadn't told Victor where they were going and Victor didn't ask. He knew what was expected of him. Rados was not a man to tolerate unnecessary questions, and anyone who asked them could not hope to gain his confidence.

It was the middle of the afternoon. The drive was short. No one chatted. There was no music or radio playing. Rados' men were neither alert nor unaware. This was not a professional security detail. They were not actively looking for threats from either outside or inside. They didn't toy with phones, but they were bored.

It was only Rados' eyes that never stopped moving.

The Range Rover parked against the kerb on a side street in one of Belgrade's poorer neighbourhoods. They were far outside of the city centre. There were lots of bars and kafanas and stores selling cheap clothes and domestic products.

Rados leaned forward between the seats to point through the windscreen. 'The frontier of my empire.'

A sign advertised massages.

Inside, the massage parlour was warm and humid and looked almost respectable. A woman in white clinical attire sat behind a counter. She was middle-aged and straight-backed, with an air of authority. Leather sofas were arranged into a waiting area with a coffee table laden with magazines and newspapers. A water-cooler stood nearby. There was nothing to suggest anything went on here beyond innocent relaxation.

Rados didn't acknowledge the woman behind the counter and she didn't acknowledge him. He walked past her, towards a door marked 'staff only'. Victor followed, as did two of Rados' men. The driver had stayed with the Range Rover.

Through the door, a set of stairs led up to the first floor. Here, it didn't look as respectable. The walls were painted pale pink. Doors were red, and numbered. Rados led Victor down a corridor and into a lobby. Victor heard grunts and squeaking mattress springs.

Zoca was there, lounging on an Ottoman couch.

He scrambled to his feet when he saw Rados. The rapid movement caused him pain, judging by the pinched expression, though he tried his best to mask it. If Rados noticed, he neither cared nor reacted.

Rados said, 'Where's the latest stock?'

Zoca clapped his hands, summoning assistance in the form of a youth with a shaved head and cystic acne all over his face. He moved awkwardly and with a pronounced shyness that made him seem more juvenile than he was.

Zoca said, 'Fetch them. Be quick.'

The youth was as scared of Zoca as Zoca was of Rados, and he hurried away, meek and subservient. Zoca avoided eye contact with his boss, but Victor caught a few glances thrown his way. They were not friendly.

Rados said to Victor, 'I have a shipment to move in a few days' time. I would like you to help secure it.'

'What kind of shipment?' Victor said, noting Zoca's shocked and displeased body language.

'The highly profitable kind.'

Victor said, 'I understand.'

A corner of Rados' mouth turned up in a precursor to a smile, as though Victor couldn't possibly understand. Which was intriguing.

'Why do you think I want you there?'

'To test me.'

Rados shrugged. 'In part, but also because I have reliability issues amongst my men.'

Zoca looked away.

Victor said, 'You don't have to worry about me.'

The Serbian considered him for a long moment. 'Such an assurance is meaningless. I place little value on words alone. It is what we do, not what we say, that defines who we are.'

Victor didn't know how to respond, but he didn't need to, because Dilas entered the room. He was as well-dressed as the last time Victor had seen him, but he looked fatigued and his cheeks were flushed.

Rados grinned. 'Shouldn't you be out there running this fair city of ours?'

Dilas returned the grin. 'One cannot rule if one is distracted by base urges.'

'I trust they were well taken care of?' Rados asked.

'Always.'

Dilas turned to Victor. 'Well played last night with the Beast. I made a small fortune betting on you against the odds.'

'You're welcome,' Victor said.

'Quite the tactician, isn't he?' Rados said to Dilas, who nodded.

The awkward youth returned, ushering four women into the room. They had all been at the scrap yard before, but now they were clean and wore new clothes.

'Take a look at my merchandise,' Rados said to Victor. 'These women are worth more than any powder or resin. These are gold.'

Victor did as instructed, his gaze taking in the women, who all had heads bowed to avoid eye contact.

'Merchandise is seasonal,' Rados explained. 'It arrives in batches, like crops gathered during the harvest. When the season is over, things are quieter. If it is a healthy season then we have a good year, everyone is happy. If it is a bad season then it is not such a good year. Do you understand?'

'I think so.'

'What I'm saying is, timing is everything. I told you I had a setback. A second, especially so soon after the last, would prove catastrophic.'

It made more sense to Victor now. Rados couldn't afford to recruit new guys the conventional way. This was harvest season. There was no time. He needed numbers and he needed them fast.

'Why seasonal?' Victor asked. 'Women grow all year round.'

'Supply and demand, as with all commodities. But these kind of crops can only be moved in batches of opportunity. The more shipments, the more distribution, the more bribes, the more expense, the more risks.'

'And the heavier the loss if something goes wrong.'

'Like I said: one setback is plenty.'

'I see,' Victor said again. 'What happened?'

'That is a most interesting question,' Rados said, eyes unblinking. 'It has been a very long time since I had a problem with a shipment. Why now?'

Victor shrugged. 'I wouldn't know.'

Rados tilted his head to one side. 'I don't expect you to.' He approached the women. 'They call it the bloom of youth; that special period where life has granted us beauty we don't deserve; that we will waste and squander and then lament its passing.'

'I've improved with age,' Victor said.

Rados smirked, then continued: 'They call it the bloom of youth because even tired and scared you can still see that bloom. Because beneath the fear and the passivity, her genes are still strong; her ability to bear children is unaffected. We alphas of the pack, we warriors, are finely tuned to that bloom. Our own genes hunger for it. We will kill for it.' Rados turned to face him. 'Don't you agree?'

'That's nature,' Victor said by way of answer.

Rados stroked a girl's cheek with the back of his hand. 'This is more precious than gold. This is more valuable than any drug. Gold is a commodity. Cocaine is a commodity. The more there is, the less valuable it is. Cocaine is temporary, it is consumable, whereas gold endures. This will hold its price long after its weight in cocaine is pissed away. Gold does nothing. It is valuable because we say it is. There is no need for it and no benefit from it if we do not decide to want it. This girl has benefit whether we want it or not, because we *need* it. We must have it. We are driven from the very depths of our soul for it. If a man is given the choice between this or gold, if he can only have one, he will choose this every single time. That is why this is what I trade in.'

Victor listened.

'They call it the bloom of youth,' Rados said once again. 'And men will pay any price to devour it.' He paused. 'Take her, she's yours.'

'I value spirit more than youth.'

'Then perhaps there is a mistake in your genome and your genes seek to balance out that imperfection of personality.'

'Perhaps,' Victor agreed.

'Pick another if you like. One with more *spirit*.'

His gaze passed over the women and rested on the one on the far right, the one with short hair who had spat in Zoca's face at the scrap yard.

'That one might have too much spirit, even for you,' Rados said.

'Why do you say that?'

'Because this is her second time with us.' Rados waited until Victor turned to question him further before continuing. 'She was here at the very beginning of the harvest season. She was trouble from the start, as some are. They do not soften to a hard hand, but strengthen. They need to be kept close by. We cannot send them away to loyal customers. This particular one stayed here in Belgrade. I liked her. Her bloom was radiant. But she left us. Now, that bloom has gone, hasn't it?'

'She escaped?'

Rados nodded. 'She ran far before we caught up with her. Her wiles are as strong as her will.'

'Yet here she is again.'

'Some people are unlucky. For some of us, the cards will never be in our favour. Now, she is back and her bloom has faded. You like her though?'

This particular one stayed here in Belgrade.

'Yes,' Victor said, 'I like her.'

THIRTY-THREE

Milan Rados watched the Hungarian leave with his choice. Zoca led them. When they were gone Rados dismissed Zoca's boy servant and the other women. Only Dilas remained. Rados took a seat behind a desk. He then sat in silence, savouring the absence of chatter, but knowing it could not endure. That's what made it so precious. That's why he treasured it so much.

It came as no surprise that it was Dilas who broke the precious silence, crushing it beneath one of his tasselled loafers.

He said, 'You can't trust him. You do know that, I take it.'

Dilas liked to make statements rather than pose questions because he thought it lent him gravitas. Rados chose not to answer.

But he persisted: 'Surely, you can't.'

Rados thought of his favourite beach and the way his feet would sink into the black sand. If he couldn't have silence, he could at least have the sweet memory of merciful times of quiet.

Rados said, 'You did as I asked?'

Dilas nodded. 'I made enquiries.'

'Speak plainly, and with an answer.'

Dilas smirked, pleased with himself. He enjoyed what little power he had over Rados, believing in his own posturing, oblivious to the fact it was permitted only because Rados tolerated it. 'I had him checked out. He's no undercover cop.'

'You're sure about that?'

'I wouldn't risk your displeasure if I was not.'

Rados said, 'You mean you wouldn't risk your own skin.'

Dilas laughed. 'Well, I have such pretty skin. But undercover cop or not, you can't trust him. Do you?'

He waited for an answer, and when one didn't come he opened his mouth to say something else, but Rados was faster. He was prepared to succumb to one of Dilas' ego games if it would put a stop to it.

'Do you know who I trust, my friend? Do you know? I don't trust any of my men. I don't trust you. I don't even trust my own reflection not to stab me in the back on a whim. So why would I trust him? Answer me that. No, don't. Instead, tell me what makes you think I trust him? What makes you believe you can see into my soul with such clarity?'

Dilas didn't answer. He had been outplayed, and he knew it, so instead he changed tack: 'You seem uncommonly open with him.'

Rados scooped a shiny red apple from a fruit bowl and used his pocketknife to begin peeling. 'You sound jealous. Do I not pat you on the head enough? Do I not rub your belly when you have been a good boy?'

Dilas didn't rise to the taunt. Instead, he asked, 'Why have you hired him?'

'We've lost men recently. We need to make up those numbers. Addition is the opposite of subtraction, is it not?'

Rados' pocketknife was razor sharp – he honed the blade every week – and so he had to use a delicate touch to slice away the skin while keeping it as an intact spiral.

'Don't you think it's convenient he's come along at the precise moment we need to replace people?'

Dilas' eyes were full of challenge and arrogance – as much as he wanted Rados to agree with him, he also wanted to demonstrate his superior powers of deduction, to be the one who was right – the only one who was right. Rados, always ready, sidestepped Dilas' gambit.

Rados said, 'You know I don't believe in coincidences.'

'Then what exactly are you doing?'

'I'm being a businessman. Hector mentioned him to us before I was forced to make the cull, let's not forget.' Rados paused, peeling the apple. 'Had he come to us afterwards then he would no longer find his skin attached to his flesh. So we can show a degree of faith, especially given his performance last night.'

'Beating the Beast doesn't mean he can protect our shipments.'

'Because we can stand straight does not mean we can stand tall.'

Dilas frowned. 'What does that mean?'

'It means: kindly stop telling me things I already know.'

Dilas unfolded his arms and held up his hands. 'It's none of my business what you do or don't do. I'm offering you counsel, that's all. Do what you like.'

'Thank you for your blessing,' Rados said with undisguised mockery. 'Look, it's quite simple: we need warm bodies, and I don't yet know who he is or what he wants, but I suspect he will be very useful to us. Until that's proved or disproved, I want to keep track of him. That's not so hard to understand, is it?'

Dilas scoffed. 'Unless you're planning on having him at your side night and day, how exactly are you going to do that? Have him watched? Great idea, Milan. Wasting more manpower watching him than you gain with his presence.'

Rados didn't respond. He continued to peel his apple. He tolerated Dilas' insolence in the same way he tolerated a bad smell – it was temporary. Clean air would follow in time.

Dilas didn't understand he was temporary. He thought he breathed the same clean air. 'This one is different,' he said. 'He's slippery. He's an eel. I knew that within seconds, which is why I bet on him. He could notice if you have him watched, and act accordingly.'

Rados shook his head, gaze still on the apple. 'I won't use my own people. I thought that would be obvious. As you said, that would not make sense and he would certainly know if I had him watched. There is no doubt in my mind. That's why I want him in my organisation if he shows himself loyal. I need a man who does not simply see, but looks.'

'Sometimes I wonder if all those books you read are good for you,' Dilas said, shaking his head. 'So who is going to watch him for you if not your own men?'

'Your people, of course. Who else is there?'

'I don't have people, Milan. I'm not a gangster, I'm a politician.'

Rados released a bark of laughter. 'Is there such a distinction? We both wield power we did not earn over those who do not deserve it. At least I do not pretend. I am honest in my criminality. You hide yours.'

'Politics is, at least, legal.'

'Ah, yes, legal,' Rados said. 'Thieves writing their own laws – the biggest irony of democracy.'

He glanced up from the apple with something in his eyes Dilas recognised.

'Oh no, no, no,' he began. 'You can't mean who I think you mean. You can't be that stupid.'

Rados' eyes narrowed. 'If I am stupid, how is it that you profit so much by your association with me?'

Dilas was quick to backtrack. 'Ah, that's not what I meant. It was a turn of phrase, nothing more. You know I don't think you are stupid, but you can't seriously be suggesting—'

'Of course. Who else would I suggest?'

Dilas was concerned. 'And what do I tell them?'

'You are a liar by profession, yet you ask me what you should say? Tut, tut. Your lack of confidence in your own deftness of tongue is most unlike you. Where is that

self-belief? Where is it hiding?' He looked beneath his desk.
'No, not here.'

Dilas huffed.

'Always remember that your friends speak the same language as you, so use words they understand. Here,' Rados said as he reached into a desk drawer and produced a strap of cash, 'have a dictionary.'

He tossed the money. Dilas was too slow to catch it before it struck him in the chest, but he managed to fumble for the strap before it fell to the floor. He wedged it into an inner pocket of his suit jacket in a well-practised move.

'Okay,' Dilas conceded. 'You win. I think I know the right person to handle this. I will ask him to make a call and—'

'But do make sure he knows the right *persons*,' Rados interrupted with quiet insistence.

'Right. Sure. I'll be clear that this needs more than one.'

'The more the merrier.'

'Quite,' Dilas said. 'They'll keep tabs on your boy and see what they can unearth. I hope you are happy to have your way once again.'

'I am a child on Christmas morning,' Rados answered with a measured smile.

Dilas sneered at the sarcasm. 'Whether they find anything out about this Hungarian or not, whether he proves uniquely useful or not, you are acting most out of character to bring someone so new, and an outsider at that, into your carefully managed world.'

'Perhaps it is in fact the opposite. Perhaps I'm acting in character after all.'

'I don't know what you mean by that.'

'You didn't fight in the war, did you?'

Dilas' voice quietened. 'You know I didn't. I was too young.'

'If you are old enough to throw a rock, then you can fight.'

Dilas didn't respond.

Rados said, 'My point is that you have never been in combat. You have never been in a battle. It is a unique experience. After you have taken a life – lives – the normal world is never the same. It is no longer normal.'

'You don't need another former soldier when you already have a platoon of them.'

'Yes, we all fought in the same war on the same side. Yet I could not be more different from them. None of them is like me. None of them think as I do.'

'I see,' Dilas said. 'So you've found yourself a kindred spirit. How very touching.'

'He interests me, yes. We are similar, yes. I want to know more about him, yes.'

'That's not enough of a motive to be taking such an unnecessary risk with this one.'

'Calculated,' Rados corrected. 'I never take unnecessary risks.'

Dilas said, 'That still doesn't explain it. I'd like to know the real reason why you're doing this.'

Rados exhaled and leaned back in his chair. 'So would I.'

When the apple was peeled he set it down on the desk before him, turning it around on the spot until it sat as he wanted it to. He placed the peel next to it and wiped his pocketknife clean. He was not hungry. He had no desire to eat the apple. Rados wanted to watch it oxidise and grow brown now it was without its skin – its protection.

He wanted to watch it die.

THIRTY-FOUR

The room Zoca led them to was small and cold. It had a bed, a wardrobe and a dressing table, and nothing else except curtains and stains. A low-wattage bulb hanging shadeless from the ceiling buzzed alight when Zoca thumbed the switch. He pushed the woman through the doorway and towards the bed, and when she resisted he raised a hand to strike that Victor caught before it reached its mark.

Zoca glared at him, enraged and humiliated, and eager to react with violence, but he also felt the incredible strength of Victor's grip compressing his wrist and knew to back down.

'Careful, Hungarian,' Zoca hissed instead of fighting.

Victor released him when he saw that passivity and Zoca left them, rubbing at his inner wrist and the vivid marks left by Victor's fingertips.

When he could no longer hear the man's footsteps,

Victor closed the door. He reached to engage the lock, but saw there was none. Only a mark in the wood remained where once a brass catch had been. He examined the room's simple furniture – bed, wardrobe, dressing table – and fixtures and fittings. There were no signs of any recording devices.

The woman's gaze followed his every move.

He kept each of his movements slow and obvious. She was scared and trying to keep control of that fear. He could hear her breathing from three metres away.

He faced her with arms down by his sides and hands open. He didn't step any closer. He wanted to be near to the door and she wanted him as far away as possible.

The woman was small and slim, but he saw the latter was through rapid weight loss. She had sturdy shoulders and hips. There was no malnourishment evident in her skin or nails. Now close, he saw she was no older than twenty-five. She was maybe fifty or fifty-one kilos and five foot three inches. He estimated she'd been about five kilos heavier when this nightmare began – at least this time around. He pictured her as well-fed and well-raised, not some impoverished peasant from a backwater village desperate for a new life. She was from a comparatively well-off background, maybe from a city, probably educated to university level. Probably she had sought to travel, perhaps to study abroad, and her quest for adventure and new experiences had been exploited. He didn't see her as naive. She wouldn't have been easy to kidnap.

He said, 'I'm not going to hurt you.'

She said, 'If you get your dick out, I'll bite it off.'

He couldn't help but adjust his footing, even if the words were delivered with more desperation than ferocity.

'I'm not going to hurt you,' he said again.

She didn't react. The words meant nothing to her. She must have heard them before and learnt how hollow they could be, no matter how presentable the speaker appeared nor how softly spoken he sounded.

'I'm not,' Victor insisted.

He resisted approaching her. He knew how to be unthreatening because he spent most of his time pretending to be no threat to anyone.

He said, 'I only want to talk. Is that okay?'

She was hesitant. She didn't believe him. 'You want to talk?'

'That's all. I'll keep standing here. You can sit down if you want to.'

She glanced at the only place to sit down – the bed – and shook her head. 'No, I don't want to sit down.'

'It's your choice,' he said. 'You don't have to do anything you don't want to.'

He spoke with his hands as well as his voice, because standing statue-still was unnatural and would only unnerve her, but he made slow gestures and kept his hands no higher than his waist.

Her expression hardened and he saw that he had tried too hard.

'Don't try and make out you're one of the nice ones. None of you are. Just because you don't hit me it doesn't mean you're a good guy. You're here, so you're responsible for what is happening to me.'

In being passive he'd made himself appear weak and had drawn her aggression as a result. He changed tack:

'And what is happening to you?' Victor asked.

'What kind of a question is that? I'm in hell. Except worse than hell, because this is real.'

'How did you get here?'

'What do you care? What do you want with me?'

'I'm going to ask you one question at a time. That's all. I'm not trying to trick you. I only want to talk to you. And so long as we're talking, we're not doing anything else.'

She stared, then looked away, but only for a moment. 'How I got here? I met a man. I trusted him. He was an asshole. Satisfied?'

'Not really,' he said. 'But you can tell me as much or as little as you like. Where are you from?'

'Armenia.'

Her hair was dark brown, cut short and choppy in a way that didn't suit her. He imagined she had cut it herself. An attempt at disguise, or maybe to make herself less attractive. She wore too much make-up, which wouldn't have been her choice. Her fingernails were cracked and broken beneath fresh polish from chewing or maybe clawing at her captors and confines.

Despite the make-up there were bags and dark circles beneath her eyes, which were green. Her lips were thin and chapped. She smelled of perfume and fear.

He said, 'Do you speak English?'

She didn't answer but he saw a flicker in her eyes.

'If we speak like this,' he said in English, 'they won't be able to overhear us.'

She understood and the hint at deception was compelling enough for her to say, 'Okay, but why don't you want them to listen?'

'You sound vaguely American.'

'I went to high school over there. A kind of scholarship. Why are you asking me all these questions?'

'Because I'm interested in who you are.'

'Why?' she asked, confused, but then a thought occurred to her and she looked at him with disgust. 'Yeah, I bet you are interested, aren't you? This is all some kind of sick fantasy for you, isn't it? You want me to like you. I bet you can't even get it up otherwise. Pervert.'

'I can help you,' Victor said.

She looked away. 'Even if you could help me, I don't believe you would.'

'I'll make a deal with you,' he began. 'If you help me, I'll help you. That's how simple it can be if you'll let it.'

She looked back, suspicious but with a glimmer of hope in her eyes. She couldn't believe he would help her selflessly, but she could dare to believe he might if he could get something out of it too.

'What do you mean by that? How can I help you?'

'You've been here before, haven't you?'

'How do you know?'

Victor said, 'You escaped.'

'For all the good it did me. When I finally made it back home they were waiting for me. I should have seen it coming. They had all my papers. They knew where I would go. It was so stupid of me to make that mistake.'

'I had my pick of the women you arrived with,' Victor

said. 'But the others were new. They hadn't been here before, like you had.'

'Why do you care if I was here before?'

'Because I want you to tell me everything you saw the first time.'

She stepped towards him, finally daring to believe that he was being truthful and searching in that truth for how it might help her in return. 'Why do you want to know what I've seen?'

Victor said, 'The older man in the suit I was speaking to, do you know who he is?'

She nodded. 'He's in charge. His name is Rados.'

Victor said, 'That's right. I'm here to kill him.'

THIRTY-FIVE

It was a risk telling her, of course. But he considered it a calculated one. She was a prisoner – a slave – kidnapped, mistreated and raped. She hated her captors and was terrified of them, with good reason. He wouldn't have long with her and he needed to gain her trust now. He had to sell her his idea fast and make sure she bought it. He couldn't leave her unless she was on his side. He couldn't risk her revealing anything to Rados or his men, which she might as a bargaining tool to procure better treatment. It wouldn't make a difference, but she might be desperate enough to try. So he had to make an instant impression.

She stared at him for a long time: analysing his eyes; searching his expression; evaluating each and every word for subtext and hidden messages and for the possibility of deceit or trickery. He said nothing further, allowing her to process the information.

In the end, she could find nothing, so her response was a simple, 'Why?'

'There is no why,' he replied, 'not really. In most cases who lives and who dies comes down to nothing more than convenience. This is no different.'

'And how will you be convenienced by that bastard's death?'

'It conveniences me only because it will convenience others a lot more.'

She understood, he saw, but she tried to hide it. She did not yet see him as anything more than an enemy, whatever he said. She needed convincing.

'The other women,' he began, 'who were transported with you. Tell me about them.'

'Why?'

He waited.

She said, 'What's to tell? They're young. They're going to fall apart. They're not going to make it.'

'They won't survive?'

She shuffled and shrugged. 'I don't mean they're going to die – I can't know that – but this will break them. They'll never be the same again, even if they're one day set free or manage to escape like I did.'

'Why do you say that?'

'They're too young. Their lives have been too easy. They haven't known any hardship. They don't know how cruel the world is. They won't be able to handle it.'

Victor nodded. She seemed to know what she was talking about, despite his evaluation that she had come from an affluent background. 'And you've known that cruelty outside of this?'

She didn't answer. Wouldn't.

He gave it a moment before he said, 'You said those other women are too young.'

'Yes.'

'Younger than you?'

'Yes.'

'Prettier?'

She hesitated, then said, 'Yes, a lot prettier. Why does that matter?'

'It matters only because I could have chosen one of them instead of you,' Victor explained. 'Any of them. Maybe even two of them. But I didn't. I chose you.'

She sneered. 'I don't give a shit about your sense of charity.'

'I didn't do it out of charity. Trust me when I say that I'm not of a charitable nature. I picked you so you can help me. In return for your help, I'll help you. I said before that it was simple, and it is.'

She was still suspicious, still confused. 'How can I help you? I'm no one. I'm nothing.'

'I've told you that too,' Victor said. 'I intend to kill Rados. But I know very little about his operations. I'm new here. I don't have the time or the opportunity to learn everything I need to know. You're on the inside too. You might find out something I can use to give me a shortcut.'

She didn't respond.

'I want you to find out everything about Rados you can. If he comes here, I want to know what time he arrived and how long he stayed. I want to know if he has other businesses and where they are. I need to know where he's going to be so I can be there first. But be careful. Don't do anything to expose yourself.'

She was staring, frown lines cracking the powder on her skin. 'You really are going to kill him, aren't you?'

'That's the only reason I'm here.'

'And if I help you,' she said, guarded and testing, 'what will you do for me in return? You said you would help me. How can you help me?'

Victor said, 'If you help me, I'll get you out of here.'

'How?'

'I don't yet know, and if I did I wouldn't tell you. Not yet. Not until you've helped me first. Once I know more about Rados' operation, I'll figure out the best way to set you free.'

'You're only one man. What can you do alone?'

'That's a good question. You'll have to take my word for it that I can do what I say I can do.'

'What are you?'

'A man with a job to do.'

'You're a killer.'

He nodded.

'If I agree,' she said, still unsure and guarded, 'how can I trust you? That's why I'm here. I trusted someone else. I fell for his good looks and friendly smile, his flattery and charm. It was all an act, but any attention is better than being utterly alone, isn't it?' Victor said nothing. 'Deep down I knew all along that he was telling me exactly what I wanted to hear, but I was desperate. I'd been without hope so long, I needed to believe I was being offered a way out, a chance of a better life. And look where it got me. How will I even be able to find out anything that could help you?'

He said, 'Don't worry about that. Just keep your eyes

and ears open. There may be some small detail that doesn't seem important to you, but could make all the difference to me.'

'Even if you're telling the truth about your intentions, that just means you're a piece of shit like Rados. How can I trust anything you say?'

'You can't,' Victor said. 'And I can't trust you either. But that's why we can help each other. We both have every incentive to help the other and a lot to lose for betrayal. Do you remember what happened the night you were brought to Belgrade?'

She hesitated as if she were about to say something, then nodded instead.

'That's good,' Victor said. 'You're telling me nothing about that night and you've told me nothing before I asked. But I know a lot about that night. I know you spat in Zoca's face. I know you were put in a shipping container with another woman while the rest were put into other containers. I know that you heard gunfire. I know when you were brought here the next day one of the youngest women had a broken nose and one who had come with you to Belgrade did not come here at all.'

'She was killed. She tried to escape.'

'I was the one who opened the shipping container. I told them to run.'

'Why did you do that?'

'I was improvising,' he explained. 'I was there to disrupt Rados' business to bring him out into the open. I didn't know how to reach him otherwise.'

'Well,' she said in a low tone, 'it worked.'

Victor nodded. 'Yes, Rados had Zoca beaten to a pulp and his men killed in punishment for their failure. He then hired me to replace his losses.'

'Exactly as you had planned.'

He ignored the spite in her voice. 'No, this was never the plan. I didn't intend on ever coming this close to Rados. He wasn't supposed to know I even existed. But now I'm here, I have to stay close to him, or I'll never get another opportunity. Like I said: I'm improvising.'

Her eyes were half closed in disgust. 'So it was your fault she died. You got her killed.'

'Yes.' Victor kept his feet pressed to the floor. 'It was my fault.'

'You've already got one woman killed. How do I know you won't get me killed too?'

'I can't make any guarantees,' he said, and she stiffened at his honesty. 'But if you help me I promise I will do all I can to help you in return. I don't make promises lightly. I'm still in single digits.'

It was the truth and he saw she believed him. But she was silent because now she had to make up her mind whether to risk helping him. He could feel her indecision trembling the air between them.

She said, 'You haven't asked my name.'

She was stalling but Victor let her. It had to be her choice. He couldn't pressure her into being his ally with any hope the arrangement would work.

He said, 'I have no right to ask something so personal about you. You can tell me if and when you're ready to.'

'Not yet.'

He nodded. 'Think of my offer as this: either take your chances here with Zoca and Rados, or take your chances with me.'

Again, he saw the effect of his words. She diverted her eyes. 'If I stay here I'm dead anyway.'

She had a survivor's mentality. He could exploit that, but he also respected it. 'Help me and you'll be able to go home.'

'I told you: they know where I'm from. They'll take me back if I return there. I'm not planning to make that mistake again.'

'I'm going to kill Rados. His organisation will fall apart without his leadership. There will be infighting amongst his senior people. Breakaway factions will form. It will be messy and it will be bloody. They won't have the resources or inclination to worry about one lost asset.'

'Assuming you're right, I don't want to go home even if I could. I don't have one, not any more. Only a memory of a place that I used to know.'

'Then you can go wherever you like,' he said. 'It's a small planet, but it's a big world.'

She was shaking her head before he had finished. She didn't understand how such a thing was possible.

He said, 'I know people. Clever people. Influential people. I can get you a whole new identity if you want. I have many of them myself. You can set up a new life, anywhere you can think of. Pick a country you've always wanted to see. You can live there. You can become a citizen. Start afresh, with this part of you left far behind. You're still young. Your whole life is out there waiting for you to take it. Make a new home. And I can make sure you're safe. I'll make sure that no one ever hurts you again.'

She stared for a moment and he was as unsure of her as she had been of him, but then her bottom lip trembled and her unreadable expression faltered. Her eyes moistened and tears spilled down her cheeks.

She nodded her agreement, and wept.

He had no idea what to do, so he just stood and watched her cry.

THIRTY-SIX

Victor met Rados at his fight club. The fights were well underway by the time Victor threaded his way through the crowd. Former combatants recovered in one corner, bloody and bruised and acting like best friends. Others were gearing themselves up to fight later. Everyone else was watching two of Rados' guys in the empty swimming pool. They were throwing punches. No one tried to kick or grapple.

'They agreed beforehand,' Rados explained. 'Boxing only. A gentleman's agreement between men who are not gentle.'

'There is no honour in combat.'

'Perhaps,' Rados said. 'But there can be once the fighting is over.'

Victor said, 'You wanted to see me.'

'No, I don't want to see you. I don't want to have to deal with men such as yourself. No offence.'

'None taken.'

'But I must. I *need*, if you will. The handover for that shipment I mentioned has been confirmed.'

'When for?'

'I'll tell you details just before we go,' Rados said. 'But tomorrow.'

Victor had wanted more warning to plan and prepare in order to exploit the situation. Less than twenty-four hours was not enough time.

He nodded. He wanted to ask where it was occurring, but he saw Rados wasn't going to tell him and it would only encourage mistrust if he persisted in asking questions when he shouldn't need to know the answers. Success depended not on winning Rados' trust – that was never going to happen – but assuaging his natural mistrust to such an extent that the Serbian would let his guard slip, if only for a moment.

A moment was all Victor needed.

Proving himself by overseeing tomorrow's handover was a necessary step. If Rados anticipated a problem then so did Victor. Rados' instincts seemed sharp, proven in battle and honed from years in organised crime. He was taking Victor along for a reason, and that wasn't because he expected Victor to be a passive observer.

The two fighters in the swimming pool were exhausted but still throwing punches. Some were blocked. Most missed. Others found their mark, hurtful and damaging, but neither man had the ability or stamina to capitalise on such successes.

Rados, watching intently, said, 'Do you know what you

do if you don't have the strength or the skill or the intelligence to succeed? You grind it out. You keep at it. You make up for your weaknesses with effort. Nothing more than rain and time are needed to bring down the mightiest castle.'

'Perseverance conquers all.'

Rados said, 'Do you like to take risks?'

Victor thought of Abigail at the Covent Garden Hotel. 'Sometimes.'

'A gambler?'

'On occasions. Blackjack or poker.'

'No roulette? No slots?'

He shook his head.

'So you don't like blind chance. You prefer to stack the odds in your favour.'

'Doesn't everyone?'

'Not everyone knows how to. I think they're called stupid people.'

'If you're stupid, how do you know you are?'

Rados smiled. 'I like your evasiveness. I like that you make me work for what I want.'

'Which is?'

The smile widened. 'Ah, I'm afraid you'll need to work for that too. I want you by my side tomorrow,' Rados went on. 'I want you there because the Slovakian buyers cannot be trusted. They're brothers. Even for criminals they are a distinctly unsavoury pair. Individually, you would not want to spend any degree of time with them. Together, you would cross the street to avoid sharing the same air. They are, quite literally, the worst of the worst.'

'What are their names?'

'Their names are unimportant. You should know that better than most.'

Victor nodded. 'Have you dealt with them before?'

'Yes, of course.'

'Then why are you now concerned about their trustworthiness?'

'Because we think in the short term. Tell a man to choose whether you're going to cut off his finger now or cut off his hand tomorrow and he'll choose the latter every time. Why?'

'Survival. Instinct. We have no choice but to think in the short term because tomorrow is uncertain.'

'Are you familiar with the hierarchy of needs? It is something I utterly believe in. We are not designed for the modern world. We are designed for the wild. We take pills for depression because if our brains are not occupied by working out how to get food, how to find water, how to avoid danger, then what is there to think about? Inconsequence. Take a man out of this thing we call civilisation and throw him on to a deserted island and see if he still worries about his advancing waistline and how he'll spend his time in retirement.'

'I'm not sure what you're saying,' Victor said.

'I'm saying this will be my third deal with the Slovaks,' Rados explained. 'The first two deals were amicable, but if their purpose had been to gain my trust so that they could betray it for greater profit, they would act now. Only a rank amateur would attempt to rip me off on the first deal.'

'And your guard is still up for the second deal.'

Rados nodded. 'Naturally, but it is more a case of what the other side believes. They are criminals so they are lazy, if not stupid. Instead of trying to understand how I operate, in their laziness they believe I am no different to them. And by the third deal they would trust the person they were dealing with, and hence become complacent in their defences.'

'Instead, you're bringing me in as an extra layer of defence.'

'Almost. You're new. You weren't present at the previous two deals. This will unnerve them. They will wonder who you are and why you are there, and this will throw them off their game. Not only that, you will be a useful second pair of eyes. Like me, you see things before they happen. You set up the Beast perfectly and did what no one else had done, all without breaking a sweat. I recognise the significance of that, even if you brought your loyalty into question by acting against my wishes. However, I shall forgive that transgression if you prove yourself during the deal. While I handle the Slovaks, you can watch their men. If this deal is bogus then you will know it.'

'Your own men can't do this?'

Rados considered his answer. 'My men are loyal and fearless, they would willingly lay down their lives for me, and I in turn trust them with my life – just as the Emperor of Constantinople trusted his Varangians to guard him night and day. But he did not entrust them with military strategy. I too know the limitations of my Varangians.'

'The Varangian Guard were mercenaries,' Victor said.

'They were only loyal because that loyalty was bought with gold.'

'They were mercenaries, yes,' Rados agreed. 'And loyalty, like any other commodity, comes with a price tag. But my own Varangians are loyal to me not just because I pay them, but out of love. They love me and believe I love them in return. They want wealth, which I provide, but they need love, as all do. And where else could they find that which they need? Because who could ever truly love a monster, but another monster?'

Victor said nothing for a moment, then, 'You're putting a lot of faith in me.'

Rados shook his head. 'I don't deal with faith, I deal with the odds, like you do. And with you at the exchange I stack the odds in my favour. You can help ensure every-thing goes well and I walk out of there in one piece.'

Not if I can help it, Victor thought.

THIRTY-SEVEN

Something was going on, she realised. She had been woken by lots of noise – voices, movement – but she knew to stay in her room and not to investigate. Surviving meant not being noticed, not causing trouble.

Yet somehow she had to get information. She had to find out anything that could be of use to the man who would help her get out of this place. She had to find out something pertinent about Rados – where he was, where he would be, or who would know.

It was difficult when she only had the other captive women to talk to, most of whom seemed to know less than she did. Rados' men just ordered her around – do this, go there, get ready, clean up – and nothing more. But she listened whenever she could, paying attention to every word exchanged between them. They assumed she only knew a few words of Serbian. They underestimated what she knew and what she was prepared to do.

When the noise quietened, she showered in the communal bathroom and dressed. None of the other girls were in sight when she emerged, but in the kitchen she found the awkward young man with acne.

He was more of a caretaker than a guard, doing menial tasks like changing light bulbs, cooking and cleaning. He didn't talk much, even to Zoca and the other men, doing whatever they told him without argument or complaint. He didn't speak to her or the other women unless he had to. He never tried to make conversation.

He avoided eye contact when she entered. She saw that he was different to the other men, not yet as cruel as them. She still disliked him as she did the others, because even if he was not as bad as they were, he aspired to be. For now, though, he had some semblance of decency, he was still weak and immature. And that could help her.

She had an idea.

She set about making herself instant coffee, filling a kettle with water and setting it on the stove. She waited for it to boil and its whistle to sound, then poured some into the waiting mug and then splashed some on her hand.

'*Ow*,' she cried out.

She cursed and grimaced and rubbed at her hand, examining the patch of skin that stood out bright red and scalded.

'Are you okay?' he asked.

'No, I burnt myself.'

'Run it under the cold tap.'

She hurried to the sink and held her hand under the stream of water, icy and soothing.

'Better?' he asked.

'Not really.'

'I'll get the first aid kit,' he said.

Pleased, albeit in pain, she sat on one of the uncomfortable sofas while he fumbled with the first aid kit and applied some balm to her hand, before applying a strip of bandage. Unnecessary, but she let him. His hands were shaking.

'Thank you,' she said.

He shrugged. 'No problem.'

She glanced around. 'Where is everyone today? It's so quiet.'

He shrugged again. 'I don't know.'

'They don't tell you?'

She made sure there was a hint of condescension in her tone, mingled with surprise. She wanted him defensive, but not angry.

'They do tell me stuff,' he replied, indignant.

'Like what?'

He hesitated.

'It's fine,' she said. 'They don't tell me anything either.'

This made him think, she saw, and doubt himself. He didn't want to be on the same level as she was – at the bottom – when he aspired to be one of the gangsters.

After a pause, he said, 'There's a deal happening. It's important.'

She made sure to look impressed, but only so it would have more effect when she added, 'They didn't take you?'

He said nothing.

She asked, 'Has the new guy gone to the deal?'

He was about to say something but nodded instead, eyes cast meekly downward.

'Why did they take him but not you?'

'I don't know,' he mumbled.

She saw this lack of knowledge made him all too aware of his status at the bottom of the pack hierarchy. His shoulders slumped because she had built him up only to bring him back down again.

'Ah,' she said, 'they need you to stay here and run the place.'

He glanced up at her, buoyed by this inescapable logic and the compliment it bestowed. 'That's right.'

'It's an important job.'

He nodded. 'It is. Very important. More important than helping move the new girls, anyway.'

'They must trust you a lot to be in charge.'

He showed a shy smile. She had him almost where she wanted him. 'They've taken all the new girls to the deal? Apart from me, I mean.'

He shook his head. 'Only three.'

She thought. There had been seven at the scrap yard including her. One had been killed and one had her nose broken, meaning she couldn't be sold on, but that left one girl unaccounted for.

'Where's the last girl then?'

He shrugged. He didn't want to say. She didn't know why.

She changed the subject to keep him on her side: 'What do you think of the new guy?'

'I haven't really spoken to him. He's a Hungarian.'

'What do the others think of him?'

His eyes glimmered again and his back straightened, because he realised or remembered something that elevated him. 'They only took him because they don't trust him.'

'How do you know that?'

He shrugged like it was nothing, like he knew everything. 'Zoca told me.'

'What did he tell you?'

'The Hungarian is being watched.'

'What does that mean?'

He felt powerful now with his privileged information, and was happy to share it to prove that power, not stopping to think about why she was asking.

'He's being followed, to find out more about him. If there is anything about him that isn't right, then they'll kill him.'

'Oh,' she said.

'Zoca doesn't like him,' the kid was in a hurry to add, to maintain his power trip. 'He hopes there is something untrustworthy about the Hungarian. He told me that—'

He stopped, catching himself in what he was doing: revealing information about his superiors to a prisoner. He didn't look pleased with himself now, but nervous.

She made a show of examining her bandaged hand, acting as though she hadn't been paying attention to him. 'Thank you for helping me. It feels much better now.'

'That's okay.' He chewed his lip. 'Don't tell anyone what I told you.'

'What do you mean? What have you told me?'

'About the Hungarian. About Zoca.'

She smiled, feigning innocence. 'You can trust me.'

THIRTY-EIGHT

They left at dawn in a motorcade of three vehicles: two Range Rovers and a minivan. Victor rode in the front Range Rover, again in the passenger seat, with Rados and two of his men in the back and another driving. He wasn't sure if this was a trust thing or because he was new – maybe to Rados and his crew sitting in the front was not an honour, it was not to be coveted. In the minivan were the shipment of women, driven by Zoca, demoted and ignored by Rados. Which seemed a dangerous miscalculation to Victor. He had known men like Zoca in the past – men whose pride remained scarred long after their physical wounds had healed. Men who let nothing go. Men who would wait and plot and keep their anger hot and ready to erupt long after their tormenters believed them dormant.

Rados was taking a show of force. In the second Range Rover were another four of his most experienced men – his Varangian Guard. They were focused, as good soldiers should be on a mission, but they were also pumped up and excited. This was proper work with a frisson of danger, a thrill impossible to replicate, pure and strong.

They drove out of the city and deep into the forests of northern Serbia. No one spoke. The radio stayed silent. The sun had risen high by the time the motorcade pulled over on a dirt track surrounded by endless trees.

The Range Rovers came to a stop and the Varangians jumped down on to the track. Victor did the same while Rados sat alone on the back seat.

The seven Varangians assembled at the back of the lead vehicle to be handed weapons from large canvas bags – AKs and Skorpion sub-machine guns – by the driver, who clearly doubled as Rados' quartermaster. No one asked for a specific gun or complained or swapped the one they were given. Ammunition was handed out next and they stuffed magazines into pockets and waistbands.

The quartermaster turned to Victor and handed him a .45 calibre Colt handgun and a spare magazine.

'I feel left out,' he said.

The quartermaster didn't react.

Victor checked the weapon. It was marked and scratched from a long life of use, but the action was good and strong. He unloaded the weapon and peered into the chamber and along the barrel. It hadn't been cleaned in a while but he didn't expect problems from the weapon. Colts were simple and effective. Accuracy, effective range, recoil, rate of fire and stopping power were all important, of course, but reliability was the trait Victor valued most. In the field, it wasn't always possible to regularly clean a weapon.

Both magazines were preloaded. Victor always preferred to do such things himself. There was something soothing about loading magazines. The repetitive nature of snapping ammunition into place, one bullet after the next, was a reminder of cause and effect and the value of proper preparation. A gun might malfunction or the shot might miss its target, but without bullets in the magazine the weapon was useless.

It was more than purely soothing though because any issue would likely come from the magazine. The first one was a little dusty – both the outside of the magazine and the top bullet were coated with a thin layer of dust, suggesting it had been stored loaded. That could be a problem. The constant tension on the spring weakened it and could lead to a malfunction when it failed to push new rounds up far enough into the chamber.

The spare magazine was the same. The quartermaster saw him examining it and a frown appeared.

'What?' he demanded.

'Nothing.'

The Varangians hadn't examined their weapons and magazines as Victor had. At most they'd made do with a cursory inspection. That was part laziness, part lack of training, but mostly because the Kalashnikov was among the most reliable automatic weapons ever made. It was a marvel of mechanical engineering even if it shouldn't be. By some standards it was thrown together. Constructed with a lack of precision, its accuracy and effective range were poor by the standard of its contemporaries, but that same lack of precision meant its parts still worked caked in grease or mud or sand or sand or snow and even under-water. Some weapons went an entire war without being cleaned and still worked as they should by the end of it.

He watched Zoca approach to collect a weapon from the quartermaster. Some of the swelling had gone down, but his eyes were black with bruising, hidden from a casual glance by sunglasses – but Victor's scrutiny, though fleeting, wasn't casual.

From behind those sunglasses, Zoca's gaze evaluated him. 'You look nervous.'

'We think we're good at reading each other,' Victor replied. 'But more often than not we are in fact projecting our own feelings and mistaking self-awareness for perception.'

Zoca frowned. 'What?'

Victor said, 'Exactly.'

He watched Rados climb out of the lead Range Rover and gesture for him to come over. Victor, gun in hand, approached his target, reminding himself the whole time about the former paramilitaries with automatic weapons behind him.

Rados said, 'The forests here are lush and green. The trees are tall and strong. Their leaves are very bright. Do you know why?'

Victor shook his head.

'It's the soil,' Rados explained. 'It's very rich and nutritious. It feeds the forest, letting it grow strong. This has happened in recent times. Why do you think the soil has so many nutrients? Where did they come from?'

Playing ignorant now would be akin to pretending to be

stupid. Either Rados would believe it, which was unlikely, else he would see through the deception. Since neither result would help Victor's objective, he said, 'The bodies buried in the soil. That's why the trees have become so strong. They've been feeding on decomposed corpses.'

Rados smiled. 'Exactly, like fertiliser. The trees have grown stronger because of the war. Death is good for life. It's always been this way.'

Victor remained silent. Rados was not just psychopathic. He was maniacal. Which made the job more difficult by an exponential degree. Victor was adept at predicting the actions of the intelligent and sane. It was a different story if the individual didn't think like a regular person. Predicting Rados' actions would therefore involve a significant element of guesswork. The Serb was intelligent and human, so to an extent he ought to be predictable. But his psychosis was an unquantifiable problem. Victor couldn't think like him, so he couldn't imagine what Rados would do in any given circumstance. Luring him into an orchestrated situation might work, or might fail for some inexplicable reason. Victor would have to revise his strategy accordingly. He would have to be prepared to improvise and perhaps act in an opportunistic, unplanned, manner. He had never liked doing so, even when there was no choice. Against a well-defended target like Rados, it was a daunting prospect.

He reminded himself that Rados' unpredictable behaviour might create a situation that he could not have imagined, and that could be a benefit as well as a hindrance. For now, there was no time pressure. He had figured it would be necessary to devote a week or two at least to building up an exploitable relationship. That was still in progress.

Rados called to Zoca, 'Bring the women.'

A minute later Zoca did. Victor recognised three of the women he had seen taken from the truck at the scrap yard and locked in containers.

'Come,' Rados said, and Zoca and the women followed him, as did Victor and one of the Varangians. The others stayed by the vehicles.

As they moved off, Victor had a clear line of sight on his target. It was tempting, but his hand was stayed by the fact he was armed with a pistol with only fourteen rounds maximum – assuming both magazines made it through without misfiring.

'You look pensive,' Rados noted, once more demonstrating his uncanny ability to read Victor.

He nodded – he didn't want to risk being trapped in a lie when his whole reason for being here was a lie – and held up the Colt. 'I feel like I'm bringing a knife to a gunfight.'

Rados smiled. 'Then turn it into a knife fight.'

They continued deeper into the forest, following another track that veered off from the main one. Within a few minutes they were out of sight of the vehicles and the odds improved, but Victor still had two men with assault rifles behind him. He could take them by surprise, probably, then kill Rados, but that left the well-armed Varangians who'd come running at the sound of gunfire.

Not yet, Victor told himself.

He saw Rados watching him, again as if he could read

his thoughts, so Victor said, 'You told me before that if someone was going to rip you off, they would wait until the third deal.'

'That's what I said.'

'You have a huge crew at your bidding.'

'Huge would be a relative term in this instance, but for the sake of argument I'll say yes.'

'Then why is it us four?'

'That's how we do business. The Slovaks bring three men. I bring three men. We agreed this at the first deal. We honoured it too for the second exchange.'

'But this is the third.'

Rados nodded. 'If they show up with more than three men, we turn around and go home. The same is true if I break the arrangement. They're not stupid and neither am I. Ah, you have but to whisper of the devil and he appears . . .'

Ahead, figures emerged through the mist.

THIRTY-NINE

The air was heavy with moisture. The wet trees and leaves and undergrowth mashed together to create a strong, natural scent. The forest was shrouded with mist. It seemed infinite. Through gaps in the canopy the grey mist blended with a grey sky.

Victor counted four men, but could not pick two who looked like brothers. When Rados walked forward alone, only one of the Slovakians followed his lead. The man who did so was thin, narrow from the shoulders through to the hips. There was at least an inch between his neck and his shirt collar. His wrists hung from cuffs so excessive he seemed a child wearing an adult's clothes. The skin of his face was pulled tight across the skull. He had prominent cheekbones and sunken cheeks, dark in the shadow. His bulbous eyes protruded from the sockets, and never stopped moving, back and forth between Victor and Rados. The Slovak's hair had unnatural thickness and texture, some kind of toupee or weave that fooled no one. He looked to be the same age as Rados, but where Rados looked strong and healthy, the Slovak seemed frail and ill.

They greeted one another like old friends, smiling and shaking hands and touching arms, despite Rados' comment about touching no one but his wife and mistresses. He played the part he needed to play. They stopped short of hugs, but their affection, had Victor not known otherwise, appeared real.

'Where's your brother?' Rados asked.

The Slovak chuckled. 'It's a funny story.'

The two of them leaned in to converse, smiling and laughing. Victor could catch only the occasional half-sentence:

... chewed it right off ...

... better, but you know how these things are ...

... don't even joke about it ...

The Slovakian's three guys stood waiting and watching, attentive but relaxed. Two vehicles were parked behind them, alongside the track. There was a four-wheel-drive Toyota, new and shiny, and a weather-beaten van.

When they had concluded their chit-chat, Rados motioned Victor over and he approached, waiting to be introduced.

'Here,' Rados began, 'this is the new man: Bartha the Hungarian.'

The Slovak looked him over, apparently neither impressed nor interested enough to care who Victor was, but playing along to humour Rados. 'You brought him to wet his ears?'

'Something like that.'

The Slovak said, 'Tell me, Bartha the Hungarian, what is it that makes you so special?'

'I can rub my stomach and tap my head at the same time.'

Rados laughed but the Slovak's expression didn't change. Rados gestured for Victor to leave them, and he backed away.

The Slovak looked away from Victor. 'How many do you have for me this time?'

'I have brought three,' Rados said.

'That's disappointing,' the Slovak said. 'I'm sure my deposit was for five.'

'True, it was for five, but our trade is more difficult now than ever. I lost two in transit, and another I would not offend you by offering as part of the package.'

'I understand,' the Slovak said. 'I take it you have brought recompense for the two I will not receive?'

'The deposits will be taken into account, yes.'

'That's not what I said. I expected five and you bring three. I have made arrangements for five. I have made promises. I have obligations for five that cannot be met by three. Your apology and refund of deposit will not travel along this chain of ours. It is not as simple as refunding my deposit. I will have to make amends. I may not lose out here and now, but I will further along.'

Rados said, 'What do you suggest we do then?'

The Slovak said, 'It is more about what *you* do. I think it would be reasonable for you to cover the costs I will incur. I promised five girls. I will deliver three. I suggest you provide the cost of those two girls, taking it from the price of the three you have brought.'

'In other words: you pay for one girl.'

The Slovak nodded. 'I am only to receive sixty per cent of the order. I will make a loss as it is.'

'In other words: you will pay twenty per cent of the original agreed fee.'

'You broke the deal,' the Slovak said, the polite tone beginning to slip away to something harder. 'You come here with three girls, not five, and excuses I care nothing about. When I break an agreement, I suffer for it. But I do not break agreements. I imagine after this day you will not break agreements either.'

Rados was silent for a long time. The Slovak was happy enough to wait for a response, neither uncomfortable nor nervous. It seemed the fear Rados inspired throughout the Belgrade underworld did not extend to Slovakia.

Victor waited too, but he used the time to scan the Slovak's men. The three of them seemed amused. In his peripheral vision he checked his flank. The Varangian stood stony faced, impassively observing the discussion, but Zoca was nervous.

As he shifted his focus back to the Slovakians, Victor registered that their amusement had an air of excitement about it, reminiscent of the crowd at Rados' fight club as they'd waited for the Beast, confident he would satisfy their expectations and inflict maximum suffering on his foe. The Slovak's men had similar expectations of their boss in this encounter with Rados.

'Fine,' Rados said. 'Twenty per cent for three it is.'

The Slovak nodded, pleased. 'Very good. You are an honourable businessman.'

'A deal is a deal.'

'This is said for a reason,' the Slovak agreed.

'It is,' Rados began, 'but you are not keeping your part of the deal, are you? I have delivered three women. Three out of five is sixty per cent. Not twenty. Not even fifty. It is sixty. Six. Zero.'

The Slovak sighed, loud and obvious with undisguised annoyance. 'I can count, Rados. I am tiring of this.'

The Slovak might be tiring of it, but his men were relishing every moment. They had known Rados would be on the back foot in these negotiations.

'Are we making a trade or not?'

'We are,' Rados said. 'But I am making sure you know that you are the one breaking the deal, not me. You are the one who is acting without honour here. I want to make absolutely sure that you know that.'

The Slovak smirked. 'Then feel good to walk away with one hundred per cent of the honour.'

His men were grinning. One slapped his comrades on the back, delighted with the boss's put-down.

Rados rubbed his chin. 'That's what I thought. That's what I always knew about you. I always knew you were a worm. So, let's get this damn exchange over with.'

There was only one way the Slovakians could have anticipated the deal going this way, thought Victor. They'd known that Rados would show up with three women instead of the agreed five. And it was impossible that they should know that – unless someone with inside information had told them beforehand.

The Slovak's smirk widened to a grin. 'I may be a worm, Rados, but this worm is tossing you the scraps from his table. And worms, lest we forget, dine on dirt.'

Victor looked behind him and found Zoca's gaze.

FORTY

Rados and the Slovak parted and returned to their respective groups. Rados appeared calm but Victor could feel the rage seeping from him. Zoca adjusted his footing, recognising that contained rage as Victor did.

Rados said, 'In this part of the world the criminals tell stories about me. They whisper to each other about the demon god that is Milan Rados, who haunts the night. I am neither god nor demon, but I am more powerful than either because I am real and the pain I can inflict is real too. This Slovak has forgotten. I need to remind him who I am.'

'Don't,' Victor said.

Rados didn't pay attention. 'Did you hear what he said to me?'

'I heard everything,' Victor answered. 'But don't.'

'When I was a child there was nothing outside my window so I created my own view. I imagined a tree, majestic and mighty; strong where I was weak; tall where

I was small. I had to imagine my own world. Now, I have my own world. What has he built? He wants to steal what he cannot build himself.'

'Don't,' Victor said again.

'Don't what?' Rados asked, as if he didn't know exactly what Victor was referring to.

'Don't do what you want to do.'

'And you know what that is, do you?'

Victor nodded again. 'You want to kill him.'

Rados shook his head. 'No, I don't want to kill him. I want to cut off his dick and force it down his throat and ask him if it tastes like dirt. That's what I want to do. That's what I'm going to do.'

'That would be a bad idea.'

'Why would it be a bad idea? Tell me why, *please*, since you seem to know absolutely everything. Tell me exactly why what I want is a bad idea.'

His voice was quiet, but menacing, snarled through clenched teeth.

'It's a set-up,' Victor said.

Rados said, 'No, it's not. It's nothing but a simple robbery. He's getting three girls for the price of one. It doesn't need to be a set-up.'

'He's getting under your skin, which was his aim all along. Because if you're angry you're not going to see this for what it is. As soon as you hand over the women, it's going to get very loud and very bloody for about four and a half seconds. Then it's going to be very quiet and very dark for us.'

Rados was shaking his head. 'No, you're wrong. He's

so stupid he thinks he's got himself a great deal. He thinks I'm going to let him go home with three girls and eighty per cent of his money. He's not going to suddenly decide to take me on. We're armed. We have the same number as he. It would be suicide.'

'I agree,' Victor said. 'If he were *suddenly deciding*. But this was decided in advance when he found out that you only had three women. He came here today knowing you couldn't fulfil the deal.'

'How in the hell do you—'

'I can't know for certain,' Victor answered. 'But if I'm right, that van wasn't brought here to take away five women. It won't be empty now. There'll be four or five guys in there with automatic weapons, and they're going to jump out and mow us all down the second the women are out of the line of fire. Four and a half seconds later their AKs will be empty and between two hundred and forty and two hundred and seventy high-velocity rounds will have passed through the space we're now occupying.'

Rados was staring. Zoca was staring even harder.

Zoca said, 'I don't know why you listen to him. He's—'

'Shut up,' Rados said, gaze still on Victor. 'Let's say you have my attention. But I can't act on guesswork. I need something solid.'

'That's simple enough to obtain. He's going to come back with the money, the twenty per cent, as agreed. All you have to do is ask to see the rest of it.'

Zoca said, 'What will that prove?'

Rados answered for Victor. 'It will prove that our Slovakian friend has no more cash to show me. If he had no intention of giving me the full amount, he won't have bothered bringing it along – all he'd need is the twenty per cent. It would prove that the negotiating, forcing the price down, driving such a hard bargain, that was all for show. A diversion, so I wouldn't suspect anything was amiss.'

Victor said, 'If he's brought the whole amount, then I'm wrong and you lose nothing by asking to see it.' He looked at Zoca. 'Right?'

Zoca shrugged.

Rados said, 'Here he comes.'

The Slovak approached with a duffle bag. He was smiling.

Rados said, 'Nothing to lose,' and walked to meet him halfway, gesturing for his man to usher the women forward.

When they had reached one another, the Slovak said, 'I hope we can remain friendly even in disagreement.'

'Of course,' Rados said, relaxed and diplomatic – the chameleon in his element. 'If everyone in business agreed on every deal then there would be no profit, would there?'

'Precisely,' the Slovak said, offering the duffle bag.

'Twenty per cent?' Rados said, taking it.

The Slovak nodded. 'As we agreed.'

'As we agreed a few moments ago.'

The Slovak nodded again.

Rados glanced inside the bag. 'You did bring the other eighty, didn't you?'

'Yes,' the Slovak said, expression tightening.

'Can I see it?'

The Slovak hesitated. 'What is this, Rados?'

'It's a simple request, isn't it? I'm not asking for it. A deal's a deal. I merely want to see it.'

'Why do you want to see it?'

'Does it matter?'

The Slovak said, 'It's a strange request, that's all. It makes me nervous. It makes me think the kind of thoughts I don't want to think.'

'There's no need,' Rados assured. If Victor didn't know better, he would have sworn the Serb's reassurance was genuine, such was his ability to lie. 'You don't have to bring it to me. I don't want to touch it. I just want to see it.'

'This makes me very uncomfortable.'

'Okay,' Rados said. 'Let's meet in the middle with this. Where is it? In the van?'

The Slovak didn't answer, but half-shrugged.

'So have one of your men hold it up. Doesn't have to be all of it. I expect you have another four bags like this one, don't you? Since the twenty per cent was already in here. I mean, I didn't see you or anyone else separate the cash, and this bag isn't big enough for much more, is it?'

The Slovak was very still.

'Like I was saying,' Rados said. 'There is no need to be nervous.'

The Slovak said, 'Sure, whatever you need to feel comfortable. I'll go fetch some more of the money. How does that sound?'

'Wonderful,' Rados said, offering back the duffle bag. 'Here, let's be friendly in disagreement.'

The Slovak took it, and said nothing. He walked back

towards his men. Rados approached where Victor stood with Zoca and the lone Varangian.

'You really should have waited,' Victor said, 'until we could formulate a plan. We're about to be outnumbered.'

'You've been right up until now. Had we waited, we would have showed our hand and given them time to prepare. Don't forget, I'm as much of a strategist as you are. Now, they've lost the initiative.'

'I wouldn't be too sure about that.'

Rados followed his gaze to where the Slovak and his men were standing. No one was making a move to collect the requested duffle bags; they were in a huddle, talking. 'Hmm. That's not a promising sign, is it?'

'Before,' Victor said, remembering, 'you asked where his brother was. What did he say?'

'Some story about a stripper biting off his nipple.'

'Did you believe it?'

Rados shrugged. 'Then, I thought it too ridiculous not to. Now ...'

Victor said, 'What do you know about this missing brother that could be relevant to our situation?'

'They're partners,' Zoca said, as if Victor was stupid. 'They run their business together. What does it matter?'

'He was a mercenary, in the war,' Rados said, understanding what Victor meant, and glancing around into the mist and trees. 'He was a sniper.'

FORTY-ONE

The forest was quiet save for the soothing sound of vegetation rustling in the breeze. Behind Rados, the Slovakians
appeared relaxed because they held the advantage.

'I'd rather they had another five men than a sniper,'
Victor said.

'It can't work,' Rados said. 'At the sound of gunfire my
men will be here in less than two minutes.'

'Not if the sniper has a suppressor and subsonic ammunition. We're at least three hundred metres away from
them with a thousand trees between us to absorb sound.'

'If he doesn't have a silenced weapon?'

'Then the gunmen in the back of the van will finish us off.'

'Four and a half seconds,' Rados said.

'Exactly,' Victor said. 'Either way, no help is going to get
to us in time. We're on our own.'

Rados said, 'We have time. As you said, we're safe until
we bring the girls out of the line of fire.'

'But not much time,' Victor said back. 'If we delay too long, we lose the initiative again.'

Rados nodded his agreement. 'If you were out there in the trees with a rifle, how would you do it? Where would you be?'

Victor looked, without making it obvious. 'There's no danger of lens glare in this light, and no danger of sun blindness, so I start with plenty of options.'

Rados nodded. 'It's all about line of sight, isn't it?'

Victor nodded too. 'The trees are widely spaced, but they weren't planted. There will be no straight lines through the forest.'

'I was never a sniper myself so I shall defer to you on this. I can see maybe sixty or seventy metres before there is nothing but mist.'

'He doesn't have to be that far out. If I were him, I would be as close as I could. The bracken is up to armpit-level in some places. I could be ten metres away and you wouldn't see me. I could be twenty and you wouldn't see me even if you knew exactly where I was crouching.'

'Won't he be lying prone?'

'No, not in this level of ground vegetation. He has to be mobile. He has to be reactive to where we are. He can't lie up and expect us to stay still. If we move a metre in any direction it would throw off his line of sight.'

'Left or right?' Rados asked. 'Fifty-fifty.'

Victor glanced in both directions. The trees and ground vegetation seemed identical in their randomness. Neither side of the track offered any particular advantage or disadvantage. Both were flat.

'No,' he said. 'Not fifty-fifty. There are three options. Two of which are exactly the same, and just as inferior.'

'Explain.'

'Where are we?'

'In a forest,' Zoca said, incredulous.

'On a track,' Rados said. 'So he's on the track too, or slightly to one side of it, crouching in the bracken, no trees impeding his line of sight. Damn, we're dead. But, wait. So long as his brother and the other Slovakians are in front of us, he wouldn't risk a shot, would he?'

'No,' Victor agreed. 'But they know what's coming. All they have to do is get into their vehicles.'

'Then we can engineer the handover. We can position ourselves.'

'That won't work,' Victor explained. 'Because I've realised he isn't further along the track in front of us, he's behind us.'

'How do you know that?'

'Because I'm thinking like a sniper. He's been out there in the trees while you've been talking to his brother, and he's spent the whole time circling around us. Don't look because you won't see him, and neither can I. But he's there, thirty to forty metres away, hidden in the bracken. We can't see him, but he's looking right at us now. And his reticle is currently hovering over your head.'

Rados took it well, calm and calculating. 'Would you miss?'

'At this range,' Victor said, 'not even if you were sprinting.'

'What are we going to do?' Rados asked. There was

no worry in his voice, no panic, but there was urgency, because the danger was real and it was imminent.

'You,' Victor began, 'are going to carry on with the exchange. I will go after the sniper. I don't have time to go into details.'

'How will I know if you have been successful?'

'Because the Slovak's guys will start dropping, one by one.'

'And what if you aren't successful?'

'You'll never know.'

Zoca said, 'What does that mean?'

Rados explained for Victor, 'It means I'll be dead before I hear the crack of the shot. Then you'll be next, dear Zoca.'

Zoca was caught in a moment of confusion as to how to react. He had set his boss up, no doubt with the intention of taking over the business, but now he was questioning whether the Slovak would spare him, or maybe he was worried about being killed in the crossfire or even scared that Victor might be successful and Rados would survive. Eventually, he made his decision and picked his side and offered Victor his AK.

Victor was fast enough to put a hand to Zoca's arm to stop him – an innocent-looking gesture to a watching sniper. 'No,' he said. 'Much as I would prefer your weapon, we can't do anything to tip them off.'

'Initiative,' Rados said. 'We only live through this if we keep it.'

Victor nodded. 'The Slovak's returning. Give him the women, but take your time about it.'

'How long do you need?'

'Every second you can give me without showing our hand.'

Rados understood. 'You'll have as much time as I can manage.'

Zoca said, 'What do I do?'

'You've done enough,' Victor said. 'For now, play along and do nothing. Then, when the time comes, don't miss.'

'Whatever you're planning on doing,' Rados said to Victor, 'is it going to work?'

'Do you remember what we talked about before?' Victor began. 'About who we are is defined by what we do?'

Rados nodded. 'I remember.'

'This is who I am.'

FORTY-TWO

Rados and Victor approached the Slovak together, but then Victor peeled away and gestured to the trees. 'I need to take a leak.'

'Be quick,' Rados said with the perfect amount of irritation in his voice.

The Slovak didn't comment. He didn't react. He bought it.

Victor left them and veered off into the undergrowth. He went right because there were vehicles on that side of the track so more obstacles to interrupt lines of sight. It would be harder for the Slovak and his men to see his route into the trees. For privacy, they might deduce, if they even bothered to think about him or what he was doing.

He walked at a hurried pace – a man trying to be quick about answering the call of nature. Nothing unusual. Nothing suspicious. The bracken rustled. He had always liked the sound. It was damp and scratched against his clothes. He had his hands before him, as if he were unfastening his belt or unzipping his trousers, but he dropped the pretence when he was fifteen metres into the trees. At this distance, no one on the track watching would see more than his head and back. At twenty metres he changed direction and quickened his pace, knowing the mist would cover him from here.

If the sniper was on the borders of the track, thirty or forty metres from the exchange, Victor had a circular distance of seventy metres to traverse before he'd come up behind him. With no time pressure he would have extended that circle and approached him from even further away, but Victor didn't know how long Rados could delay the exchange.

He wasn't concerned about the sniper shooting before he was in position. If the Slovak's brother succeeded, Victor's contract would be fulfilled with no further effort on his part. Ahead, lay nothing but forest; he could make a clean escape without difficulty. But it was not an option.

There was no way of knowing how competent a marksman the sniper was, or the quality of his weapon. Anyone with a rifle could claim to be a sniper, and even if the guy had made a name for himself in the war, he might have lost his edge since then. Moreover, if the Slovakian's maintenance of his firearm was on a par with the Varangians', it could misfire at the crucial moment. There was too much that could go wrong if that first shot missed its target. Rados' men would jump into their vehicles and rush to the scene, turning it into a drawn-out firefight – with no guarantees who'd come out alive. And if Rados did survive,

Victor would never get close enough to him for another opportunity.

His best course of action was to take out the sniper and use the weapon himself. That way Rados was guaranteed to die. And if Victor was to continue living afterwards, he wanted to have a rifle in case he encountered any of the Varangians responding to the gunfire.

As the track came into view ahead of him, Victor slowed to a careful, quiet pace. It was impossible to be silent in a forest, but a forest wasn't silent either. He reached the edge of the track and looked right: from this vantage point he had a clear view of the three women, guarded by Zoca and the single Varangian present. He could see Rados and the Slovak too, a few metres further away in the centre of the track.

Forty metres from them, and ten metres from Victor, was the sniper.

He was kneeling next to the track. Beneath the bracken, the ground was stony, but he had come prepared for that. Over his jeans, he wore the kind of kneepads skateboarders used for protection: hard plastic armour. Excessive for his purposes, maybe, but Victor knew as well as anyone it was better to be over-prepared than under.

He couldn't make out the sniper's weapon, but he could see the two fat magazines lying on the ground next to him. Victor recognised them. They were for the Dragunov he had asked Georg to supply. Soviet and Russian weapons had been common during the Balkan conflict. It wasn't surprising the Slovak's brother had opted for the same model he had used back then. Maybe it was the exact same weapon.

Victor didn't draw the pistol from his waistband. Even if it had been suppressed it would have remained in place. Any gunfire would create chaos, with gunmen bursting out of the Slovaks' van and Rados' Varangians piling in two minutes later. Victor did not plan on any shots being fired until he was behind the Dragunov. The first shot would be the one that killed Rados. He could leave the Slovak and his guys to deal with Zoca and the Varangian, and then by the time that was over, Rados' remaining men would turn up. Victor wanted to be long gone by then. He wanted to be out of the country by the time anyone started to question what had happened.

A choke would do it. The sniper, by kneeling, was at the perfect height for Victor to wrap an arm around his throat, locking his hands and squeezing the neck so hard, the blood pressure inside his head would make him think his skull was about to explode.

The sniper would have no more than five short seconds to save himself. The surprise of the attack, the incredible pain, and the sheer terror of breathlessness would cost him at least three of those. Two seconds was never going to be enough to loosen Victor's hold on him, even if he maintained his composure in impossible circumstances to try and use the Dragunov in a desperate blind shot.

The sniper had no chance. He would be incapable of fighting back after five seconds; unconscious by seven; never waking up again by sixty.

Ten metres.

Each one more difficult to traverse than the last, with every footfall growing louder and the danger of a snapping twig or rustling branch growing at an exponential rate.

But the sniper was not watching his back. He had no spotter. He was alone. All his focus was on his target, and waiting for a prearranged signal to squeeze the trigger.

Victor crept towards his own target with footsteps so light the breeze rustling the bracken around him was louder. His heart beat at a slow, steady rhythm, his gaze locked on the back of the sniper's neck, picturing the twin pulsing arteries.

Ahead along the track, Victor saw Zoca bringing the women forward. The sniper tensed in readiness. He couldn't be more unaware. He couldn't be more vulnerable. Victor could almost feel the man's pulse as a tremor in the air between them.

Victor, three metres away, opened his hands, ready.

Everything that could go wrong did.

FORTY-THREE

The sniper sensed him.

Maybe it was the sound of undergrowth crunching beneath Victor's feet; maybe Victor's extended absence had made him paranoid; maybe the sniper detected Victor's scent on the breeze.

It didn't matter why, but the sniper did a quick half-turn and glance that became a rapid twist when he saw for sure someone was behind him, switching with expert moves from one knee to the other, the Dragunov swinging through a 180-degree arc.

The sniper was fast and assured in his movements; there was no time for Victor to close the distance, but he was already snapping the Colt from his waistband and squeezing the trigger.

Click.

Misfire. A dud round; a bad primer, maybe. He racked the slide to eject the bullet and load another, and fired again. Nothing happened. The magazine spring, too long under tension, failed to push the .45 calibre round into the chamber.

Victor hurled the handgun.

The sniper lurched to avoid it striking his head, but in doing so lost his chance to take aim with the Dragunov.

Victor charged into him at full speed – too much distance to cover otherwise – and they hit the track together, wrestling for control of the rifle. Victor – bigger, stronger, faster – won, and tore it from the sniper's hands.

Before Victor could turn the rifle around, the sniper, knowing he was outmatched, yelled, 'POMOC.'

Victor didn't speak Slovakian, but a frantic cry for help sounded the same in any language. Victor batted the sniper's desperate grasp aside, pushed the muzzle into his mouth and fired.

The man's head near enough disintegrated beneath him.

Victor jumped off the corpse and raised the Dragunov, peering down the scope as blood hissed and steamed along the barrel.

He saw chaos unfolding through the lens, blurred by a smear of the sniper's blood –

– the three women panicking at the sound of the gunshot and the cry for help –

– Rados drawing his pistol and executing the Slovak with a double-tap to the head –

– Zoca and the single Varangian unleashing their weapons on the Slovak's three men, taken by surprise like their boss –

Victor swung the reticle over Rados' centre mass – not willing to risk a headshot with a scope he hadn't zeroed himself, and through a bloodied scope lens at that – but didn't fire because one of the women had made a run for it and Rados grabbed her as she passed him.

She fought him with everything she had, the two of them becoming a tumble of limbs in the centre of the crosshair, ruining any hope of a hit.

Get out of the way, Victor willed her.

More gunfire roared as five Slovakian reinforcements poured out of the back of the van.

Rados' Varangian took down one before the other four gunmen, all armed with AKs, massacred him in a storm of gunfire.

Victor, on the track and in the line of fire, felt rounds burning the air around him, and darted into the treeline to avoid being hit by a stray bullet. He glimpsed Zoca doing the same, seeking cover off-track, and Rados too, having released the escaping woman to save himself.

The Slovakians were pumping rounds into the trees, shooting at everyone and no one because they didn't know what was happening, only that the ambush had gone wrong.

No plan survives first contact with the enemy.

Victor ignored them, and went after Rados.

The problem was, so did three of the Slovakians. They knew who Rados was, knew he had killed their boss, and were after revenge or still following orders out of loyalty or simple conditioning. They darted through the trees, shooting and moving.

Rados had a narrow head start, enough to keep him alive for the time being, given the Slovakians' inaccurate fire and the irregular distribution of trees interrupting line of sight.

The fourth Slovakian must have gone after Zoca or the escaping women. Victor couldn't see him and didn't have time to look because Rados was pulling away from the Slovakians.

He was older than his hunters, but he was fit and healthy whereas they were hard smokers and hard drinkers who ate junk while he ate well and played cards while he ran on the treadmill. Most importantly, he was running for his life and they could not replicate that sense of urgency.

Rados was making a mistake, however, because he was taking a curved route through the trees in the hope of making it back to the Range Rovers and his men. That let the Slovakians close the distance.

Victor converged fast. Speed and stamina were top of the list of requirements in his line of work. He was a league ahead of the Slovakians, and even though Rados was fit and fast himself, Victor was over a decade younger.

He veered, running towards where Rados was going to be, heading to where their paths would converge. Victor sprinted through the bracken, rounding trees and jumping fallen branches.

He stopped when he judged he was in the right place, and took up position in the undergrowth, a tree to his right and as clear a line of sight through the trees to where Rados would come as possible.

With a sleeve, Victor wiped some of the sniper's blood

from the lens and raised the scope to his eye. The lens now had a pink filter of blurred blood.

He saw Rados through the mist, moving fast and well – lots of lateral movements to make his pursuers' shots more difficult. They weren't far behind now. Rados' curved path had let them close in; like Victor they had moved to intercept him. They were out of shape but they had some tactical awareness.

Victor lined up the reticle over Rados' weaving centre mass and fired.

The Dragunov's recoil thumped against his shoulder and the crack of the shot echoed through the forest.

A miss.

Victor slowed his breathing, followed Rados' movements and took a second shot.

Another miss, but Victor saw the bullet strike a tree where Rados had been an instant before.

Rados was close now, only thirty metres away, and the Slovakians were all visible, coming out of the mist fifteen or twenty metres behind him, shooting as they moved.

A stray AK47 shot hit the tree trunk next to Victor. Bark pelted his face. Some found his eye. He blinked the bark away, adjusted his aim once again, peering through the flood of tears and smeared blood on the lens.

Rados didn't see Victor, but he ran towards him, unaware he was running towards his death.

Victor fired.

A hit.

FORTY-FOUR

The bullet struck Rados high on the left shoulder and he dropped into the bracken below a mist of blood. It wasn't a kill shot – Victor could tell that from the split-second glimpse of the impact he witnessed before Rados went out of sight.

Victor rose out of cover to create a better angle to finish off his target. He could only see swaying bracken where Rados had been. Blood glistened on bright green foliage.

Behind where Rados fell, came the Slovakians.

They didn't see Rados drop, but the lead one saw Victor and didn't hesitate. The Slovakian squeezed off a burst that shredded nearby leaves. Victor returned fire – a snapshot that had little chance of hitting – and ran, because the others had now seen him, and their guns were coming up.

Fire spat from the muzzle of the lead man's AK in intermittent gouts of yellow. The shooter yelled as he tracked

Victor, the war cry only audible in the brief pauses between squeezes of the trigger.

Victor kept running, concerned only with creating distance for the next few seconds. He was outgunned three-to-one; his enemies had fully automatic weapons while his was semi-automatic.

He twisted around to return inaccurate fire. There was no time to aim, but his enemies weren't fearless. Even inaccurate rounds coming their way made them hesitant and increased the distance between them and Victor.

The sound of gunfire filled his ears. The thick canopy above enhanced the roar of the AKs into a deafening hurricane of noise. If he survived, his ears would be ringing for days. He kept moving, ducking and weaving, hearing rounds zip and snap around him and crunch through foliage or thump into solid tree trunks.

He couldn't run forever. He could outpace them, but what then? Rados was behind him, alive but injured and alone. Victor would never have a better chance of finishing the job. If he delayed, the Varangians would arrive.

The AKs stopped firing.

He had created enough distance to disappear into the mist. He positioned himself behind a tree to make sure he stayed out of sight and removed the scope from the Dragunov. It was no use for close quarters combat, even properly zeroed.

He breathed slow and steady to control his heart rate, elevated from the exertion. He noticed a small smear of blood on his trousers and realised the knife wound in his thigh had opened a little from all of the running. He waited. He couldn't see them, but he knew they were coming. They were hurrying after him, crashing through the bracken, unconcerned because they were the aggressors, full of adrenaline and bloodlust and self-belief in their numbers and his place as the victim, running for his life.

He heard them slow down as they neared his position, realising they should see him running ahead, and if he wasn't then he could be hiding. They exchanged a few words then split up to cover more ground.

One entered his peripheral vision some thirty metres to his right. He was too far away to engage with, so Victor waited.

Another gunman stalked right by him.

Victor waited a moment then slid out behind him. Five fast steps, noise deadened by the man's own movements, and Victor was close enough to loop his right arm over the guy's right, dragging and locking it behind his back with the AK pointed at the forest floor while Victor's left snaked around the throat to apply a choke.

The man gasped and fought, but a kick to the back of his knee took his legs out from under him and increased the pressure on his carotids. He slackened long before his free arm could reach Victor's eyes.

He kept the choke on with his left while he scanned the immediate area, gun back up now he no longer needed his right arm to maintain the lock. He saw a shadow, twisted and turned using the unconscious man as a shield as—

The third gunman appeared, coming out of the trees.

Victor shot first, bullet hitting the man in the throat, but he returned fire as he fell. Victor's human shield took a spray of rounds to the chest, but the big 7.62 mm rounds were designed to tumble soon after leaving the barrel, to continue doing so inside the human body to create extensive internal trauma, so they did not exit out of the man's back as a conventional high-velocity round might have done.

The human shield flinched and jigged, hit multiple times, his AK firing on full-auto into the dirt as his dying central nervous system sent his muscles into spasm.

Victor released the man – soon-to-be-corpse – because the one thirty metres away was joining the firefight, shooting as he ran closer. Victor dropped the Dragunov and scooped up his human shield's AK.

He loosed off an unbraced burst – no time to adopt a proper firing position – that missed, but came close enough to make the charging Slovak think twice and head for cover.

Victor shot again, the AK low on rounds after the muscle spasms, and searched for a spare magazine from the jacket of the corpse at his feet. Nothing. The man must have used up the rest of his rounds chasing Rados.

He tugged the magazine free and saw he had nine rounds remaining. He thumbed the selector back down to single shot and peered out of cover. Swaying bracken told him the gunman had moved position. He had learned by the death of two of his comrades that this foe was no easy victim.

Victor could neither see nor hear him, but moved to where the man he'd shot in the neck lay twitching on the forest floor, seeking more ammunition. His eyes were open and staring. His lips trembled in some post-death activity of the nervous system, still responding to signals sent while there had been a working brain inside his skull.

At a noise from behind him, Victor leapt to the side, diving into the undergrowth as a gun roared and bullets tore through the air where his head had been.

The fourth gunman – the one who had gone after Zoca – had changed his priorities.

Victor took a shot at the new threat, aiming through the mist and undergrowth, unable to see if the bullet found its mark. Return fire gave him the answer, muzzle flashing, the rounds hitting far wide of his position, the gunman a poor shot even without the mist and limited visibility. Victor adjusted his aim and shot again. He couldn't see whether the bullet hit, but the gunman flinched and dropped to his knees. Maybe from a glancing hit, or maybe just through fear.

Hanging around to find out would only increase the risk of being flanked by the Slovakian at his back, so Victor hurried away, moving from tree to tree, knowing his enemies had no comms and scant tactical sense but could still catch him in crossfire without even trying.

He heard one AK47 shooting at him, bullets following him because the shooter was unskilled and chasing him with rounds instead of aiming ahead, and then a second rifle – the flanking gunman lured into exposing himself.

Victor changed direction, still moving fast, aware the fourth man had managed to get around his flank and would be nearing with every passing second, not yet knowing two of the others had been killed by Victor, not yet knowing that Victor was the aggressor now.

He changed positions while the second shooter was reloading, moving to where he could ambush the new-comer. The timing was crucial. It was impossible to face them both at once, and while he dealt with one, the other had his back.

Victor found a cluster of trees with little space between them, and settled into place. While the AK's rounds were excellent at piercing flesh and bone, the thick tree trunks around him provided impenetrable cover. But only from one direction at a time.

The new guy appeared through the mist. He was cautious and wary but as unskilled as the others, moving along the corridor of space, not utilising the cover as well as Victor –

– who squeezed off a double-tap that hit the man in the chest. He contorted but stayed on his feet, so Victor put a third bullet through his forehead. The man dropped to his knees, wide-eyed, then disappeared into the undergrowth.

Victor was already rolling backwards over his shoulder, facing the opposite way in time to see the other gunman pop out of concealment in response to the gunshots.

They fired at the same time, muzzles flashing, cordite and gunsmoke perfuming the air, rounds slicing leaves and fragmenting bark.

All misses.

Victor ran because he was down to his last bullet.

The gunman lost line of sight and the firing stopped, but only for a moment. He chased after Victor, shooting as he moved, the resulting spray wide and inaccurate. The gunman ran and fired in erratic bursts. There was more danger of being hit by a ricochet than a deliberate shot. Victor kept moving, not seeking cover because he was counting the bursts. The AK47 had a cyclical rate of six hundred rounds per minute, which equated to a fraction over nine every second. The gunman was firing in quick squeezes of the trigger, quarter-second bursts, sending three or four rounds at a time.

Victor stopped running after the seventh burst, turning to see the gunman tugging free the empty magazine. His eyes were wide with panic because he had been caught out by the dreaded dead man's click.

Victor approached him. The gunman was fumbling with the fresh magazine, struggling to get it out of his jacket pocket and into the weapon's feeder. He was high on adrenaline, his heart rate probably 90 per cent of maximum, fine motor skills impeded, not used to reloading when his life depended on it.

Victor waited until the man had the magazine in the feeder and the breech knocked forward before shooting him in the face with his final round. It saved him reloading the man's rifle himself.

With the fully loaded weapon, Victor hurried back through the forest to where Rados had dropped.

He found blood glistening on bracken leaves, but no Rados. With the AK up and his gaze peering along the iron sights, Victor stalked through the forest, moving from tree to tree as he approached the track, following the route marked by bent branches, crushed foliage and the occasional drop of blood.

He heard, and then saw, Rados clutching his bloody

shoulder, wounded but alive and safe, protected by the second Range Rover of Varangians who had arrived in response to the firefight. Zoca had returned too. The women weren't there. They had used the chaos to make their escape.

Victor considered for a moment, then lowered the rifle. Rados' Varangians were a league above the Slovakian guys. He wasn't going to engage a whole group of them in a gunfight for the sake of completing his job.

He stepped out on to the track.

'You're alive,' Rados said when he saw Victor.

He nodded in response.

'The Slovakians?' Rados asked.

Victor shook his head.

Rados smiled. 'Shame you didn't spare the one who shot me.' He grimaced, taking his hand away from the wound. 'Through and through, but let's say that pain is a woefully insufficient word.'

'It could have been a lot worse,' Victor said, thinking a hit three inches down would have been enough to puncture a lung and rupture major blood vessels.

'These were amateurs,' Rados agreed. 'Thankfully.'

'But it would have gone a lot smoother,' Victor said to the quartermaster, 'had you given me a working firearm.'

Rados laughed. 'I think you've earned that at the very least. But there'll be time for a proper after action report later. Now, we need to take our leave.'

FORTY-FIVE

London, Krieger thought, was not all it was made out to be. He was no fan of the city. It wasn't because of the weather – not as bad as some said. It wasn't the people – dour, but not sour. It was the lack of character. London was a city of history and culture, of civilisation itself, but its identity was its very lack of anything resembling cohesion. He heard a dozen different languages on the street. He saw magnificent historic buildings in the shadow of monstrous skyscrapers. It was an indescribable mess of peoples, cultures and architecture.

Krieger felt as if he were trapped in a maze of dirty mirrors.

He was here to work, not discover, but he couldn't wait to leave. The proper preparations of a professional meant he journeyed far and wide throughout the city for counter surveillance and in doing so felt as though he'd traversed a hundred different towns and not one would he wish to return to.

His target lived on a quiet leafy street on the north side of the river, far away from the congestion of the inner city, where the air was crisp and people crisper. This was more Krieger's kind of environment. He could even imagine settling down in a place such as this when he hung up his boots. If the fates played fair with him, he might be able to soon.

Krieger waited in his stolen car – a fine German vehicle – until his target pulled on to the driveway in a vintage MG coupe and came to a halt next to a sensible family people carrier. Krieger rolled the stolen car forward so that he was alongside the target's driveway at the same time the man climbed out of the MG.

Three measured squeezes of the lightweight trigger were all that was required. Krieger's weapon was a .22 calibre pistol, equipped with a high-quality suppressor. He timed the first two shots to coincide with the MG's door shutting, and the quiet thwack-thwack did not even cause a dog to bark. Krieger then took a third shot, as insurance, as he revved the car's engine. He fired from within the vehicle, so the ejected shell cases were contained and rattled in the footwell.

Job done, he drove away in a pleasant mood. The ease of completion helped soothe the lingering pain of the failure on the train to St Petersburg. He could now turn his attention back to that unfinished contract.

I'll see you again soon, he had told the man they called Cleric.

Krieger was a man of his word.

FORTY-SIX

The doctor was young and short and had to muscle his way through the Varangians to get to Rados. They formed a shield around their emperor, who lay on an examining table, grimacing and holding gauze to his wound. Victor stood in one corner of the doctor's office, quiet and watchful.

The doctor frowned when he examined the twin bullet holes on either side of Rados' shoulder.

'You boys really shouldn't play so rough.'

'Golfing accident,' Rados replied.

'This is why I prefer tennis. You're a lucky man, Milan. A clean-up and a few stitches and you'll be fine.'

'Scars?'

'Oh yes,' the doctor said, 'but we can take care of those once you've healed. For now, the priority is to make sure the wound is sterile. We don't want a nasty bacterial infection to complicate matters and ruin your, uh, golf swing, do we?'

'No, we do not.'

The doctor said, 'Incidentally, I'm a pretty sharp putter myself.'

'Of course you are.'

The doctor gestured to the Varangians. 'Do you think we can have some privacy?'

Rados told his men to wait outside, then addressed Victor.

'Take some down time, and I'll contact you in a few days,' Rados said. 'And thank you. You saved my life.'

Victor remained silent.

Zoca was lounging in the upstairs lobby of the massage parlour when Victor arrived. He sat toying with a lighter, snapping it open with a thumb and forefinger, and extinguishing the resulting flame with his palm.

He didn't look up. 'I take it you are here to see the Armenian woman? The one with the sad eyes.'

Victor nodded. 'That's correct.'

'Again?' Zoca asked, as if surprised by Victor's answer, though he wasn't.

'Again,' Victor agreed, as if he didn't notice the man's tone.

'That's twice in one week.'

'Your powers of arithmetic are second to none.'

Zoca smirked at that. 'You must like her.'

'I take back my previous statement,' Victor said. 'Your powers of deduction are even better.'

The smirk became a chuckle and Zoca stood. 'What makes her so special? Is her vagina so deliciously tight?'

Victor went to step past Zoca, who sidestepped to block him.

Zoca said, 'Are you in love with her or it?' When no answer came he added, 'You're an outsider. You shouldn't forget that. You think because Rados talks with you that somehow you are special, but you are no Serb. You are nothing.'

'If I am nothing then why do you take the time to watch me and talk with me? If I am nothing then I should not be worth your time, yet you always find time for me.'

The lighter flame continued to burn.

'But I understand what you are saying,' Victor said. 'You are concerned that Rados will find out that you set him up. You are worried that I'll tell him. You don't need to be. I don't have any proof and he wouldn't simply take my word for it.'

Zoca said nothing, but the beginning of a smile formed.

'Of course,' Victor said, 'what you should really be concerned about is why Rados has recruited me in the first place, so soon after you failed him with the shipment. What you should be concerned about is the answer to a very simple question: did he hire me so that there would be someone to replace you?'

Zoca snapped the lighter shut.

Victor knocked on the door before he opened it. She looked up from the bed with eyes even more absent of hope or life than on his previous visit because he wasn't rushing to rescue her.

'He's still alive then?' she said.

Victor was quick to close the door behind him. 'Yes,' he said. 'Of course he's still alive.'

Her eyes were red and the dark beneath them was deeper. He saw she had new bruises on her upper arms.

She was somewhere between angry and sad. 'He took you to some deal. You said you needed to be close to him to kill him. Surely you were.'

It was a simple equation for her: he had said what he needed in order to kill Rados, so if he had had that, it meant Rados should be dead. She had been working without variables.

'It's complicated,' he said, thinking of the firefight in the forest. 'These things take time.'

She was shaking her head, refusing to accept this. 'Why? How? Kill that monster. What are you waiting for? You have a gun, don't you?'

'You think I should draw my weapon the next time I see him and shoot him in the head? Bang. Bang. Like that?'

'Yes,' she insisted, 'just like that.'

It was his turn to shake his head. 'That's not how it works, I'm afraid. If I do that, I'll be gunned down by Rados' men within seconds.'

She tried to hide it but he read her eyes: *So what?*

'While I appreciate your single-mindedness,' Victor said, 'you need to think of the long game. If I'm killed after I kill Rados, who do you think is going to get you out of here? Have any of Rados' men hinted that they would come to your aid?'

Her eyes dropped to her clawed cuticles.

'I requested your assistance for a reason,' Victor continued. 'I need to find a way to kill Rados without killing myself in the process. I'm working on that. He doesn't yet trust me enough to let down his guard in my presence, and he might never, so I need to engineer a way to get him alone or vulnerable.'

'He's never without his men. He doesn't trust anyone.'

'Good for him. Given my intentions, he's right not to trust people. Least of all me. But that's where the problem lies. That's why he's not yet dead.'

'Can't you poison him?'

He stopped himself sighing. 'Listen, poisons aren't as easy to use as you might think – I would need access to his food or his drink, which I don't have – and they don't just make someone drop dead. More importantly, I don't have any, and I have no way of acquiring some here. I'm no chemist. I'm no botanist.'

She slumped rather than sat on the bed, depressed and defeated.

Victor said, 'You don't need to concern yourself with how. Leave the methodology to me. That's what I do.'

'You need to work faster. I can't stay here any longer. I can't.'

He nodded. 'I understand your desire to leave this place, but you're going to have to wait. Rushing these things rarely ever works. Hurrying almost always leads to mistakes. And mistakes in this business are usually fatal. That would be no use to you, and it's certainly no use to me.'

She sat quiet for a moment, head bowed, hands in her lap, her fears made worse because the hope that had buoyed her up before had been deflated. There was nothing Victor could do about that, even if he knew how. He wasn't prepared to expedite his methods and it wasn't his nature to placate. He could lie to her – *he'll be dead in a few days, I have it all worked out* – but that seemed an unnecessary cruelty.

'I came close,' he said to reassure her, stepping closer. 'But it didn't work out. Next time could be better, but you need to be patient.'

She didn't respond. Only Rados' death was going to make any difference to her mindset.

'Do you have any new information for me?'

'Rados doesn't trust you,' she said.

Victor nodded. 'I know he doesn't.'

'He's having you followed.'

'What makes you say that?'

'I heard it from the young one who works here. Zoca told him.'

Victor had seen no signs of surveillance since he had been in Belgrade. That didn't mean there wasn't any, but Rados' guys stood out even on their home turf. There was no way they could follow him without his being aware of it.

'Okay,' he said, 'that's useful to know.'

She shrugged. She didn't want his thanks, only his help.

'Anything else?' he asked.

She shook her head. 'Nothing.'

'Okay,' he said. 'It's still early days. Keep listening. Pay attention to everything.'

'I know,' she said. 'You already told me that.'

There was frustration and annoyance and condescension in her tone. He didn't blame her for that.

'We have a deal,' he reminded her. It was better than saying he was only helping her so she could help him in return. 'Did you have a chance to speak to the other woman you arrived with?'

'No,' she replied. 'And now I'm the only one left. She's gone too.'

'So where is she?'

She shrugged, sad but also numb to the inevitability. 'Dead.'

'Not necessarily. Rados considers the women he's trafficking to be valuable assets. Remember he had three of his men killed and Zoca beaten as punishment for losing two women the night you arrived. He wouldn't have tolerated losing a third, so if this other woman isn't here, she must have been moved on somewhere else.'

'What was she like?' she asked. 'I don't remember.'

He said, 'Young,' thinking she wasn't as young as the blonde girl with blue eyes.

'Prettiest?'

'That's subjective,' he said, 'but yes, you could say that.'

'So he has another brothel. Where the youngest and prettiest women are,' she said, mimicking his own conclusion.

'Yes,' Victor agreed. 'Somewhere I don't know about. Somewhere that Rados probably goes to himself. Maybe the one place he will be without his guards in the room.'

'Maybe he keeps the best girls only for himself.'

'I don't think so,' Victor said. 'Rados is a man, yes, but a businessman first. He wouldn't have a harem. It would be a waste of assets. He would rent out his best women for top prices from the wealthiest clients. Somewhere respectable but anonymous.'

She saw a plan emerging. 'Then you need to get invited there.'

'Indeed. But first we need to find out where it is.'

'Why?'

'So that when I'm invited there with Rados I know the layout and have a plan in place. Maybe even a weapon hidden. I want to be prepared. I need to be, if this is going to work.'

She nodded, understanding the generalities he was talking with, even if the nuances of his profession were beyond her comprehension. He saw the elevation of her mood now that she was a survivor with a plan one step closer to success.

She said, 'If there is another place like this, I'll find it for you.'

FORTY-SEVEN

Banik wanted to meet. He required some more face time. It was far from ideal to interrupt preparations at this stage, but Victor was working to his own schedule and Rados didn't need him for anything at the moment. He was still recovering from the bullet wound. Victor was still on down time.

He didn't know what Banik wanted, but there were only two subjects that would warrant another meeting. Either there had been a development in the Rados contract that couldn't be transmitted digitally, or Banik had learned more about the contract on Victor's head. He envisioned some new intelligence gathered from Leonard Fletcher's phone or laptop, or by tracing his movements; maybe some electronic fingerprint he had left behind before Victor had convinced him to kill himself.

He caught a flight out of Serbia to Hungary, and from there a train took him to Austria where a taxi ferried him across the border into Germany, before another train took him back into Austria for a flight to Scotland and a domestic flight over the UK brought him to London. In total he was on the move for almost twenty-four hours, but when he arrived at Stansted airport he could almost be sure no one was following him.

He was tired from the travelling but airports always made him alert. He passed through without incident and picked a hotel at random, taking a room on the second floor and falling asleep within minutes of securing the door behind him.

When he woke he sent a coded message to Banik giving him a time and place to meet. Both the hour and venue were Victor's choice; he was in no mood to tolerate another excuse for Banik to watch his team on company time.

A club in north London was hosting a Romanian music festival. Victor bought a couple of tickets in the daytime, paying cash at the door, and received two plastic wristbands to allow in-and-out access. He performed a reconnoitre of the club and the surrounding area in the afternoon, ready for the meeting with Banik in the evening.

The club was little more than a hall with a stage at one end and a bar at the other, but the acts were seasoned pros. Victor was early, as per protocol, and listened to a band performing with relish and skill. He didn't watch, because with his ears full of rock music – the band had two drummers – he had to rely on his eyes alone to warn him of potential threats. It wasn't something he liked to do, but the trade-off was worth it. The club's patrons were almost all Romanians and almost all under twenty-five.

Any professional would stand out as obviously as Victor did, especially a German assassin with greying hair.

The band were as popular as they were talented and the previously subdued crowd were going wild by the end of the set.

A set Victor listened to the whole of, because Banik didn't show.

Traffic was hell in London, and even with an extensive public transport network, it could still take forever to cross the city – tube strikes, signal problems and suicides could all have delayed Victor's handler.

When it was obvious Banik wasn't coming, Victor waited. He waited because protocol said to leave with haste. If this was a set-up, he wasn't going to do what they expected. The crowded club was a terrible place for anyone to move against him even if he wouldn't see them coming a mile away. A team would be outside. They would make their move when he was on the street, empty at this time of night apart from Romanian kids smoking outside on the pavement.

He waited because he had taken the precaution of providing himself with a protected exit. He waited until the band had finished their set and returned for a much-appreciated encore. He waited until the encore had finished and they had left the stage for the last time. He waited until the crowd began filing out of the club and slipped away among them.

He stood out, but no sniper could hope to make a shot and no grab team could get anywhere near him. He saw no evidence of either, but stayed within the bulk of the

Romanians until he was in the nearest tube station, where he waited again to see if anyone followed.

No one did that he could see, but he spent two hours on the tube, swapping trains and doubling back and waiting on platforms and circling stations before he headed to Heathrow for the next flight out of the country.

He didn't return to his hotel. He didn't check his messages. He spent another day on the move – trains and flights and taxis – before he returned to Belgrade. It was a risk returning, of course, but there was as much chance of a message waiting for him from Banik with an innocent explanation as there was of any danger. Victor wasn't prepared to abandon his preparations without good reason when he had made so much progress.

It was late in the day when he disembarked the plane and made his way through the airport. He saw no one that caused a tremor on his threat radar until he neared the exit.

Victor didn't like surprises. There were few things he disliked more. He needed to be in control to survive. A surprise demonstrated his inability to orchestrate every facet of his existence. He knew this was impossible, of course, but the less he could control the more at risk he found himself. He'd spotted the woman and read her sign from across the hall, which gave him a little time to decide on his response.

She stood out because her skin had a dark brown tone and her features were sub-Saharan. She was the only non-white person in the terminal as far as Victor could see. Serbia's only notable immigrant population hailed from

China, and even they made up an insignificant percentage of the population.

She also stood out because she held a sign before her stomach.

It was an A4-sized whiteboard with a name written on in thick black marker.

Leonard Fletcher.

FORTY-EIGHT

She ate with the other women, those that had been here for weeks or months, who didn't talk to her because she was trouble. She would get them in trouble. There was always plenty of nutritious food available to keep them healthy and looking their best. The kid with the bad skin did all the cooking, and though not a chef, he knew his way around a kitchen well enough to create decent meals. She had no appetite these days. She couldn't remember the last time she had craved food. She ate because it would be noted if she didn't. Those who didn't follow the rules were disciplined by Zoca.

There was no conversation around the dinner table. A few words were exchanged, but no one knew anyone else, and everyone was too afraid to say something wrong that might trigger Zoca's wrath.

She washed and cleaned up afterwards, shooing away anyone who wanted to assist her, so it was just her and the kid.

'That was nice,' she said. 'You're not bad at cooking.'

He shrugged, awkward and shy.

'I can teach you a few tricks someday,' she said. 'If you like.'

He nodded. 'Sure.'

'Can I ask you a question?'

'What kind of question?'

'A simple question. I'm curious about you, that's all.'

He frowned, nervous and unsure how to respond.

'What are you doing here? You seem nice. You seem normal.'

He shrugged. He couldn't answer.

'You're cute too.'

He reddened. 'What?'

'You heard me. It's a shame we couldn't have met in the normal world. Instead of in here.'

'Why?'

'You know why.'

He couldn't look at her. He found a dish to dry.

'You should let your hair grow,' she said. 'It'll suit you better.'

He fumbled to put the dish away.

'Why do you work for Rados?' she asked. 'You want to be a gangster? You want to be a tough guy?'

The kid shrugged. 'I suppose.'

Then he was an idiot, but she kept the thought to herself. 'Do you like Rados?'

'He's the boss.'

'That's not the same thing. Don't worry, I'm not going to tell anyone anything. I'm only making conversation.

Don't you get bored only ever talking with Zoca? He can't be much fun.'

He sniggered to himself.

'What happened to Zoca's face? He was ugly anyway, but now …'

He chuckled. 'Rados was mad at him.'

'Why? What did he do?'

'He messed up. He lost Rados money.'

She tried not to think about the reality of what that meant. She had to focus on her objective. 'The other woman who wasn't taken for the Slovakians, the one who went elsewhere. She went to the other massage parlour, right?'

He was reluctant to answer.

'Don't worry if you don't know.'

He frowned. 'This is the only one.'

She nudged him on the arm with a playful elbow. 'Rados has her for himself?'

'No, he's married,' the young guy said, as if Rados was some upstanding citizen. 'He keeps some girls for his special parties.'

She acted as if this was inconsequential. 'Parties are fun. Do you go to them?'

She knew the answer before he shook his head. 'They're only for his friends. I've never been to one.'

'That's a shame,' she said, pretending to offer sympathy, 'I'm sure you'll be invited to one eventually, like Zoca.'

He was quick to shake his head. 'Zoca isn't allowed to go either. He only delivers the champagne to the house.' He smirked again, happy to talk down his superior.

'How often does Rados have these parties?'

He shrugged. 'I don't know.'

The kid stiffened, and she felt uneasy. She glanced over her shoulder to see Zoca standing in the doorway. She had no idea how long he had been there.

'Why are you asking all these questions?' he asked.

'I'm making conversation. There's nothing else to do.'

'You should only have time to work.'

'When there are no clients?'

Zoca approached and she tensed, uncertain of his intent or even mood. He gestured to the young kid. 'Get out of here.' When he was gone, Zoca said, 'Your new lover came to see you again, I see.'

'He's not my lover.'

'He likes you.'

She exhaled. 'Well, I don't like him.'

'I think you do.'

'Think what you like.'

He said, 'I think you're asking questions at his bidding.'

She did everything she could not to react.

'I don't know who he is or what he's after,' Zoca said. 'But don't make your life any harder than it needs to be. Don't be fooled by him. Don't be taken in by his suit and his air of superiority. He doesn't care about you. He'll grow bored of you in time. He'll move on to someone else. However kind he seems to you, he's not. He's just like the rest of us.'

'I know that,' she said, because she did.

FORTY-NINE

Her skin was a few shades too light to be a native African, so it wasn't a stretch to make her as British of Afro-Caribbean descent, and therefore one of Banik's people. MI6. A spy.

Even without Victor's photographs on file she would have his general description or had maybe even seen a sketch, but she didn't seem to notice him. He was used to hiding in plain sight. Nothing about his attire or actions made him stand out here. He didn't slow his pace or adjust his trajectory. He continued his walk towards the exit with his gaze on the middle distance – a business traveller like many around him.

Her woollen overcoat disguised her build but her long neck and solid calves revealed she was slender but fit. Thick tights covered her exposed legs and her shoes were plain and black. Her lack of boots told him that this had been a last-minute assignment. Anyone with time to pack would have brought more appropriate footwear. The coat, shoes and tights were adequate protection from the chill of the UK at this time of year, but not the cold of Serbia.

She had been standing there a long time. The sign, even though it couldn't have weighed more than a couple of hundred grams, was resting on one of the buttons of her coat, which was still fastened. She hadn't been waiting for him at arrivals because she hadn't known which flight he was coming in on. That was something, but he didn't like that anyone had been able to predict the day of his arrival, even if the trip to London would have provided a big hint.

Why was she here? The easiest way to find out would be to approach and ask, but nothing useful ever came out of taking the easiest option. Victor continued on his way and exited through the automated doors. He stepped through the downward blast of hot air from the overhead heating vents and into frigid air that stung his face and made his eyes water.

Presumably Banik had an urgent message for him, or an explanation as to why he'd missed their meeting in London. He'd had no communication from the MI6 man since that initial request for face time. Then again, he'd been in transit the last twenty-four hours and unable to check his messages, so it was conceivable that Banik had tried to contact him and panicked when Victor hadn't replied. Either the woman had been sent in the hope of intercepting him, else the message had to be delivered in person and the woman was the only person able, or trustworthy enough, to deliver it. It was possible she was tired not through waiting for a long time but because she was operating on a sleep deficit; Victor couldn't be sure. Either way, her presence was significant and foretold bad news.

He waited in the cold and dim afternoon light. He figured he had less than an hour to wait in total. Flights would be arriving for another seven or eight hours, but the woman wouldn't be standing there the whole time. Not because fatigue would force her to give up – she could time rest breaks between arrivals – but because she wouldn't be alone.

There would be someone backing her up. If the information was critical enough for Banik to want it delivered in person, it would be too valuable to risk to one courier. The same principle applied if there was something else going on – a set-up in the making; there was no way she would be alone.

Victor hadn't noted anyone else inside the airport, so they must be outside, waiting in a nearby vehicle, ready to ferry the woman away or rush to her aid. He didn't know if this second person would swap roles with the woman inside, or if they had already swapped, and he didn't know which of the two had the message if they were rotating roles. They wouldn't both know it. Whoever was the more senior would be the messenger.

Victor figured on the sub-hour waiting time because the backup would spot him given enough time. Either they had eyes on the main entrance and taxi line from their vehicle, or they would make regular passes on foot. With people coming and going to disguise his presence, and without a photograph to go on, it would take time for the second person to identify him.

In the end, it took only half an hour. There was a lull

between flights and the line for the taxis became thin. It was the woman from inside the airport who approached him. The second pair of eyes must have called her. Victor hadn't seen them in return, which meant it had to be a skilled operative or someone keeping surveillance with a pair of binoculars so that he had no hope of making them.

She walked towards him at a slow pace to give him plenty of time to see her coming, as if she might catch him unawares otherwise. Victor acted as though he spotted her long after he had.

He allowed her to draw near and turned to face her square on.

She was maybe thirty-five, but it was hard to be sure. She had the firm smoothness of youth but her eyes seemed to have the wisdom of age and experience. Her make-up was minimal, except on her lips, which shone with gloss. Her hair was short and straightened by chemicals. She had no earrings but he saw the scars to her lobes.

She said, 'Would you like to see my identification?'

Her voice was quiet. She sounded dehydrated.

Victor said, 'I don't need to, do I? I saw the sign.'

'But I'm going to need to know it's definitely you.'

There couldn't be a prearranged code because this wasn't prearranged, so he said, 'You were sent by a West Ham fan.'

She caught herself before she said something she didn't want to. Instead, she first composed the words in her mind, then asked, 'How many siblings are there?'

'He's the eldest of seven.'

'Okay, that's good enough. You need to come with me.'

She'd started to walk away before he could say, 'No chance.'

She slowed but didn't stop. It seemed beyond her comprehension that he might refuse. 'I'll give you a lift into the city.'

'I don't need a lift. And I certainly don't get into cars with strangers.' He paused. 'Even ones as attractive as you.'

She was attractive, albeit tired and stressed, but he said so only to catch her off guard. He wanted to test her. She might not have seen his photograph, but she knew more about him than he knew about her. He wanted to redress that balance.

She absorbed his comment and didn't react apart from the absence of a reaction, which wasn't the same thing. 'You need to hear what I have to say.'

'You can tell me now. We don't have to get into a car to talk.'

'It's freezing out here. Let's go somewhere warm and sit down. Are you hungry? I know I am. I could eat a horse, I tell you. If not then I'll buy you a coffee. Or a beer.'

Victor said, 'I like how you're trying to be friendly with me after I said you were attractive. Trying to hook me by appealing to my maleness. But there's really no need. I don't actually find you attractive.'

'Okay.'

'You rushed to Belgrade to give me a message in person, so it can't be new files; you haven't had time to memorise anything significant. Therefore it won't take long enough for you to get that cold.'

'You're wrong. It is significant.'

'I don't care. I'm not going anywhere until you tell me what it is.'

Her glossy lips pursed instead of arguing further. She saw he was inflexible.

'Okay,' she said. 'I concede. We don't have time to argue, so I'll tell you now. You need to hear it.'

'Go on.'

'Banik's dead. He was murdered.'

FIFTY

The British woman's car was parked some thirty metres from the main airport entrance, over the access road and beyond steel barriers in a short-stay parking lot. It was a boxy Lada, old and cheap. Not a rental, so it must be one of the Embassy's or owned by the local MI6 station. It wouldn't be a personal vehicle. The guy behind the wheel was slumped down in his seat, which was reclined way back so his head was level with the dashboard. He was big and out of shape. A camera with a large lens sat on the dash, obvious when they were close, but impossible to detect at range.

'I want that memory stick,' Victor said as the woman opened the passenger-side rear door. She held it open for him.

The man behind the wheel worked the manual adjuster and the driver's seat inclined in jerky movements. The whole car rocked.

'It wasn't recording,' he said. 'I was only using the zoom.'

Victor reached a hand into the vehicle, but didn't climb inside. 'The memory card.'

'Chill,' he said. 'It's empty. There's nothing on it to be worried about.'

'Then there's no reason not to give it to me, is there?'

The guy hesitated.

'You either give it to me,' Victor said. 'Or I take it.'

There was no challenge or threat in his tone, but the British man understood what Victor meant and he didn't like it one bit. He stared hard at Victor, reacting with a challenge. It was hard to square up when twisted around in a car seat, but he tried his best.

'Hand him the bloody disk,' the woman said. 'It's not like you bought it yourself.'

The guy behind the wheel sighed and dragged the camera from its perch. He spent a moment digging his nail into a groove and prising open a sliver of plastic. He used a fat finger and thumb to drag out the card and tossed it in Victor's general direction with a fast, un-telegraphed throw, hoping to catch him off guard and salvage some kind of personal victory or revenge.

Victor snatched it out of the air and crushed it in his fist.

The guy looked away. 'There was nothing on it.'

Whether he was telling the truth or not, it didn't matter now, so Victor saw no point in commenting further. If the guy wanted the last word that bad, he could have it. Victor's ego didn't need it.

He slipped the crushed memory card into a pocket of his

suit trousers. There was no point keeping what remained, but he couldn't abide littering. He disliked it even more than cursing.

The woman said, 'Have a seat.'

'You first.'

She looked at him, trying to decipher his intention, but there was nothing in his expression to enlighten her. He watched her eyes glance down – to his pocket – and he saw she concluded that if he intended to kill them then he would not have needed to first destroy the card. That could be done afterwards. He softened his face a little so she wouldn't continue the line of thought and conclude destroying the memory card first was a good way to lower their guard in case he decided on killing them later.

The woman nodded and climbed into the back of the Lada. Despite her fatigue she was limber and her movements were effortless and almost graceful. He imagined she had been a gymnast as a child or practised yoga as an adult.

Victor waited until she had shuffled behind the driver's seat before climbing in himself. Had they been preparing to go somewhere he would have preferred to sit in her place to better attack the driver, but he was only here to talk. He wasn't going to let them take him anywhere, whatever their plans.

The Lada was old and he could see the locking mechanism on the far rear door was up and disengaged. No child lock activated. He closed the door behind him.

'I'm Monique,' the woman said. 'This is Dennis.'

Victor remained silent.

The woman who called herself Monique was half-turned in the back seat so she could face him. He didn't mirror her position. He sat with his feet in the footwell, knees parallel to one another and facing the passenger seat so he could be out of the door fast if necessary. He didn't want to lose time repositioning in an enclosed environment. Having to turn his head to look over his right shoulder was a small price to pay to gain that small advantage, should he need it.

'Thank you for coming with me,' Monique said. 'Thank you for making this about as easy as it could be. You could have made my life a lot more difficult.'

I still might, Victor thought.

She continued: 'As I said, Banik was murdered. He was shot and killed on his driveway, climbing out of his car. Two shots to the heart from a .22, followed by one to the head once he was on the ground. No one heard the shots.'

Victor wasn't surprised. Guns were never silent, but a low-powered subsonic bullet fired from a top-of-the-range suppressor could be quiet enough that even had people heard the sound they would have failed to recognise it as a gunshot. Given the low proliferation of firearms in the UK, it made sense that neighbours wouldn't identify a gunshot when they heard one. A car backfiring or even a firework would be the first thought a Londoner had.

'Sounds like a professional hit so far, right?' the woman said.

Victor nodded. He had killed people using the same method. For a brief moment he thought of a contract in Paris he had fulfilled – one that he had considered simple,

311

even easy – but it had caused his life to spiral out of control. He was still trying to put it back together.

'What?' the woman asked, seeing his expression change. She was observant or he was slipping.

'No powder burns at the wound sites,' Victor said, to change the subject.

'That's right. Because he would have taken a headshot at point-blank range?'

'Not necessarily. A .22 can ricochet off the skull if the angle is right. That's why he went for the heart. The headshot was insurance. No such thing as overkill.'

'Then how did you know there were no powder burns?'

'I guessed,' Victor said, and she seemed satisfied. Any thought of his face changing as he remembered that fateful job in Paris had been forgotten and any chance of her understanding him better had disappeared along with it.

'It gets worse, I'm afraid.'

Victor raised an eyebrow. 'Doesn't it always?'

'You know why we're here, right?'

He looked from her to the guy. 'I didn't at first, but I do now. This isn't a courtesy call to let me know my handler is dead. You're investigating Banik's murder and I'm a suspect.'

'Prime suspect,' the woman corrected.

FIFTY-ONE

They were both watching him with unblinking eyes. The roar of planes taking off, descending to land and circling overhead filled the silence. It was not the calm rumble of trains coming and going, but angry. The Brits were tense, worried about a violent reaction, but he sat still and calm. He wanted more information before he did anything.

'Ah,' Victor said. 'Of course I am.'

'Can you prove you weren't in London recently?'

'I have been in London,' he answered. 'As you already know. I was there to meet Banik, as you also know. But you're getting nothing else from me. Don't even think I'll provide proof of anything I've done or haven't done.'

'I thought you might say something along those lines.'

'You can't arrest me. This isn't London. This is Belgrade. You have no jurisdiction here in Serbia, and even if you had, you have no evidence because the killer knew what he was doing. And I'm sure I don't have to tell you that the last thing you want to do is try and take me into custody.'

'I know you didn't do it,' the woman said. 'I don't know anything about you – anything *real*, I mean – but I know you're not stupid.'

'Flattery will get you everywhere.'

'Maybe I phrased that clumsily, but you're not going to shoot dead your own handler outside his house, are you?'

There was no need to answer or discuss the point any further. He glanced between them. 'Why am I prime suspect?'

'I'll get to that in a minute.'

'Then why are you here?'

'I've told you,' the woman said. 'We're here to talk to you about Banik's death.'

'What else?'

A moment of silence followed. The guy behind the wheel avoided eye contact.

Victor said, 'You've made it clear you don't think I killed Banik, so you didn't need to come here to tell me that. You didn't even need to tell me he was dead, let alone assassinated. You could have waited until I'd completed my job, but here you are. I want to know why, and I want to know now. I understand why you've told me about Banik and why you've told me you don't think it's me. You want to encourage trust. You want me to be grateful. You want me to be more on side when you present me with the real reason why you're here. Those MI6 classes in pop psychology you sat through aren't going to pay off with me. So let's not waste time. Tell me now.'

The woman had turned her gaze to the man before Victor had finished speaking.

She said, 'We need your help.'

'Obviously,' he said. 'And I'm still waiting for you to get to the point.'

She rubbed her hands together. It was almost as cold inside the car as outside. The guy had kept the engine off to maintain covert surveillance, so there wasn't any heat. He had better clothes for the temperature and about double the woman's natural insulation. His window was open a crack too, so the glass wouldn't steam up while he was conducting surveillance. Victor felt the chill but he had a high threshold for discomfort even if his level of physical fitness didn't ensure his fast metabolism doubled as a portable furnace.

'London still wants you to kill Rados,' the woman explained. 'I appreciate it if you feel resistance now that your handler is dead.'

'Dead is a heart attack or hit by a bus. A double-tap to the heart followed by one in the head is an execution.'

'Like I said, it's understandable if you want to back out.'

'I don't need to back out,' Victor said. 'I'm already out.'

'Then this is when I reel you back in.'

He thought of the Armenian woman in Rados' brothel, the woman he had made a deal with. *If you help me, I'll help you. That's how simple it can be if you'll let it*, he had told her and meant it.

Monique noted a change in his expression, so he said, 'When you *try* to reel me back in.'

She exhaled. 'Okay, I hear what you're saying and

you've been right so far. But there's still a job to be done that is separate from Banik's ... execution. He presented you with the contract, but it wasn't his call. He was only a messenger.'

'It's bad manners to speak ill of the dead. You're here to bring me a message. I'm a messenger too, when it comes down to it.'

She nodded in a sign of placatory agreement. 'Banik told you about Leonard Fletcher, I'm sure. He told you how Fletcher was selling secrets ... the girl ... the affair ... Chinese intelligence. Yes?'

Victor nodded and said, 'Okay,' so she would continue.

'And I bet he even told you Fletcher had sold your file.'

He had an idea what she was getting at. 'Go on.'

She shot a glance to the guy and he looked pleased, as if it was a foregone conclusion they had Victor on board. Then she said, 'But that last part was bullshit. It was—'

'You can say bogus, if you want. Or you can say incorrect or false or a lie.'

She frowned, confused. 'Yeah,' she said, still unsure what point he was trying to make. 'It was a lie. Fletcher didn't sell your file, Banik did.'

'Hence I'm prime suspect in his murder.'

She nodded. 'Of course. Banik sells you out to the broker named Phoenix and puts killers looking for a big payday on your trail. You find out, and kill him. It's logical. It makes sense. Some of us would even say it's justified.'

'Was Banik working with Fletcher?'

'We don't know. Maybe he got the idea from him. Maybe they were collaborating.'

'They killed each other,' Victor said. 'Banik sent me after Fletcher, but Fletcher had already sent someone after Banik. It just took them longer to fulfil the contract than I did.'

'I'm looking into that idea,' she said. He saw she was telling the truth. It was reassuring to deal with people who could think more than one step ahead. 'There is a contract out on you, brokered as Banik said by an agent named Phoenix. That's been there for a few months, at least. But Banik tried to cash in on that fact to help his own cause. Fletcher wanted him dead. He wanted Fletcher dead. To hide that, he would have you fall victim to another contract killer who was after the bounty on your head. No one would question that. He hasn't sent anyone after you. He's simply made the right people aware of your movements, taking advantage of your – how shall we put this? – *popularity*. We know for certain that one freelancer was in London at the same time as you when you met up with Banik.'

Victor didn't react.

'You're lucky you didn't cross paths.'

'I think I see where this is going.'

'I wouldn't have expected anything less.'

Victor said, 'You're about to threaten me.'

She shook her head, a groove between her eyebrows. 'I wouldn't do that. I'm here to help.'

'No,' Victor said. 'You're here to offer help. You're going to tell me that if I continue with the Rados contract you'll help me with my own problem.'

'We can help each other, yes.'

'Such as offer me intelligence on this female professional on my tail, I'm guessing.'

She nodded. 'We have a whole file on her. She's a bad-ass. You'll never see her coming.'

'Burn the file,' Victor said. 'She's at the bottom of the Thames in six neat pieces.'

The woman stared at him, searching for the untruth. 'You're lying.'

'You didn't tell me she was female. Check the guest list at the Covent Garden Hotel. A woman matching her description checked in nearly two weeks ago but hasn't checked out. Vanished into thin air, in fact.'

'I am going to check, you know.'

Victor said, 'What else do you have to offer?'

'Okay, assuming you're telling the truth, your file is still out there with a powerful broker chasing a big payday. One tried and failed, so all credit to you. But you know as well as I do that there could be others.'

Victor thought about the German with greying hair on the train to St Petersburg. The assassin who had tricked him and stabbed him. That assassin was still out there. The residual pain in his thigh seemed to worsen for a moment. The wound hadn't yet healed fully. He was going to have another ugly scar.

'The sooner that file is retrieved, the easier you'll sleep.'

'How do I even know you can find Phoenix?'

'It's what I do.'

There was enough weight behind her voice that he almost believed her. She was confident in herself.

'And until Phoenix is found, we'll do everything we can to watch your back. That sounds like a pretty sweet deal to me.'

'A deal I wouldn't need if your organisation didn't suffer from endemic corruption. Every single one of your people I've dealt with or come across in the last few years has been playing by their own rules. That's an even higher hit rate than the CIA, which is saying something.'

She said, 'I'm sorry about your situation, if it helps.'

'It doesn't.'

'I won't tell you that you can trust me. I know such a claim would be meaningless right now. I won't say I'm the one who is different from all the rest. I won't insult your intelligence. But I didn't have to tell you about Banik's death. I could have let you continue with the contract and you wouldn't have been any the wiser, would you?'

Victor remained silent because she was right. However he looked at it, it made no sense to tell him about Banik's assassination if she wasn't being truthful now.

'So,' she said after a moment, 'will you do the job?'

'Are you staying in Belgrade?' Victor asked.

'Yes, until this is over. But this is Dennis' turf. He's attached to the Embassy, so he can assist you. He knows this part of the world well. He knows land. He knows people. He can get things done. You have a problem, he can help solve it.'

Victor looked at the big, out-of-shape guy who lost his cool over a blank memory card. 'He can't even solve his own problems. No, thanks.'

Dennis said, 'Whatever.'

The woman shrugged. 'It's your choice. Please know that, if you need anything, I'll be waiting to assist you.'

Victor said, 'What are you offering?'

'Anything,' Monique said. 'And everything. Whatever you need.'

'Whatever I need?' Victor echoed.

She nodded. 'That's right. I can act as backup, surveillance, logistics, intelligence. Whatever you need me to do, you only have to say.'

'Intelligence?' Victor said. 'It's funny you should say that when SIS gave me bad intel from the very start. Rados isn't a drug dealer. He's a people trafficker.'

She looked at the guy in the front seat, who shrugged in response.

'How do you know that?' she asked Victor.

'Because I'm doing my job. Women are more precious than gold, to use Rados' own words.'

She frowned. 'Wait, what? His own words? You've heard him say them or have heard that's what he said?'

'That's what he told me himself,' Victor said. 'Didn't I mention it? I'm working for him.'

Her eyes were huge. 'You're *what*?'

FIFTY-TWO

For a second she looked at him as if he were speaking a
foreign language she didn't understand. 'You're working
for him? You've actually met Rados? You've spent time in
his company. Yet ... he's still alive?'

He said, 'Rados has been walking free unopposed for
six years.'

'What's your point?'

'I don't have one. Do you?'

She was quiet.

'He's paranoid,' Victor said. 'He hasn't given me an
opportunity to kill him. These things take time. I still have
five years and three hundred and fifty days before you are
allowed to criticise my pace.'

'Noted. I'm surprised, that's all. I didn't expect you
to have located him this soon. And I never expected you
would have infiltrated his organisation too.'

'I'm a fast worker,' Victor said, 'but he hasn't really been hiding. If you had known how to look, you would have found him years ago.'

Dennis made sure his gaze was anywhere but Victor.

'I guess we should have hired you sooner,' she said.

He nodded. 'I can't take all the credit. He's done a lot of the work for me. He's done some spring-cleaning recently and needs new recruits. I'm on probation, you might call it.'

'Everything I know about Rados suggests he's insular, that he wouldn't use an outsider like you.'

'True enough, but I think he's modernising. I think he realises that his crew is made up of hard cases when to succeed he needs hard thinkers. Aside from that, I think he likes me.'

Her eyebrows formed perfect arches. 'He likes you?'

Victor nodded again. 'He called himself an emperor surrounded by barbarians. He likes to think of himself as a philosopher. He likes to think he's an intellectual. Whether his men really are as lacking as he believes is irrelevant. It fits his narrative to think that. It elevates him, satisfying his ego in the process, but there is a price to pay for that satisfaction. Because he believes himself to think at a higher level than that of his men he derives no pleasure from conversing with them.'

'What does he get from you exactly?'

'I'm able to talk to him on his level. It's not often I get to talk openly with someone and that resonates with him, even if my reasons for doing so are duplicitous.'

'It does sound as if he likes you,' Monique said again. 'But it also sounds dangerously like you feel the same way about him.'

'He's a target,' Victor said.

'A target who you've been getting to know. Is that going to be a problem? Before you make a pithy retort, I'm asking as part of me watching your back.'

'Is it a problem that you like that handsome asset of yours? The one with the nice smile and strong back.'

She said, 'How did you know about—' but stopped herself.

It had been a carefully generic statement. She probably ran two dozen assets. There was bound to be at least one man she found attractive. Her lips pursed because she was annoyed at herself for falling into his trap.

'Well played,' she said. 'I won't question your objectivity again.'

'It'll save us both a lot of time if you don't question me at all.'

'In which case I won't mention there have been reports of gunfire several nights ago. At a scrap yard linked to Milan Rados. I won't ask if that was anything to do with you.'

She watched his face, waiting and expecting a reaction, whatever he said.

'Yes,' said Victor. 'That was me. Who else would it be?'

'Belgrade police are investigating. Even if Rados doesn't want cops sniffing around, they can't ignore it – people heard gunshots.'

'Gunshots are loud.'

She waited a moment, but when it was obvious he wasn't going to answer, she said, 'I won't ask you to tell me what happened.'

'I'm doing my job. It's not all going to be smooth sailing. If it was easy to kill Rados, you wouldn't be paying me so much money, would you?'

'Going back to Rados,' she began, 'what else can you tell me about him?'

'He's psychotic, but he believes himself to be highly rational. He puts a high value on intelligence and mental fortitude. I demonstrated those things to him early, which put a big mark in my favour.'

'Even if you do say so yourself.'

Victor said, 'I don't think I'll respond to that.'

'Sorry,' she said. 'Continue, please.'

'This is all one long interview,' Victor said. 'He's tested me a couple of times, and I've passed so far. Hopefully that means if I can continue to do well I will no doubt gain more of his trust.'

'It sounds like he wants to offer you the job. It sounds to me like he's hoping you prove yourself worthy.'

'I've drawn the same conclusions.'

Monique watched him with a careful gaze. 'It also sounds to me like you're actually considering it.'

'That depends,' Victor said.

'On what?' she asked.

'On whether he offers me more money than you.'

She sighed. 'I'm not going to rise to that. You do what you need to do and we'll watch your back.'

'Make sure you keep out of my way,' Victor said. 'Both of you. I work alone. You watch my back while I kill Rados, but you do it from afar.'

She showed her palms. 'Like I said, do it your way.'

'If you're lying to me about anything at all I'm going to kill you.' He looked to the man in the driver's seat. 'And I'm going to kill you too.'

She stiffened and the guy looked pale.

She said, 'I'm not lying.'

'Then I'll do it. Because I believe you're telling me the truth now.' He stared into her eyes. 'But you need me to believe you later too.'

She swallowed, but held his gaze. 'Perhaps we'd work better together without the threats.'

'I don't make threats,' Victor said. 'What I'm doing is establishing the rules and ensuring you both know who you are dealing with. Because, whatever your previous priorities, your new number one goal in life is to make sure I don't see either of you as my enemy.'

She took it well. 'We're taking a risk associating with you, as you are with us, so we can at least be cordial.'

'I assure you, this is me on my very best behaviour.'

FIFTY-THREE

The rain had stopped. The city looked drowned. Belgrade meant white city, but now it was grey. Buildings were wet and dark. Puddles lined the kerbs and filled the grooves between cobbles. Trees were weighed down by rainwater, soaked and crooked.

Victor nursed his coffee in a well-heated kafana while he conducted counter surveillance and considered what the British woman had told him – Banik's assassination, and his handler betraying him. Such things were not uncommon in Victor's world, but familiarity was small comfort. He rubbed his thigh.

On a table across from him a woman was using a laptop. She wore a green sweater with white flowers and wore large headphones. Throughout the entire time he drank his coffee she had a constant smile. Victor couldn't help but wonder why she was so happy. At another time, in another life, he might have asked her. Victor looked away before she noticed his gaze.

Banik selling him out meant the danger he was in was real and close, but he behaved the same. He operated on the assumption that enemies were always closing in, so there was nothing more that could be done. He was on the lookout for the German assassin with greying hair but he was careful not to give himself tunnel vision. Anyone could be a threat so he assessed everyone he met, and whom he might meet. He noticed height and weight and body composition the way regular people noticed hair and eye colour. He examined bone density, limberness of movement and strength of posture. He looked to the intensity of gaze as much as their breadth to determine threat, because a person needed the willingness to use their strength for it to be effective. Speed and reflexes were harder to assess, as was skill, but a person's physical appearance was only one of many signs of potential threat.

A person's gait told him a lot. The length of stride and the speed of movement revealed flexibility and agility. A tall man with long legs may have a long stride and cover distance faster as a result, but slow strides suggested a general slowness of movement, due to a lack of cardiovascular fitness or inflexible joints. Both had measurably different effects in a confrontation, but were equally valuable for Victor to exploit.

He sat near the window so he could see who was nearing the kafana before they entered. His chair was small and uncomfortable, but he enjoyed the rare swathe of sunlight that found its way through the clouds to his face. The street outside the window was narrow, one lane, and had little through traffic, letting him check for threats with relative ease.

A man turned on to the street and walked in Victor's direction. He was in his early forties, tall and broad – waist as well as shoulders. His hair was short and neat and thinning, but still had plenty of orange and red hues. His face had a permanent flush. His eyes were blue behind smart glasses. The grey suit was inexpensive but fit well. His black oxfords were old but polished.

Victor saw him as physical, but rusty. He had the natural strength gained from plenty of protein and calories, but his lifestyle was sedentary. He might throw a volley of effective punches, but he would be exhausted by it.

No threat.

The man didn't notice Victor looking, didn't notice the assessment and evaluation, and continued on his way.

The next was a lot younger. He came from the opposite direction. His hair was blond and wavy, swept back from a high forehead and receding at the temples. He had a sparse growth of stubble, darker and thicker than his hair. There were shadows under his red-rimmed eyes. He had a boyish face but he carried a man's width in his upper body, across his chest and shoulders. His clothes were casual and unrestrictive. Victor's gaze lingered a moment longer.

He was in shape, but his neck was thin and his back narrow. The young guy exercised, but was building muscle for aesthetics, not power. He was fit and young, but tired and weak. He looked eager – for food; for knowledge; for purpose – but nothing more.

No threat.

The waiter asked if Victor wanted another coffee, so he paid his bill, walked a while, then caught a bus. He didn't check its number or its route. He didn't know where it was going, which was the point. If he didn't know, no one else could; no ambush could be prepared for him at his destination. A man with glasses caught the bus at the next stop. He was out of breath.

The bus was busy and Victor had to stand, as did the man in glasses. Victor made sure to keep him in his peripheral vision at all times, because maybe that man was out of breath because he had been following Victor on foot and had been forced to sprint ahead of the bus. The man wore a leather jacket and tan scarf. He was about thirty, short but strong.

The man played with his phone, as most people did. Standing helped Victor assess the other travellers. The prevalence of mobile phones and other devices helped with identification of potential threats. On trains and buses people looked down. They always had, to an extent, with newspapers and books, but it was even rarer now for eyes to be looking up or ahead. Victor liked that, even if he stood out with no handheld device to distract him. It was hard to be watchful without appearing so. It was the thing that gave away most surveillance. It was easy to be anonymous – to be one more person in the crowd – but hiding in plain sight was no use if the target slipped away.

The balance between anonymity and awareness was almost impossible to perfect. It was fluid. It varied with circumstance, situation and surroundings. It was influenced by opposition and their intent, as well as Victor's own objective. Like any other aspect of Victor's profession, compromise was key. A loss in awareness here might help him stay unseen and therefore lessen the necessity for that awareness. Else, if in making himself more visible he had nothing to lose – if the enemy were already aware of him or knew he would appear – then it might assist his ability to identify and hence counter the threat.

A kid ate six marshmallows from a packet, so Victor left the bus at the sixth stop. He waited at the stop until the bus had faded into the distance. The man in glasses had stayed on the bus, never looking up from his phone. On the pavement, a woman with a pushchair smiled and waved, stretching her hand higher and higher in an effort to catch the attention of someone Victor couldn't see.

He stayed on the move. He didn't know Belgrade well and that helped keep his routes and method of transport random. His threat radar hummed the entire time. Every car that passed him seemed to slow down as it neared. Every person seemed to have their jacket unzipped. Every window had a shadow behind the open pane.

He saw him again – the man wearing glasses. Short. Strong. Leather jacket and tan scarf. It was enough to make Victor change direction. Not because he wanted to lose the man, but because he wanted to see if the man followed.

He did.

It was all Victor needed to know. Seeing him twice could be put down to coincidence, but three times was too many to ignore. Victor paused outside a street vendor, a fishmonger selling off the last of the day's fresh stock cheap, for cash only. Old women fought for the best of the remaining fish and haggled over the price. Victor joined the small crowd and acted like them – perusing fish and ignoring the smell, gaze passing over the polystyrene boxes, wet with melted ice and blood, old and stained – but used the time and the excuse to glance up and watch the street in the plate-glass windows of a florist next door. He didn't look to see what the man in glasses was doing. He didn't need to look to know he would have slowed or stopped to maintain distance. Looking would achieve nothing except alerting the shadow that Victor had made him.

He crossed the street, walking at a slow, casual pace. A crowd was huddled under the scaffolding outside a bank because someone was lying prone on the pavement, having fainted or otherwise been taken ill. Some people were trying to help, others just wanted to see what was happening.

Victor veered towards the crowd, so that he had to thread and weave and sidestep through the mass of bodies. In doing so he had the excuse to survey a wide angle of the street. The man in glasses was nowhere to be seen.

Which was a serious problem.

Victor hadn't been trying to lose him, so the man had voluntarily held back. A shadow would only do that if he feared he would be made otherwise, or because other shadows were taking over.

The first was simple enough to identify because he knew what he was doing. He wore the right clothes and carried himself in the right manner and acted in the right way someone stalking a target should. It was a process of elimination. There were several men in the vicinity who could be Victor's enemy, but he ignored those who were too old or too young or too out of shape for a competent professional.

A strong-looking forty-something was dismissed because he wore thick gloves to fight off the cold. Those gloves were no doubt effective at keeping digits warm, but would make it hard to slip an index finger through a narrow trigger guard or allow fine enough purchase to cock a hammer or release a safety catch. A handful of men wore bulky coats that would weigh them down or risk becoming caught on objects or trapped in doors. They too were dismissed by Victor. As were those with zippers or buttons fully fastened, keeping out the wind chill but restricting upper body movement.

In the shelter of an awning a man sipped from a big thermos flask of steaming coffee or tea. Caffeinated beverages would not be drunk because of their diuretic effects. Even if the coffee or tea was decaffeinated, no assassin on the hunt would choose to compromise his hands – his ability to attack and defend himself – with such an unwieldy object, especially one that he left his DNA on and could not be disposed of as readily as a waxed paper cup.

Which left just two men.

The first was tall and broad while the second was shorter and slim. The height and build of the first was not ideal for a professional who needed to remain unnoticed by targets and enemies alike, but the strength that size resulted would prove a useful attribute for a man who worked with aggression before stealth. The second man was less noticeable. He could hide in a crowd better or in shadows or anywhere else the taller man's size would make problematic. But it was harder to shadow a target from a low vantage point. Size alone would not reveal the identity of an enemy.

They both wore the right clothes – dull, muted colours; loose but not baggy; unrestrictive but plenty of material for an assailant to grab and manipulate, or to snag and catch and otherwise get in the way.

Not killers then, Victor deduced with a little surprise. These men weren't connected to Phoenix and looking for the bounty on his head, or sent by one of his many enemies for revenge or to send a message or for self-preservation.

Three shadows.

The Armenian woman had warned him Rados was having him followed, but these men weren't Rados' Varangians. He didn't think they were SIS watchers keeping an eye on him either. He had believed what Monique had told him, so it didn't make sense she would have him followed. But, he reminded himself, he had believed Banik too. Even if they weren't killers, they were also too sloppy for the kind of professional that would come after Victor.

So, who were they?

FIFTY-FOUR

He had to find out. It wasn't in his nature to ignore threats, and even if these three weren't shooters they could be a local crew in the employ of one. Which made a lot of sense if Victor had already encountered that killer and knew his face. Hiring a local crew to keep tabs on him was less risky than doing it personally.

Traffic was slow-moving. Even Victor's casual gait was faster. He kept going, as yet unsure of his course of action. He stepped aside to allow a short woman carrying brown paper bags of groceries to pass by. She smiled in appreciation.

He reached the end of the block. Traffic was at a standstill at the four-way intersection. Drivers were getting restless because one of the lights was faulty and no one wanted to be the good guy and let the others through first.

Victor crossed, turned side on to pass between two stationary taxis. He glimpsed the man in glasses again, hanging back while the two on the other side of the road had closed the distance, now walking side by side.

The tall man wore a hip-length brown leather jacket. He had a bald head and grey stubble. The second man had a blue sports coat, open over a chequered shirt. They walked side by side without talking or gesturing to one another, which was rare for two men, especially when they walked at the same slow pace as Victor, despite the cold and drizzle.

Either it was a prearranged exchange in lead position, or they feared he had become suspicious of the man behind him.

Half a block later, he saw that it was the latter, because the tall man in the leather jacket had broken off from the man in the blue sports coat and was now lead. The man in glasses had fallen way back out of line of sight. If Victor turned, he was sure he would see him, but for now casual glances and reflections were not revealing him.

The light was fading and headlights glowed from roads slick with rainwater. An old man in a stinking trench coat asked Victor if he had some spare change. Victor kept on walking. He turned a corner and crossed the street, earning a blast of horns from drivers who had to slow down even more to accommodate him.

In the windscreen of a parked removal van he saw the man in the blue sports coat pick up his pace. They were willing to take risks in order to maintain contact with him.

He saw a row of payphones, all of which were unused. Victor liked payphones, and lamented the days when they could be found almost everywhere. Cell phones were more use to the wider public, but almost useless to him. He approached the row of phones, picked the cleanest-looking one, inserted coins into the slot, and punched random buttons with a knuckle.

With the receiver to his ear, he recited the Lord's Prayer to give his lips something natural to say as he turned and rotated and peered around as people did when talking on the phone. He saw the tall man in the leather jacket loitering at a bus stop. The man in the blue sports coat had stopped to tie a shoelace. The man in glasses with the tan scarf was still walking because he had a lot of distance to cover.

They were operating on a classic, if poorly executed, switch routine; alternating who kept close to Victor to prevent him from spotting them. They had no idea he had made them a long time ago. That was his advantage and he planned to exploit it in full.

He left the payphone and went for a walk, keeping his movements slow and predictable while he waited for the right moment. He wanted them in a bored rhythm. There had been no indication that they possessed superb powers of alertness. The easier he made it for them, the quicker their focus would slide.

He headed to Knez Mihajlova, a long pedestrian street in the centre of the city. It ran from the main square, Trg Republike, to Belgrade's imposing fortress and Kalemegdan Park. It was busy, even in the rain, and he passed along until he saw a dense crowd watching a street magician perform tricks. Victor kept his pace slow as he headed towards the crowd, as if he had no interest in seeing the magician and he was merely taking a route that would pass through the crowd. He didn't want his shadows to shift a gear.

A crowd meant numbers. Numbers meant anonymity. Victor became a singular fragment of a much larger whole. Outside observers saw the crowd, not its composite parts. Those parts were hard to identify as individuals, made harder by limitations in line of sight and the ever-shifting nature of the mass. He liked crowds for this reason. He dressed to blend in – muted colours; common garments. In a crowd of any decent number he was almost invisible. He acted to appear unremarkable, to disappear against the background. Longer and longer strides reduced his height little by little. He waited until he was as deep into the crowd as he could be, and stopped walking.

The shadows would be looking for a man on the move; a man maintaining the same route and pace he had been using. Their eyes would be programmed to spot such telltale signs. They would be looking for someone of his height. They would ignore those men standing still. There wasn't time to evaluate them all.

They ignored Victor.

It was one of the reasons he preferred to go up against professionals. He knew how such opposition acted. He could predict a sensible response to most situations. With amateurs it was harder to anticipate their actions. They were prone to impetuousness, apt to impulsivity, happy to improvise. Professionals had training and experience; they had protocols and modus operandi.

The tall man in the leather jacket and the shorter man in the blue sports coat walked on by.

Victor gave it a moment and then moved in the opposite direction until he spotted the man in glasses and the tan scarf. Victor fell in behind him.

They passed out of the crowd and continued on the route Victor had looked like he was taking. It led them down an alleyway.

Not long now, Victor knew, because all three had lost sight of him. They would have to communicate.

It took another fifteen seconds, which surprised Victor – the man seemed even less patient than he imagined – but the slip in discipline came anyway.

The man sighed, shoved a hand into his trouser pocket and withdrew a mobile phone, the phone Victor had seen him playing with – pretending to play with – on the bus. He thumbed the screen to enter a code to unlock it.

There was a brief conversation.

... No, me neither ... he can't have ... keeping looking ...

Victor was behind him when the call finished.

He tapped the man on the left shoulder as he stepped to the right, so when the man turned Victor was out of his line of sight. Victor wrapped an arm around his neck, applying a choke hold, and dragged him backwards behind the cover of wheelie bins and a fire escape.

The phone fell from the man's hands as they snapped up to grab Victor's to relieve the pressure, but Victor was strong and the man was too slow and too unskilled to have a hope of saving himself.

He went slack as oxygen deprivation convinced the brain it was dying and to shut down non-essential functions like consciousness in an attempt to stay alive as long as possible.

Victor released the man and let him drop on to the ground. He was no threat, and there was no need to kill him. At least yet.

He took a step and retrieved the phone from the ground. It had survived the fall, but with cracks across the screen. It still functioned though. The inaction had caused the brightness to dim, but it would remain unlocked for another few seconds.

He used a knuckle to operate the screen, finding the man had been using his personal phone. It was full of apps and notifications. He was not surprised by this. These guys were not good enough to be operating sterile.

Victor navigated to the phone's settings and then to the location settings and then to its location history.

A calendar and a map filled the screen. On the map was a red line and a number of dots that marked everywhere the phone had been today. Victor used a thumb and finger to zoom into the map and saw where the man had walked from to the point where he had begun following Victor. He zoomed out of the map and saw where he had spent the rest of the day. Victor memorised the address.

He checked the previous day's entry. The man had travelled to, then from, the same location. Whatever was there was significant.

Victor slipped the phone back inside the man's jacket and searched for a wallet. There was one, worn from use, but it only contained cash. The slots for cards were empty.

No receipts either. An attempt at operating sterile, but a half-hearted one, given the personal phone.

He checked the man's pulse to make sure he hadn't killed him by mistake – it happened sometimes – but felt the thump of blood pressure through the carotid. He would wake up fine, without sign of injury. It was doubtful he would even remember being choked out.

Victor glanced around in case his buddies had come to check on him, and walked away.

The address corresponded to a beautiful old stone building designed by a true artist and built by artisans. It looked like a grand office building from the late nineteenth century, the kind of place that was commissioned by a rich merchant to show off his success and had been sold by squabbling heirs of heirs. The once lavish interior would have been gutted decades ago during the communist era. Where once had been solid oak tables, brass light fixtures and Persian rugs, now there was chipboard veneer, stained plastic and linoleum.

The people coming and going through the entrance were blue-collar workers and the civilians they dealt with.

Even without the sign, Victor knew a police station when he saw one.

FIFTY-FIVE

Cops. He hadn't been expecting law enforcement to be after him. He had kept a low profile in Belgrade despite the incident at the scrap yard and the hospitalised attempted muggers. He couldn't imagine having left enough evidence of criminal activity to have put the police on his tail. Which meant Rados, with all his connections, had done so instead.

Not a true surprise, but an unexpected development nonetheless. He knew Rados didn't trust him as an outsider and a newcomer, even without the Armenian woman's warning, but he hadn't anticipated Rados would put police assets on his tail to find out more about him.

Since when?

It made no sense for him to have done so after the Slovakian deal. Rados believed Victor had saved him, and if he hadn't, there was no need to go through the pretence. So the cops must have been following him earlier, before Victor had proven himself.

He hadn't seen these three prior to the Slovakian deal, but there could have been different cops shadowing him. They might have seen him leave the country or witnessed his return and conversation with the British woman. Or his counter surveillance techniques could have kept them away until now. There was no way to know for sure.

A long, circuitous route took Victor back to the apartment via cab, bus and foot. The neighbourhood was almost deserted at this time of night. Scant few lights were on in windows and whole minutes went by between passing cars. The lack of foot traffic meant it was easier to look out for enemies, but he stood out more as a result. A sniper on a rooftop or at one of the black windows would have a simple shot to make.

No shot came and he detected no signs of cops or killers. It was impossible to be sure, of course, but that was why he didn't rely only on his own perception for protection. The location, the legend, the counter surveillance techniques all combined to form a multi-faceted defence. He could be tracked down, as the German on the train and Abigail in the hotel and many others had shown, but both had had to reveal themselves to corner him.

He checked his watch and waited in an alleyway at the back of his block until it was time to move. The wait was a long one, because of the hour, but he was used to waiting and he'd done his research. There was no need to pass the time because his mind was occupied each and every second – paying attention to every sight and sound and smell that might warn him of an approaching attacker.

When the time was right he left the alleyway and circled

the block until he was on the corner of his street with the apartment building's entrance visible in the spill of sodium streetlight. The heavy door offered a great deal of safety, but it was also a chokepoint. If an enemy or enemies had tracked him down and knew of the apartment they could lie in wait for him to return.

With as little exposure as was possible he scanned the building opposite – the windows and rooftop overlooking the apartment's front door. He saw no open windows or out-of-place shape on the parapet above, but he carried on waiting regardless. He didn't rely on his own perception.

He didn't check his watch again but he kept track of the time and was surprised when the bus was late. At this time of night there was almost no traffic on the roads to slow it down, so he imagined some other issue had delayed it – a drunk passenger without the right fare, arguing with the driver.

He heard its approach before he turned to see how far away and work out its speed – thirty to thirty-five miles per hour. No traffic and no lights to interrupt. It had half a mile to travel, which it would cover in less than thirty seconds. But it would slow as it reached its destination, adding another ten seconds. Victor had fifty metres to cover, which he would traverse at four miles per hour – a quick walk, but not attention worthy. After the count in his head reached fifteen, he set off along the pavement.

When he was five metres from the steps leading to the apartment, the bus slowed to a stop at the bus stop outside, shielding him from any marksman hidden out of sight on the rooftop of the building opposite. He unlocked the front door as the bus doors hissed open and a man stepped out.

He was young, maybe twenty and maybe high. His hair was lank and his clothes shabby. He wore headphones and was lighting a roll-up cigarette before the bus doors shut behind him. No threat.

Victor entered the building, spent the rest of the night awake and alert, and fell asleep at first light.

The phone woke him up. He checked the message.

The club. Now.

The fights were well underway when Victor arrived. He detected nothing from Rados' crew outside or on the way in to suggest anything was amiss. He didn't believe they would be able to hide it from him if their opinion of him had changed.

Rados was dressed in a fine suit, shirt and tie. He looked fresh and rested and without the sling supporting his left arm, he appeared in excellent health.

'My hero,' Rados said with a warm smile.

Victor said, 'How's the arm?'

'I'm going to have a nasty scar. But otherwise, I'm fine. It doesn't even hurt that much. My doctor – you met him, right? – is a religious man, and said that angels had been watching out for me. Hilarious, isn't it?' Rados continued: 'He is wrong, of course. If I am protected, it is by the prince of darkness himself.'

'I almost believe that,' Victor admitted.

Rados smiled. 'I hear you have been spending a lot of time with the Armenian woman.'

Victor nodded. 'I've seen her a second time, yes.'

'You like her?'

'You could say that.'

'How interesting.'

Victor said, 'I like familiarity.'

Rados said, 'I'll bear that in mind. It's a funny thing, isn't it? Why do we like what we like?'

'What do you mean?'

'We like sweet things. We like meat. We like fat. Why?'

'Simple. Our bodies need carbohydrates and protein and fats. Our taste buds respond to the macronutrients to make sure we eat them, to make sure we stay alive.'

Rados had expected such an answer. 'Then why don't we like water in the same way? We need it more than anything else but air. We can survive weeks without food, but a matter of days without water and we will never recover. Water should taste like pure joy. Why doesn't it?'

'Because it never had to compete. We had no choice. Water to quench our thirst or death.'

'So, we don't always like what we need. Sometimes we don't know what is good for us. Sometimes, having no choice is actually the best thing for us.'

Victor said, 'Is that what you tell your men so they don't question you?'

'You see through my tricks with a rare gaze.' Rados laughed. 'How are you fixed for later?'

'I don't have any plans.'

'Great,' Rados said. 'I would like to invite you to a special gathering tonight.'

'What kind of a gathering?'

'A coming together of like-minded fellows of means. I hold them every so often for esteemed associates.'

'I'm honoured to receive an invite.'

'You have earned your place in the court of your king where riches of all kinds can be yours.'

Victor said, 'I like the sound of that.'

'I thought you might. Make sure you're suitably attired.'

FIFTY-SIX

When Victor entered her room, she was lying on the bed, on top of the covers, half-naked in the only slip of clothing she was allowed, her face pinched and damp with sweat, eyes shut tight. She didn't hear him enter, but her unconscious detected his presence and she bolted awake, jumping to her feet – at first because she feared all who entered this place, but when she saw it was him she did not fall back to the bed on which she had been sleeping. Anticipation maintained her momentum.

She had fresh bruises. These ones were on her legs. Victor recognised them as marks left by fingers gripping far tighter than any finger needed to grip.

'We're running out of time,' he said. 'You were right about Rados having me followed, but it wasn't his own men. It was cops. They might not yet have witnessed anything to expose me, but if they're following me it's inevitable they'll also be investigating my alias. It's inevitable they'll realise

I'm not who I'm supposed to be. I have to act fast or I might not get another chance, so I really hope you've found out where the other brothel is located.'

'Rados doesn't have another brothel,' she said. 'He keeps the best women for parties.'

'What kind of parties?'

'They're for his friends,' she explained. 'At one of his houses.'

'I think I've been invited to one, tonight. Rados told me he has gatherings every so often for esteemed associates. The women must be there as entertainment for those he wants to impress and curry favour with.'

'Good for you,' she said, pushing tendrils of damp hair from her face. 'He must like you.'

He didn't tell her why – that Rados believed he had saved his life – but he said, 'It's no help to me. I don't know where his house is nor what to expect when I get to the party. I can't go in blind and unarmed with all Rados' men there protecting him.'

'Zoca won't be there,' she said.

'Because he looks a mess.'

She shook her head. 'He never gets invited.'

'He doesn't?'

'That's right,' she said. 'And if he doesn't go to the parties then the rest of Rados' thugs won't either.'

She approached the wardrobe.

He thought about Zoca and the Varangians: hardened criminals and paramilitaries; Rados' barbarians. He wouldn't have them littering up the place and drawing attention while making the wealthy clients uncomfortable.

'Yes,' he agreed. 'That makes sense. But it still doesn't mean I can get a weapon inside.'

'Maybe you can't,' she said, opening the wardrobe, 'but I can.'

Inside, hung a black evening gown, fresh from a dry cleaner, still inside a cellophane protector.

'You're going to be there?' he asked.

'The dress was brought up earlier. I didn't realise why until now. Why else would they have given it to me? I'm obviously going to be there for you. Because they think you like me.'

He thought back to his previous conversation with Rados. *I prefer familiarity ... I'll bear that in mind.*

'You have a gun?' she asked, and he nodded. 'They won't search me. I'm a prisoner. I'm no one. They won't think even for a second that I might have a weapon.'

He hesitated.

She continued, 'You said yourself, time is running out. This is your best chance to kill Rados. I can sneak your gun in there, and you can take it from me once you're inside too.'

It was a simple plan, but it had merit. In the absence of any other he drew his Five-seveN. She recoiled from it, frightened by the sight of a gun even though she was expecting to see it.

He released the magazine and slipped it into a pocket.

'What are you doing?'

'I can sneak the mag inside myself,' he said.

'Why do you need to?'

He didn't answer.

She said, 'You don't trust me with a loaded gun?'

He shook his head. 'You could be tempted to use it, and I wouldn't blame you for doing so. But Rados' men have guns of their own and it'll only end badly.'

'Maybe I don't care about dying any more.'

'My point, exactly.'

She said, 'You don't want me to get killed with your gun in my hand, do you?'

'That's right. It wouldn't help either of us. I'll kill Rados at the party, then I'll get us both out of there.'

'Will it work?'

She wanted assurance. She wanted guarantees. He could provide neither. She saw this and her head slumped. Whatever hope he had given her had been diminished already.

'I think you were having a nightmare when I came in,' he said to change the subject.

She didn't react straight away. Then she became self-conscious – aware of her half-nakedness and her unkempt appearance. She pulled her knees up to her chest, ankles touching, and tried to comb her hair with her fingers. He made sure not to watch her.

She said, 'I didn't mind the nightmares when I was here before. They meant I was asleep, not awake. Nothing I dreamed about could ever be as bad as reality.' Her head rose and she looked at him. 'I didn't thank you before, for not asking my name.' She couldn't smile, but for a second her face didn't look as pained. 'Thank you for giving me some degree of privacy in this place. My name is the only thing I have left that's truly mine.'

'I know how you feel.'

'I don't want you to feel sorry for me,' she said, mis-understanding. 'I don't want your sympathy and I don't need it.'

Victor said nothing, but he nodded to show agreement. It seemed polite.

'Maybe if you do get me out of here I'll tell you my name then.'

'That's up to you,' he said.

The silence lasted a while. She looked at the gun, exam-ining it as if she had never seen one up close before. Maybe she hadn't.

'What happens if those cops have found out something about you?' she asked. 'What if they've told Rados?'

It was a good question. He considered his answer, but she didn't like the pause.

'He'll kill you, won't he? And if he tries and fails, then you won't come back here for me, will you?'

Victor remained silent.

She said, 'Then you need to give me the bullets.'

'No.'

'Give them to me.'

Victor said, 'We stick to the plan. You do your part and I'll do mine.'

'I don't believe you. I want out of here. *Now*.'

'That's impossible. You're going to have to wait until tonight.'

'You're full of shit. I'm never going to see you again. Once you walk out of that door then it's over, isn't it?'

'I have a job to finish and I'm going to finish it. You help me do it, and you'll be free.'

She shook her head. 'I don't believe you. If you don't get me out of here I'm going to tell them what you're doing here. I'm going to scream at the top of my lungs and then you're going to take the gun back and get us both out of here, because if you don't I'm going to tell them what you told me. I'm going to tell them you plan to kill—'

In an instant she was against the wall and he had his hand on her throat. She was as shocked by the speed of his transformation as she was scared by it. Her gaze was fixed on his own.

'It's really not smart to threaten me,' Victor said. 'If there is one thing you don't want it's for me to think of this arrangement as not worth the risk.'

She said nothing.

He said, 'We have a deal that I will stick to. I'll get you out of here. You have my word. But after I've done my job. We do it my way and you had better stick to your part of the deal. Do not play games with me. Do not threaten me. Do not make yourself the kind of problem I don't need. I'm the worst enemy you could have. Worse than Rados and his thugs, so do the smart thing and take the offer to be my ally – because I'm the only ally you're going to get.'

Again, she was silent, but her eyes said everything that words could and better too: anger, fear, hate, helplessness but also understanding and acceptance.

He said, 'Keep the gun hidden and don't do anything stupid, then tonight Rados will be dead and you can have your life back. All you have to do is wait. Can you do that?'

She nodded.

When he removed his hand he saw there were livid red marks on her throat – four fingers and his thumb, visible and obvious to the point of the creases and lines of his skin showing. He realised she hadn't responded because she hadn't been able.

'I didn't mean to hold you that hard.'

'Yes you did,' she said, her voice quiet but her tone pure rage. 'And you can't threaten me. What are you threatening me with? What are you going to do, hurt me? Kill me? I told you before: if I stay here I'm dead anyway. Are you going to hurt me worse than these scum?'

'And I told you before: you're a survivor. You're not going to give up, so don't try to pretend you have nothing to lose. While you're alive, there is always a chance. That's how you escaped before. That's why you're risking everything to help me. You have the same survival instinct I have. While you're breathing you'll keep fighting.'

'Okay,' she admitted, 'I don't want to die. Especially not here. Not like this. But you're bluffing too. You can't do anything to me. If you do, you'll also kill any of the trust you've gained with Rados. Even if he places no value on my life he isn't going to trust someone so reckless. We're in central Belgrade. There are clients in the building and people on the street outside. He doesn't want gunshots. He doesn't want a dead body to deal with in one of his businesses.'

She was right, of course, but he kept that from his expression even if to deny it would be futile. 'Supposing you're right, you're forgetting the single most important fact here.'

She was not hesitant because she knew she had gained the upper hand. 'And what would that be?'

He pointed. 'That's the door.'

'It is,' she said.

'And I can walk through it any time I like and never come back.'

Her lips stayed closed.

He said, 'This is a job to me, nothing more. If I don't kill Rados I don't get paid. It's worth a lot of money to me, but that's all. I'll simply wait for the next contract to come my way. I'll go skiing. I'll read.'

She looked away.

'Am I making myself clear?'

'Yes,' she answered. 'Don't worry about that.'

'I never worry.'

'I understand exactly what you're telling me. I don't have any choice but to do as you want. I'm a prisoner here, but I'm your prisoner too.'

'That's one way of looking at it.'

She stepped towards him. 'I hope you feel good about that. I hope that makes you feel powerful. Do you?'

Victor didn't answer.

FIFTY-SEVEN

Victor was early, because it was always his preference to arrive before he was expected. It was simple protocol. He was early because he liked to see trouble coming instead of walking into it. He was expecting trouble, because the British SIS officer needed to see him. It could only be more bad news.

She hadn't arrived. He was glad. He didn't like people being earlier than him. He didn't like people thinking the way he thought.

But she had sent someone ahead.

The watcher looked and acted like almost every other man in the bar. He wore the same kind of stylish business suit, jacket off. The tie was loose and the top button of the shirt undone in the same kind of expression of freedom and release. He leaned against the bar with one elbow as if fatigued after a long day. He was perspiring and his hair was unruly from constantly pushing it back with his fingers. He sipped from a tall glass of premium beer. His glass was three-quarters full. Alcohol and work rarely mixed well, but it enhanced his cover in the way a full glass or a non-alcoholic beverage could not. The attire, behaviour and beer marked him out as a pro. He blended in perfectly in his surroundings. Had Victor not been expecting trouble he might have missed him.

The watcher was working alone but he was not alone. He was chatting and flirting with a redhead in a pinstripe trouser suit. It was a risky move. The interaction could not help but draw attention and the energy and effort it required to maintain meant less could be used to watch. But he was pulling it off with ease. He had the redhead positioned in such a way that he could look at her and see Victor in his peripheral vision.

His shirt gave him away. He had his jacket hanging off the back of a tall chair because it was hot in the bar but it was cold outside. The creases in the shirt gave him away – specifically their absence. He had the right clothes, the right attitude, the right actions, but his shirt did not show the wrinkles that a day in the office would acquire. It was too fresh and well pressed – either because he had not been wearing it long or because he had spent most of the day as foot surveillance, not slumped in a chair or hunched over a desk.

Excellent, but not perfect.

He was not surprised that SIS had sent backup. Monique might be convinced of Victor's innocence in Banik's assassination, but the jury would still be out so far as her bosses were concerned. Either she would be told to send the watcher, else someone higher up had made that decision without her consent. Victor didn't like being watched, but for the time being it was an irritant rather than an interference so he was prepared to ignore it.

When Monique arrived she found him in a quiet corner. No one was seated within earshot.

There was no sign of the other one – Dennis. Maybe they had discussed it beforehand and decided it was best if he didn't come too. Maybe that had been Monique's idea. *I think it would be best if I dealt with him alone ... Don't worry, I'll take a pavement artist for backup.*

Monique was in civilian attire: jeans and a sweater. Ankle boots made her even taller. She looked a lot fresher than the last time he had seen her at the airport. Her skin was so smooth it looked polished under the bar's spotlights.

'Thank you for meeting me,' she said. 'I know it's short notice.'

'There's no need to thank me. There is no need for any pleasantries. Let's get on with it. I'm pushed for time and it's a risk meeting you at all.'

She didn't react to his belligerent words or blunt tone. She gestured. 'Have a seat, please.'

Victor said, 'Why am I here?' as he adjusted a stool to give him the best viewing angle, and sat down.

'I'm watching your back,' Monique insisted. 'And I'm doing a great job of it.'

'I hope you didn't hurt your shoulder when you gave yourself a pat on the back.'

'I was a gymnast,' she said, 'but I have good reason for my grandiose statements, I assure you.'

'I'm waiting.'

Monique said, 'It turns out that Fletcher and Banik had a nice sideline going, using company assets for personal business. Also turns out they both used the same professional killer for most of these jobs.'

'He wouldn't be German by any chance?'

'Yes, and his name is Krieger. Banik used you to get rid of Fletcher, but Fletcher had by that time hired Krieger to take out Banik.'

So Krieger had prioritised Victor as the bigger payday, he realised, only going after Banik after the unsuccessful attempt on the train to St Petersburg.

He said, 'Why are you telling me this?'

'Because you have a problem,' she said, 'a serious one, but I managed to see it coming. One of Krieger's aliases showed up in Belgrade yesterday.'

'Great,' Victor said. 'He knows about my current contract then.'

'I'm afraid it appears that way.'

'You said Banik was killed on his driveway, not interrogated. How could he have passed on my whereabouts to Krieger?'

'He didn't,' Monique explained. 'Fletcher did. Banik was telling you the truth after all. He may have sent you after Fletcher for his own benefit, but otherwise he was playing straight with you.'

I also see you as a friend, Banik had said to Victor.

She said, 'Thankfully there's a simple solution to this mess.' She paused. 'You can leave Belgrade and never come back. Krieger knows where you are, not where you are going to be.'

'What about the contract? What about Rados?'

'Forget Rados. Forget the job. It's over. In light of this Krieger situation, London has pulled the plug. They've already lost two case officers to infighting and they don't want any more blood spilled, even if it's a freelancer's.'

He sat in silence.

'You can stand down with immediate effect,' she continued. 'Get the next flight out. I can provide security if you want it, or we'll happily let you fly alone.'

He thought of the watcher at the bar. There for his protection, as well as Monique's.

'London appreciates its case of cold feet has put you out and apologises profusely, ditto for Fletcher's actions putting your life at risk. In recompense, you are to be paid in full for the Rados contract, so you won't be out of pocket due to events beyond your control. They hope if you are aggrieved by all this the payment will satisfy you.'

He read her tone and imagined her pleading with her superiors to make sure he was paid because she remembered what he had said in the back of the Lada.

'Are you okay?' she asked. 'You haven't said anything in a long time.'

He nodded, thinking how close he had come to killing Rados in the forest and how everything he had done so far had been for nothing.

I'll get you out of here. You have my word.

'I appreciate the offer of protection,' Victor said, 'but I'll leave alone and to my own timeframe.'

She nodded. 'I thought you would say that, but you can

change your mind at any time. All you have to do is let me know.'

'The first time I met you,' Victor said, 'you told me you would do anything to help me, provide any assistance I needed.'

'I did.'

'Does that still stand, given the job is over?'

She took a moment to think about the answer. 'While you're still in Belgrade, that offer stands. Once you've left, my ability to assist will be severely limited.'

'But while I'm here I'm still considered here on SIS's behalf?'

She nodded. 'That's right.'

'Then there are two things I need: transportation out of the city, and then out of the country – but not for me, for a civilian, a woman. Armenian national, and here without documentation. You're going to take her somewhere secure and then send her abroad, to the UK if that suits, or any-where in the EU where you can guarantee her safety.'

'Why? Who is she?'

He said, 'The second thing is for you not to ask ques-tions. From the moment I leave here you need to be ready for my call and be ready to move out at a moment's notice. Bring back-up. Put together an extraction team. Bring your guy standing at the bar, and whoever else you have who can help. Make sure you're all armed and do not under any circumstances let the Belgrade police catch wind of your actions. I can't tell you any more than that because I don't yet know any more. But I need you on side and ready.'

'Okay,' she said. 'I think I can do what you're asking

me to, but I don't understand why. I only say that because it will help your cause if you tell me what's going on. I'm going to need authorisation for this.'

'London doesn't want me to feel aggrieved for Fletcher putting me in danger, right?'

She nodded. 'That's correct. We really are very sorry.'

Victor stood. 'This is the price of my forgiveness.'

FIFTY-EIGHT

Krieger liked Belgrade. In some ways it was as inconsequential as any other city – the young played with their
phones; couples smiled and chatted over coffee; old men
sat alone with their beers – but he liked the cold and the
architecture, and more than either he liked the wind. The
wind in Belgrade whistled more than blew; it slipped and
slithered between the buildings; a high pitch along the
narrow avenues and alleyways, lower down the boulevards
and through the parks. It was a mournful sound, tinged
with introspection and regret.

Had he been an emotional man he might have wept.

He was a little behind his target, he knew. The information, detailed and thorough, had been of considerable
use, but Krieger was not going to rush a second time. He
had learned that lesson on the train to St Petersburg. No
one was infallible, but mistakes had to be acknowledged
and absorbed with a conscious self-examination if they

were to become useful experience and not remain as failure.

Life was but one lesson after another. Test followed by test. Krieger enjoyed climbing the learning curve.

Did his target?

He was a tough man to corner, and tougher still to execute. Krieger shook his head. He was wrong to downplay. This target was not *tough*. Tough was landing a long-range headshot in high wind. Krieger had bled. He reprimanded himself. It was foolish to underestimate. He had learned from that first mistake. He would not repeat it.

Krieger did not know exactly where to find his target, but he did not need to. As on the train to St Petersburg, all Krieger had to do was find his target's target. Krieger had the same dossier to work from, and he had come to inarguable conclusions about his target's preparations.

Krieger had spent his time in the city learning about Milan Rados as he imagined his target had done beforehand. Krieger spoke to drug dealers and prostitutes, the homeless and corrupt cops, each time adding to his store of knowledge, drawing closer.

He found that many knew Rados' name, but few had come in contact with him beyond brushes with those associated with his chief lieutenant, Zoca. Krieger investigated the warehouse at the docks and the scrap yard near the river. He read about reports of gunfire in the vicinity of the latter, and could almost smell his target's scent, still fresh on the air. Krieger was near.

The most useful piece of information Krieger acquired came from a kind old man with one leg he met inside a veterans' club in a bad part of town. A club near to a location where three local addicts had been hospitalised in a savage beating rumoured to have been the work of a single man. Krieger discovered from the drunk amputee inside the club that Rados was generous to those who had served in Serbia's military. He helped them, sometimes with food or money, and sometimes in other, no less essential, ways.

Krieger pushed open a door, acting shy with lowered eyes and hunched shoulders, and approached the woman behind the counter who asked him how she could be of help. His response made it seem he was unsure, nervous.

But he wanted everything that could be provided. Money was no object. He fumbled open a wallet full of crisp banknotes.

This led him upstairs to pink-painted corridors and red doors. A youth with acne directed him to a couch. While Krieger waited, a man with white hair and a black eye entered. The man gave him a look of suspicion.

'It's my first time,' Krieger said with his most innocent of smiles.

FIFTY-NINE

Victor headed straight for the massage parlour. He didn't
conduct counter surveillance because time was short. If he
was still being followed by the cops then they already knew
where he would likely be heading. If the German assassin –
Krieger – had somehow tracked him down, then getting the
Armenian woman and getting out of Belgrade as fast as
possible was the priority.

He parked nearby, and walked fast along the back
alley to the courtyard outside the parlour's rear entrance,
trusting to speed instead of stealth in case there was a rifle
aimed at him from an overlooking window.

It was his own fault they cornered him. He was too
focused on his objective and the threat posed by Krieger to
notice their intentions until it was too late.

They were waiting for him outside the massage parlour – Zoca and four of his guys – seemingly hanging
around outside the rear entrance, smoking and passing the

time. Zoca had a casual air about him, but his men were different. They were hyped up. They couldn't hide their anticipation.

Victor was amongst them before he realised.

Zoca said, 'In a hurry to see your wife?'

'What's this about?' Victor asked.

Zoca shrugged. 'What do you mean? We're just standing here.'

'Waiting for me,' Victor finished.

'What makes you think you're so special? Who the hell are you anyway?'

'I'm the only reason you didn't die in the forest.'

Hate dripped from Zoca's smile as he said, 'You have my eternal thanks. Let me buy you a beer.'

'I'll pass.'

'I insist,' Zoca said. 'Let's be friends. You can see your lady afterwards. She will wait for you. It's not like she's going anywhere, is it?'

'I have too many friends as it is. And I know how you treat your friends.'

Zoca's smile faded. 'You've told him, haven't you?'

'About the deal you had with the Slovakians? No. As I said before, he wouldn't take my word over yours. We both know that.'

'And thanks to your actions in the woods he will never know, will he? I really should buy you two beers.'

'I'm not thirsty.'

'Come on,' Zoca pleaded. 'You'll be guest of honour.'

'Then why don't I feel welcome?'

Zoca motioned with his chin. 'Please, let's go for a drive.'

'I prefer to walk.'

'You don't have a choice.'

Victor said, 'I thought we were dancing around that issue.'

'I'm bored of playing,' Zoca said. 'Get in the car or we'll shoot you right here.'

They showed their guns.

'Does Rados know about this?'

Zoca smiled. 'You think he'll save you? You're nothing to him. Do you know what you are? You're his new puppy. You're cute and adorable and make him smile, but you're a pet. You're an animal. He will grow bored of you soon enough.'

'That's a no then,' Victor said.

'He'll know,' Zoca replied. 'When the time is right, when you've told me who you really are, then he'll know. Then he'll want to know. Then he'll be ever so grateful to me.'

Zoca's guys moved closer. One in front withdrew a hand from under his long sports coat. He was holding the stock of a sawn-off shotgun. The others had handguns. Including Zoca, there were five armed men surrounding him. No way to kill them all without at least one gunman getting shots off. At this range, even amateurs wouldn't miss.

Victor had a fully loaded magazine in his pocket, but no gun. That was upstairs with the Armenian woman.

'Take him,' Zoca said.

Two of the four approached. Victor glanced at both, deciding to attack the one to his left, who was smaller and weaker; dropping him fast and stepping behind the man to the right, preventing the other two from having a clear shot. Then, as the larger man was disabled and turned into a human shield, he would seize his gun and take out the other two.

But he let the approaching two men grab his arms because as they neared they put away their weapons. His plan was no longer viable. He couldn't waste time drawing a weapon from someone else and get it into a firing position fast enough to catch the others by surprise.

He would have to wait for another opportunity.

Zoca said, 'Let's go.'

He gestured with the muzzle of his gun and the two holding Victor led him away. They held him with tight grips, one clasping his forearm, the second controlling him by the triceps.

Zoca and the other two walked behind, which was the worst position they could be from Victor's perspective. Had they walked in front he could gain a second or so before they reacted to the noise behind them and turned to respond. Behind, they could see all. But there was no tactical consideration to this.

There was no tactical consideration to anything they did. This was not a tactical course of action. Their excitement told Victor they planned to do more than just shoot him. Something more crowd-pleasing was on the cards. Which was a mistake. There wasn't much he could do against five weapons pointed at him, so any other situation would be a huge improvement on those odds.

He let them march him over to Zoca's Land Rover and

shove him on to the back seat. Two of Zoca's men joined him in the back, one on either side. Zoca drove with a third man in the passenger seat. The fourth man stayed at the massage parlour. He waved them goodbye with a mocking grin.

As the Land Rover turned out of the courtyard Victor glimpsed a silhouette at one of the parlour windows. A man.

'Where are you taking me?' he asked.

Zoca grinned, showing almost every yellow tooth. 'Where fun happens.'

'Why do I get the impression I won't be the one having fun?'

They drove to the scrap yard. Victor knew within a few minutes where they were heading. He sat in silence, feigning ignorance as well as passivity. Had they positioned him behind the driver he would have made a move, but with two strong guys boxing him in, anything he did would be immediately compromised.

He pictured sending elbows and sideways head-butts into the two in the back, but in the time it took to incapacitate the first, the second would be attacking. Without room to manoeuvre, Victor would inevitably become entangled. The Varangians were not professionals, but they were tough.

The Land Rover would screech to a stop and Zoca and the third Serb would become involved. By then maybe Victor would have choked out the remaining man in the back seat but he would be defenceless when Zoca opened fire.

He had to wait. The longer he did nothing in their presence, the less of a threat they would perceive him to be.

Then, when the time was right, he would kill them all.

'Don't be scared,' Zoca said as they arrived at the scrap yard. 'All I want to do is get to know the real you.'

'You will,' Victor assured.

SIXTY

She knew next-to-nothing about weapons, but she knew the gun was useless to her without bullets. Which was why he had not given them to her. He feared she wouldn't wait until the party. He feared she would turn it on her captors the first chance she had, get herself killed and ruin his chance to kill Rados.

He was right.

The desperate part of her wanted to try anyway, to point it at the arseholes keeping her here, to enjoy watching them cower from her while she marched out. The calculating part of her knew they wouldn't be fooled for long. Her best chance was to wait, to trust he would stick to his side of the deal and get her out of here once Rados was dead.

She didn't trust him though. She didn't trust anyone. Not any more.

There was no reason why a man like him, like her captors, would honour his word. Once he had the gun, once he had killed Rados, there was no need for him to help her. He would have no more use for her. He could make good his own escape and leave her behind.

She had an idea.

He needed the gun. She needed the bullets.

At the party, he had to retrieve the gun from her to do his job and kill Rados. She didn't have to give it to him.

Give me the gun, he would say.

No, she would say in return. *Give me the bullets and get me out of here, then you can have both to go kill Rados.*

The man at the window had his back to her. He was a man of few words. He hadn't even tried to touch her yet. He had left her alone with her thoughts.

'Are you okay?' she asked, because she knew how to appear caring and had learned that in doing so she would be treated better.

She had been doing her best to smile and be polite and attentive. *Don't cause any trouble*, he had told her. She only had to wait until the evening, until the party. A few hours, that was all. She could do that.

The man said, 'May I ask you a question, please?'

'Of course,' she replied, always glad to talk in preference to anything else.

'Who is the man with white hair?'

'His name is Zoca. He's in charge here. Like a manager, I suppose.'

'Thank you,' he said. 'That's what I thought.'

'Do you know who the man in the suit is? The outsider. He has dark hair and eyes. He's a bit taller than me. A bit slimmer.'

She tensed at the question. He sensed it, else saw it in her reflection on the windowpane. He turned. He had a kind face and greying hair. A German, she deduced, from his accent.

'You've met him then,' the German said.

Not a question. A statement. He knew. There seemed no reason to lie but at the same time she felt she should.

'Ah,' the German said, reading her expression. 'You've done more than meet him. Do you happen to know his name?'

She shook her head. 'I only know he works for the man who owns this place. Zoca's boss.'

The German seemed surprised, but also impressed. 'How very interesting. Unexpected, yet on reflection an entirely logical course of action. For how long has he worked for Rados?'

How did he know about Rados? Who was this German? Her unease grew by the second.

'Not long,' she said. 'A week, maybe.'

'But Zoca and he do not get along from what I witnessed.'

She shrugged. 'I wouldn't know anything about that. I only work here.'

They were instructed to call it work. Clients were put off by the truth, she had been told.

'I can see that,' the German said. 'But I also see that you are surprisingly well informed.'

She said nothing, afraid to confirm as much as she was to deny.

'Don't be scared,' the German said, soft and reassuring.

'I'm not going to cause you any trouble. I'm an old friend of the man in the suit.'

She didn't believe him, but she tried to hide that fact.

He saw, and corrected himself. 'Well, I say old friends, but perhaps it's more accurate to say we're business acquaintances. Colleagues, of sorts. It would be nice to catch up. Where would he be going with Zoca?'

'How would I know?'

'A better question is how do you know anything at all?'

She didn't answer.

'If it matters, I think Zoca is going to hurt your friend.'

Her eyes widened before she could stop them. She tried to compose herself, but her freedom – her life – was slipping away. The German's gaze drank in her fear and seemed satisfied by it.

'I don't care what your relationship with him is. I don't care what you've had to do to survive here, and no one will know anything about what you tell me. Perhaps I can even help you, if you help me in return.'

'What kind of help do you mean? What do you want with me?'

'I want information. Information that I already possess, but you can help expedite my processing of it.' He read her confusion, and added, 'You can save me some time.'

'How? What kind of information?'

He tilted his head to one side. 'You're a smart woman. I think you know exactly what I require.'

She did. 'What do I get in return?'

'That depends on the value of the information you provide,' the German answered. 'But if it helps me *catch up* with my acquaintance, then I will be generous in providing compensation.'

'How generous?'

The German held out his hand, palm upturned. 'Do you know what I'm holding here?'

She shook her head. 'There's nothing there.'

The German shook his head too. 'No, you're mistaken. In my hand is anything you desire. Look at how effortlessly I hold it. Look at how easy it is for you to take.'

She did look. 'You don't know what I want.'

'I know exactly what you want,' he said. 'You want to see the blue sky above your head. You want to buy yourself a cup of coffee.'

She fought, but couldn't stop her eyes moistening.

The German said, 'I think the man I'm after knows that too. I think he offered you what I'm offering, but he has not delivered. What is he waiting for? Did he really have to make you wait so long?'

She had a deal with the other man, but that deal rested on him killing Rados. That rested on him surviving Zoca. The German offered the same, but for information only. Her throat was still sore.

She placed her palm on top of the German's own.

'You've made the right choice,' he said. 'Once I've concluded my business we can go for that coffee.'

He laid his other hand on top of hers, like a bizarre handshake to seal her betrayal. Her stomach knotted, but she met the German's gaze without blinking.

'Now,' he continued. 'Rados owns a warehouse at the docks and a salvage yard, does he not?'

375

'I don't know anything about a warehouse. I swear I don't.'

'I believe you. But you know about the salvage yard?'

She nodded. 'I do. I've been there. It's a horrible place. When I was first brought here they put us in shipping containers overnight.'

'How awful for you,' he said. 'And when you were there, who was in charge?'

'Zoca was.'

The German smiled. 'That's precisely what I was hoping to hear.'

SIXTY-ONE

The Land Rover pulled to a stop outside the office cabin at the centre of the scrap yard, near to the three shipping containers. Zoca and the Varangian in the passenger seat climbed out first and drew their weapons. They weren't professionals, but they weren't stupid. They didn't know who Victor was, but they knew he was dangerous. The two either side of him in the back followed and did the same with their guns.

No one ordered him out so he sat there, unmoving.

'What are you waiting for?' Zoca asked.

'A pretty please, naturally.'

Zoca gestured with his pistol. 'This isn't my car, so I don't mind making a mess over the interior.'

Victor didn't move until Zoca drew back the hammer, then he shuffled out of the vehicle, his expression neutral but pleased to have caused frustration. Any emotional response affected rational thought, and with it Victor gained a small advantage. While Zoca was annoyed with Victor, he would forget to be scared of him.

'Belgrade might belong to Rados,' Zoca said, 'but this is my own kingdom.'

Victor glanced around at the mountains of scrap metal, dirty and rusted. 'It suits you.'

'Here you are nothing,' Zoca continued. 'Here, you are at my mercy.'

'You're not a fan of understatement, are you?'

Zoca's jaw flexed and he motioned to one of his men, who struck Victor in the abdomen with the butt of his rifle.

Victor dropped to his knees, coughing. He had seen it coming – had wanted it – and had been doubling over before the impact. It hurt, but there was no real damage, and the man who hit him wasn't about to tell Zoca he thought he hadn't done a good enough job even if he had noticed.

'Rados may value your tongue,' Zoca hissed, 'but I might have to remove it.'

Victor stayed on his knees in the cold mud until he was heaved standing again. He made himself a deadweight so the man who lifted him up had to work at it. Victor carried no excess, but he was still one hundred and eighty pounds of muscle and bone and the guy was red-faced and rubbing his lower back afterwards. He didn't complain, of course. He didn't want to be seen as weak.

But now he was a little weakened.

One unlocked the office cabin and pushed open the door. Zoca pointed at the opening with his gun. Victor didn't move.

'Get inside,' Zoca growled.

Victor took his time, climbing the short steps and entering through the doorway. The interior lights were off and the blinds were drawn. No one had gone inside before him because they had no idea who they were dealing with.

They filed in behind him, jostling for room because he had stopped near the door. He turned. Zoca closed the door and glared at him.

'Sit yourself down or I'll break your legs right now.'

Victor reached for an office chair, took the back in two hands, and swung it like a bat at the closest Varangian's head. There wasn't enough room for the five of them, let alone for the man to dodge the chair rushing at him.

It was cheap plastic, not wood or metal, but it did the job, striking the guy in the face and sending him reeling back into the others before he fell to the floor, dazed and bleeding. Just as there was no room to dodge, there was no room to aim long rifles – too many friendlies in the way, too much risk of hitting the wrong person.

One imitated Victor, using his AK like a club. Victor used the chair to parry the attack with enough force to knock the gun out of the man's hands.

Victor heard it clatter against a wall, out of sight, and then strike the floor. He didn't see where. Turning to look would only leave himself exposed.

He released the chair when the man grabbed at it, expecting to have to wrestle for control, and Victor took advantage of the man's surprise and inability to defend himself to throw punches and elbows, driving him back, overwhelmed and bleeding.

Another of Zoca's men attacked and Victor caught the looping punches on forearms and shoulders, feeling the heavy sting of each blow, but where the only effect was pain, not unconsciousness.

Fighting more than one at a time meant he didn't see the elbow that sent him stumbling backwards, hitting the cabin wall and window, rattling and flattening the aluminium venetian blinds. He had his guard up to protect against the following blows. None found their way through.

Frustrated, the Serb grabbed Victor's jacket to pull him closer, to grapple, but in doing so gave Victor a stationary target: the man's hand.

He grabbed it across the knuckle line, rotating clockwise to twist the man's wrist into a lock, with his arm straight out to break at the upturned elbow, which Victor did, slamming his free forearm down against the joint.

The *crack* was lost in the Serb's wail.

Victor released the arm and struck up with an open palm at the next man's face, catching him on the nose, and breaking it.

The man grunted, blood gushing from his nostrils, and stumbled forward against the window, tearing down the blinds in a clatter of plastic and aluminium. Glass smashed and clattered to the floor.

Bright daylight spilled into the dark cabin, shining into Zoca's eyes as he tried to line up a shot. He flinched and squinted, shooting but missing, bullet punching a neat hole in the wall.

Victor grabbed a shard of broken window glass and hurled it Zoca's way.

It shattered against Zoca's face. He screamed, dropping the gun to clutch at his wounds.

The one with the broken nose grabbed another shard and went to stab Victor, who took control of the attacking wrist and the man's collar and turned him on the spot, taking away his balance, and shoved him backwards against the wall and broken window. More glass smashed. This opponent was strong and determined and hung on to the shard despite the pressure Victor applied to his wrist, so Victor drove the man's fist through a jutting fragment of windowpane.

He howled as his hand was shredded. Victor dragged it downwards, smashing more glass and cutting and tearing the hand until it was too slippery with blood for the man to keep hold of the shard.

Victor drew him closer, put a head-butt into his already-broken nose and then, while the man was still dazed, grabbed him by the head and slammed his neck down on to the jagged shards of glass protruding from the window frame.

The one with the broken arm lay on the floor, writhing and moaning. Victor stamped on his throat to finish him off and faced Zoca and the remaining Varangian.

Zoca's face was slick with blood where the glass had struck him, but he could still see. He held a hunting knife with an ice-pick grip, blade protruding from the bottom of his fist. It wasn't Victor's preferred way of holding the weapon – it limited range and available attacks – but some knife fighters fought that way. They held the weapon low at hip to bring up in arcs that sought out arteries in the thighs, groin, neck and under the arms.

The Varangian on the right had no weapon and adopted a fighting stance – left foot forward, angled in ten degrees and hands up at head height. Those fists were not tight for punching, but loose to grab.

They didn't rush Victor like the others had. They weren't going to make that mistake.

Zoca was wounded but the cuts were superficial. Victor had seen his speed and ferocity, and knew he was dangerous. The other man looked like a competent fighter. Neither man displayed the signs of an adrenaline overload. They were cautious, but they weren't scared. They had known combat before, and were still here. But had they fought alongside one another before? If not, then Victor had an advantage. He had no one to get in his way.

No was the answer, because Zoca stepped forward first, moving between Victor and the other man. That was his first mistake. He had helped Victor that way. The second man could not engage him at the same time. His line of sight was blocked and he had a man-sized obstacle in the way.

You should have come at me from either side, Victor didn't say. You should have flanked me.

Zoca bounced forward, left arm out for protection as the right whipped up in the predicted arc, aiming for Victor's neck.

He dodged back a step, moving out of range, and the knife sliced through the air before his face. He made no move to catch the attacking wrist. Before he'd had no idea of Zoca's skill with a blade. Now Victor knew everything about him that he needed to know.

Zoca attacked again, this time to the groin, and, when Victor dodged, he pushed forward and brought the knife back in a backhanded slash at Victor's abdomen, looking to split him open in a horizontal line across the navel, spilling out a tangle of intestines.

Victor danced away, and, as the knife recoiled, he timed his move and leapt forward into the empty space with his wrists crossed, palms facing inward to protect his arteries, and hammered the crossed arms against Zoca's inner wrist as he tried to counter-attack.

The force of Victor's two arms beat Zoca's one, and he grimaced in pain – hard bone striking tendons protected only by a thin layer of soft flesh – then yelled as Victor adjusted his hands to grab wrist and triceps, twisting and pulling the arm tight against his chest for an arm bar. Victor wrenched downwards, seeking to snap it at the elbow, but Zoca was quick enough to drop low at the same time to ease the pressure.

Victor slammed him with a knee to the abdomen and tore the knife from his grip as he dropped.

The second attacker was already coming forward, and by the time he realised Victor now had the knife, it was too late.

Victor stabbed him in the chest, between the fourth and fifth ribs on the left side of the sternum.

The man stayed standing, but Victor released the knife and turned away from him because he would be dead in moments, as soon as the brain worked out there were several inches of steel piercing the heart.

Zoca had recovered enough from the knee in his guts

to begin to rise and face Victor, but seeing he was now the only one left, tried to flee. He tripped in the tangle of corpses covering the floor and fell.

The guy with the knife in his chest tumbled on top of Zoca before he could scramble to his feet.

Victor squatted next to where Zoca lay, now whimpering in terror because he was pinned in place. He was only brave when he was in control.

'Please,' Zoca wailed. 'I'll do anything.'

'I only need one thing from you,' Victor said as he reached towards Zoca's throat.

SIXTY-TWO

Victor took a moment to get his breath back, then pushed open the door to the office cabin and stepped outside into the cooling rain.

He had an instant's warning before the shot came because he saw mountains of scrap and the crane opposite the office cabin across the empty space – shapes he knew well enough to notice the irregular contour on top of the crane's cab; a man lying prone – Krieger.

Victor threw himself backwards through the doorway as the muzzle flashed.

It was only a hundred metres away, but it still took the bullet a tenth of a second to cover the distance and Victor's head was already out of its path.

The bullet punctured an office desk and went through the floor.

There was no snap because the round was subsonic, but the rifle's suppressor could not contain the escaping superheated gases to eliminate the telltale crack of a gunshot that arrived an instant later.

Victor scrambled further into the cabin, over the corpses, keeping as low as possible because the door was wide open and his enemy had a clear view inside from up on the crane.

Another shot. This one buried itself in Zoca. The corpse trembled. Blood misted.

Victor grabbed one of the AKs and returned fire from the floor, using the corpses as cover. He had no scope to help his aim, but he had automatic fire and his enemy had no cover.

He saw the sparks of rounds hitting the crane, and Krieger slid backwards until the crane cab's solid steel structure impeded line of sight. Victor could no longer see him, but could no longer be seen in return.

Victor jumped to his feet and pulled the body from where it hung from the window, dragging away most of the broken glass in the process, and dropped the AK through before squeezing out himself.

He dropped down into the mud outside the office cabin, grabbed the rifle, and sprinted across the open space.

Bullets raked the mud ahead of him, but he made it into the cover of an impenetrable mountain of scrap metal. He had the AK, but there had been no spare magazines to grab. He'd put four three-round bursts at the crane, so there were eighteen remaining.

He crouched low, mud caking his trousers, rain soaking his jacket, judging angles and lines of sight and coming to the conclusion his enemy wouldn't be able to see him from any perch on the crane. He would have to descend, else risk losing Victor altogether, who could use all the piles of metal to his advantage, staying in cover the whole time while he made his escape from the scrap yard.

If the assassin wanted to finish his job, he would have to engage Victor on the ground.

Krieger had come to the same conclusion, beginning his descent as soon as he realised his target would make it into cover. The crane was metal and slippery in the rain, but he was strong and sure of foot. He reached the bottom and removed the scope from his Armalite assault rifle. He preferred the iron sights for a close-range engagement.

He removed his coat too, not wanting to be restricted against so fast an opponent. What he had wanted was to execute his target with a 5.56 × 45 mm projectile to the brain, but the man's instincts were razor-sharp. He was moving by the time Krieger squeezed the rifle's trigger.

Like on the train, another not-quite-good-enough attempt. Krieger recognised an unfair hand when he was dealt one.

Instead, he would make his own luck.

Victor moved at a slow pace, staying near cover, only increasing his speed when he had to cross open ground. He wasn't one to rush for the exit and hope the assassin had failed to reach it in time to intercept. He couldn't move fast anyway, because the rain was turning the ground into a sodden mire that sucked and squelched underfoot. He had to tug his shoes free from its grasp with every step.

He blinked water from his eyes, breathing more often as the cold seeped into him and his body fought to stay warm. The air was icy and full of moisture. Clouds of steam ascended with every exhale. He pushed on towards the exit. He wasn't prepared to scale the fence that surrounded the scrap yard. If he tried to climb it at speed the noise of it rattling was sure to bring Krieger into range; if he climbed with an attempt at stealth he would only give his enemy even more time to come across him defenceless.

It was the main exit or nothing.

Krieger knew this too. He was approaching it as he pictured his target doing likewise. Krieger had begun from a closer position, and so would arrive first and could lie in wait to ambush the troublesome quarry. No wonder the bounty offered on his head was so high. Krieger could rationalise the meddlesome hand of the universe involving itself in the encounter on the train – robbing him of his rightful success as Zeus and Hades denied ancient heroes of victories they deserved – but to lose out twice seemed beyond malicious.

The rain was coming down hard and fast. It glowed and sparkled in the twilight. Krieger's hair and clothes were soaked in the relentless ice-cold barrage. Goose pimples rose across his skin. His breathing quickened and he shivered as his body fought to maintain its core temperature. The rain restricted visibility and the barrage of raindrops pelting the thousand tons of scrap metal around him drowned out other sounds.

Through the haze of rain and shadows he saw a shape

move. Krieger stayed low, stepping without need to lessen the noise of his footsteps because the rain did that for him. He stopped when he reached the edge of a scrap mound, his left shoulder pressed against a rusting air conditioning unit, and waited for the shape to reappear.

It did, and Krieger opened fire.

Victor was sprinting, staying clear of the open spaces between mounds of scrap metal. He ran as fast as the sucking mud let him, weaving left and right, trying to make himself a harder target as the rounds hissed and snapped through the air. Incoming shots pinged and thunked into scrap metal. The zigzagging increased the chances of a slip, but though he lost his footing more than once, he did not fall. Falling meant being stationary, however briefly. A stationary target was a dead one.

He threw himself behind the cover provided by the stacks of disused and dismantled firearms, rolling and sliding in the mud, coming to his feet fast and controlled, utilising the cover to return fire.

The AK barked in his hand, muzzle lifting with each expulsion of white-hot gas. Brass splashed into the mud around him as his gaze fought to keep track of his enemy through the rain.

The shooting stopped.

Victor maintained his position. He'd not been able to see where the bullets had struck. The cessation in incoming fire could have come from a kill shot or a scratch on the ear. Victor wasn't going to leave cover to find out.

A cry through the rain did nothing to convince him

either way. He continued to wait, peering along the AK's iron sights.

The target wasn't buying Krieger's play-acting. Not surprising, but it would have made things easier for the target to come to him instead of the other way around. Pretending had never been one of Krieger's strengths.

He rose to re-engage but grimaced.

Chance was on his target's side because a round had grazed Krieger's flank.

Krieger used a finger to taste his blood for the second time in memory.

Sudden shock and pain interrupted his balance and he had to steady himself on one knee. He stayed behind cover to check the wound. The skin over his left oblique was split and torn in a short horizontal line, but the muscle beneath was uninjured. Blood seeped from the wound.

There was no danger from the wound itself. At this rate blood loss would take hours to kill him, and the blood would clot long before then. He could ignore it for now. It wasn't bleeding enough to leave a trail for his target to follow.

It wasn't the first time this foe had wounded him and he knew it wouldn't be the last, so he bit through the pain and rose to fire.

The target was waiting for him to do just that and bullets pinged near his head. Krieger squeezed off a shot of his own and ducked low to load a fresh magazine.

A cluster of rounds clattered on nearby metal – a blind shot, wasting rounds, the target rolling the dice in the hopes of a miracle hit. This time he wasn't so lucky.

Krieger popped up to return fire, not waiting long enough to aim or to be aimed at in return before he dropped back down.

He achieved the effect he wanted as another volley of bullets passed by, the target fooled into thinking Krieger was going to engage. It was a fair trade of wasted rounds – his one for the shooter's burst of three or four.

Krieger, who was well prepared with backup magazines on his tactical harness, had not seen the target fleeing from the office cabin with any spares of his own.

Chance favoured the prepared mind.

Victor was low on ammunition. He couldn't hope to win a sustained gun battle with fewer than half a dozen rounds, even if he only needed one decent hit to end it. He had to move.

He risked leaving cover and hurried toward the exit. Two paths lay ahead, forking either side of a mound of washing machines and tumble-dryers, dishwashers and microwaves. Victor took the left path, keeping low, staying close to the scrap metal.

He rushed through the rain and mud, weaving left, then right, picturing the assassin behind him rising from cover and spotting him.

The first shot sounded earlier than he had anticipated – the German was fearless – but Victor kept moving, not seeking cover because he would only find himself pinned once more. Speed and distance were his defences. Rounds pinged and clanged behind him.

He struggled to stay on his feet, shoes sinking deeper

into the mud as the rain continued to soak into the ground.

The path branched into two again, and he selected the longer route, seeking the protection of the corner ahead, which would offer both cover and a firing position that overlooked the exit and the open space before it.

The target had given up the fight and fled, but so would Krieger if he had been so outmatched. He pursued, hurrying because his target was fleeing for his life. He let off shots when he could – he had ammo to burn – but he couldn't risk pausing to aim and further the target's lead. The paths through the scrap yard were too twisting; there was too much hard cover impeding line of sight.

He reloaded on the move, then rounded a mountain of piled cars, expecting to see him in the distance, making for the exit, but instead the target had stopped and turned and was waiting to shoot Krieger as he appeared.

A trap.

It didn't work, because Krieger slipped in the mud, moving too fast and with too much eagerness.

The target missed with his burst of automatic fire, and as Krieger fell down into the mud, his own weapon escaping his grasp, he prepared himself for death, but the shooting stopped and he saw the target was out of rounds because he was tossing the AK aside and sprinting straight at Krieger.

SIXTY-THREE

The distance was short, but covering it felt like an eternity. Victor fought the mud and the freezing rain as he watched Krieger recovering from the fall, climbing fast to his knees, then regaining his footing, and turning, whipping out a back-up handgun, small and compact –

– which Victor grabbed as it swung his way, catching it by the barrel in his left hand and wrenching it up in a sharp circle that twisted Krieger's hand back the wrong way.

The enormous pressure on his wrist joint forced Krieger to release the weapon, but rapid strikes to the abdomen and face caught Victor defenceless before he could turn it around to fire. A backhand blow sent the gun out of his grip.

He heard it splash into the mud.

Victor backed away to shake off the effects of the strikes, guard up and ready to block more. Krieger didn't follow. He welcomed the pause to strip away his tactical harness. He didn't want to give Victor any handholds.

They faced each other across a few metres of mud.

'We've been in this situation before,' Victor said.

Krieger nodded. 'I was thinking the same thing. History, as we are bearing witness, has a tendency to repeat itself.'

'And those who do not heed its lessons are doomed to repeat the same mistakes.'

'I know the saying.'

Victor said, 'So let's change that record.'

'This would be a lot less painful for both of us had you allowed those Serbs to kill you.'

'I will not go gentle into that good night.'

Krieger smiled, edging forward. 'I too know the value of persistence.'

Now in range, he threw himself at Victor, body-slamming him and sending them both over the bonnet of a rusting car.

They hit the mud at the same time, Victor underneath, but he used the slick ground to slip out from under Krieger before he could capitalise on his position. Both men were on their feet in seconds, Krieger attacking first with a jabbing punch that Victor was quick enough to catch on his left forearm.

It was a feint to distract him for a stomp kick that Victor didn't see coming, but the German missed his knee and struck his thigh, near the site of the knife wound, not yet healed. The jolting agony made him retreat a step.

Krieger charged again. Victor was ready for him, side-stepping to divert his attacker's momentum past him and into a wall of metal.

A smear of blood appeared on galvanised steel before the relentless rain washed it clean again.

The German spun around, a jagged gash across his scalp that stained his hair red. His eyes were a little glassy – dazed from the impact – but the pain in Victor's thigh kept him from rushing in to take advantage. He knew he had lost some speed.

'You don't give up, do you?' Victor said.

'It's not about giving up. It's about self-belief.'

'Am I really worth all this?'

Krieger touched his head wound. 'This is nothing. *This* is a workout.'

They approached one another, circling, attacking with more caution, more attentive of defence and not over-exposing themselves. Victor was shivering in the downpour despite the adrenaline surging through him. Krieger's skin had paled almost to white. Both men sent clouds of moisture skyward with every heavy breath.

Victor said, 'We don't have to do this.'

'It's what we're paid for.'

'You'll only get paid if you kill me,' Victor said. 'I get nothing for going through this.'

Krieger said, 'This is the price you must pay for getting paid all those times before. This is the inevitable conclusion to the life you have led. It was always going to end like this.'

'I've known that for a long time,' he admitted. 'And you must know it's the same for you.'

Krieger's chin lowered in a small nod of agreement. 'We are paid in gold, but we pay it back in blood.'

'Doesn't sound like such a good deal when you put it like that, does it?'

'Alas, we don't get to renegotiate our terms once we've signed our lives away.'

He heard Abigail's voice in his head: *We can always negotiate.*

Krieger gestured for Victor to come at him, so Victor grabbed a rock from the mud and hurled it at Krieger, which was dodged easily enough, but Victor used the moment of distraction to attack with a storm of strikes – throwing punches at Krieger's body; elbows at his head.

One slipped through the German's guard.

Blood fell to the ground with the rain, but Krieger was as tough as he was strong and threw his arms around Victor's hips, forcing him back and tipping him backwards.

He stumbled, feet working fast to keep from falling, but he had no purchase and Krieger roared, determined and powerful, taking Victor off his feet.

The ground was sodden mud, absorbing the impact and taking away the brunt of its energy that would have stunned him otherwise. Victor wrapped his legs around Krieger's waist and began working the man's right arm into an elbow bar.

Krieger was skilled enough to slip out of it and tried to stand, but Victor's legs were so tight around him that he had to lift their combined weight.

His face reddened from the exertion, the mud robbing any hope of secure footing. Victor exploited that by grabbing Krieger at the back of the neck and wrenching downwards, pulling him off balance. Again Victor's back hit the mud, but the momentum carried Krieger over his head.

The German flipped over, and he too landed on his back in the mud.

His mistake was moving on to his front to push himself upright, giving his opponent his back, because Victor was already rising and was standing over Krieger before he could too.

With both hands, Victor pushed Krieger's head down, using all the muscles of his back and shoulders to force the German's face deep into the mud.

Krieger tried to force himself upwards. He was stronger than Victor, but his knees were trapped beneath him and his head was too far away from his hips to maximise that strength. Victor fought him with his superior position, his own strength keeping his enemy's nose and mouth in the mud, denying him air and making him weaker with every passing second.

He felt the German's strength fading – then fading too fast when he stopped resisting with one arm. Krieger's face sank deeper into the mud and Victor had to catch himself not to lose his balance with the sudden loss of resistance. He glanced left and right at the ground for anything Krieger could be reaching for as he had with the knife on the train, but there was nothing.

He maintained his position, all his energy focused on pushing downwards and suffocating his enemy, only realising what Krieger was doing when he felt fingers on his thigh.

Krieger's thumb found where the knife had pierced

Victor, pressed against it, and then when the wound burst open from the pressure, pushed inside Victor's flesh.

He roared, even stronger waves of agony crashing through him than when the knife had first stabbed him.

Instinct made him grab Krieger's exposed hand and wrench it clear, breaking the wrist before he threw himself back, overcome by pain.

He lost his footing as he swayed against the dizziness and approaching unconsciousness.

Victor fell, blackness encroaching on the periphery of his vision. Passing out meant an end to the pain, to sweet bliss, but he would never awake again. He fought it away.

Through his hazy vision he saw Krieger stand, but he didn't come after Victor. Instead, he stumbled for where his Armalite lay in the mud.

Victor headed for the pistol.

They reached the weapons at the same time, and turned to face each other.

SIXTY-FOUR

Dark rain clouds blocked out the last of the sun. The gloom was enough for Victor to see Krieger's eyes, half-closed but unblinking. The German was a wreck, injured and bloody, soaked with rain and sweat and filthy with mud. His greying hair was flattened against his skull. His stubble was caked with filth. His clothes were soaked, stained and torn. Only his eyes were untouched. They had the same relentless intensity Victor had seen on the train, when Victor had Krieger pinned beneath him – about to die before stabbing Victor with a blunt knife. When faced with certain death the German had found a way to survive.

He had done so again a moment ago. The pain made Victor want to vomit.

The German held the rifle one-handed, because his left arm was useless and hung down by his side, fist coated in bright blood that dripped in a steady rhythm to the ground because the broken wrist bone had pierced through his skin. The relentless rain washed the mud from his face, leaving it streaked and dark. His chest rose and fell with heavy breaths. The gun-holding hand was steady, though, and the arm extended to support it was strong and unwavering.

His expression was neutral – no anger; fighting back the pain – but his eyes were calculating.

Krieger said, 'You should know the Armenian woman helped me find you.'

'Good for her,' Victor said back. 'She's a survivor. She took the better deal.'

'I'm glad you see it that way, but whatever your arrangement you shouldn't have made her wait so long. That was unnecessary. That was cruel.'

'Maybe,' Victor said. 'But I'm going to get her out of there as soon as I leave here.'

'*If,*' Krieger corrected. 'You haven't squeezed that trigger yet for a reason.'

'What reason would that be?'

Victor kept his own weapon stable, muzzle aimed for centre mass because even at this short range the small-barrelled gun he was holding would group at about two inches. Like Krieger, he was fatigued and hurt. He couldn't rely on his aim being perfect. If Victor went for a head shot, a two-inch displacement plus his own inaccuracy was as likely to send a round straight past Krieger's ear as hit its mark.

Victor said, 'And you haven't fired because you can't hope to shoot a rifle accurately with one hand.'

The German nodded. 'Each of us needs a perfect shot

to brain or spine in order to ensure the other man will not return fire.'

Victor nodded too. His weapon weighed less than two pounds even with a full magazine. Krieger's weapon was far heavier. Victor noticed it was starting to tremble. Ever so slightly, but it was there. Krieger had only one hand to hold more than three times the weight Victor held with two.

'I know statistics,' the German said. 'Two out of three gunshot victims survive.'

'Exactly,' Victor said.

'But perhaps most shooters are scared or else are not very able with their weapon. I, however, am an excellent shot.'

'So am I.'

Krieger said, 'I'm not scared.'

Victor said, 'Neither am I.'

'You're injured,' the German said.

'So are you,' Victor said back.

They were silent for a moment.

'Yes, we're both skilled marksmen, both tired and hurt,' Krieger said. 'We're a little out of point-blank range. It's getting darker by the second. The chances of scoring a one-shot drop are negligible. In all likelihood, once one of us begins shooting we will kill each other.'

Victor watched the trembling gun in his enemy's hand. 'Like you said a moment ago: we both understand how this works. But we don't have to do this. There's another way.'

'What do you propose?' Krieger said, echoing what he had said on the train to St Petersburg.

'Easy,' Victor replied. 'We lower our guns.'

Krieger said, 'Then what?'

'Then we walk away, but for good this time. We both leave Belgrade tonight. You don't try and complete the contract again and I won't come after you to eliminate the threat. I think we both know by now that these encounters are bad for our health.'

Krieger shrugged and smirked. He couldn't argue with that.

Victor said, 'I want to live. I'm sure you do too. This is just a job, after all. It's not worth dying for, is it? I have nothing to gain by killing you and everything to lose by trying to. You're in a better position than me. You actually have something to gain, but whatever price is on my head is not worth rolling the dice for – not when it could cost you your life.'

Krieger's gun was trembling more now, but even Victor's arms were feeling the strain of maintaining his aim while he fought the constant pain in his thigh.

The German nodded. 'You negotiate well, but there is no need to convince me. I told myself after our first tryst on the train that I would try again, but only once more. I learn my lessons. I know when to quit. Like you said: this is only a job. We are both professionals. It is only amateurs that are willing to die in pursuit of a paycheque. But more than professionals we are gentlemen, as we showed in Russia. What do they say? Work to live, not live to work. This is business. This is not personal. We are killers, but that's not all we are. We can show the other some humanity, can't we?'

'Yes,' Victor said, 'we can.'

Victor lowered his weapon, inch by inch, slow and deliberate – gaze focused not on Krieger's eyes or the gun, but the German's index finger wrapped around the trigger – until it was down by his thigh and pointed at the cold mud.

Krieger maintained his trembling aim, grimacing as his pain worsened. 'Do you believe in fate?'

Victor shook his head. 'We make our own fate.'

'I disagree. I think our lives are mapped out for us. They are too complex, too perfect to be an accident of randomness. They have an inescapable narrative – a beginning, middle and end – unnecessary except by design. Birth, life and death, neatly separated and sequenced. Authored, if you will, by the universe's own hand. We are gifted existence in three acts, but we can only ever understand our middle third. We cannot control our birth, yet though we have no power over this first act of ours we believe we can manipulate our second act, our life, to control our death. We cannot choose either, and it is right that we cannot. We think we are the lightning or the thunder, but we're merely raindrops in a storm. We forget that we are ordained a time to live and a time to die. They are chosen for us, only when that time is right.' The German paused. 'Now, for you and I, it is not our time to die.'

He maintained his aim for a moment more, but only because that moment meant something – the surprise humanity found between mortal enemies who had minutes before been trying to kill the other.

He lowered the Armalite to his side, as Victor had with the pistol, but then Krieger dropped it by his feet as a sign of faith, of commonality. He smiled despite his pain – no longer enemy to enemy, or even professional to professional, but brother to brother.

Victor shot him twice in the chest.

He snapped his hand up, firing once on the move before his arm had risen and again a split-second later when it was at full extension. *Bam. Bam.*

He didn't attempt the headshot for the reasons they had discussed. The first bullet hit Krieger in the sternum, the second striking a few inches higher and to the left. Neither struck the spine and severed the spinal cord. Had the gun still been in Krieger's hand he could have shot in return. But he had no gun.

The German's face contorted in both pain and surprise. He staggered backwards a step, but remained standing, somehow, through some last defiant force of will, forged in outrage, tempered by betrayal.

'You were half right,' Victor agreed, walking forward.

He shot Krieger a third time – a well-aimed shot to the head, and the German's corpse fell face-down into the mud.

SIXTY-FIVE

She was a survivor, the man in the suit had said. She would do anything to survive. That's what she had done. He was helping her so he could kill Rados, no more. She had done what she had to, telling the German about the scrap yard. The German hadn't hurt her, hadn't threatened her, so why did she feel guilt?

She knew. They'd had a deal and she had broken it. A moment of weakness, maybe, or was it strength? Because now there were two people who had said they would help her. She didn't know what would happen at the scrap yard – she didn't want to know – but it didn't matter who returned to get her out of this hell.

No one cared about her, so she cared about no one in return.

She had to prepare for either eventuality, so she kept looking at the gun. It was futuristic to her eye, lighter than she had believed, and no use to her.

A part of her regretted what she had done, but she had no choice. She couldn't rely on anyone. He had made it clear he was only helping her to help himself in return. She owed him nothing.

A polite knock at the door interrupted her thoughts.

She barely had time to hide the gun under her bed before the politician, Dilas, entered, smiling because he was in a happy mood. She returned the smile because that's what she had learned to do. He always seemed pleased to see her, always acted friendly, but he was the same as all the others and she hated him as much as anyone could hate.

'How are you?' he asked, and the imitation of caring made her hate him even more.

'I'm sorry,' she said, 'but I need to get ready for the party.'

'All for the Hungarian's benefit. I wonder why that is.'

She shrugged. 'I don't know. He likes me, I guess.'

'And why would he like you?'

She didn't know how to answer. Her indecision seemed to displease him.

He sat on the bed. 'What do you do for him that you don't do for me?'

'Nothing,' she was quick to answer.

He nodded as if he accepted this, but his tapping fingers revealed his displeasure. 'He's taller than me. And stronger. Is that it? Is that why?'

She sat next to him and rested a hand on his thigh. She despised touching him, but she knew she needed to. She could see that his ego was fragile, but his anger was strong. A volcano was just a hill until it erupted.

'Rados will kill him,' Dilas said.

She stiffened and he felt it. Liked it.

'Rados doesn't trust him. He's curious about him, that's all. He wants to know who he really is and what he really wants. Has he told you anything about himself?'

'No,' she said, 'he doesn't tell me anything.'

Dilas regarded her, eyes searching hers for any hint of untruth. It took every iota of will not to blink. At last, he looked away and she could succumb.

'If you had a choice,' Dilas began, 'would you rather go to the party as his date or mine?'

'I don't have a choice.'

'Of course you do,' he insisted, ignorant or oblivious to her true situation or unable to escape his own fantasy.

She didn't want to answer. If she said Dilas then she was afraid he would use his influence with Rados to make it happen. Then, she might never get out of here. But if she didn't give him the answer he wanted she was afraid of what he might do now.

'You,' she had to say.

'I don't believe you. You're telling me what I want to hear.'

He seemed more sad than angry. Despite herself, she felt sympathy for him because he felt worthless, and that's how she felt.

'Don't feel sorry for me,' he said, seeing her expression. The volume of his voice rose, startling her. 'Don't you dare.'

'Okay,' she said.

He stood and approached the window. He yanked

back a curtain and put his forehead to the pane. His fists bunched at his sides. His breath misted on the glass.

'I missed you when you left before,' he began, almost tender, but with something in his voice. 'I'm glad you came back to me.'

She stood too. 'I need to finish getting ready for the party.'

He sighed, eyes closed, and nodded. 'Okay, get your things together.'

'We're going now? I thought it wasn't until later.'

'You can get ready there. It'll be beneficial to be early. I can show you around the estate. It's very beautiful.'

He stood now, back to the window, waiting. Watching.

The gun was under the bed, wedged between mattress and wooden slat. There was no way to retrieve it with him standing there. She needed it. If the man in the suit was the one to return from the scrap yard, she had to have it for him to help her escape. Assuming he honoured his word.

She thought fast and walked towards the door.

Dilas said, 'Didn't you hear me? We're going now, so grab your things.'

'I heard you. I need my hairbrush from the bathroom. Unless you want me to look a mess.'

'I'll fetch it. You get your things together.'

She shrugged. 'If you want.'

She waited until Dilas had gone and padded to the door to listen, to make sure his footsteps were growing quieter, then retrieved the gun from under the bed. She wrapped it in a pair of tights and packed it in her bag.

When Dilas returned, he said, 'There's no hairbrush in the bathroom.'

'It was here after all.' She held up an overnight bag. 'All set.'

He sighed as though it was all a huge inconvenience for him, and gestured for her to go ahead. She did, clutching the bag in a tight grip, knowing that if anyone looked inside they would find the gun without any trouble and she would be dead soon afterwards.

She was the only woman from the massage parlour going to the party. She was led to a vehicle parked outside and told to get into the passenger seat.

'Hand me your bag,' Dilas said.

She hesitated, afraid; caught between the instinct to hang on to it for dear life and the knowledge that to do so would only draw suspicion. Her heart pounding, she handed it over and Dilas slung it in the boot.

'Put your seat belt on,' he told her.

She did as instructed, playing the part of the passive prisoner and not someone determined to escape, whatever it took, whatever the cost.

SIXTY-SIX

Victor took Zoca's Land Rover back to his apartment, where he grabbed his go-bag from the basement. Back in the vehicle, he bound his reopened thigh wound with the first aid kit, cleaned himself as much as he could, and changed his clothes. Within fifteen minutes he was almost presentable enough to move out.

He would have liked to have questioned Krieger, to learn more about Phoenix and the contract on his head, but the German had been too dangerous to keep alive any longer than necessary. Krieger had paid the price for not removing the threat posed by Victor when he had the chance. Now, Victor had only one thing left to do in Belgrade.

Zoca wasn't at the massage parlour because he was dead at the scrap yard, along with several of his men, but the awkward young guy with the cystic acne was upstairs, holding the fort alone. He shot to his feet when he saw Victor. He hadn't expected to see him again.

'Stand there,' Victor said, 'and don't even breathe until I'm back.'

The kid said nothing in return.

Victor left him and headed into the pink-painted corridor. He worked the catch and opened the door, saying, 'Time to go.'

She wasn't there.

When Victor returned, the young guy's lips were locked and his face was almost purple. He literally hadn't been breathing.

'Where is she?'

He released a lungful of carbon dioxide and gasped and spluttered. Victor strode towards him.

'The party,' the young guy said, stumbling backwards as fast as Victor was approaching. 'She's already... left.'

'Okay,' Victor said with a nod. 'Relax.'

The kid's face was slick with sweat.

'Who do you work for?' Victor asked. 'Zoca or Rados?'

'Rados, of course.'

'Then take a seat.'

The young guy couldn't fall on to the sofa fast enough.

'This party,' Victor began, 'tell me everything you know about it.'

Rados' house was practically a castle. It stood in a huge estate, surrounded by woodland, accessible via a private road almost a mile long. Perfectly maintained lawns and flower gardens bright with winter flowers and illuminated by ground lights flanked the driveway. More ground lights lit up the neoclassical façade and glowed off the polished bodywork of limousines and sports cars parked out front. There were no Range Rovers in sight. No Varangians in evidence, apart from two heavies standing outside in tuxedos.

They were young but had the hard faces of ex-military men. Private security, presentable and professional.

One held out a palm as Victor approached. 'Name?'

'The Hungarian,' Victor said. 'Bartha.'

The palm lowered and he nodded in recognition. The other stepped forward to pat Victor down. He raised his arms. The man was checking for guns, so didn't frisk along Victor's lower arms. He didn't find the Five-seveN's magazine taped under his left wrist nor the suppressor taped under the right.

'Clear,' the man said.

The other one said, 'Have a pleasant evening, sir.'

'That's what I came here for.'

Inside, Rados' house was as impressive as it appeared on the outside. The entrance hall was huge and grand, with marble floor and statues. A chandelier the size of a small car glimmered from a ceiling decorated with elaborate frescoes.

Soft piano music played and Victor headed towards its sound until he entered a music room where eight men in fine suits were entertained by young women who moved with the grace of catwalk models. They wore designer dresses and were groomed to sultry perfection. Each one was as beautiful as she was elegant. The Armenian woman was not among them.

He recognised none of the women, but the young politician, Dilas, was there and waved him over.

'You're rather under-dressed,' Dilas said, looking him over.

'It's been a long day.'

'Well, this is the perfect place to relax and unwind.'

Victor nodded. 'Where's Zoca and the rest of the Varangians?'

Dilas laughed. 'Are you serious? You think Rados would bring his barbarians here? Oh, no. These gatherings are for friends. Belgrade's fat and finest only.'

So that meant it really was just the two private security guys. Armed and competent, but avoidable. 'Where's the man himself?'

Dilas sipped some champagne. 'Rados? He slipped away to pop some painkillers. He's putting a brave face on, but he's suffering. I can't imagine what being shot feels like.'

'It's not pleasant,' Victor assured.

'I think I'll go have a cigarette,' Dilas said. 'Would you like to join me?'

'Later,' Victor said. 'Excuse me, please.'

Dilas' gaze was on one of the women. 'No problem.'

Victor left the ballroom to find Rados.

SIXTY-SEVEN

Victor found Rados in the drawing room. As with the rest of the house it was a tasteful and elegant space, opulent but at the same time understated, with hardwood flooring and subtle wallpaper. The light fixtures were brass and turned to a low glow. Rados sat in an armchair by an open fire. He was swilling a glass of brandy around in his hand and putting his nose to the glass. A crystal decanter sat on a silver tray on top of a small table nearby. Next to the tray sat a fruit bowl of bright apples and a hardback book, resting open.

'The hero returns,' Rados said with a smile.

He stood to greet Victor. Like his guests, Rados was in evening wear. He wore a black suit, with a white shirt and white tie. His left arm was still in a sling, but this sling was black silk.

'Shame you couldn't make an effort,' he said.

'My apologies,' Victor said. 'I almost didn't make it at all.'

'Sounds like there's a story in that statement, but let's keep things on the right side of levity. Tales of woe are best reserved for when the embers are fading. Anyway, I'm glad you came. I wouldn't have taken it well had you been absent, but more than that it would have been a terrible shame to miss this, now you have earned your place in my inner circle. It is here that you will come to understand why it's so very good to be alive.'

Victor thought of the women he had seen and Rados' guests, all of whom would be powerful or influential, the wealthy or the well-connected. Rados had invited him to be part of this gathering and Victor had to continue to play the man Rados had invited. He didn't yet know where to find the Armenian woman or the best way to leave with her. He had to be patient. He had to stay in character.

'How's the shoulder?' he said.

Rados pointed to the brandy. 'I'm keeping it well medicated.'

'What are you reading?' Victor asked.

Rados set down his brandy to lift up the book. 'Marcus Aurelius.'

'Didn't you say you had no desire to rule the world?'

'If we can't learn about the perils of weakness from an emperor of Rome, who can we learn from?'

'Weakness?'

Rados said, 'Rome fell not because of barbarians at the gates but weakness within. They conquered and they enslaved and as a result they ruled. They should have gone on ruling, but instead they began to govern and in doing so they sowed the seeds of their own annihilation. The whole

415

world suffered as a result and human progress did worse than stand still, it regressed. It took Europe a thousand years to regain what had been forgotten. A whole millennia lost because Rome became ... nice. Where might we be now had the Romans built upon the walls of their fathers instead of tearing them down? It's a lesson for us all.'

'No empire has ever endured,' Victor said. 'People will not submit to foreign rulers. After a while, they fight back. Whether with war or diplomacy, they resist. They do not give up. History has taught us that, countless times. Rome would have fallen, weakness or not.'

'But not then,' Rados insisted. 'Civilisation would have sustained.'

'Maybe for a while longer.'

'Civilisation,' Rados said again, but this time as if testing the word to see how it tasted. Having rolled it around his mouth, he pulled a face, finding it unpleasant. 'Has there ever been such a thing? Will there ever be such a thing?'

'That sounds like a rhetorical question.'

Rados shook his head. 'No, it is a genuine question, because I really don't know the answer, and I would like to.'

'I'm not qualified to answer.'

'Of course you're not,' Rados agreed. 'No one is. But the asking is perhaps more important than the answer. The pursuit of knowledge can only be undertaken if one first understands that the goal is in fact unobtainable.'

'We continue to build the sandcastle our ancestors began, one grain at a time.'

Rados smiled, but frowned at the same time. 'I like

that. I really do. The acceptance that we cannot truly comprehend what we are accomplishing, but at the same time we can take comfort in knowing that, even if the bricks are beyond our understanding, we can begin to lay the mortar.'

Victor shrugged. 'I prefer the way I said it.'

Rados smiled. 'I don't find humour often, but your tightrope-walk of arrogance is quite amusing to witness.'

'I don't even have a net.'

Rados chuckled and returned to his seat. He gestured for Victor to take a chair near the fire.

He did so, maintaining the façade of friendliness while in his mind he rehearsed what he would do if the two security guards came rushing in. He felt Rados' watchful gaze, so said in distraction, 'I have a question to ask, if I may.'

'Sure.'

'Why did you hire me? The real reason, I mean. It wasn't because you needed additional manpower because of – what did you call it? – corporate restructuring. You had more than enough men for that deal with the Slovakians.'

'You don't miss a thing, do you? And you're right, of course. I didn't need a new recruit for that. But that served as a useful excuse to bring in an outsider. I didn't want my men questioning the decision, because what I really wanted was an outsider to do the kind of job I couldn't ask one of my own to do.'

'Which is?'

'Killing Zoca. He's always been a liability, and he had finally managed to hang himself on the rope of my patience, even before he betrayed me to those Slovakians.' He paused, 'I can see you had already worked that out for yourself.'

'I had no proof.'

'It doesn't matter,' Rados said. 'It's not your job to keep my men in check. Zoca is a relic from another era. This business, like any other, must change with the times, and Zoca will never change. The ability to adapt is perhaps the most important any of us can possess. You, Mr Chameleon, know that better than most.'

'You said "at first".'

He nodded. 'Yes, at first. At first because I would have had you killed afterwards. But that was then. That was before you proved to me I wasn't mistaken. I wasn't wrong when we first met and I saw something in you I've never seen in another.'

'Which is?'

'Myself.'

'I'll take that as a compliment,' Victor said.

Rados said, 'It's the highest compliment I can pay.'

'What did you say about arrogance?'

Rados nodded and said, 'Touché,' before adding, 'so, I would be grateful if you could get rid of Zoca at your earliest convenience.'

'I killed him earlier,' Victor admitted. 'At the scrap yard, along with some of his men. I would say it was self-defence, but I didn't like him anyway.'

Rados' eyes widened, not believing Victor initially, but then he laughed when he saw it was no joke. 'That's hysterical. And it goes to show how right I was to hire you.

You have earned your place here tenfold. I'm sorry, I didn't offer you a drink. Would you join me?'

'Of course.'

Rados stood to pour a couple of brandies. It took him a minute, with the use of only one hand, but Victor didn't offer assistance – Rados didn't want any. He handed Victor a glass.

'What shall we drink to?'

Rados said, 'To shadows.'

'I don't understand.'

Rados smelled the brandy. 'A writer once said that you should face the sun so the shadows fall behind you. I disagree. Have the sun to your back. Face the shadows head on, so they can see you coming. Give them fair warning that you are not afraid, that you are the darkness blocking the light. Then watch them run away from you.'

They clinked glasses.

'To shadows,' Victor said.

They sipped in unison.

Rados was in close proximity, yet the ever-present Varangians were absent, and the only security guards were out of sight because Rados now trusted him. This was what Victor had been working towards. He was alone with him, at last. He could kill the man at his leisure – a choke or neck break – and stroll out of the building unopposed. Rados only had the use of one arm. It would be simple. Even easy.

Except Victor wasn't going to kill him.

SIXTY-EIGHT

There were two reasons, each as important as the other. The first was a practical consideration. Victor had made a deal with the Armenian woman and he was going to stick to it. He didn't yet know where she was in the building – or even if she was in the building – and finding her and improvising a means of escape while Rados' corpse lay waiting to be discovered was no plan.

The second was because, even if Victor knew where to find her, London had called off the contract. Rados was no longer a target. He was just a man, albeit as abhorrent an individual as Victor had ever encountered, but Victor was well aware he had no moral authority to judge anyone.

He killed who he was paid to and who he had to, and because Rados was neither of those he would live through this conversation.

'You're looking at me differently,' Rados said.

'You're looking at me differently too.'

'Something's changed between us and I'd like to know what it is.'

'Maybe we didn't really know each other before, and now we do.'

Rados thought about this. 'It could be that.'

'Or,' Victor said, 'maybe it's because we've made up our minds not to kill the other.'

Rados chuckled. 'Now *that* sounds far more likely. And as we have finally passed that momentous barrier we can be true friends and not simply friendly.'

'I've never had any true friends,' Victor said.

'Never?'

'Maybe one or two I thought of as such, but can you be friends with someone who doesn't really know you?'

Rados shook his head. 'That's exactly why we can be friends. And as a token of my friendship you may have first choice of any of the women. To keep, if you like.'

'To keep?'

Rados smiled. 'Yes, to keep, because not only are you my friend but you saved my life in those woods. Do you think I don't appreciate that? Do you think I don't reward such service?'

'That's not what I meant. What do you mean by saying I can keep one of the women?'

Rados said, 'I mean if there is a girl you like, you can have her all to yourself. You can have her for your exclusive use. You may sell her. You can take her away to live with you. Or even introduce her to your mother, if you wish.' He smiled.

Victor smiled too, thinking he didn't even need the

smuggled gun; he didn't even need to avoid the two security guards. There was no need for any violence. He could walk out the front door with her, not just unopposed but encouraged.

'I don't know what to say,' was all he could say.

'Words are meaningless,' Rados said. 'We both know that. Remember, it's what we do, not what we say, that defines us. Pick any girl here. She's yours.'

'That's incredibly kind,' Victor said. 'Thank you.'

Rados shook his head. 'I don't want your thanks. This is my gift to you. This is my thanks to you. This is who I am.'

Victor nodded his understanding. He said, 'The women here are all very beautiful, but maybe I wasn't clear before. I'm the kind of man who likes familiarity. I hope that doesn't offend you.'

Rados took an apple from the fruit bowl and opened his pocketknife to peel it. He could hold the apple in his left hand, but it pained him. There was something in his expression Victor couldn't read.

Rados said, 'I believe you're talking about the Armenian woman, Eva.'

Eva.

'Yes . . . ' Victor said. 'That's who I mean.'

Rados continued to peel the apple with small, awkward movements: 'Unfortunately, she couldn't be with us tonight. But, familiarity or not, I'm sure one of these heavenly creatures will help with that need of yours.'

'What do you mean she – Eva – can't be with us tonight?'

'I know you requested her, but I'm afraid I have to let

you down. I did try to have her here, of course, as per your wishes, and I did my best.' He paused, sighing. 'Look, we should have known she couldn't be relied on after leaving us before. But I didn't realise how unpredictable she could be.'

'What are you telling me?'

Rados said, 'My friend Mr Dilas has a heavy hand with women, even if he does not look the sort, and she reacted badly. There was an altercation.'

'Where is she now?'

Rados sighed. He placed the pocketknife and the apple down next to the decanter. 'What does it matter? She would not have been a good match for you even if she had behaved impeccably. Her bloom had faded. A shame, but it happens eventually. You can become familiar with another.'

'Where is she?' Victor said again, unable to control the tone of his voice.

Rados made a floating gesture with his hand. 'She has left us to pursue environmental concerns.'

'*Where?*'

'She is helping the forests stay so very green.'

Victor was as still as he had ever been.

'You can only tolerate so much bad behaviour,' Rados explained, 'before that bad behaviour is a reflection on yourself, and your tolerance becomes weakness. Which is in itself intolerable. I am no Marcus Aurelius, after all.'

Rados stood and opened a drawer of a cabinet that stood near to the fireplace. 'It's a funny thing. She had a gun on her.' He removed Victor's Five-seveN from the drawer. 'Quite the weapon, isn't it? Empty, thankfully. She waved it around before she was overpowered. She even tried to make out that you had given it to her. Had you not risked your own life to protect mine in the forest, I might have believed her, but people will say anything to save themselves, won't they? I'm sure you know that more than most. I can only assume she stole it from one of the clients. I've been trying to think who would have been so armed. It's something of a curiosity, no?'

He set the gun down next to the decanter of brandy.

Victor's gaze remained on the weapon. An image flashed in his mind of Eva pointing the gun in desperation, knowing it was empty, hoping the threat would be enough, but knowing it couldn't save her.

Rados regarded him. 'I'm sorry you've taken it badly. I didn't realise you were quite so fond of her. You'll forget her soon enough. Let's face it, she was nothing to you but someone to use.'

I'll make sure no one ever hurts you again.

Rados said, 'You look like you could use another drink.'

He took Victor's glass to pour him another, struggling as before.

Victor joined him at the decanter. 'We are the same, aren't we?'

Rados wasn't sure of his tone, but he nodded anyway. He placed his good hand on Victor's shoulder. 'That's why we get on so well.'

Victor nodded too, then grabbed Rados' pocketknife from the silver tray and stabbed him in the abdomen, driving the blade deep until only Victor's own hand prevented it thrusting any further.

The blade was short but razor sharp. It perforated the small intestine, and severed the abdominal aorta beyond. Victor twisted as he ripped the weapon free.

Rados sank to his knees, gasping; shock paralysing him as much as pain; grabbing at Victor's jacket with the single hand he could use in a vain effort to stay standing. Victor lowered himself too, until Rados' grip failed and he collapsed on to his back. In seconds his white shirt and tie were soaked red. A keening exhale escaped from his lips.

Victor knelt beside him. 'I didn't stab you in the heart, because I want you to know you're going to die. I want you to feel yourself dying.'

Rados' head lolled backwards. His skin was now as white as his shirt and tie had been. His eyes closed.

'No,' Victor said. 'Don't die yet. Open your eyes. Look at me. Look at me.'

Rados did, eyelids fluttering as death neared, but he was still conscious, still aware.

'Good,' Victor said. 'Now my face is the last thing you'll see in this world.'

Rados' eyes closed for the final time and Victor stood and backed away from the growing pool of blood. He took the Five-seveN from where Rados had left it, loaded the magazine torn free from one wrist, and screwed on the suppressor from the other.

He found Dilas outside, alone, enjoying a cigarette on the terrace while he gazed at the moonlit mountains in the distance. Dilas heard his footsteps on the paving stones and turned, smiling at first because he was enjoying the party and he welcomed the company, but then frowning because he saw Victor's expression as he emerged through the shadows.

Dilas said, 'Why do you look so serious?'

Victor shot him five times in the chest.

SIXTY-NINE

The bar was noisy with music and people trying to talk over it. It had a soft glow, flattering and atmospheric, but only because some of the light fixtures were not working. No one seemed to mind. The patrons were almost all men, hanging out in small groups or standing alone. The women were all accompanied. The only females not in couples were the barmaids, of which there were two. Both looked as though they had been on their feet far too long for far too little pay. Their faces brightened when there was a customer to serve, but Victor could see through their smiles even if those they served could not.

Today, the sun was shining and London had a rare air of winter brightness. Pedestrians walked slower and motorists didn't use their horns with the same frequency. People were friendlier too. There were fewer frowns and more smiles.

The establishment was somewhere between a bar and a pub. There was no technical difference that Victor knew of or cared to know, but his rule was to never order lunch in a bar nor ask for a cocktail in a pub. Anything more specific could be left for the purists to argue.

He was a regular drinker to keep his tolerance high. He needed to be able to handle alcohol in his line of work. A lone man drinking lemonade after lemonade in a bar attracted attention; one that sipped beer was part of the scenery.

He took his time moving from the entrance to the bar itself, giving himself plenty of opportunity to scan the scene and its occupants before he arrived. Lots of bars had mirrors behind them. Victor was never sure why sellers of alcohol believed the recipients wanted to see themselves inebriated. This establishment didn't have one. Maybe that made it a pub.

'Thank you for meeting me,' Monique said.

She was sitting in a loud corner, under a wall-mounted speaker so the music would ensure no one could overhear their conversation.

She said, 'I appreciate why you were hesitant after all we've put you through.'

He took a seat at a right angle from her so his back wasn't to the rest of the room. This time there were no watchers for either her protection or his own. She wore a well-cut business suit and thin-framed glasses. Together, they seemed another pair of corporate colleagues escaping the office.

She continued: 'When you didn't contact me that evening in Belgrade I thought you were dead, else had disappeared. I spent the whole night on standby with an extraction team waiting to hear from you.'

'That's why I'm granting you this courtesy.'

He managed to stop himself stating he always paid his debts.

'I'm sure it comes as no surprise to you to learn that Rados was murdered that night at one of his houses. Apparently there were several influential Serbs at his house at the time, but surprise surprise no one knows anything at all and the investigators are under enormous political pressure to bury the case as a burglary gone wrong. Which means said influential people won't have to answer difficult questions about what they were doing there. Which also means that no one is looking for an assassin in the pay of the British government.'

Victor said, 'What do you want?'

'London wants to thank you for a job well done. You may have disobeyed the directive to stand down for your own safety, but no one is complaining, not when you managed to complete the contract. In fact, given that the blame for Rados' death has been nicely diverted, your stock has risen even higher within our hallowed halls. We've been missing a man who can get things done.'

'Your thanks is unnecessary, but that's not the only reason you're here, is it?'

She nodded. 'There are two other reasons why I wanted to speak to you. The first is because London would like to retain your services on a more permanent basis. While we appreciate you have been put at risk by your association with Banik, we will continue to make every effort to watch out for you and provide intelligence on your enemies as well as a significant increase in your payment. If you accept, there is another job you would be perfect for. This time we know exactly where the target is. The groundwork has all been done. You simply have to, uh, execute. Can I tell them you'll consider it?'

He thought of his conversation with Leonard Fletcher on the train to St Petersburg.

'The answer is no.'

She didn't react. 'I told them you would say that, even if I hoped it could be different. I think we could be very useful to each other.'

Victor remained silent.

Monique said, 'London doesn't care why you went against orders, but I'd really like to know. Especially as several of Rados' men, including his chief lieutenant, were also murdered that same day. Along with an unidentified male of German descent. Obviously, I can guess why you had reason to kill the latter, but that doesn't explain why you went after Rados when you didn't need to, nor why you requested an extraction team.'

He glanced towards the door. 'I hope you have an umbrella in your bag. I think the weather is about to turn.'

'Okay,' she said. 'You're reluctant to reveal your motives – I would be too if I were you – but I'm sure you understand, I had to ask anyway.'

'You said two reasons.'

She said, 'We can call the second a parting gift. One that I hope will convince you to give me a call some day.'

'Doubtful, but knock yourself out.'

'I'm sure you can work it out from what I've said. Well, from what I've not said.'

He thought for a moment, then understood.

She explained.

When she had finished, he said, 'Thank you.'

It was rare he said those two words together, and rarer still with any degree of honesty.

Monique could tell. 'You can thank me by not forgetting who your friends are.'

She held out her card.

He took it.

SEVENTY

The ceiling was a chessboard of polystyrene tiles. They had been there for thirty years and looked their age. Once white and clean, they now had the appearance of a desert landscape, cracked and yellow. He had mistaken them as such, as he drifted in and out of consciousness during that first night when his heart stuttered and stumbled to keep going. But it had. A touch-and-go night had become a weekend of uncertainty that had become a morning of hope followed by an afternoon of relief. He had made it.

He had survived.

A miracle, he heard a doctor say when he was still only semi-conscious. He hadn't understood the precariousness of his situation at first. He hadn't even known what he was doing here. Memories had first come back in patches hazes, unformed and nonsensical. As his blood pressure had continued to rise to a normal range and his brain was supplied with a steady flow of oxygen, the jigsaw of sounds and sights had reconstructed and reformed and reordered.

And when he understood, when he knew, the pain came, and soon after the sedation because his screams and moans were frightening other patients and the wild movements were threatening to burst open his many stitches. More drugs had followed. Sweet, sweet sedation.

Now, he was awake and alert for the first time.

Life was cracked and yellowed because he could see nothing but the ceiling tiles because he couldn't move his head. It was in a brace, fixing his gaze forward, limiting his range of vision. He was too weak to sit up in bed so the ceiling tiles were all he had to look upon.

There had been no visitors yet because today was the first day he was fully awake and no longer under heavy sedation for his own safety. He had used the last couple of hours to think. He had to work out a story to explain why he had ended up in hospital. The thought of police officers, honest and true, interrogating him at his bedside made him feel faint. Bravery was not his forte.

Until then he had the sound of the TV for company. All day long it played dubbed US sitcoms – the same ones that had been playing since the Americans bombed Serbia.

He had the best care, at least. The nurses and doctors knew he was a man of no small importance. They knew he was an influential man – a connected man – who had to be well looked after. Maybe he wouldn't have made it through that first terrible night and the days that followed without that extra attention paid to him. It was a scary thought. Life, he thought, was but a flower: beautiful and delicate.

Dilas swallowed and his heart monitor showed a sudden spike in pulse and blood pressure. It was hard not to be terrified of the fallout, of having to explain himself; to justify his association with Rados and the man's criminal network. *Why exactly were you at the house of a wanted man?* But that was only his first reaction, because he remembered that night at the mansion clearly – the girls, the Hungarian killer, the gunshots, the moment of agony followed by nothing.

Rados was dead, Dilas had overheard. The organisation had been ruined by the Hungarian. It would be scattered. It would be fragmented.

Dilas had lived through it all. He was excited.

He heard his door open and in his blurry peripheral vision he glimpsed the shape of a nurse enter the room and hurry to the heart monitor. An alarm had been initiated because of his spiking pulse and blood pressure.

'Are you feeling okay?' he asked Dilas.

Dilas felt the nurse looking even if he couldn't see him in return, so he nodded in answer and breathed and his heart rate began to settle.

The nurse made adjustments to the monitor and said, 'Try and keep calm.'

'Okay. I'll try.'

He shifted on the bed and grimaced.

'Are you in pain?' the nurse asked.

Of course he was. Dilas nodded. 'A bit.'

'I'll give you something for that, if you like.'

'Thank you.'

The nurse detached the cannula in Dilas' arm from the

saline drip. 'No sharp needle scratch this way. You've had your fill of pain, I'm sure.'

Dilas nodded along because he couldn't be bothered with idle chit-chat. He only wanted some more drugs and some time to plot.

'What happened to me?' he asked. 'I can't remember anything.'

He was an exceptional liar, he knew. He tried to twist his head to look at the nurse, but the neck brace kept his vision on those annoying ceiling tiles.

'You were shot,' the nurse explained. 'You have five gunshot wounds to your chest. You are exceptionally fortunate to be alive.'

'I don't feel lucky at the moment. But how am I alive? Is it really a miracle?'

The nurse's tone was placatory. Dilas couldn't see his face, but he pictured a look of condescension. 'Not exactly. You have a very rare condition called dextrocardia. Simply put: your heart is on the right side of your chest instead of the left. Had your heart been in the conventional location you would have been killed instantly.' The nurse removed the needle. 'All done.'

'I see,' Dilas said, trying and failing to look down at his bandaged chest. 'The bullets have been taken out? They're not still inside me, are they? I'm going to be okay, aren't I?'

When the drip was reinserted into the cannula the nurse said, 'They were removed straight away. Aside from tissue damage and some blood loss, you are in remarkable condition. Dextrocardia is something you are born with, and, looking at your notes, you are quite healthy otherwise. Aside from the recent bullet wounds, I mean.'

You didn't fight in the war, did you? Rados had taunted because it was true, and spoke of deeper truth: Dilas was weak and he was a coward. He was quick of thought and tongue, but he had no macho credentials to draw support within certain demographics. Until now.

He had been shot, but he had survived. A miracle.

Vote for Dilas. Vote for invincibility.

Dilas made sure not to smile too much and asked, 'What about my head? Why am I in this thing?'

'You landed hard on paving stones when you fell and cracked two vertebrae. There's no damage to your spinal cord, so don't worry. The brace is merely to let the bones heal without further damage. You're going to be fine, physically, but this is a lot to process. Try to get some sleep. You'll wake up feeling a lot better.'

'Right. Could you shut off the TV, please?' Dilas asked.

'Sure,' the nurse said, and a moment later the TV fell blissfully silent. He placed the remote control next to Dilas' hand on the bed. 'In case you want it back on. Simply raise it in the air and thumb the top right button.'

'Thanks,' Dilas said, touched by the simple act of compassion.

The nurse then said, 'I'll check on you later,' and left the room.

Dilas lay in silence for a moment, feeling tired but also not wanting to sleep after all – he was too alert – so he did as the nurse had instructed and raised the remote and found the top right button with his thumb and switched the TV back on.

Dilas was happy.

Even shot, even bedridden, even pained, he could still play the angles. It was something Rados had been incapable of, and it had cost him. He'd made the mistake of trusting that Hungarian, whoever he was. Dilas had never trusted the outsider, and he planned to find out the man's true identity. He had politicians who owed him and cops he had paid off and many other useful people Rados had intimidated on his behalf. Would the latter still help him now Rados was gone? Of course not, but then they would suffer because all those leaderless barbarians needed a new purpose, a new emperor to protect – an emperor proven to be even tougher than them; even tougher than Rados himself.

Everything Dilas wanted would now come to fruition. He wanted power, he wanted respect, he wanted to induce fear.

He also wanted vengeance. He wanted the Hungarian dead. He would do everything in his soon-to-be-considerable power to make sure of it. Vengeance would be his.

Dilas was smiling at a sitcom one-liner when the door eased open.

A shape appeared in the corner of his peripheral vision. A man. Not the nurse. Someone else.

Careful footsteps approached his bed.

The shape stopped before it came into Dilas' view and a man asked, 'How are you feeling?'

The voice was quiet. The accent hard to pinpoint.

Annoyed by another intrusion, Dilas replied with a curt, 'I'm fine.'

The man – a doctor by the glimpse Dilas had of his white coat – passed the bed and approached the heart monitor.

With his back to Dilas, the doctor said, 'You're a very lucky man.'

'Yes,' Dilas said, feeling smug. 'I guess I'm blessed.'

'Yes,' the man echoed. 'Blessed.'

The white coat drifted by Dilas and the man stood at the head of the bed, where Dilas couldn't see him. He heard the rustle of paper as his notes were checked.

The doctor said, 'I'm going to give you something for your pain.'

'I've had an injection.'

The junior doctor remained silent.

Dilas heard his notes being set back in the slot at the end of the bed and felt the doctor standing there – a blurred hint of white at the very edge of his vision. It made Dilas uneasy. He had a sudden horrible thought that quickened his heart with terror, but he dismissed it as an attack of cowardice when the doctor left the room.

He would ask for police protection, he decided. Best not take risks when that asshole was still out there. At least until he was in command of Rados' brutes, and after: the whole country. He smiled, thinking of a glorious future.

Vote for Dilas. Vote for invincibility.

The junior doctor was new and unsure of himself, but he understood protocol and left the room to check who had administered the patient's pain relief without updating the notes. None of the nurses had, it appeared, and he believed them because they were as honest as they were hard working. The patient probably dreamt the whole incident. It was not unexpected. Heavy sedation could blur the distinction between imagination and reality. The junior doctor often experimented with the many mind-altering chemicals easily 'lost' from the hospital pharmacy.

By the time the doctor returned to administer some real pain relief, Dilas was dead from massive cardiac arrest. He had put up a brave fight, people would later say, but it was not surprising that he had succumbed to his injuries, grievous as they were.

He might have been saved had his heart monitor not failed to initiate an alarm when he flat-lined. An internal investigation concluded that the machine had developed a technical fault. Unexpected and unexplained, but these things happened from time to time.

No one was to blame.